THE RETURN OF KAVIN

THE RETURN OF KAVIN

David Mason

WILDSIDE PRESS
BERKELEY HEIGHTS, NJ • 1999

THE RETURN OF KAVIN

Published by:

Wildside Press
P.O. Box 45
Gillette, NJ 07933-0045
www.wildsidepress.com

THE LORD OF NIGHT

The black glass of the table was glowing, and flickering, as though currents of light flowed deep within the material; it cleared, into a tiny, perfect image . . . a great city, webs of streets and houses, walls and towers. A glimmer of sea, beyond, and the green hills that crowned the other shore of the Narrows.

"Mazain," Hugon said.

There was a lake, a long oval of shining water; reflected in it, the groves and tall palaces that surrounded it. Just beyond, at the island's tip, a dark mass of building.

"The Temple of the Lord of Night," the dragon said. "So he has revealed himself, to the Emperor. And the Emperor is now his servant, building that which is no temple, but a gate."

"I came because of this," said Thuramon. "The Egg of Fire . . ."

"He has it," the dragon said. With the Egg of Fire in place, that gate will open to all worlds and places, even the place where Ess now lies . . ."

A NOTE

For the authority concerning the events described in this and the preceding work (*Kavin's World*), we have principally used the great work of Geryonis the Younger, referred to as *Chronicle of the Kingdoms*. Geryonis assigns the events of Prince Kavin's life to approximately the ninth century of the Third Cycle, probably correctly.

According to the *Chronicle*, "There came into the world Three Lords, who being either demons or allied with demons, sent forth evil things, and sought to slay all men that lived, or to make of them slaves.

"These Three sent wars and plagues against that kingdom which was called Dorada, which lies eastward of Meryon, over against the Southern Sea. Then the Prince Kavin, of the house of Hostan, went with all of the people of Dorada, into another land, fleeing from that which had been sent against them."

In that land, which is called Koremon, they of Dorada dwelt, and became great; since also there were certain ancient and wise folk of the Dragon kind, who made compact with the folk of Koremon, and did thereby aid them greatly.

But the Prince Kavin, knowing of those Three Evil Lords, went with ten companions, and journeyed to the place where these Three were, and all their servants, with many armed men. There, it is said, the Prince caused the Three to be slain, so that the evil they did was no more upon the earth.

Yet, it was also said that the Prince Kavin was cast into a magical sleep, and stayed for seven lifetimes in that sleep; till he awoke again, and returned to Koremon. There, it is said, he lived, but told none of his name or what he was.

Yet, this tale cannot be true, since it is known that the Prince returned, and sat once more on the throne of that kingdom of Koremon. He lived and ruled, for the space of fifty years, or some say fifty-five; then, he died and lies with his ancestors.

It is also said of this King Kavin that he was wise, and that he ruled justly; also, that he had a certain spiritual being, who was not seen by any, yet was heard to speak with him in the voice of a woman upon certain private occasions. However, of this matter the chronicler knows nothing.

ONE

The galley came north by east, through the straits of Chema, rolling slightly in the wave-chop. Her long oars beat steadily to the dull thudding of a drum; ahead, the dawn reddened the sky, as the land fell away on either side. Now, the prow dipped and rose in the deeper waves of the open sea; the cruel bronze beak, slung upward for sailing, was whitened with salt.

On the high poop, men in thick seacloaks waited, watching the sky, while the steersmen leaned against the long whipstaff, holding the course.

A chill whisper of wind came from the north to the galley's port quarter; the broad white pennant at the foremast top flapped and spread in the breeze, the golden eagle of imperial Mazain gleaming on its surface.

The steersmen thrust at the staff, and the galley turned, slowly; men hauled on deck, and her two triangular sails rose, creaking, and filled. The drumbeat ceased; the oars swung up, and locked back, with a clashing thunder.

The wind blew a little more strongly as the sun rose; the galley coursed ahead, steadily, south and east.

Below, men moved along the oarbanks, passing bowls of food to the ragged, weary rowers who sat, chained to their benches. It was dark down there, and the smell was memorable, a stench of sweat, human excrement, unwashed bodies, and bilge. It was silent, except for the creaking and murmuring of the ship itself.

The Amabar was a single-banker, two men to an oar, and forty oars to a side; one hundred and sixty men sat

7

in the odorous dark, and there they would live, till they died. There was no reprieve likely from the imperial galleys.

The two men who sat on a midship bench were an odd pair; one a huge black, the other a lean, small man with light brown hair, pale skinned. The black man was nearly naked, except for the ragged kilt worn by most of the galley-slaves, not for modesty but to protect the bottom from the hard bench. He was bearded, heavily; he had odd blue markings on both cheeks, and his wide face was grim.

The smaller man wore the remnants of a fine linen shirt, and torn leather breeches. His beard was stubbled and new, as were the lash marks on his back; he had, even in his present condition, an oddly aristocratic look about his long-nosed face. At the moment, the long nose was wrinkling in disgust as he examined the bowl in his lap; he looked as if he were being presented with a serious dilemma.

"Something's died in the porridge, Zamor," the lean man said, still staring into his bowl.

"Whatever it was, it was lucky," the black man said. He lifted his bowl and drained it off in a single gulp, and proceeded to munch on the lump of hard bread that was the second course. His strong white teeth clamped down, and he chewed slowly and swallowed. "I wouldn't doubt they'd drop a rower into the pot, at that. Hate to waste money, these Mazain folk."

"If I don't eat it, I'll likely drop at the oar," the lean man said, thoughtfully. "If I do, I may be poisoned by it." He shrugged and lifted the bowl, grimacing. "Ugh."

"You'd best get used to it," Zamor grunted, munching. He glanced curiously at his oarmate. "You pull well, for such a runtish one as you look . . . what did you say your name was? Hugon? A Meryonish name, isn't that?"

"Hugon, yes," the other said, with difficulty; he was trying to chew the bread. He gulped it down, and grinned. "As hard as Darina's heart. Yes, my large friend, I was born in Meryon, and I wish I were there now."

8

"You might be," Zamor said, darkly.

"Eh?" Hugon stared at him.

"Well, if seeing your homeland through an oarhole will do," Zamor said, grinning widely. "There's talk. That bloody madman, the glorious and ever beloved of the gods, might yet decide to try a new war against the east."

"You don't sound like a loyal subject of the emperor," Hugon observed.

Zamor spat. "Why do you think I'm here?"

"Why?"

"I'm a Numori," Zamor said. His eyes gleamed oddly. "I am . . . I was . . . of some importance, once. As you seem to have been, sprat." He shrugged. "Now . . . I'm what you are, and what we will be till we go through an oarport to feed the sharks."

"I don't know if I want to . . . ah, resign myself to that," Hugon said in a low voice, staring at his hands, blistered and raw.

"You haven't much choice, have you?"

Hugon was silent for a minute; then, he glanced at the black man.

"It depends," he said.

"On what?" Zamor asked, and chuckled, grimly. "No doubt you're a magician?"

"Well, now, as a matter of fact," Hugon said, and stopped, rubbing his stubbled chin with the back of his hand.

"Are you?" Zamor said, in a low, fierce voice. "Use your art, man; break this iron on my ankle! Let me get up to that deck, long enough to lay hands on one or two of those fine Mazainian peacocks and pluck 'em . . ." His hands knotted.

"I may be, ah, exaggerating," Hugon said, glumly. "True, I've studied the Great Art for a short time, but . . ."

Zamor relaxed, and grunted.

"On the other hand, I may be able to think of something," Hugon said, staring once more at his hands.

9

"You'll understand, I'm a man of some wit. I came to Mazain to add to my small store of knowledge, in fact . . . though I hardly expected to end in a galley. Most inhospitable, I'd say, these folk."

"What was it?" Zamor asked.

"An unfortunate accident," Hugon said. "There was a lady whose husband returned from his work too soon. He was a man of some importance, I'm afraid. But he neglected to tell me that, and he was a very poor swordsman, rest his soul."

Zamor laughed, in spite of himself, a deep chuckle.

"But, about our problem," Hugon went on. "I have been thinking hard. Now, I'm sure there's not a man down here who would not like to see freedom again . . . and there's a good many of us."

"There are three score armed marines up there," Zamor said, pointing upward. "Not to mention another score of seamen, and their officers . . . though they're a poor enough lot. And then there's these bits of jewelry." He jangled his leg iron.

"It was just that I was thinking about," Hugon said, and held out his hand under Zamor's nose, opening it.

A thin, shining blade, with a finely serrated edge, lay in his palm. Zamor studied it and shrugged.

"So you've a knife," he said, disinterestedly. "What use is that, except to cut your own throat?"

"It's no mere knife," Hugon told him. "Look closely. It's a saw. But no common saw; it's a blade made of metal for which there's no name. It will cut iron as though the stuff were cheese." He glanced down at the leg manacles. "Common iron, nothing to this tool."

Zamor stared at him, with increasing interest now. "If what you say is true . . ."

"It is."

"You could have escaped from the prison ashore, then," Zamor said.

"I could have sliced bars away," Hugon said. "And ended, speared like a fish, by some clod of a guardsman. That prison's well guarded, damn it."

10

"How did you hide such a thing, little man?" Zamor asked, staring.

"I had a way," Hugon said, with an odd expression. "It doesn't matter . . . but now, listen. If I were to manage to loosen every man below here, what then? You know this ship well. What would happen?"

"If you could do that . . ." Zamor said slowly. "The oarmasters come here too often . . . but if you could. Well, at night would be best, of course. Then, rush the deck, try to take weapons wherever they may be had. But damn it, these are beaten men down here. Many of them have been here so long . . ." Zamor paused, but there was a fire in his black eyes. "It would be worth it, even if we died," he muttered.

Hugon's lean face was expressionless; his hand was closed around the tool, and he watched Zamor, silently.

"This ship's bound southward, along the lower coasts of Quenda province," Zamor said, almost to himself. "There must be trouble . . . sea raiders from the southern seas, perhaps. Or smuggling, it may be." He looked up, and his fierce eyes met Hugon's. "Sea raiders, now. D'ye know what becomes of us, in a sea fight, man? The oars, cracking us like fleas in a pinch, when the other ship drives down the oarbanks. The fire-ball to roast us, or the sea to take us down, if we lose the fight; and if we win, we can hear the cheers . . . up there. And maybe, if the victory's fine enough, they'll send us down a skin or two of sour wine."

Hugon nodded. "Then we'd best not wait for all that, eh?" he suggested.

"Let me see the thing again," Zamor said.

Hugon chuckled. "I'll do better than that," he said, and bent down. "Watch." He sawed the blade briskly, for a moment; and Zamor's eyes widened incredulously. The thin saw slid into the black metal of the leg iron, clear through in a few strokes. The iron was still in place, but a gap showed in the circle; a second cut would have freed Hugon completely.

11

"By the Great Snake, it did it!" Zamor muttered, amazed.

"Then we'll begin," Hugon said, and leaned forward. He tapped the shoulder of the man ahead, a gaunt gray man who sat slumped over his bench. "Listen, friend . . ." Hugon began.

The Amabar sailed on under the steady wind; the sun rose higher, and the dark inner world grew hotter, and more odorous. Unknowing marines walked the upper deck, and officers stood, watching the sea ahead, while below, man whispered to man, each telling the one ahead of the plan.

At the forward end of the gallery above the rowers, a guard nodded, half asleep in the heat; and sometimes one or another of the two oarmasters passed through, along the narrow walk above the oarbenches, staring down contemptuously into the shadows, and swinging long whips, idly. None of those above noticed the muttering and whispering that ran, like a slow wave, down the benches as the hours passed.

Late in the day, a tall man, cloaked, long plumes sweeping from his cap, stepped down onto the walk and paused there. Behind him, another such stood, and the sailing-master next to that one, looking properly deferential; these were nobles of the empire, plainly enough.

"Phew," Lord Barazan said, lifting a gold pomander to his nose. He spoke, over his shoulder. "Good Pharash, the stench! My lady spoke of it an hour ago, reaching up to the cabin itself."

"I'll order the banks hosed down, milord," the sailing master said, anxiously. "As soon as possible . . . but, milord, the water fills the bilge when we hose these men down, and your lordship knows, the matter of the pumping . . ."

"May the Nine Gods preserve me," Barazan said, in the general direction of the sky. "Orsha, you perceive the burdens I bear," he said to the other noble. "My Amabar, allowed to go to leaking ruin through lack of care . . . while in trust with my good fool here, Pharash. Pumps

12

that draw no water, seams untarred, and untrained scum at the oars." He spread his hands in dramatic despair, and Orsha clucked sympathetically.

"Ah, well," Barazan said. "We must do with what we have, in the Glorious Emperor's service. But these oarsmen . . . Pharash, how many new hands are there below?"

"A hundred, my lord," Pharash said.

"So many?" Barazan looked amazed. "No more than sixty still lived, then?"

"True, my lord," Pharash said. "Disease, in the shore barrack where we kept them last month while we lay in dock, repairing. They do not do as well in the unhealthy air ashore."

"A weak-looking lot, too, I perceive," Barazan said, moving slowly along the walk, peering down. He paused and stared downward, hard-eyed. When he spoke again, his voice rang loudly, echoing under the deck. "All of you, there, hear. You've had a fine day's rest, lolling about at your ease. We've a fine wind, good for another such day or two, so enjoy yourselves, lads." He laughed harshly. "But we'll meet the southern trades off Quenda shore, and then I'll expect you to work a while. You'll pull to the beat, and keep on pulling while there's breath in you. And if there's a man of you who doesn't pull, then . . ." Barazan paused, and his teeth gleamed in the shadows. "Why, he'll not need to pull an oar again."

Behind Barazan, Orsha snickered. Otherwise, there was a deathly silence.

"Good, then," Barazan said, after a moment. "I'm understood, eh, lads? Sleep well, and think about your sins. Here, you'll have a great chance to atone for all you've ever done, and serve the emperor while you do that." He turned and went out with the others; overhead, the hatch clanged shut.

"Now, there's a fine one that I would love to hold some further conversation with," Hugon muttered. Beside him, Zamor grunted, a bitterly amused sound.

13

"The sun is low," Hugon said, peering through the narrow oar slit, past Zamor's black bulk.

"Be patient," Zamor muttered. He sat, hunched, his big hands clenching and opening, slowly. "You have been here only a day. I have been here half a year."

The low murmuring went on, and the chuckle of the sea past the ports. The sky grew red, and then grayed to darkness.

In the great cabin, there were voices, and laughter; the sound of a woman singing came softly in the night wind. On deck, men moved about, trimming sail; then, the night watch came on, and lanterns were lit. Once there was the sound of hoarse laughter, smothered; a wine jar stood in the shadow of the cook's deckhouse. The leading steersman glanced skyward, reading the familiar stars; behind him, the Axe turned, while the Dolphin's green eye gleamed directly over the masthead, as it should.

In the pitch blackness, the blade passed, from man to man; each man cut, and cut again, and leg irons opened, one after another. Hugon and Zamor, already free, sat tensely, listening; twice, guards walked along the gangway in the dim yellow lamplight, but passed along, seeing nothing amiss.

And once, a man gibbered insanely in the dark, feeling his foot move freely after so long; a moment's crazy yammering, cut short by his oarmate's hand clamped on his mouth. The guard glanced up, sleepily, and shouted a warning curse, but did nothing. Such lunatic sounds were not so unusual in the oarbanks.

It was midnight before the saw had finished its long journey up one bank and down the other. The whisper came back from man to man; and there was a rustle as men began to stand up.

Near the forward gangway, where the drummer usually sat, and where the guard now squatted, four men came sliding, swiftly, like seasnakes; up, onto the boards, two from either side. The yellow light fell on their maddened, bearded faces; gleamed in their wild eyes as they

14

sprang. The guard went down beneath them, with only a choked gasp of terror; one of them snatched at his short sword and stabbed, again and again.

The whole act had taken only a moment. Now, more men swarmed up, climbing onto the gangway, panting, but wordless. Zamor, his face grim as carved black stone, thrust forward, through the others; his size made it easy for him to move in spite of the jammed walkway, and Hugon came close in his wake.

Under the closed hatch, there was a muttered conversation; then, Zamor lifted himself up onto the ladder, and his huge shoulder pushed, slowly and carefully, but with enormous force. A hinge gave, with a ripping noise; then, the hatchway was open. The men behind saw the stars overhead, and the glimmer of the masthead light.

Zamor lifted his head and peered across the darkened deck. Then, with a single thrust, he lifted himself up and out, and the others came pouring out behind him, still in terrible silence.

The big black sprang, in a wolf's bound, toward the half dozen marines who squatted or stood near the break of the poop; the men had barely time to see him before he was upon them.

They were all big men, wearing the leather armor and round helmets of their corps; but Zamor was not merely bigger, but a man in whom rage had waited a long, long time. More than that, he was an Almor of the Numori; that race whose fighters were said to be the best in the world, men who lived for the art of war.

Zamor's extended hands thrust like swordblades, and two marines went down; his right hand snatched a short sword, which slashed across a third man's belly in the same movement. The force of the blow was so great as to cut partly through the heavy leather of the marine's cuirasse, and he staggered back with a scream of agony. But Zamor's left hand had seized still another man's neck already; he thrust the man forward, into the sword another lifted, and both men reeled backward, one spitted and screaming.

15

Hugon, close behind the giant black, had already seized an abandoned blade that came spinning along the deck; he laughed aloud, and cried out, a wordless sound. A moment later, he met a charging marine, blade to blade; the heavy, short weapons met, with a clang like pots falling in a kitchen. The marine tried to thrust, and was deftly parried; he snarled, and drew back his blade, to cut, axe-wise. It was a serious error, but he had no time to regret it. Hugon's blade entered his throat.

As he drew the sword back, Hugon thought, in a flashing moment of queer regret, "Another poor fool." He hated killing, and especially men whose skill with the sword was so small.

By now, the silence that had reigned before was lost completely; the roar of battle replaced it. Galley slaves hurled themselves upon marines, clawing, snatching, and shrieking; here and there, men who had already gained weapons slashed and cut at knots of seamen and marines backed against the forward bulkheads and against the mast.

On the quarterdeck, men were emerging, half-dressed, shouting, with whatever weapons they had snatched. Out on the main deck, the crazy rush of the slaves had swept the last defender away; and now, the ragged mob moved purposefully aft, toward the great cabin. Zamor, splashed with blood, a sword in each hand, was first; he came up the ladder toward the last defenders, looking like a demon out of the pit, with a wild yell as he sprang up. The knot of men on the quarterdeck shrank back before him, their faces white with terror. But near the port rail, a seaman stood, legs apart, leveling a heavy crossbow and taking aim at Zamor.

Hugon, at that moment, swung a leg lightly over the quarterdeck railing, starboard; he was behind the group of defenders, and Zamor faced them, moving tigerishly toward them. Hugon saw the crossbowman; he narrowed his eyes, thoughtfully, and swung back his right hand over his shoulder, with the sword. Bringing it forward, he let go; the sword flew, like a huge dart, and nailed the

16

crossbow wielder to the rail. The bolt flew up, as the trigger snapped.

Zamor paused, and his eyes flicked to the falling body of the crossbowman, back to Hugon, who grinned at him. Then, Zamor roared, a sound that might have been either a giant laugh or a war cry in an unknown tongue, and met the first defender.

It was no longer a battle, now; the others had reached the quarterdeck, and the officers and nobles went down. Orsha broke free and ran, screaming, toward a door; a dozen swords swung at him as he clawed at the door, and he was down, hacked into pieces. For a moment, the sailing master held his own, his back against a rail; then, two slaves grappled with him, and all three fell into the black sea below. Others leaped into the darkness.

Lord Barazan fought well; there were dead men piled against his legs as he hacked and slashed. But a dozen swords thrust at him, and a half dead slave clutched at his knees; he went down, like the others.

The doors to the great cabin were flung open; beyond, in the light of lamps, figures moved in a panicked rush, and women screamed wildly.

Hugon, knocked against a bulkhead in the rush of men, saw a big slave with a hideously scarred face turn, grinning insanely, his arms spread wide.

"There's women!" the slave roared; and the mob howled in demonic answer as they burst in.

In the turmoil, Hugon was carried forward; a door opened, and he fell forward, into an inner cabin. He saw the woman, and, lightning-fast, he kicked shut the door, placing his back against it. Behind him, he heard screams; the other women.

The woman was tall, with a breathtaking body, plainly visible; she had drawn a sheet around herself, but that was all she wore. She had a mass of dark red hair, loose on her shoulders; her eyes flashed, green, wide with fury as she stared at Hugon.

"You traitorous dirt!" the redhead spat, staring at him. "You . . . here!"

17

"My Lady Gwynna," Hugon said, and grinned. "What, a traitor? I? Would you care to discuss it, lady, as to which of us . . ."

Men were thrusting at the door behind him, and a hand tried to enter the crack of the opening; Hugon rapped the hand with his sword hilt, and leaned close to the door, turning.

"Zamor!" he roared. "Zamor, here, quickly!"

There was renewed noise outside; then, Zamor's deep voice bellowed in answer. Hugon moved, and the door opened; Zamor's bulk filled the narrow opening, as he stared in.

"Zamor!" Hugon barked. "There's a prize pigeon here we'll need to keep alive! Keep the others out, man!"

Zamor turned, his body still blocking the door, and roared out, "There's enough, all of you! This one's mine!"

A couple of slaves tried a moment's protest, and Zamor's fists slammed out; then, as he backed into the cabin, there was no more dissension. He kicked the door shut, and turned with a puzzled look toward Hugon.

"Let me introduce you, friend Zamor," Hugon said, in a queer, strained voice. He made a sweeping bow, a strange figure in his rags. "The Lady Gwynna . . . formerly of Armadoc, and lately wife of the late lord Barazan. We've made her a widow, poor lass." His teeth gleamed in the dim lamplight. "But she made many another widow, not too long ago, and she's welcome to the new estate."

The girl who stood, her back pressed against the carved panels, was tall, pale, with a loosened mass of dark red hair flowing over her bare shoulders. She was beautiful, like a trapped panther; her green eyes flared with hate as she stared at Hugon and Zamor. She was in near-nakedness, but she seemed unconscious of her near nudity, and there was no fear in her face, only rage.

"Hugon," she said, in an icy voice. "Pimp, thief, and scribbler of bad rhymes. You filth . . ."

"Ah, not that, my lady," Hugon said, smiling. "My rhymes have been said to be quite good . . . the rest,

18

perhaps, true enough." His expression changed slightly. "But I doubt there's time for an exchange of wit, lady. I shall make no mention of . . . your first widowing."

"Araaak!"

At the sound, Zamor crouched, his sword up, and Hugon leaped back. They froze, eyes searching; then, the voice came again, high and screeching, and they saw its source.

"Aaak! Who you?"

A cage was hung near the ceiling, which was why they had not seen it at first; and the voice came from there.

Between the bars, a triangular, scaled and whiskered head poked, inquisitive bright eyes fixed on the two men. A long tongue flickered out, and there was a slight puff of smoke.

"Aak, what men? What you do?"

"A dragonet!" Zamor said, staring.

"Eee!" the dragonet said, in a pleased tone.

"The lord Barazan had an expensive taste in pets," Hugon said, straightening up and peering at the creature. He glanced at the girl. "Two such beasties must have cost him many a gold piece. I know what price he paid for you, my lady, of course . . ."

There was a renewed banging at the door, and Hugon looked in that direction, worriedly.

"Zamor," he said, hastily, "Listen. This woman might be held for ransom . . . there are those who will pay well for her. It would be a waste to let her be raped and flung over the side."

The Lady Gwynna laughed, suddenly and coldly. "You! And you called yourself a gentleman!"

"Oh, no, never," Hugon told her. "I've never had the wealth for that. Not yet."

"Aaak!" the dragonet, in its cage, said. "I like you, man."

"And I like you as well, small ugly one," Hugon said. "But I've no time for conversation, I fear. You, woman . . . I'd assume you want to live. Get you into that closet, there . . ." He opened a door, and yanked out masses of

19

garments, making room. The woman glared at him, and he seized her arm, impatiently. "In, damn it!" He thrust her inside, and slammed the door.

Someone was banging drunkenly on the cabin door, and Zamor, with a quick glance at Hugon, moved to open it. A bearded face appeared.

"Where'sh women?"

"No women, bucko," Hugon said, with a broad grin. "Got wine, though. Here." He tossed a bottle from the cabin sideboard.

The other took the bottle and upended it, gulping; he moved back, leaving the door half open.

"I could use a pair of boots, at that," Hugon said, loudly, kneeling beside the piles of clothing tossed out of the closet. "Ah, now . . ."

"If that woman has sense enough to keep quiet . . ." Zamor muttered, beside him. "It's a mad scheme, man. Ransom . . ."

"Mad?" Hugon whispered, pawing at the clothes. "You'll see, Zamor."

The uproar outside was deafening. As the two of them found garments and put them on, they could see others in the outer cabin who had the same idea. Men reeled to and fro, waving wine bottles, dressed in fragments of the finery looted from the cabins beyond. There were wild shrieks from other parts of the ship, where the women had been dragged to their fate; and quarreling over them had evidently broken out, from the sounds.

"We'd be no more than twenty or thirty miles from the Quenda shore," Zamor said, frowning. "And there's no man at the rudder now."

"Could we find a sober man," Hugon said, and moved into the riot, Zamor behind him. He pushed open the door to the quarterdeck, and stepped out into the torch-splashed darkness. He stopped, staring into the night, and stiffened.

"Damnation!"

The starlight on the sea was bright enough to outline a row of jagged masses, black against the dim light. Beneath, flashes of lightness appeared, and there was a distant thunder.

"Surf," Zamor said, behind him.

"You were wrong about the coast, I think," Hugon said. He stared at the chaos on the deck, and then glanced up at the slanted sails. "Could we tack, with no hands at the lines?"

"It's worth trying," Zamor grunted. "Else we'll be aboard those breakers in another hour."

Together, they went swiftly aft, to where the twelve-foot whipstaff swung idly; stepping over bodies as they went. There were three more dead men, one hanging limply over the staff itself; Zamor plucked the corpse away, and dropped it as Hugon seized the staff and thrust it hard over.

Slowly, the galley began to turn away from the threatening white line of surf. As the sails caught on the other tack, the booms slammed over, and the ship heeled slightly; Zamor lent his own huge strength to the work, holding the turn.

Now, the ship moved in a straighter course, with more speed, since the wind set slightly away from the land. Hugon let go, and found a line coiled on deck, which he looped around the staff, holding it in place.

"Knowing something of that lady down there," Hugon said, "I'd feel better if I could see her with my eyes. Come on, Zamor."

The cabin was undisturbed; the dragonet, in its cage, squawked a greeting, and the closet door was still closed.

"Hello, aak!" the dragonet squawked. Hugon chuckled, and moved closer to the silver cage; he lifted the hook that closed its door, and opened it.

The dragonet uttered a high, musical trill and leaped out, its wings spreading for a moment. Hugon's arm was extended, like a falconer's, and the creature landed there, and clung, its tail wrapping around Hugon's arm. It emitted a thrumming musical note, and a small puff of smoke, obviously pleased.

21

"My name is Fraak!" it sang, preening. "I like you, man!"

It was a handsome little monster, its scales a coppery red, shading into purple, bright yellow eyes, and whiskers that seemed to be made of gold wire. Zamor reached out and touched it, gingerly, and it uttered another pleased note.

"I've seen the bones of such a beast, in the west country," Zamor said, "but much larger, bigger than ten horses. This one is so small. Is it a young one?"

"It seems full grown," Hugon answered, absently. He was staring at the closet. "Lady Gwynna?" he called out, softly.

"Pig," came the muffled reply.

"Good, our prize is untouched," Hugon said, satisfied. He stroked the dragonet's scaled head. "A beautiful specimen, this one. Male, I think . . . they are rare, and hard to catch, but some wealthy lords like to keep them, as we keep falcons in the west. Also, they sing beautifully, and talk most amusingly."

"I *like* you," Fraak repeated, emphatically, lifting his wings. "You let me out of cage." He trilled a scale, and sailed off, flying to a cornice where he sat, chuckling.

Zamor had been rummaging in chests and cabinets; now, he straightened, with a broad grin, holding a long scabbard and belt out before him.

"A decent sword!" he crowed, drawing the blade half out and testing its edge with his thumb. "A piece of Grothan steel, by Lord Snake! Ach, if I've had this beauty in my hand an hour back . . ."

"You did well enough with what you had," Hugon said. "Here, is that another blade there?"

"Take it, little man," Zamor said, passing a second handsome weapon. "But this one's mine. Ha, you've no idea what it feels like to stand free, with a sword in your hand again, after the oarbanks this last half year!"

Hugon, weighing the sword thoughtfully, nodded. "A day was enough for me." He buckled the weapon around his waist, and picked up a bottle from a shelf. "Good

22

wine, too." He upended the bottle, drank, and passed it
to Zamor. As the other drank, Hugon moved restlessly
about the cabin, prying and searching.

"A few jewels, but enough to pay our way," he muttered, pawing about in a small chest. "Ah, some silver
pieces . . ."

"Yo!"

The door was open, and grinning, drunken faces appeared in the lamplight, fists and weapons waving.
Zamor and Hugon turned, hands dropping to their own
weapons, but the leading invader came in, grinning.

"Ye're the lads got us loose, ain't you?" the man said, in
a wine-blurred voice. "Come out on deck, we're aholdin'
a meetin'." He stared curiously about the room. "Found a
bit of loot, eh? Good for you, you're entitled to it, seeing
you're the clever ones that got us all out of this."

The dragonet hissed from his high perch, and the man
recoiled, wide-eyed; a knife lifted in his hand, but
Hugon seized his wrist.

"No, man, it's nothing but a pet beast!" he said hastily.
"Brings good luck . . . let it be, now."

"Eh, if you say so . . ." the other grunted, putting
back his knife. "Fair scared me, it did . . . but come
along, will you?"

Out on the main deck, a good half of the mutineers
stood, reeling, or sprawled in the scuppers; some were
drunker than others, but there had been plenty of wine
in the hold, and none were sober. The ship still drove
steadily, under the two big sails, unattended; the wind
seemed to be rising, too, from the sound in the rigging.
But the noise on deck drowned out the other sound.

Some of them cheered drunkenly, seeing Hugon and
Zamor; several others, making speeches to each other,
paid no attention. Dead men rolled in the scuppers, and
drunken men, hardly different in appearance, lolled next
to them.

"Now, that's not an encouraging sight," Hugon said,
surveying the deck from the doorway above. Zamor, behind him, grunted in agreement.

23

"Listen, little man, you've cleverness enough," Zamor said, coming up beside him. "What's next, now?"

Hugon glanced at the big man, scowling. "Damn it, would you leave off calling me little man? I've got height enough, among ordinary folk."

Zamor grinned, but said nothing.

"Cleverness won't get the wine out of that lot, anyway," Hugon muttered, staring down at the motley mob. "We can't take this blasted sea-cow anywhere without a few hands to work sail. And where in the Mother's name she's heading now is a grand mystery to me. I'm no sea-tracker." He glanced skyward. "South, I think . . . damn it, what's south of Quenda Cape? Nothing at all but sea, and more sea . . . I've never heard of land in this direction at all."

There was a loud argument progressing among the least drunken of the mutineers on the deck below, led by the man who had called them out.

"Ye'll not get me to put my hands on any turd-covered oar again, not if you kill me where I stand!" someone roared, and several others agreed with him, loudly. Another, bracing himself on spread legs, pointed at the billowed sail. "Why in hell row? We've wind enough!"

"But damn your eyes, we've got to make easting!" the first man shouted. "There's land, eastward, the capes of Meryon . . ."

The argument grew hotter. Hugon, listening, shrugged.

"No chance at all," he told Zamor. "They'll yell till they remember they've got weapons, and then . . . aha, there it begins."

The knot had exploded into combat, and several other fights spawned from the first, spreading across the deck. The two men stood, on their vantage of the quarter deck, and watched grimly.

"Ha, little man . . . excuse me, friend Hugon!" Zamor corrected himself. He was staring at the top of the nearer mast.

24

"Clouds," Zamor said, thoughtfully. "The stars are gone."

"And the wind's rising," Hugon said. "Hm. Had you noticed any sort of boat, perhaps, about this ship?"

"There's none at all," Zamor answered. He glanced out, to the darkness. "Not that it would help us much, anyway. The sea is growing heavier by the minute."

Hugon rubbed his chin and laughed, sharply. "Do you know, it looks as if we've jumped off the roasting spit and into the soup pot, as the saying goes, doesn't it?"

"If we drown, we drown free men," Zamor said.

"Yes, but it's not the best of company to be entering the Rainbow Gates with," Hugon said. "You and I are the only honest men aboard, at that."

The ship heeled sharply, and he clutched at the rail; as she swayed slowly back, men on deck rolled into the scuppers, or sprawled where they had fallen. But those who could still stand were continuing to fight.

"To hell with the lot of them," Hugon grunted. "Come, let's go back and see whether there's another flask of that excellent wine left. Also, I intend to keep an eye on our prize to the last. I'm not giving up hope of fetching her to market till the breath's gone out of me."

They went back, through the doors, and into the inner cabin; within, the lamp swung in long arcs, and fallen objects rolled back and forth on the floor. The dragonet was talking quietly to itself, in despairing tones, as it clung to its perch. Seeing Hugon enter, it squawked with joy and spread its wings.

The Lady Gwynna had emerged from her hiding place, and sat on the bunk now, wrapped in a white woolen cloak, stiff backed and stony faced. She stared at them, her green eyes lit with silent fury, and said nothing.

Zamor kicked the door shut and braced himself against the deepening roll of the ship; Hugon held a stanchion with one hand, watching the girl with a wry grin on his face.

25

"We may all die soon, Lady Gwynna," he said, quietly.

"Good," she snapped.

The ship rolled heavily, again.

"Well . . . it was my thought that it was only fair to let you be warned," Hugon said, lightly, and gripped the stanchion with his other hand against a wilder lurch. He glanced toward Zamor. The big black man's face was without a sign of fear, but his lips moved, silently, as though praying to his Numori Snake God.

Outside, above the now strident wind, there was a sudden new uproar, and the sound of running feet, and shouting. And then, a terrific thud made the deck shake under their feet; there was a steady roaring, and over it the explosive cracking sound of breaking masts and splintered planks. The cabin began to tilt.

"We've struck!" Hugon shouted over the noise, as he clung to the stanchion. The cabin lamp slammed over and went out, and everything in the place fell, seemingly all at once.

TWO

The great galley lay broken among jagged black rocks; only the high-pooped after end was entire. The ship had turned as it struck, coming in stern first. Beyond, in the boiling surf, parts of the ship lay; and on the gray sand, there was a drift of smaller fragments, oars and planks, and the bodies of drowned men.

Hugon, soaked and staggering, came up the slope of sand, toward the scrubby trees at the upper edge. The dragonet clung to his shoulder, whimpering and terrified. Behind him, Zamor came, as wet and weary as he, but lugging the girl over his wide shoulder, slung like a sack. Behind them a man crawled out of the surf, and a few moments later, another; both followed the dimly seen forms ahead, by some vague instinct.

Among the trees there was some shelter from the wind, and Hugon halted; he scratched together the drier bits of fallen wood, shuddering with cold as he worked. Zamor, arriving, dropped the girl and aided Hugon's search until they had a small pile.

Hugon squatted beside the wood, and coaxed the dragonet down, holding it in his blue hands near the wood.

"Ah, now, Fraak, try hard," he murmured, through chattering teeth. "You can do it, handsome laddo that you are, just one puff . . . ah!" Fraak had emitted a tiny orange flame, and a stick of wood caught. As the flames crackled up, Fraak crowed softly with pride, and Hugon stroked his scales, complimenting him.

"Eh, what a useful wee creature it is!" Zamor grunted, and hunched over the blaze, his cloak steaming. Hugon

27

stood up, and went to pull the girl closer to the fire; he sat her up, chafing her arms and face till she began to return to consciousness.

Behind them, a hoarse voice called out, and the two other men came hobbling up to the grateful warmth.

"Any more get ashore?" Hugon asked, squatting back on his heels as warmth returned.

"Nah, not a one but us," one of the men said. "I'm Gorash. You'd be the smart lad that had the queer knife, wouldn't you?"

Hugon nodded. Gwynna was sitting up now, staring about dazedly. The other man stared at her, interestedly.

"Ye've saved one of the wenches, too, haven't you?" he said. "Come in handy, may be, for one thing or t'other." He chuckled hoarsely. "Good tender meat's got more than one use, it has. This looks like a hungry place we've hit . . ."

"She's not for cooking," Hugon said, with a cold grin. "Hands off the one, bucko."

"Ah, now . . ." the man said, apologetically. "I didn't mean no harm . . . my name's Hazarsh, by the way. Two years in that stinkin' sea-sty I was, and as innocent as a child, too, at least as far as what they said I did . . ." He was staring at Gwynna, and licking his salt-crusted lips. "And never no sight of a handy trollop . . . missed out on what there was aboard last night, because I was too drunk. Not being used to drinkin' either, after all that time, you understand . . ." His eyes were still on the girl. "Be we goin' to share her around, likely?"

"Not likely at all, Hazarsh lad," Hugon told him, and laid a hand meaningfully on his sword hilt. "Get the thought out of your head, or I'll bleed you for your health."

Hazarsh grunted and fell silent, looking carefully away from the girl.

She was huddling close to the fire, and she looked sideward at Hugon, with a strange expression for a moment. Then she said, hoarsely but with a note of mockery, "Ah, still a gentleman at heart, good Hugon."

28

"It's not your honor I'm worried about, Gwynna girl," he told her. "That's gone long since. But I'd like to offer you for sale in at least as good a condition as I got you in."

Zamor, listening, chuckled, and Gwynna glared silently.

Hugon stood up, drier now, and stretcned, staring at the sky.

"It's possible the sun may yet decide to come out," he said thoughtfully. "And the wind's lessening, at least. Has anyone any idea where we might be?" He looked around, but the others were silent.

After a moment, Gwynna said, coldly, "I think I know."

"Ah?" Hugon turned. "Where, then?"

"An island," she said, indifferently. "I recall a map that shows a few such in the southern sea. Mere rocks. of no value and impossible to land on . . ."

"As we've already discovered," Hugon said. "Are there any folk here, do you know?"

"Who knows?" she said, with a shrug.

"Ah, well, girl, you're no Laquellian Lexicon, but you tried," Hugon told her with a shrug, squatting down again. "Another momeni of warmth, and then I'll see what can be done about food. Ha, Fraak, my winged beauty, I just remembered your skills." He reached out and the dragonet climbed to his wrist, trilling. "Had you learned to hunt with the late Lord who owned you?" Hugon asked.

The dragonet snorted. "Not hunt for that one. I not like him. He put me in cage!"

Hugon chuckled at the creature's anger.

"I help *you*," Fraak said, and uttered the oboe note that meant pleasure. "You good."

"That's fine," Hugon said, and stood up. "Would you help me now?" he asked, coaxingly. "Catch a bird, or a rabbit if we find one?"

The dragonet spread its wings, uttered a fierce cawing cry, and sprang into the air, circling Hugon's head.

29

"I'm off to the hunt," Hugon said, and strode into the scrubby wood, the dragonet sailing above him.

"Ungrateful little beast," Gwynna said, staring after Hugon.

Zamor, sitting next to her, glanced at her and chuckled.

"Your dragonet?" he asked.

"My lord . . ." she stopped, and bit her lip, then regained her control. "My Lord Barazan gave that . . . *creature* . . . the best of food, bright toys, a handsome cage . . . and now it seems to have fallen completely in love with that filthy renegade vagabond, that . . ."

"A handsome cage, you said?" Zamor asked, calmly. "Better than the cage he gave us, below there, I suppose." He grinned at her. "Many beasts dislike a cage, no matter how cunningly made it may be. As we Numori, for instance . . ."

She shrugged. After a moment, she looked at him, oddly.

"You . . . your people were rebels against the Emperor, weren't you?" she asked.

"Our Queens were rulers when your Emperor's ancestors scratched each other's fleas in a cave," Zamor said, coldly.

After a while she said, in a conciliatory tone, "I am sorry. I meant no . . . well, I have little knowledge of such things. Wars and conquests and the like." She grimaced. "Dull lists of names and deeds. My . . . husband's . . . only source of conversation, except for court gossip." She stared into the fire.

Another time passed. Then she spoke again, with a forced calm. "Poor dog, I'm sorry he's dead. He had a lusty way about him . . . but that was all he had, alas. I . . . I learned to seek for more in a man than a stallion's skill, in Armadoc."

"You seem to know Hugon, lady," Zamor said. "How is that?"

Her teeth gleamed in a mirthless smile. "Ah, I know him. And he knows me, too well. Would you like to hear

30

it all, big one? Listen, then. I was mistress of Armadoc, there on the north coast of Meryon. Mistress alone, my parents dead, none to say no to anything I wished . . ." She stopped, staring into the fire.

"Armadoc is a great hold, there where the river enters the sea," Gwynna went on. "It is a key to the north of Meryon, held since the first days, by my own family. No army can pass Armadoc, toward the High King's seat. Well, he that is King in Meryon now, prince that was, gave me cause for anger, and I gave Armadoc to his great enemy, the Emperor." She laughed, suddenly. "If the Emperor had slain all, laid Meryon waste, I would have counted it no more than fair return for that insult. But he sent Barazan, who could not hold even Armadoc, in the end. He offered me marriage, at any rate, and high honor in Mazain . . . and since I had nothing left otherwise . . ." She shrugged, eloquently.

"Ah," Zamor said, nodding. He had heard of that war, in some small part. The Mazainians had struck at Meryon, across the sea, on some pretext; in a summer's time, they had been thrust out again, and since then an uneasy peace had been made.

"Your friend, that Hugon," Gwynna said. "The second son of a house with a great name . . . and no wealth at all. A maker of poems, I've heard, and one that was forever traveling about, pretending to study one sort of wisdom or another. There are many like that in Mervon land. Too many. My people . . . love to talk and lie and sing, but for anything of use . . ."

Zamor grunted, carefully noncommittal.

"He sent me a poem once," she said, after a while. "A bad one. I've written better myself."

"Ah," Zamor said.

There was a long silence. He could feel her green eyes on him, probing.

"You seem a man of . . . some nobility," Gwynna said, in a low voice. Zamor glanced at her, but said nothing.

"I do not wish to die," she said.

"No one does," he said.

31

"Ii Hugon sells me to the High King of Meryon . . .
Rhys will kill me."

Zamor shrugged. "You have friends in Mazain, too,"
he pointed out.

"The High King may offer more," she said, desperately. "Listen . . . you are a handsome man, a strong
one . . ." Her hand touched his bare shoulder, ca-
ressingly. "You could . . . do whatever you liked with
me . . . and drive Hugon away. If we could find a way
back to Mazain; you could be a great man, with my
help . . ."

Abruptly, Zamor laughed, throwing back his head, a
deep bellow of pure pleasure.

"Hugon!"

Hugon came out of the wood, something dangling
from his hand; the dragonet perched on his shoulder,
singing.

Zamor stood up and called again. "Hugon! Come back,
I'm in great danger!" And again, he roared with laughter.

Hugon came, at a faster pace; at the fire, he dropped
his prize, grinning.

"Hey, one of you two clean the pair of them," he said,
toward the two other survivors. "Hazarsh, you've a knife
there. Gorash, scramble a bit more wood, and we'll have
breakfast. I don't know what the beasts are called, but
they're fat, and like enough to rabbits to eat."

"Hugon, you're barely in time," Zamor told him, grinning. "I've nearly been seduced by your prize here."

Hugon stared, and Gwynna's eyes burned in rage, at
Zamor.

"Truth!" Zamor said. "She's offered me a taste of her
pretty flesh, and then I'm to be Captain of Imperial Eu-
nuchs, later, no doubt, after I take her away from you
and back to Mazain."

Hugon burst into a full-throated laugh of his own,
dropping to a seat beside the girl, who glared at both of
them.

"I . . . oh, Great Mother . . ." Hugon controlled his
laugh with difficulty. "I should have warned you, Zamor.

32

The girl's a widow, and a Meryon lass. Now, all our girls are most notoriously hot-fleshed, and widows, especially newly made ones, even more so!"

"Damn you both," Gwynna said, harshly. "May you rot with the blue pestilence, both of you." She hunched herself up and stared into the fire.

"I'll take your advice, Hugon," Zamor said, still grinning. "I've heard you know much of women. I'll avoid all widows, I swear it."

"Maidens, too," Hugon told him. "Stick to wives. They're much the best. Hey, Gorash, spit those two beasts, and let's begin the roast!"

Whatever they were, they smelled delicious, turning on a green stick above the fire. Before they were ready, Gwynna was staring at them, avidly; and in a moment, Hugon gallantly offered her a choice portion, on a sharpened stick. She took it, silently, and ate with haste.

On Hugon's shoulder, Fraak nibbled delicately at a tender morsel held between his slim-clawed forefeet; satiated, he belched, a foot-long pencil of fire.

"Careful, Fraak!" Hugon warned, almost dropping his own portion. "You'll burn me bald, there!"

"Much sorry, please," the creature said. "I be careful, yes."

"What's the land back there?" Zamor asked, through a mouthful.

Hugon shrugged. "An island, I'm afraid, though I did not go all around it. There are no signs of live folk, but . . . well, there have been people here, some time."

"How?"

"Broken walls, stones, carved rock," Hugon said, looking oddly nervous He glanced back toward the wood, uneasily. "A stone road . . . but it begins nowhere, and goes nowhere."

The two oarsmen were listening, as they ate. Now, Hazarsh glanced uneasily at Gorash, and cleared his throat.

"Listen, sirs . . ." he said, in a low voice. "Road, you said? And stones . . . but you saw nothing alive?"

33

"Nothing except these beasts, which Fraak took handily," Hugon said. "Why?"

"There's a sailor's tale," Hazarsh said, slowly, and stopped.

"The Island of the Old Ones," Gorash said. He was pale.

"Old Ones?" Hugon, stared at the two of them. "What Old Ones?"

"It's a tale," Hazarsh said. "A crew landed on such an island in the south. It would be . . . about where we are." He bit his lip nervously, and glanced toward the wood again. "Of course, it needn't be this'n, but they did say . . . there were stones, and old walls, and a road that went nowhere . . ."

Hugon considered him, thoughtfully. "Why did they call it the Island of the Old Ones, then?"

"Well, sir, there's a tale that there used to be . . . different people, once," Hazarsh said. "Before we was, you know. Like as if the Great Goddess tried out different kinds a long time back, before anybody." He shifted a little closer to the fire, but shivered anyway. "They say there used to be a big country, here in the southern sea, and these . . . Old Ones, whatever they might be, they lived here." He shivered again. "Suppose there was a bit of the place left, you understand . . . and maybe . . . maybe there was some of . . of *them* left."

Zamor chuckled. "Old Ones? Aah, what white man's nonsense?"

"I've heard such a tale," Hugon said. "That there were others, before humankind. But nothing about any of them being left alive. I'd like to see them, if . . . ah, but it's only seaman's nightmares."

"Perhaps not," Gwynna said, in a low voice.

Hugon looked at her, and thought, privately, that it was the first time he had heard her speak a word that was not an angry thrust at himself. Fear? He wondered what could make that iron-willed young woman feel even so much as a trace of fear . . . she who had not shown fear of the storm, or the sword.

34

"It's recorded, in certain places . . . old, rare books," she said, staring into the fire. "There were many others, before mankind . . . uncountable years ago. As there are many others, creatures as wise as man but not like man, in other worlds. Worlds that touch our own, sometimes. You know of tales that say the first High King of Meryon, and many folk with him, came to this world out of another, across the northern seas. And others tell tales, like that . . ."

"Tales, my lady, not certain truth," Hugon said. "I have always sought truth, myself . . ." He chuckled. "And found very little of it, I fear. But a great deal of what the world holds wisdom I've found to be the sheerest nonsense, too."

"Oh, so?" Gwynna looked at him. "You, a truth-hunter? I heard differently, Hugon. I thought it was gold you sought, not truth."

"The two aren't enemies, lady," he said, smiling. "One may often buy one with the other, in fact. But, alas, I've found little of either commodity." He leaned back against a log, stretching his toes toward the fire luxuriously, and scratched himself. "You know my name and something of the rest. I might have stayed at home, in the glens and rocks, and my ancestor's drafty halls . . . not my own, since I'm a second son. Indulged myself in the customary amusements of my folk . . . peasant girls, hunting, drinking and eating, and the music of the bagpipe . . ." Hugon laughed, looking around the circle of faces. "I'm something of a performer on that monstrous instrument; I left a fine one in Mazain, with all else I possess, except my honor." He sighed, dramatically rolling his eyes skyward.

"Your honor, sir pirate?" Gwynna asked, ironically.

"Of course," he said, gravely. "Look you, lady. I have killed no man who did not first threaten my life. I've stolen nothing from any poor man, and tupped no woman who was not willing enough. I have never broken my given word, nor raised sword against my king . . ." He stopped and looked at her, hard. "Ah. A tender point?"

35

"The High King offended *me*, before I did what I did," she said, her green eyes meeting his unflinchingly.

He shrugged. "A point I'd not argue, having little knowledge of the ins and outs of high policy. But I have my own honor, and it seems undamaged, so far."

Zamor grunted, and his teeth gleamed in a smile. "As I do, Hugon." He looked at the girl, his face like black stone. "The lady seemed to think otherwise when she whispered to me a little while ago. It might be better if I make the matter clear." He looked toward Hugon. "You flung that sword, that slew a man whose arrow would have killed me. By Numori custom, we are spear brothers, each to the other, and I now declare this before witnesses." His huge black hand stretched out, and clasped Hugon's wrist. "Before the Great Snake, I call you brother."

"And I, you, before the Snake," Hugon said, in a formal voice, and grasped the black wrist with his own hand. They let go, simultaneously, and Hugon rubbed his wrist, grinning.

"Great Goddess, but you've a grip on you, man," he said. He glanced around. "As for witnesses, well . . ." He chuckled. "These two gentlemen, and a lady . . ."

Hazarsh had risen, and was prowling restlessly on the other side of the fire, casting glances toward the darker areas of the scrubby woodland. Gorash had lain back, and was apparently asleep, and the dragonet was curled at Hugon's side, also with closed eyes.

Suddenly, Hazarsh bent low, prodding at the ground with his finger, and uttered a grunt of surprise. He picked something up, and came toward the fire, holding it out.

"Hey! Look y'here!"

Hugon came to his feet and took the object.

"A gold bezand!" he said, and whistled in surprise. "And with the head of the Emperor Avor II . . . barely a generation gone!"

"Here now, sir, let me have that back, will 'e?" Hazarsh said, anxiously, and Hugon returned it with a grin.

"If you find anywhere to spend it, be sure and tell me," he told Hazarsh. Zamor, too, had risen to his feet and seen the round gold coin; he rubbed his chin, thoughtfully.

"It could be sea raiders, leaving treasure hidden here," he said.

"Not impossible," Hugon agreed. "But I wish they'd left a boat, instead. I've no ambition to stay here forever."

"Well, now, brother," Zamor said slowly, hitching his swordbelt up, "I'm fairly full, warm enough, and there's a day of light left. If this place has been visited before, there might be a boat."

"Or at least the means to make one," Hugon agreed. "Shall we explore a while?"

"Hey, now, I don't know . . ." Hazarsh said, uneasily. "It might be that this is the Island of the Old Ones, like the tale . . ."

"Stay here, then, if you want to," Hugon said, agreeably. "Myself, I doubt there are any Old Ones left alive, here or anywhere else, but if there are, they can eat you as well in one place as another, can't they?"

"Ow," Hazarsh said, thoughtfully. "Might be best we stay together, yes?"

Gorash had awakened; he sat up with a grunt. "I'm coming too, gentles. Four's better than two." He got to his feet, glancing enviously at the swords worn by Hugon and Zamor. "But I'd feel safer wi' a blade of me own, I would."

"Have you been down yonder beach yet, Gorash lad?" Hugon asked, lifting an eyebrow. "There were half a dozen of our late shipmates, feeding the crabs there. If the tides haven't taken them, there might be a weapon or two among 'em. Go search . . . we'll wait, willingly."

Hazarsh followed Gorash, and the two went down toward the gray sands. For a while, Hugon and Zamor stood watching their distant figures roaming along the

37

tidepools, and pausing whenever some dark shape lay still. Then they heard a shout, and saw the two returning, each waving a short sea-sword triumphantly.

Gwynna had sat, watching the proceedings without a word. Now she lithely stood up and stretched.

"It seems I have little choice," she said to Hugon. "I must accompany you, I suppose."

"I've seen no signs of danger here," Hugon said. "You may remain by the fire, if you choose."

"Men are always offering me that woman's privilege," Gwynna said, and smiled slightly. "I think I'd prefer to go with you. With any luck, I may be able to see you fall into some really unpleasant misfortune . . . eaten by wild beasts, perhaps. Or, if this is really the Island of the Old Ones . . ."

"Please, lady, I'd rather not hear about that," Gorash said, hastily.

The group moved slowly off, following the shore's direction, along the upper ridge; through scattered, wind-bent pines, walking watchfully. Hugon, Fraak seated on his shoulder, led the way; once, he glanced back and noticed the Lady Gwynna following with long strides, apparently not hampered at all by her thin sandals. Unwillingly, he felt a liking for the wench, though, as he thought, she had a tongue like a razor and the mind of a serpent.

But a real woman, not a delicate court flower as he'd thought her to be, at first. A woman of Meryon, the best kind, Hugon thought.

"Here," he said suddenly, halting. The others came up beside him as he pointed ahead. "There's a bit of a wall, like the others I saw inland. Matter of fact, this wall seems in better shape. Let's have a look."

Seen closer, the wall was obviously the work of hands . . . but not necessarily human hands, Hugon thought, with a slight chill. It could be the foundation of a building, a long course of gigantic blocks that seemed to melt back into the rocky hillside.

But the blocks were huge. smooth masses of something

that looked like black volcanic glass, and each fitted to the next with hairline tightness. Looking at them, Hugon could not think of any craftsmen of his world who could work such stone so well.

"It's only a wall," Zamor said, and prodded at it with his sheathed sword. "Anyone could have built it."

But Gwynna was looking at it, her fine-boned face pale.

"Could anyone?" she said, in a low voice, and turned away.

There was nothing else for another quarter of a mile; then, they came to the road.

It began in the gray beach sand, and ran, straight as an arrow's flight, inland. Wide, and made of the same glassy black stuff, it was certainly a road.

"Well, now," Zamor said. "A road goes to a place, doesn't it? A village, perhaps, or a castle . . ."

"I saw another road like this, back among the pines," Hugon said. "It ran a short distance, and stopped. From nowhere to nowhere. You'll perceive that this one appears to begin nowhere."

"No reason for both ends of a road to resemble each other," Zamor pointed out, and turned, to stride forward along the black stone. "It's easier walking than yonder gravel, anyway."

The rest followed.

The road ran, slanting slightly upward, but undeviatingly straight, between piled ridges of rock on which the twisted pines grew sparsely. The sun was higher now, and the air warmer; it suddenly occurred to Hugon that their only drink was the wine in that single jar they had brought from the beach, slung now on Zamor's shoulder.

"Fraak?" he said, softly. The dragonet peered down from Hugon's shoulder.

"Could you fly up, and look about?" Hugon asked. "Look for water, especially . . . a pool, perhaps, or a river. Or people."

Fraak trilled a falling note. "I do!" he said, and

launched himself from Hugon's shoulder, wings beating, upward at a sharp angle. The group of people stood, watching the dragonet flying higher and higher, until he was only a speck against the brightness. He circled in wide swooping curves; then he descended, arrowing almost straight down with folded wings, until he was dangerously close to the ground. His wings opened, with an audible snap, and he swooped in, to Hugon's shoulder.

"Eeee!" Fraak cried excitedly; his wings opened and closed, and he panted puffs of pale smoke. "I saw something!"

"All right, all right, be calm," Hugon told the little dragonet, stroking its scales. "What did you see?"

"Something!" Fraak panted. "Big, big, moving. There, there, that side, and that side!"

Zamor's hand dropped to his sword hilt; Hazarsh and Gorash stared at the rocky slopes, and Gorash muttered something under his breath. Gwynna made no sign, except that her green eyes widened somewhat.

"What was moving, Fraak? People? Animals?"

"No, no, not people," Fraak said, and moved his whiskers in a puzzled way. "Not animals. Like people, but bigger, and not right. Long arms, long, long arms, and all gray. Many! Hugon, we run, run, now!"

"Long arms and gray color?" Zamor asked, frowning. "What could that be? Little lizardkin, what did you see, anyway?"

"I am afraid!" Fraak said, and flapped his wings again. "Please, run! Run!"

"It might be a fine notion to take his advice," Gwynna said. Hazarsh had already done so; he was pelting away, down the road in the direction from which they had come, back toward the sea. Gorash was behind him, but not far behind.

"No!" Fraak squalled, suddenly, rising a few feet in the air, and then settling back on Hugon's shoulder. He flapped with wild agitation, crying out again. "No, no, wrong way!"

Hazarsh was a tiny form, now, far down the road.

Then, from either side, something moved, coming out of the gray rock, something that seemed almost the same color as the rock. Whatever they were, they were twice the size of the running figure; erect, walking . . . but they were not men. Two came from one side, and three from the other, moving with surprising speed, and blocking Hazarsh's path. He seemed to stop and try to run back, but there was another behind nim.

Gorash, still a distance behind Hazarsh, had turned, and was returning at an even faster speed, head downward and arms flailing wildly. The gray shapes hid Hazarsh briefly; then they seemed to move back into the slopes. And Hazarsh was . . . gone.

"Run away!" Fraak cried again. Hugon shuddered, staring back down the road; he grasped Gwynna's hand with his left, and drew the long blade with his right. Beside him Zamor's sword slid out, with a snicking sound.

"Let's make haste," Hugon said, making an effort to sound calm. Gwynna's hand tightened suddenly on his own as they began to move. Then, gasping horribly, Gorash arrived; he was unable to run farther, but he kept on, moving as fast as he could, choking out words as he went.

"Demons!" he choked, looking back at the others. "Gh-ghosts! No . . . FACES!" He staggered on, his breath tearing in huge gulps.

Hugon broke into a trot, and Gwynna with him; Zamor came beside them, his sword out, his long legs loping easily along.

"No . . . faces, he . . . says!" Hugon panted. "Sounds . . . inconvenient!"

Zamor barked a deep laugh, but with a note of tension; and the dragonet lifted into the air, sailing just over their heads and uttering a rising and falling whistle of excitement.

Then, just ahead, Hugon saw the odd structure, and called out, pointing. It was atop the ridge on the right of the road, a round, squat tower of black stone. As they came closer, abreast of it, it loomed against the sky; a narrow path led from the road, up to a single narrow doorway in the tower's wall. Hugon came to a stop, panting.

"Zamor, look there!" he puffed. "Like . . . a guard tower, it might be . . . one door, and no windows!"

"Better than an open place like this," Zamor said, staring at it. "Unless . . . ah, but there's nothing alive in that." He began to mount the path, and the others followed. Gorash, seeing them go, returned, and went up after the other three, chattering with fear as he went.

Zamor, at the narrow doorway of the tower, paused to stare into the shadowy interior; he turned, and called out, "Empty!"

Then, they were all inside, gasping for breath; Hugon leaned against a wall and stared about him, while Gorash collapsed in a gibbering heap, and Gwynna leaned on Hugon's shoulder, her breath coming hard.

The tower's interior was simply a stone floor, some thirty feet across, strewn with rubble. Overhead, a round circle of bright sky admitted light; there was no roof at all, and no window of any kind. The door through which they had come was oddly made; twice the height of a man, but so narrow that Zamor had some trouble squeezing his big body through it. Not a door for large folk, Hugon thought. Or . . . a door at all, then? ·

"If we're pursued, it'll be hard on any man that comes through that," Zamor grunted. "It's tight as a virgin." He moved to stand at one side of the slit door, and Hugon moved to the other. Cautiously, Hugon peered out.

"We are pursued, brother," he said, in a low voice. "But I'll be damned if I know by what. Look, and see."

Zamor hazarded a look and drew back, eyes wide. His black face was grayer.

"Great Snake!" he muttered.

They were on the road below, standing in a close group, seeming to look toward the tower. They were like thickened smoke, Hugon thought. Oddly insubstantial, cylindrical, somehow like an ill-made imitation of an

42

enormous human shape. But the heads were merely oval blank forms, without a single feature. And there were too many arms. How many, it was hard to tell; the Things seemed to shimmer, edgeless and ill-defined, as heat rising from a desert.

But misty as they were, there was an air of purposeful menace about them that sent a prickle of cold down Hugon's back. And there was no sign of Hazarsh; the creatures were capable of some harm, certainly.

"The question is," Hugon said, balancing the long sword thoughtfully, "can they feel a sword's edge?"

"We'll know in a moment," Zamor said, grimly. "One comes."

The Thing moved up the path toward the tower; Hugon, risking another glance, had the odd impression that it *slid*, rather than walked. It was obviously too large to pass the narrow door, though, he thought.

Gorash, huddled against the wall, shrieked as he saw it through the slit door. He scrabbled at the wall behind him, as if trying to dig through it. The Thing was not in Hugon or Zamor's sight, but, between them, a long gray arm suddenly emerged through the door. It stretched, impossibly; there seemed to be a hand, with clutching tentacular fingers, searching. The arm shot clear across the tower's width, toward the squalling Gorash, and snatched at him, seizing a kicking leg. Then it drew him, writhing, across the stone floor.

Zamor and Hugon swung together, their blades whistling into the gray stuff. The steel sank in, but seemed to stick. as if in thick clay; both men wrenched desperately, freeing their swords to hack again. There was a deep gash where each blade had cut, but no blood.

Then, from outside, there was a whistling scream, an inhuman sound; but clearly a sound of pain from the Thing. The fingers writhed wildly, but did not release Gorash, who was now howling with mindless terror.

Zamor hacked again, and Hugon slashed as well; but the gray tentacle drew back, still clutching Gorash, yank-

43

ing him brutally through the narrow slit and out of sight. The Thing outside screamed again, and then again, and was silent. But the missing Gorash was equally silent.

"It . . . feels something!" Hugon gasped. "You heard that noise!"

"Yes," Zamor said, his face grim. "But it doesn't bleed."

"Look out, it's back again!" Hugon cried, and swung. The exploring finger of gray sprang out of sight, and there was another whistle of pain from outside.

"It seems to respect the sword, anyway," Zamor grunted. They waited, but no further attempt came.

"What in the name of the thirteen demons is that creature?" Zamor asked, his back flat against the wall and his eyes on the door. "Do you know, Hugon? You say you've studied such matters."

"It's not in any book of monsters I've yet read," Hugon told him, grimly.

Gwynna, white as milk, came to her feet, and walked to the other side of the tower; she bent, and found the shortsword that Gorash had dropped at the last, scooped it up, and came back to stand beside Hugon.

"Now, we are three," Hugon said, grinning sideward at her.

"The creatures cannot be killed," the girl said, with an icy calm. "I think they are . . . guards. Left here by the Old Ones."

Hugon glanced at her in surprise. "You seem to know more than I do," he said. "What else do you know of all this?"

"More than you think," she said in a low voice. "I have read much . . ."

There was a sudden tremendous thud against the tower wall, a blow that seemed to shake the whole structure. Fragments of loose stone fell, powdering and raining down.

Hugon barked an oath, and looked incautiously around the door edge. Outside, he saw gray shapes standing massed and silent, their enormous arms raised, drawn back. A moment later, the arms swung forward, in uni-

44

son, and a second thundering blow shook the tower again.

"They're breaking down the wall!" Hugon cried, and drew the girl away from the vibrating stone, toward the center. Zamor, too, moved back; they stood, swords out, waiting grimly back to back.

"I think we die soon." Zamor said, calmly.

Fraak, uttering a wild note, shot up from the corner where he had been crouching, and sailed up toward the open roof, out into the sky.

"One of us will survive, at any rate," Hugon said. "Now, if only the Great Goddess had seen fit to give a man wings . . ."

There was a third earthquake blow, and a section of stone fell inward, like an opening portal. Through the cloud of dust, the silent gray shapes were visible, standing in a row; and now they moved forward, inexorably, their featureless faces turned toward their prey, long arms raised and reaching.

THREE

"Ha . . . aaah!" Zamor cried, and the long blade slashed out, matched by Hugon's lunging steel beside him. Gwynna, between them, leaned slightly forward, knees bent, and her shorter blade thrust forward. Hugon saw her action from the corner of his eye, and felt a moment of bright wonder at the girl's bravery . . . and at her skill. She held the shortsword like a skilled fighter, he saw . . . and then, there was no more time to think, as a snaking gray arm came at him, and he cut at it.

His blade sank in, but the spreading fingers caught at his arm, and held. An icy cold spread from the touch, and he gasped with pain, involuntarily.

Then a weird howling came, the voices of all of those gray Things in chorus; the icy touch relaxed, and the fingers drew back. Hugon held himself on his feet with difficulty, pain lancing through his arm, and his eyes watering with the agony of the touch. He swayed against Gwynna, who held him upright; he heard her outcry of surprise, and tried to focus his swimming eyes.

The gray creatures were moving back, slowly, making a moaning noise as they did so, back in a line on both sides of the broken wall. Beyond, a man came, walking toward the tower, and the creatures fell back away from him.

He was a small, fat man, in a long brown robe. He had a grizzled beard, and was bald; across one shoulder he lugged a leather sack, and in the other hand he carried a curious staff. It was nearly as long as he was, and it had a round knob at either end; it seemed to be made of dark

47

wood, and he carried it horizontally, across his chest as he came toward those who waited in the tower.

The gray Things whistled again, and the small man shook the staff impatiently, glancing at them. They slid soundlessly back, and then were gone.

"Here, now," the small fat man said, halting at the broken wall and staring. "What have we here?"

And then Fraak came swooping down, to circle wildly about Hugon's head, ululating with joy; he skidded to a landing, and puffed a perfect smoke ring.

"Aaak!" he cried. "Good, good!"

"Your small friend here saw me a moment ago," the fat man said, and stepped over the broken stones to come inside. "Had he not called me . . . well, the Moroloi are dangerous without this rod to protect you." He peered at the three and stiffened, suddenly. "By the Holy Nine!" he said in a different voice, his eyes on Hugon's face. "You there, young man! Who are you?"

Hugon swept his sword up in a salute, returned it to his scabbard. "Hugon of Meryon and clan Kerrin, good sir," he said, formally. "And my deepest thanks to you."

"Accepted," said the fat man. He still studied Hugon oddly. "Hugon, you say. My name is Thuramon, warlock by profession."

"Zamor, I am called," the big black man said, and sheathed his own blade with a grin.

"And the lady is Gwynna of . . . ah, simply Gwynna," Hugon said, cautiously. It might be best to keep some things to oneself, he thought, especially in the presence of a warlock.

But Thuramon's curiously intent gaze was still on Hugon's face.

"Young sir, tell me," he said slowly. "Clan Kerrin, you said? Know you the name Kavin, by any chance?"

"My great ancestor, you mean?" Hugon said. "Of course, sir. Our line is traced directly from that son of his who came back to Meryon, four generations back. If you wish, I could recite every name and sib . . ." He

48

laughed. "Driven into my head, name by name, when I was still a weanling."

"Oho," Thuramon said, and nodded. "That explains it. You startled me greatly, young man. You bear a great resemblance to that ancestor of yours . . . except for your hair, of course." He pulled at his grizzled beard, still staring. "His was silver gray, though he was hardly older than you . . . then."

Hugon stared at the fat man, and Gwynna frowned, puzzled.

"You sound as if you knew Kavin in the flesh," Gwynna said. "If you mean that Kavin who was first king of far Koremon, he died long ago."

"Did he, indeed?" Thuramon asked, his gray eyebrows lifted. "So . . ." He chuckled. "I informed you of my profession. We are a long-lived sort, we wizards."

"I don't care a walnut's worth for your age, old fellow," Zamor said. "But we'd have been no older than today, if you hadn't come with your fine stick, there. What in the Snake's name were those hellish things?"

"Moroloi," Thuramon said. "Guardians, left here . . . a long, long time ago. They were set here to ward a treasure . . ."

"A treasure, you say?" Hugon asked, his eyes brighter.

Thuramon chuckled. "No, lad, I'm sorry . . . no gems nor gold. Much more valuable than that, but of no worth at all to most men. Only to me, and a few like myself . . . and now, I am about to see it, at last!" His eyes were glowing avidly.

"You have a boat, no doubt," Hugon said. "Now, there's a treasure, as far as I'm concerned. And while I think of it . . . Zamor, could you unsling that wine? I've a thirst could drain a lake of wine, now, what with dust and this morning's work."

"A moment," Zamor said, and unslung the jar from his shoulder. "Leave a little for me, brother."

But Gwynna snatched the jar from Hugon's hand, with a green-eyed glare, lifted it to her lips, and took a long draught.

49

"Here, clod," she said, handing to Hugon. "Had you no thought for my own thirst, you peasant lump?"

He laughed, and drank, handing the jar back to Zamor.

"There's water beyond here," Thuramon said. He studied Gwynna, and nodded. "The lady's tongue work alone would name her, if I had not heard her name elsewhere. Gwynna, of Armadoc."

She stared at him boldly, and shrugged. "Well, then, another of you, is it?" she said, and turned away.

Thuramon grinned at her erect back.

"How came you here, tell me?" he asked, cocking his bald head. "A Meryon man, a man of far Numori land, and a lady with . . . a remarkable history for one still young."

"A shipwreck," Hugon answered, shortly. Thuramon nodded.

"I have a boat, true," he said. "But there are Moroloi everywhere. This staff keeps them back." He held up the black rod. "A most expensively acquired tool, but indispensable. You must stay with me while I complete the work I came for . . and then, we shall leave this island." He grinned. "So that you may fully realize your luck . . . you may be the first to leave here alive, out of many who have come here over the years. Your famous ancestor, Hugon . . . he was known for his luck. It may be you've inherited it." He gestured with the staff. "Come with me."

Thuramon turned and went toward the road below; the two men and the girl followed closely, looking about. There was no sign of the gray Things anywhere; nor any sign of Gorash, either, not even a spot of blood.

Thuramon led them along the road, walking swiftly for such a small and pudgy man, clucking occasionally to Fraak in an odd language full of musical sounds, to which Fraak replied with joyful notes.

"I learned the ancient speech of the dragon folk a long time ago," Thuramon said as they strode along. He stretched out a hand to scratch Fraak's head, where the little beast sat curled on Hugon's shoulder. The dragonet closed its eyes in ecstasy, purring.

"You're most fortunate, young man," Thuramon told Hugon. "These small dragons are difficult to tame, giving their love rarely, but when they do, they are the best of beasts."

"I've found him most useful, indeed," Hugon said. "As a firelighter, and as a gerfalcon of skill."

"While his discourses may contain little wisdom," Thuramon said, pursing his lips thoughtfully, "he sings most charmingly, as you have doubtless found."

"I do, I do!" Fraak carolled, and puffed.

"He has other uses," Thuramon said. "I myself have written somewhat on the subject of dragons . . . his droppings, for example, may be made into several electuaries of great potency, one which can be used to calm nervous horses, and another an aphrodisiac of mighty power . . ."

Far ahead, a curious shape appeared on the horizon; the road appeared to run straight to that point, and Hugon stared hard, trying to make it out. Then, as they drew closer, he began to see details.

It was a dome, but so enormous that it seemed almost a mountain. In the distance, its sweeping curve glittered, as if studded with jewels that reflected the sunlight. Around it, thin needle shapes, convoluted and bent in odd angles, rose, and as they came nearer, Hugon could see angular shapes too, like small pyramids and cones among the needle forms.

They strode on and on, still at the same swift pace set by Thuramon, who seemed tireless. From time to time, Hugon glanced at the girl, but she kept up, without complaint, though her face was damp with sweat.

It was nearly another hour before they came close enough to see that gigantic dome looming over them; and before them, a path of black stone that led straight to a tall, narrow doorway.

"We are here," Thuramon said, his eyes bright with triumph. "Keep close, all of you. There are Moroloi among these buildings."

"Buildings?" Hugon asked, staring about him. The eerie stone blocks and skyward-pointing needles bore no resemblance to any building he had ever seen.

"The Old Ones were very different from you and I," Thuramon told him. They were at the doorway now, a doorway as narrow and tall as that of the tower had been; the warlock squeezed through, and the others followed, one by one, Zamor grunting with effort as he came last.

"Welcome to the most ancient archive in the world," Thuramon said, his voice echoing hollowly under the mighty dome.

Above, light slanted down in multicolored rays from a thousand openings of colored glass. Hugon, staring upward, realized that these were the glitterings on the dome; looking up, it was as if he looked into a sky filled with great glowing stars in unfamiliar patterns.

All around, in the light-stippled shadows, shapes stood; cylinders, spheres, squat blocks, row on row stretching away into the enormous circle under the dome. Thuramon's face was alight with joy; he gave a curious skip, and uttered a wordless sound of excited pleasure.

"So many years . . ." He muttered. "So many . . . and now, at last, the keys are here, under my hand . . ." He drew a small roll of paper out of his sleeve and spread it out, studying it.

"Yes, yes . . ." he muttered again. He glanced at the two men. "You may earn your passage with me, if you like," he said with a grin. "I had thought I would have to bear away only as much as I could carry myself, but with two strong backs . . . three, if the lady wishes to be of help . . ." He chortled again, and moved swiftly toward one of the nearest objects, a tall, columnar thing of shining metal.

"Now, a moment, sir wizard," Hugon said, coming

52

after him. "I wouldn't for the world hold you back from your worthy work, but a little explanation, if you would . . ."

"I told you," Thuramon said, pausing before the cylinder. He leaned close, and Hugon saw that there were twisting letters engraved on the thing. "This is an archive," Thuramon said, impatiently. "A library, if you will, a museum . . ." He followed the letters, muttering under his breath. "Ah! If this is Gwa, then Vang must be . . . there!" He straightened up and trotted away, purposefully. Hugon shrugged, and grinned at Zamor and Gwynna; they followed.

He had stopped at another tall cylinder, and now he was moving his hands intently, pressing against the coppery metal. As the others arrived, Thuramon uttered a cry of joy; the cylinder seemed to split down its length, and swung apart into two halves. Within, there were thousands of small divisions, like the cells of a giant honeycomb, each no larger than a hand; at these, Thuramon looked with the expression of a bridegroom regarding his new life.

"So many . . ." he crooned. "So many!" Hastily, he consulted his paper roll again, and peered at the divisions, which bore tiny labels of metal. His hands flew in one and then another, drawing out small cylinders the size of a finger, brightly colored. There were red ones, green ones, yellow and blue and a dozen glittering colors beside; and at each one Thuramon crowed, and thrust it into his leather sack.

"More than I can possibly read through in years!" he cried, grasping more of the rolls. "By the Nine . . . no, I must choose well. Quickly, to the next!" He galloped off again, swinging the sack.

The next was another cylinder, where Thuramon repeated his performance while the three watched in puzzled wonder. Now the sack was full, and heavy; silently, Zamor took it on his shoulder. Thuramon scuttled on.

This time, he paused at a squat pyramid; opened, this

53

disclosed a supply of flat, smooth plates that seemed to be made of greenish glass. He selected a number of these and wrapped them with great care in a scrap of cloth, giving them to Hugon to carry.

Then came another cylinder, but here the divisions held oddly shaped boxes of all sizes and colors. Thuramon danced impatiently, selecting and changing his mind time and again. He pressed four of the objects into Gwynna's hands; she took them without complaint, though she held them with difficulty, Hugon noticed, as though they were strangely heavy for their small size. Thuramon himself made a crude sling of a part of his brown garment, to carry another six of the objects. He paused, staring around, and sighed deeply.

"There's so much . . ." he said in a low voice. "Still . . . I have what I came for. And much else, besides. Things I've taken out of . . . no more than greed; that's all it is, greed." He shook his bald head and grinned wryly at the three. "Come now, let's go, quickly, before I yield to temptation still further. We cannot remain here too long, and we must return to my boat before dark."

They emerged again through the narrow door, carrying their loads. Once Thuramon cautioned Hugon nervously about the glass plates he carried, but otherwise he said nothing more. As he strode along, he seemed almost sad, compared with his former excitement.

They went swiftly along the road, back toward the sea, pausing to drink at a small spring among the rocks. Then, on, as the sun sank lower ahead of them.

Occasionally, Hugon thought he saw movements among the rocks, and his hand shifted toward his sword; but none of the gray Things showed themselves. Thuramon still carried the rod on his shoulder as he marched.

The sun had almost reached the sea's rim as they came down the road toward the beach. They were weary, now. Hugon had an arm supporting Gwynna, who limped but refused to let her load be carried by Hugon. Her face was set and white, but she had uttered no word of complaint.

The boat lay, drawn high on the beach, not far from the road's end. Hugon, seeing it, realized that they might have seen it on their earlier passing had they gone but a few paces further. And those two poor sods might still be alive, he thought, wryly. But then, of course, Thuramon would have been left here. Not that the old warlock couldn't take fine care of himself, though.

It was a common fisherman's boat, high prowed, with a single mast; the painted eye was on either side, a custom of Meryon fisher folk.

"I'd have expected something more . . . well, stately," Hugon said, as they came wearily across the sand toward the boat. Thuramon chuckled, and put his burden over the side, tenderly; he did the same with the other loads, one by one. Then he clambered up and over the side; leaned over, extending his hands to Gwynna.

"Up, lass," he said, grasping her wrists. "Now, you two, heave away."

Zamor and Hugon leaned against the prow and thrust; the boat slid down the sand, till they waded in water. The two men grasped the gunwales and swung up into the boat, and now she lifted on the first wave, rocking.

"Oars?" Hugon said, glancing around. Thuramon shook his head.

"No need," he said, and leaned over the prow, muttering. The boat swung seaward and out, taking the deeper swells as if there were oars pulling . . . but there were none.

"Now, the sail," Thuramon told the two men, and they helped him lift the triangular sheet, bracing it up. The evening wind took it, and the boat slanted away into the twilight. Thuramon dropped a steering oar over and sat down, holding it.

"You'll find food there, in the forepeak," the warlock said in a tired voice. "I . . . am not hungry, but you most certainly are."

55

"Damn me, yes!" Zamor said, and moved forward to rummage. Gwynna yawned and settled herself in a fold of sailcloth. She stared at Hugon, and said, "You may bring me something, please. Whatever there is . . ." and she yawned again.

Hugon awoke, feeling the gentle sway of the boat and the sun's warmth on his face. From the height of the sun, it was late morning already; he sat up stiffly and stretched.

"Aho, brother," Zamor's voice came from aft. "Last awake, then?"

Zamor sat at the steering oar, relaxed and grinning. At the fore end of the boat Gwynna knelt, carefully washing her face in a small pannikin, working away with the neatness of a cat. Beside Zamor, the warlock lay curled in a blanket, snoring.

"East by north, the old man said," Zamor told Hugon. "Before he went off to sleep. Says we'll sight land before tomorrow noon, with any luck."

Hugon moved stiffly, coming to sit beside Zamor. He glanced down at the snoring figure.

"What land?" he asked.

"Called it the Grassy Land, and said we're not to go in there," Zamor said. "But from there, it's only a bit farther to where he wants to go. Koremon, he says."

"Koremon!" Hugon sat up. "I've heard much of that land, but never gone there. You heard the old man speak of that ancestor of mine, Kavin . . . he was its first king. The folk that went there came from Dorada, fleeing some sort of pestilence, then . . ." Hugon paused, and looked around the boat. "Where's that dragonet? Still with us?"

"Eee!" The voice came from overhead. Hugon looked up, to see the creature wheeling above the mast. It cried out again, and swooped in beside him.

"I catch fish!" Fraak said, triumphantly. His long tongue flicked out, delicately cleaning silver scales from his whiskers.

56

"You like fish, do you?" Hugon asked, grinning down at Fraak

"Like fish!" Fraak declared. "In cage. they make me eat dead meat. Pfff!" He made a disgusted sound. "Like live meat. Especiaily fisn." He curled his tail around himself and relaxed.

"He's been sieeping since dawn," Zamor said, indicating Thuramon. "A man of his age needs sleep . . ."

The warlock opened a bright eye and fixed it on the big man.

"If you knew my age, you would be surprised," he said, and sat up, fully awake.

In the bows, Gwynna had completed her toilet, and turned to look toward the men. She studied them a moment, then came aft, moving with surefooted grace and looking completely rested.

"I see a cooking stone, there where I was," she said, looking from Hugon to Zamor. "And there is food to be prepared." She smiled, cool and composed. "Surely one of you can prepare some sort of breakfast?"

Hugon looked at her thoughtfully, and rubbed his chin. Zamor looked at the sky and chuckled, deep in his throat, and Thuramon turned his head to study the sternpost with deep interest.

"My lady, there's something you seem to forget," Hugon said, slowly. "We are no longer aboard the galley." He stood up and braced himself against the boat's roll, spread-legged. His eyes fixed on her green ones, holding them. "You, now . . . till I find a proper buyer, you're . . . should we say, in my custody? Now, I find the idea of having service done me very appealing. I've never been able to afford it before."

"You unutterable . . ." Gwynna began, her eyes blazing.

"Ah, ah!" Hugon lifted a hand. "If it's unutterable, don't utter it. Now . . ." He smiled, benevolently. "All of us require breakfast. Knowing your lack of experience, I shall forgive small errors in your work . . . but not sulkiness." He stared at her. "Breakfast, girl. Now!"

57

"You . . ." she almost stuttered in her rage. "You'd dare to order me . . ."

He moved a step closer, and looked into her furious face, his eyes coldly certain.

"If you refuse, girl, I'll lay my swordbelt across your pretty rear till you'll not sit for a week," Hugon said without raising his voice. "Go now."

"You wouldn't dare . . ." she began, and saw his eyes.

"You . . . would," she said in a low voice, and turned to move slowly forward to the cookstone.

The wind held, not a strong one, but steady. The boat forged on, and the sea was a smooth swell under her keel.

Gwynna had done very well about the breakfast, though she had worked with an expression that implied much.

"I think she'd have gladly poisoned us all," Zamor muttered to Hugon; they sat, picking the last of the breakfast from their wooden bowls. Beside them, Thuramon was delving among the strange items of his cargo, crooning to himself; Gwynna sat, far in the bows, her back turned regally.

"Why, the girl's got the hand of a fine cook indeed," Hugon answered, lifting an eyebrow. "Look you, if we can't sell her for a decent price, we'd do well to keep her by us. Why, one of us could marry her, perhaps."

"It was yourself warned *me* concerning widows," Zamor told him. "You'd not live any longer than it took that wench to find a suitable potion . . . unless she preferred to find some more painful way, considering how she looked at you."

"Well, then, wed her yourself," Hugon suggested.

"If ever I find my way back to Numori land, I've three good wives there already," Zamor said. "Or I did, at any rate." He sighed. "No Numori lass would stay unwed all the time I've been away. But I doubt I could get used to that queer color . . . no offense, brother, but in a woman . . . no. And she's most unhealthily lean, too, for my taste." He leaned on the steering oar and looked gloomy.

58

"As long as I've had to do without a pair of busy thighs, though, almost anything would seem good."

Thuramon glanced up from his business and grinned. "We'll land at Koremon's port, called Drakona, a fine great town," Thuramon said. "There are ships come there from all the world, and willing girls enough, I think."

Zamor sighed, but said nothing. Hugon stared curiously at the objects in Thuramon's lap, the small cylinders. The warlock held one, like an old fashioned scrollbook, unwound; but he held it upward, peering at it through the sunlight.

"A book?" Hugon asked.

"A most ancient book," Thuramon said, still turning the roll in his fingers. "But not made to be read by men's eyes. See how the light shines through it, thus . . . the letters, so small . . ." He sighed. "It will be difficult, very difficult." He rolled it up again, and put it back in the pile.

"Whose eyes, then?" Hugon asked.

"The Old Ones," Thuramon said. "An ancient race, dead before man came. There was a greater land there, in the southern sea, when they lived . . . and once they set up certain places where their books and other things might be kept. For the future . . ." He stared at the objects in his lap, darkly. "I don't know why they did so much, to be honest. For their own kind, or for others that they thought might come . . . who knows? But there, on that island, is the last of their archive halls. I learned of its existence a long time ago, in another place. And of the guardians, those Moroloi, unkillable and mindless, who would slay any who came near."

"Your staff seemed to be a perfectly sound defense, sir," Hugon said. "It saved us, too."

"It is a simple thing, that staff," Thuramon told him. "And like most simple things, it took me long years to make it. And more years than that to discover that it could be made at all. I sought the clues, in one place and another . . . for this." He touched the pile of small cylinders and grinned.

"Listen, young man," Thuramon went on, leaning closer, his eyes brightly intent. "I am very old, older than you would credit if I told you. I'll die someday, like any other man . but I've much to do before then, much. Once, a great evil was done. a thing so evil that it should not be spoken of . . and you have no need to know it, in any case. But because of this evil thing. many worlds were shaken . . . not your world alone, but many."

His eyes held Hugon's, intently. "If you live long enough, you may understand what I say . . . or in another life, in time. But I can tell you as much as you need to know, now. I came to these lands, a long time ago, to work a certain task; a work that others like me do, in other places . . . a work that may never be finished. And I found a man who could serve that work."

Hugon, still and quiet with his back against the rough wood of the boat's side, listened. He felt a strange awe, a new thing in him who had always been a mocker and a skeptic. Thuramon's eyes glowed as he spoke, and Hugon heard.

"He was . . . like any other man, good, bad, and middling," Thuramon said, and smiled to himself. "Better than some, worse than others. What else can I say? He had honor, and courage . . . and a little wisdom. Enough wisdom not to want to be a king . . ."

"Now, that's a considerable wisdom," Hugon said.

"You understand that, do you?" Thuramon said. "Good. Well, I tricked him, in the warlock's way. Gained his word to help me in a struggle which he never fully understood . . . more for my benefit than ever for his own, though the evil we fought had already touched him and his folk, to their great sorrow."

There was a silence, broken only by the lap of waves and the creak of the rigging. High overhead, a seabird cried, and the dragonet stirred, staring upward but not moving. Zamor, listening at the oar, was as still as Hugon.

"The man I speak of was called Kavin, once prince of the lost land Dorada," Thuramon said, slowly. "I was

·with him; and when he and the remnant of his people fled in the end from their destroyed valley, I was also there. And when they came to the land to the east, Kore-Imon, which lies near the Isle of Dragons . . . there too. went with Kavin, and a few companions, out of Kore-mon, into the great mountain, where we found a place of evil. A place that was one of the seedlings of that evil I spoke of . . . and we destroyed it."

Hugon nodded. "I know the tale," he said, "though it seems difficult to believe even a warlock can live so long as that. Old man, that story is of a time . . . why, you would be two hundred!"

"Well, then?" Thuramon said, and grinned again.

"I wish I knew how it is," Hugon said, shrugging. "I've been able to resist the artful tales of fine charlatans in a hundred places . . . and here I sit, believing your wild story. I do believe it . . . and I cannot understand why." He chuckled, "But go on, then."

"There's so little truth in the world that it's easy to distinguish its face in a crowd, by reason of its oddity," Thuramon said.

"I believe him," Zamor said suddenly, and fell silent again, watching Thuramon.

"I've heard the tale of Kavin," Hugon said, resting his chin in his hand. "How he fared forth to the Black City, where three evil ones ruled; broke their power, and returned to Koremon. Ruled there, and left numerous offspring . . . one of whom was an ancestor of my own, founder of my clan." Hugon chuckled. "A wild rogue, too, it's said, who had to flee Koremon and return to the mountains of Meryon for something of the same reasons I've had myself, at times."

"All true," Thuramon said, solemnly. "But . . . there was a tale never told. I shall tell it to you now . . . for a reason."

Beware magician's reasons, Hugon thought, but said nothing.

"The last and greatest of those evil ones whom Kavin fought was called . . . Ess. He was not human. There

61

was nothing at all of humanity in him; he came from a world no man could know. I called him evil . . . but he was not. He was neither evil nor good, only so much a stranger to this world that such words had no meaning. And what he was, the things he desired . . . no human could know. And one thing more . . . he could not die."

Hugon stared. "I had heard of some such monster . . . but didn't Kavin slay him, as the story goes?"

Thuramon shook his head. "Here, there lies a deep mystery. Kavin went to the place where Ess dwelled, and then . . ." He stopped and pulled his beard, staring at Hugon. "There are deep things here; it may be too deep for your mind. But let me try. Think now of time, the progression of days and nights as you know it . . . and of the world, the lands and seas and folk, known to you. Of . . . reality."

In the silence, Hugon felt cold. He listened, trying to understand.

"Think now of worlds folded upon worlds, time turning upon itself like the spiral shell of a sea worm, and days that return again, the same yet changing," the old man said. His eyes held steady, earnest. "Yesterday becomes today . . . and today, yesterday, and worlds spread on, through an endless time and space . . . and only one thing remains constant and real through the spinning mist. One thing alone." He stared, hard, into Hugon's eyes. "The living spark that shapes itself, into man. Or into other beasts, who live, spawn, and die . . . but the spark lives."

"This I know already," Zamor said in his deep voice. "We are taught, in our Almor lodge . . ."

"Were you taught this, too?" Thuramon asked. "That a man may live in two, in a hundred places and times . . . at once? That he may move in many worlds at once, in one as a prince, another a beggar . . or that his life may fold backward upon itself, so that he meets his own form in a shadowed street?"

Zamor grunted. "Certain things were told us," he said.

"And we also learned that other things should not be told."

"Now, there's wisdom," Hugon said.

Thuramon paused a moment, then went on. "Kavin . . . returned, as the tale has it. But Kavin . . . not another Kavin, understand, the same Kavin . . . slept, gripped in the sorcery of the creature called Ess. A third Kavin, too, had once passed through such a magic . . . but I will not speak of that. Then, Kavin awoke, and returned at last, to find a land grown great, and his name a legend."

"That's like the ballad of Ernas the Lost," Hugon said, slowly. "How he spent a night in a magic hall, and came back to find he had been gone a hundred years . . ."

"And it might be that tale was true, too," Thuramon said. "Kavin returned, as Ernas did. But, in one way, the Great Goddess gave him a gift . . . unearned, like most of Her gifts. That in spite of his rejection of that Goddess, thrice repeated."

"She is known to be whimsical," Hugon said.

"Indeed," Thuramon said. "Whimsical. I said that Kavin came back, to a land that had forgotten him except as a tale, ruled by his distant descendants . . . and there was still one who waited. A curious . . . person. You may say a witch woman, if you like; one not at all like other women, but still . . . more a woman than most. She had waited for Kavin. Now his wishes are fulfilled. He did not wish to be a ruler, and he is no ruler; he desired peace, and he has it."

Hugon stared. "You speak as if he lived . . . now?"

"He does," Thuramon said. "He is horse master to a lord of Koremon . . . one of his own descent. He lives, contentedly, with a fine woman . . . who is, to all appearances, no more than a woman . . . beside a lake, in which he sometimes fishes."

Hugon leaned back and blew a deep breath, eyes wide.

"Now there's a tale," he said, quietly.

63

"A tale, indeed," Zamor said. "Lord Snake, what a tale. This Kavin, then . . . he's found what he wishes, eh?"

"Certainly," Thuramon said, and he smiled, wryly. "So, surely he will be discontented, in due time."

"Wait, now," Hugon said. "If that's so . . . then who returned to Koremon, as the story has it? Who ruled, in Kavin's name, spawned my own ancestor and all the rest . . . and who's buried there in Kavin's tomb? Some imposter?"

"Kavin himself," Thuramon said. "Both are the same."

"I don't understand," Hugon said, and shrugged.

"I didn't think you would," Thuramon told him. The warlock began to smile, slowly and disquietingly. "You too have a most curious fate, young man . . . and I doubt not you will find it just as hard to understand, though you struggle a lifetime's worth."

"Ah, now, no prophecy, please!" Hugon cried, grinning. "Look you, old sir, I'm willing to believe your tale, take my oath I do. But my blood's been cooled enough . . . no more wizardry for now, I beg you. Those strange wee books you've got there . . . have they more of these mysteries in 'em? Or maybe these Old Ones liked a comic tale, or a romance, as we common humans do . . . or possibly there's a bawdy verse written there? Can you read them?"

Thuramon chuckled. "There might be anything here . . . even what you suggest, though I doubt it. No, I cannot read them, not with ease. A few words, here and there . . ." He sighed. "There's the lengthy work before me. Somewhere, among these books, or in those other things you helped me carry, there's a secret I require. I think I found the correct books . . . but it will be very long before I find that key, itself."

"What key?" Hugon asked. "Something of magic, then?"

"Call it that," Thuramon said. "A key . . . that will find a way back for me . . . no, I can't say more."

Hugon was silent for a while. The talk had disturbed him. Yet he could not understand why that should be so,

64

and that fact also disturbed him. He leaned back, and stared at Gwynna's straight back, in the forward end, biting his lip.

Finally, he stood up and made his way forward, to pause just behind her.

"My Lady," he said, quietly.

"I would prefer not to speak with you," she said, distantly.

"Will you accept my compliments, at least?" he said.

"Compliments?" Her eyes blazed, as she looked back at him. "A compliment, from you? I'd prefer an insult."

"You have a fine handed way with a meal, lady," he said, smiling down at her. "And with a sword. Also, you held the march with us, without complaint. For all that, accept compliment."

"Spit your damned flattery on a rusty swordblade, and go sit upon it," she said, in a level voice.

Hugon chuckled, and returned to the after end, smiling.

"Ah, but that's a fine lass," he said, to Zamor. "A fine, fine lass." And he chuckled again.

FOUR

A stiff morning breeze propelled the boat along the green coast of Lower Koremon. Ahead, the dark mass of rock lifted on the horizon; the fabled Isle of Dragons. The boat tacked, and sailed through the sound that lay between that island and the mainland of Koremon itself. On Thuramon's advice, they kept as well away from that dark rock as possible; but even so, Hugon saw a distant flying thing, high overhead, that was no bird. He watched it as he steered. It slanted down toward the island and vanished there.

Fraak perched on the prow, his triangular head lifted, his bright eyes following that distant flight with silent wonder. As he watched, his wings lifted, moving uneasily, and he sang a low deep note.

"Like me?" Fraak asked, turning his head. "Eee?"

"Like you, handsome one," Thuramon told him. "But a great deal larger." He scratched the dragonet's head. "And wiser, small one. Much wiser."

"Not as pretty?" Fraak asked.

"Well. Probably not," Thuramon said, and chuckled quietly.

Hugon glanced at the dragonet and laughed; then, he watched the shore again, intently.

Far ahead, white sails lifted on the horizon, a ship that moved across the boat's course, going landward. Now it was visible, a tall-prowed, round-bellied merchantman, rolling in the swell.

"That one would be going into Drakosa town,"

Thuramon said. "There, you can see towers, and the outer seawall."

Hugon steered in the merchant's wake, watching the town grow clearer on the skyline. Now, a slim swift ship came, sliding past toward the open sea, a long pennant flying from its topmast; and on the beam, Hugon saw the masts of fishing boats in a distant convey. Gulls wheeled overhead, crying.

"Now my day of ease is over," Hugon said, gloomily. He shifted on the seat and sighed.

"What's your woe, brother?" Zamor, who had been lying with closed eyes on a fold of sail, sat up on one elbow, grinning at Hugon. "Ah, there's the town! Ha!" He stretched and licked his lips. "I swear by the Snake, I'll not set foot on any ship again if I'm not compelled to at sword's point . . ."

"We've problems in plenty," Hugon said. He jerked his thumb at the still-aloof Gwynna. "There's our prime one. The warlock here's told me much about the customs of Koremon, and it seems we'll have to be watchful, or our bird will fly."

Zamor looked inquiring. "Customs?"

"If she's called a slave, we'll have no right to bring her ashore," Hugon said. "They've a law against it, being civilized folk. She'll never keep her teeth together, damn it; the moment we're ashore, she need only cry for the civil protection, and we've no merchandise left. Ah, well . . ." He shrugged.

"I hadn't any special wish to become rich," Zamor said, teeth flashing. "Not woman-selling, at any rate."

"Ah, but I did," Hugon said. "Never having had more than two or three gold pieces together, I wondered what it might be like to have . . . oh, a bagful. Possibly to ride home to the glen with a jingling pocket, on a fine horse . . ."

Thuramon listened, and now he leaned closer, with a thin smile, stroking his beard.

"You've done me some small service, you two," he said, in a low voice, and glanced at the girl's back. "Also . . .

68

I've another reason for . . . ah, assisting the gods' will, as it concerns you, Hugon. Will you accept my assistance?"

Hugon felt a warning memory; magicians' help was often a surprisingly overpriced article, he thought. But still . . .

"Assistance?"

"A small spell," Thuramon said. "I must admit, in spite of long years of study, there are still many things I cannot do. To render a woman tame and venomless, permanently . . . I doubt any warlock can manage so mighty a wonder. But to calm her, and make her silent . . . or as silent as she can be, without injuring her to any degree . . . that, I may do."

"Hm." Hugon considered the matter.

"Best speak soon, young man," Thuramon said. "There's the quayside in sight."

"It would seem the only way," Hugon muttered. "Do it, then."

Thuramon rose, and moved toward the prow. He called out, in a soft voice, "My Lady Gwynna."

She turned, and looked up toward him. He drew something from his sleeve, a small bright object, that swung from a silver chain, and held it out, swinging it slowly.

"See . . . see . . ." Thuramon said, in a low, singing voice. He was staring down at the girl, whose eyes seemed glassy, as she watched. Now, he bent lower, and began to whisper in her ear. She sat, eyes fixed, as he backed slowly away; she seemed not to see anything.

Thuramon continued to move back, till he came to the steering seat, where Hugon waited; he lowered his plump body down, grinning.

"Now, lad, take this," Thuramon said, holding out the bright object. Hugon took it, and looked at it; it was a small, flat disc of crystal, on which an odd, angular letter had been deeply cut. It was suspended from a thin silver chain; and as it lay in his palm, it seemed almost living, warm.

"The lady will do as you say," Thuramon told him. "At

69

least, in most things. Only an amateur of the Art would guarantee what a woman will do in all particulars, certainly not I. And the spell will last at least an hour or two, possibly as long as half a day, though no longer. She will awake, then, with no memory of what has happened, but completely herself again."

"Herself," Hugon said, flatly. "Oh, well . . ."

"Wait," Thuramon told him. "Keep that bauble; whenever it seems necessary, you need only show it to her, and in a moment, she will again be as she is now."

"Ah," Hugon said, more cheerfully. He put the jewel away.

"But there's a slight flaw."

"I thought as much."

"Each time 'tis used, she will resist it more," Thuramon said. "The duration of her enchantment will grow a little shorter each time, and then, at last, the time will come when the jewel will no longer work at all. I cannot say how often it can be used; a dozen times, possibly more. But not much more, you understand. So, use it sparingly, with care."

Hugon glanced ahead; the girl still sat, eyes fixed. He called out, "Gwynna, come here."

The long quays of the city were closer. Hugon watched the girl as she came obediently toward him, and kept an eye on the nearing docks as well. She stood, waiting, and he told her to sit down. She did it, without a word.

"Gods," Hugon said fervently, and paid attention to his task again. The boat swung and ran in beside a stone wharf; Zamor leaped ashore, and drew a line around a squat pillar, tying it. Then, Thuramon lifted his treasures ashore, handling them as if they were children, delicately.

A man in an embroidered cloak, and a jerkin with a glittering emblem on its front, was descending to the dock, followed by two fat individuals bearing staves. Hugon, looking up, had no doubt that these were Drako-

70

sa's civic guards; in all towns, he thought, such functionaries seem to have the same look.

But they seemed to know Thuramon; the cloaked man bent, in a deep courtesy, to greet him.

"These others are guests of mine," Thuramon told the man, with an inclusive gesture. "There's no need to require a port tax." And the fellow departed, with a few more bows.

Hugon lifted the girl ashore, and followed her himself.

"You seem to be a citizen, here," he said to Thuramon.

"I have a sentimental feeling for the town," Thuramon said. "I returned here, a few years ago, and keep a house in the city. Ah, that reminds me. Would you gentlemen care to aid me in carrying these small matters?" He indicated the sack and the other things.

"Why not?" Zamor said, and gathered up a load; Hugon followed suit. Fraak, chuckling, settled on his shoulder, and the girl followed, her eyes still empty. They followed the warlock up the stone stair to the level of the street.

The streets that led into the town were crowded with people, busy with life and noise. As the four moved through the narrow roads, Hugon and Zamor stared about, curious as a pair of country yokels, and Fraak's head swiveled to and fro as he too drank in the sights.

The houses were tall and ornate, brightly painted in many colors, and the town was cleaner to Hugon's nose than many such places where he had been before. The people looked to be a handsome, cheerful-looking breed; they were much like the Meryon folk from whom they had come. Hugon noticed that there was another type as well, small, brown-skinned folk who seemed to mix with the others on equal terms.

They passed into a broad square, lined with ancient trees, past a squat round temple that bore the glyph of Orcas, the Sea God; across the rooftops Hugon glimpsed the arches of other temples. A tolerant place, he thought, recalling that these people worshipped the Great Mother

71

in their own tradition; but it seemed evident that they permitted other gods as well.

He saw men of a dozen races passing; once, a couple of kilted Grothans, and then a white-robed, hawk-nosed nomad of the western plain beyond the sea. There were three or four sallow men with slanting eyes, dressed in furs and barbaric jewelry, who passed chattering in a singing tongue that Hugon did not recognize. And there were still others of nations that he did not know; seamen and traders, he guessed, from the general look of them.

Thuramon turned up a street lined with busy shops, where merchants chattered loudly with buyers; past shelves loaded with all sorts of goods.

"Great Snake, what I'd give for such a spell as you've laid on that lass," Zamor observed, grinning. "Look there, Hugon. She's passed every shop without turning her head. If I could use such sorcery on my own wives . . ."

Thuramon beckoned them on. They turned into a broader, less noisy street, lined with tall houses, and came at last to a low green door in a white wall. Thuramon knocked.

The door swung open almost at once; a squat, extremely hairy man stood there, so short that he was almost a dwarf. He grinned up at Thuramon, and bounced on his heels, making a curious chittering sound as he swung the door wide, but saying nothing.

"Come, and welcome to my humble home," Thuramon said, and they followed him within; the hairy one closed the door behind them and bounced ahead, still chittering.

They were in a garden, where oddly shaped trees overhung neat plots of flowers and herbs. Beyond, the white stone front of a great house rose, and a wider door stood open on a broad hall. Two more of the hairy servitors stood waiting, dressed, like the first, in brown leather, and like him uttering pleased and wordless sounds, and bouncing up and down.

"Sir wizard," Zamor said, staring at those servants, "if

72

I offend, forgive me . . . but there's something most familiar about these housemen of yours. Haven't I seen their like swinging in trees in my own land?"

Thuramon glanced at him and chuckled. "True," he said. "They are indeed apes. I find them the best of servants, being cleaner and more dexterous than some of human kind . . . and also, they cannot speak any word of human kind, and therefore do not gossip at all."

He led them into the great hall and paused, motioning to an ape servant. The servant took their bundles, gathering all together in his long arms, and scuttled away purposefully. Another servant grinned and bounced on his heels, waiting.

"This one will lead you to your rooms," Thuramon said. "You may remain my guests as long as you wish. I myself am a somewhat solitary sort, and may seem lacking in politeness . . . forgive me, if you will, if I am not seen often." He paused, pulling his beard thoughtfully, and stared at the girl. She stood, like a statue, staring at nothing. "There's another matter, however," the warlock said, slowly. "Are you still resolved to hold this woman to some ransom?"

Hugon shrugged. "If possible," he said.

"As you wish," Thuramon said. "But in this, I will not aid you, beyond that small spell I gave you. Nor hinder you, either. If you can keep the girl, do so. But she is clever, and no law of this land will aid you to hold her." He sighed. "For a time, until you decide your course, I will instruct my servants not to permit her to leave this house. But I will do no more, and if she insists, I must give way finally."

Hugon nodded. "Understood," he said. "I'll ask no more than that, and thank you for so much."

In the upper story of the house, there were high-ceilinged, cool rooms, furnished richly; and to Hugon's vast pleasure, a great pool of warm water steamed in a marble-walled room beyond the others. Glancing into that room, he chuckled with pleasure, and scratched his salt-crusted head, anticipating.

73

Hugon took the girl's arm, and led her into one of the rooms; he had her sit down, and left her there. In another room, he found Zamor, already busy with a table full of hot food that a hairy servant had brought. The big black glanced up, grinning, his mouth full.

"Mmpf!" he said, gesturing. "You'll find some fine bits of clothing piled there . . . ought to tickle your foppish ways, brother. It's a fine host indeed, our wizard is."

"A bath'll be even more to the point," Hugon said. "I've gone unwashed since I was first flung into the galleys, except for rain and the sea. I'm off to drown my fleas. Save some of that wine for me, eh?"

When he returned, Zamor was sprawled on a pile of furs, grunting in satiate comfort; and there was still ample food and wine left, which Hugon assaulted. Zamor, opening one eye, commented on the other's newly donned finery with a deep laugh.

"I don't deny it, friend Zamor," Hugon said, and selected a fat bird from his plate. "I've a touch of peacock in my nature, but it does no harm. Alas, it's a world where a man's judged too readily by his cloak and not his works."

"How long, think you, will it be before the girl returns to herself?" Zamor asked, closing his eyes again.

"I've no idea," Hugon said. He drank some wine, and pushed back his chair. "But I've regained my strength to deal with her, thanks to Lord Thuramon's excellent cook . . . whoever or whatever that one is."

"I've trouble thinking of the matter of his cook," Zamor said. "In Numori, a monkey makes a fine dinner, too, but not in quite the same way."

Hugon laughed, and leaned back. He stared around the big room, and suddenly sat up in his chair, with an exclamation.

"Oho, a lute?" He stood up and went to where the instrument leaned against a wall, picked it up and turned it around admiringly. "A fine one, too . . ." Hugon plucked a string. "Though not in tune. La, la . . ." He tried the pegs, turning them up.

74

Under the table, Fraak had been sitting quietly, nibbling on bones that both men had been giving him as they ate. Now he walked out, on his short legs, and lifted his snout at the sound of the lute string.

"Eee!" the dragonet said, and emitted a pipe-note.

"Perfect!" Hugon said, and matched the note with a string. He twanged another, and then a third, tuning them to Fraak's piping scale.

"You've the makings of a duet, there," Zamor observed. Hugon ran his fingers across the strings, and found a tune, uncertainly at first, and then with masterly skill. Fraak puffed a jet of smoke, and began to emit flute sounds in perfect counterpoint to the strings.

"Fine," Zamor said, lifting himself on an elbow to listen. "Oh, very fine," and grinned.

"Of my own composition," Hugon told him, running a rapid series of notes on the lute as he spoke. He grinned down at Fraak. "But never with such accompaniment before."

He played again, a rippling tune, and sang in a clear high voice.

"Beware of love, and from her hide,
Make prayer her arrows miss you,
And if a lass should kiss you,
Flee swiftly from her side . . .
For love but leads to sorrow . . .
And joy will be but grief,
Yet I shall yet still play love's fool,
And then be wise, tomorrow . . ."

He stopped, and Zamor opened his eyes; Gwynna stood in the door, and her green eyes were brilliantly awake again, and angry.

"A musician, as well as a thief and pirate," she commented acidly. "Gods send me the pleasure of hearing you sing on a rack, some day. Now, will you tell me where I am, and what filthy trickery's been played on me?"

Hugon grinned at her. "Why, we are guests of the warlock," he said mildly. "And trickery . . . well, you must admit our way was less disturbing to your dignity than if I'd been forced to lug you here, crammed in a sack like a piglet for market day."

Her glare was withering, but he paid no attention. "There will be fine clothes in that room I left you in," he went on. "And I recommend the food most highly. Otherwise, lady, you may find things dull for a while, but I'll make as much haste as I can to finish our dealings."

She stared at him for a moment. "Then, you're still about this lunatic scheme to ask for ransom for me?" she said slowly. He nodded, and twanged a string. She spoke, "Well, then, I'd best help you, since you haven't the wit to set about it properly yourself. Bring me pen and paper, and I'll write a letter to the stewards of my estates in Mazain, ordering them to send whatever sum your greed requires."

Hugon chuckled. "But lady, I'd thought that possibly I might offer the High King of Meryon a part in this auction. His wealth is considerable . . ." Hugon grinned maliciously, "And I've heard his feeling concerning you is strong."

"You would do that?" she said in a low voice. "Let me go back . . . to be spat on by my kinsmen. Before I lose my head . . ."

"It seems a dismal notion," Hugon agreed. "But I'm a loyal vassal of the High King, alas. And a poor man, too. Now, just how much . . . in gold, to make the reckoning easier . . . would you say was fair?"

She uttered a remarkably crude word, and whirled out of the room. Hugon put the lute against the wall and stood up.

"Business calls," he said to Zamor. "I'll go to the docks again, and see if any ship sails soon for Mazain that can bear the lady's letter. There will be many ships going north to Meryon, of course, so I'll write my own letter to the High King's presence later."

There were ships lying in the port whose destination would be the Empire and the imperial city itself; Hugon, asking along the quays, found them without difficulty. Also, a round Grothan trader ship was loading cargo for the north, and a message for distant Meryon might be easily sent with that. But Hugon, puzzling at his own dilatory thoughts, did not go back to write those messages, or to take the Lady Gwynna's letter either. Instead, he walked slowly, along one street and down another, jingling a handful of coins that he had conveniently found in the room in Thuramon's house.

He took one out and twirled it thoughtfully, looking at it. It bore the head of the current king of Koremon, Garth; Hugon remembered that this land had an odd tradition of having two brother kings, one a temporal monarch, and the other some sort of advisor, bearing the title of Dragon's Friend . . . whatever that meant. Garth, it appeared, was the temporal lord; a man of middle age, said to be a good king as kings go. The image on the coin flattered him, Hugon did not doubt.

Hugon was conducting a prolonged and fruitless inner debate as he walked. An inner voice kept exhorting him, with a rather nauseatingly proper tone, and constant references to honor. Hugon noticed a sharp resemblance in the voice to that of his late father; the old man had held equally firm views on what was right and what was wrong, and what a Kerrin did or did not do.

A Kerrin, it seemed, did not hold women to ransom. While it might be perfectly correct to ambush a male enemy, and, if he survived one's first assault, to drop him in a dungeon until such time as his relations delivered him . . . one didn't do that with women.

But, Hugon argued with the voice . . . the lady was a traitoress, and also other things like as not. And properly seized, in fair combat, too. And rich, while Hugon himself had seldom owned much more than the few coins he jingled now. Her ransom would purchase much, Hugon thought. A few good horses, for example, and possibly a fine cloak or two, among other things. And since she now held her late lord's wealth by right, she would never miss

77

a few bags of gold at all. Didn't that make a difference, Hugon inquired, silently.

It did not, the other voice answered smugly.

"Aaah," Hugon said aloud, and paused to watch an interesting sight. Through a wide tavern window he saw a half dozen men, seamen from their looks, crowding about a wooden table where mugs and bottles stood. One of them shook his closed hand above his head, calling upon the gods, and spun a pair of dice on the wood.

Well, now, Hugon thought. If I'm to do without the lady's ransom, I'd best set about continuing to earn my living in the ways I'm used to. These seamen had the air of men recently paid, and trusting lads, too, he thought; and he turned into the tavern, whistling a tune softly.

Much later he emerged, rolling slightly as he walked; and now there were gold pieces among the silver ones in his pouch, and a good many more of the silver ones. He was not entirely sober, but not drunk either, not by his own standards in such matters.

Also, he had still been unable to make up his mind about the matter of the Lady Gwynna. If he returned to the house of Thuramon, he realized, he would have to make some sort of decision; else, that infuriating nagging conscience would begin its smug discourse again. Hugon grunted, and turned toward streets that seemed more promisingly vulgar.

Still later, long after sundown, Hugon sprawled on a wide bed that was well rumpled, playing idly with a long black braid that belonged to his companion in the bed. She giggled sleepily; he yawned, and reached for a wine jar beside the bed. He was now somewhat drunker than he had been, he noticed, but not nearly drunk enough; he chuckled, and lifted the jar to his lips.

At that moment, a thunderous knock shook the door; the girl beside him shrieked and sat up, and Hugon dropped the wine jar, swinging his legs nimbly to the floor and reaching for his garments and his sword.

"Your husband, of course," Hugon said, backing toward a window. The girl screamed again, and the door

78

shook a second time as he found the window's catch and opened it.

"Somehow, I find this too familiar," Hugon grunted, glancing down into the street. The door gave way, and a large and angry man charged in, barely missing Hugon with a wild swing; but Hugon was already half over the window ledge by then.

Hugon passed a squatting ape-servant at the entrance to the guest rooms, who grinned cheerfully at him as he went by. The dwarfish creature was obviously there to prevent Gwynna's exit, as Thuramon had promised.

Beyond, curiously shaped lamps burned with a yellow light, but the archways of the rooms were darkened. Hugon swayed a little as he studied the various doorways, trying to remember which was the one assigned to him. He scratched his head, selected one at random, and moved into the shadowed room, blundering into a low table with a grunt of pain.

There was a flare of light, and a lamp came into full flowering; Gwynna sat up in bed, glaring at him.

"It's not enough, is it?" she asked, icily. "You must add rape to your other foul impositions upon me? You fatherless sewer worm, I'd submit to one of those dwarf apes before I'd let you lay your scabby hand on me . . ." At which point she threw some object, whose nature Hugon could not make out; whatever it was, it shattered, with a loud noise, on his forehead.

Gwynna seemed to find the effect pleasing; through a haze, Hugon saw her searching for another missile. He backed out, in some haste, and collided with Zamor, who laughed.

"You've been about the town, haven't you?" Zamor grunted, sniffing.

"I have," Hugon said, with owlish solemnity. "Been seeking truth. Considering things, that I have." He rubbed his forehead. "Mother of All, that's a woman, there!"

Gwynna, holding a robe about her, came to the room

door; she stood glaring, and there was the glitter of a pair of scissors in her hand.

"Try it again, peasant," she invited him. "A little closer, and I'll geld you with these."

"Don't doubt you would . . ." Hugon said, and laughed. "But take my word . . . was a mistake. No such intentions. Can't tell one room from another."

"You're drunk, too," she said, more calmly.

"Not too . . . drunk," Hugon said. "Or just drunk enough. I . . . find it necessary to . . . change m'plans. With my brother Zamor's consent . . . seeing that we're, ah, partners in the matter so to speak . . . I hereby give you leave to go. No ransom, no rewards."

Zamor, beside him, grinned. "I'd prefer it, brother," he said. "The enterprise sounded like much work and little reward, in the end. By all means, let the lady go her way."

Gwynna stared at both of them, eyes wide and puzzled; for a long time she was silent.

Then, "You're speaking truth?"

"As I always do," Hugon said grandly. "With a few necessary exceptions."

"You're free to go anywhere you like," Zamor explained, with a broader grin. "Back to your home in Mazain, if you choose."

Gwynna's expression was oddly panic-stricken; her hand went to her mouth.

"Why?" she said, in a low voice. "Why are you doing this?"

"I've had trouble with what, for lack of a better word, I'll call my conscience," Hugon explained, and hiccuped. "I beg you, lady, don't trouble me for long explanations just now."

"An attack of what's called honor," Zamor told her. "I've noticed that it doesn't last too long in white men. You'd best take your luck and be off to Mazain, girl, before either of us regrets this."

"Mazain?" she said, low voiced. "I . . . hate the place. And I cannot go back to Armadoc . . . never again."

80

She stood for another moment, staring at the two of them; then turned and vanished into her own room.

Fraak put his head around the door of another room, and peered at the two men in the hall; he uttered a sleepy sound, questioningly.

Hugon hiccuped again, and turned toward his room. Zamor watched him go, and chuckled once more as Hugon disappeared within.

"You were serious, then," Gwynna said.

The three sat at a great table in the high-ceilinged dining hall of Thuramon's house; a late morning sun slanted through narrow windows overhead, and the ape servants moved in and out, bearing breakfast.

"Yes, I was," Hugon told her. He rubbed his forehead, where a blue bruise showed. "I'll forgive you this, too," he said. "I must have seemed a trifle ominous last night."

She gave an unexpectedly open laugh. "I did suspect you'd grown impatient," she said. "And I've an odd distaste for being raped."

"So," Hugon said, and thrust a bit of meat about his plate, staring down at it abstractedly. "Then, if you've a mind to, you'll find a merchant ship in harbor . . . a sound-looking craft, if smelly. Called the Waterbird or something equally unfitting, if I remember it rightly. Her master told me she would sail for the imperial city within another day or two; you may be back upon your own lands in hardly any time at all."

She stared at him for a long time; then her lips curved in a strained smile, and she shook her head slowly.

"How little you know of my . . . friends!" she said quietly. "Hugon, you weren't long in the city of Mazain, were you? No, not long enough to know those folk, I think." Gwynna was silent for a moment, then she shrugged. "I . . . ask your pardon, for many things I've said to you."

The two men looked at her, amazed; Zamor grunted, and Hugon slapped his own head, hard.

"I'm in a warlock's house, and illusions are as thick as

81

fleas would be in a common man's hall," Hugon said, faintly. "I wouldn't dare repeat what I thought I heard just now."

She shook her head. "I asked your pardon," she said again. "I called you false, among other things. I'm the false one, sir Hugon. If you had continued with your notions of ransom, you'd have discovered that, soon enough." She picked up a glass, and sipped slowly; set it down. "I knew, when you first spoke of ransom back aboard the galley, that you would see to my safety until you gained that ransom. Otherwise . . . I'd be skewered and slain, as the other women aboard were slain. Then, later, I spoke to you as I did . . . because . . . oh, for several reasons. But I never admitted the largest matter." She paused, and then, "There will be no ransom, I think. Not from Mazain, at least."

Hugon looked at her in silence. Finally, "Stab me! I do think you're speaking truth!"

"I am," she said. "If you were not such an honest man . . . no, I mean the word . . . you could know nothing of the black webs of intrigue in the court of the Emperor and among the lords and great ones of Mazain. Like . . . like nothing else on earth."

"I may not be quite so ignorant of those things as you think, lady," Hugon told her. "Then, your wealth, and your husband's estates . . ."

"By now, a hundred kinsmen are tearing those estates to fragments," she said. "Each with a train of lawspeakers, and a retinue of forgers creating false documents daily. Not one of Barazan's kinsmen would aid my return, believe me. Ransom? Why, there are some of my cousins-by-marriage who'd gladly pay you for evidence of my death."

"So," Hugon said, and stared down at his plate. "And so much for my attack of . . . honorable feelings. Why, by the Great Mother, I'm not even given the choice of doing rightly, damn it."

"Now, friend," Zamor said, and grinned. "Can we not

82

make the other arrangement and hand the lady over to your own king?"

Hugon looked up. "Well . . . no. No, I think not."

"Sometimes . . ." Gwynna said, in a low voice, "sometimes I think I would accept the axe for a day in Armadoc again." She sighed.

Zamor looked at her gravely. "As I would see Numori land again," he said in a low voice.

Hugon looked from one to the other. "Well, I don't pine for the windy glens of home, myself," he said, but then, "not . . . too often at any rate. And I need only remember my oath, taken loudly in my clan's hall the day I left . . . that I'd return only when I'd made both fame and fortune." He grinned. "Wherefore, my clansmen bade me goodbye forever, having no confidence at all in me."

"But you *could* return, if you chose," Gwynna said. "Or Zamor could."

"I shall," Zamor said. "One day . . . though it'll be a long journey. You know where Numori lies?"

"North of the Empire of Mazain," Hugon said. "But that's like saying nothing at all; there's much land north, and no maps worth having of it all."

"That's the worm in the winecup," Zamor said. "The Empire lies sprawled across any path I might take to my own land. And I've no ambition to find myself back in the Empire's grip, or pulling another oar in one of their galleys." He leaned back and sighed. "It may be a long road home. Around the edges of the world, so to speak. For instance, I might find a ship from here to northern lands, even as far as Thulan. Thence, cross the northern end of the Middle Sea at the narrowest part, and go into the hot lands there, where there are jungles and naked savages . . ." His eyes became intense. "And then southward again, till I come to the Numori kingdoms . . . it is possible."

Hugon nodded. "It could be done, though a long journey, as you say. But I wonder . . ." He frowned thoughtfully. "I've heard tales of an ancient land, like a great island, east of here . . ."

"East, from Koremon?" Zamor shook his head. "No. This is the most easterly of all the kingdoms of men. There's nothing south but the sea of ice, nothing east but the world's edge. And anyway, brother, it's north and west I'd want; there's Numori. What's east to do with it?"

Hugon stared at the big black man. "Why, if one sailed east, in time you'd come upon the western shores of the Empire, of course. Or the deserts, north of the Empire. Unless there's another land, in the east, between . . . as I said, there are tales."

"East, to end in the west?" Zamor looked at Hugon, puzzled.

"But the world's round, man," Hugon told him. "Round, like an apple, d'you see?"

"Oh, come," Zamor said, and laughed. "More of your joking?"

"No, I swear it," Hugon said. "Many wise men, nowadays, know of this. Some seamen, too. In the Imperial Schools, for example, there is a map, made in the form of a globe . . . and I've seen another such in the schools in Grotha . . ."

"Round, you say?" Zamor said again. "Well. Round, then, though only the Snake knows how that can be . . . but round, or shaped like a dish, or whatever, I've no taste for sailing any more than I have to, and certainly not into a sea I don't know. Man, I *know* my way home, as it is." He chuckled. "And I'm in no great hurry, anyway. Numori will remain where it has always been till I get there. Eh, now, you could come with me, brother. I'll find you a pair of fine plump girls for wives, and there's all else you could ask for in life there. Why not?"

Hugon grinned. "Why not, indeed? Who knows, I may do that!"

Gwynna looked from one to the other and laughed, sharply.

"Gods, I'd give anything to be a man, and free to choose any road I wanted," she said in a bitter voice.

"The two of you, with nothing to hold you anywhere . . ."

"And not much to pay our way with, either," Hugon
pointed out.

She put her chin in her hands, looking down at the
table. "While I . . . I dare not go back to Armadoc, and
I am a stranger in this land. And who knows what's left
for me in Mazain . . ." Her eyes were shadowed. "Except what I've already had of it, and that's more than I
wanted."

Both men were silent, looking at the girl. Hugon
shrugged, "I've no advice, lady. Though . . . well, if the
warlock can ever be brought away from his treasure of
books, Thuramon might . . ."

"Thuramon might do what?"

The warlock stood in the door of the room, looking at
the three. Hugon pushed back his chair and stood up.

"Why, give the lady the benefit of your wisdom, sir,"
Hugon said. "A wizard as learned as you are might aid
her to decide her fate."

Thuramon's eyes turned on Gwynna. "Decide? She
chose her own fate long ago, as we all do. But, if she
likes, I'll give her this much." He came toward the table,
and Gwynna turned to look up at him. Hugon saw her
eyes as she stared up at Thuramon; and for the first time
since he had known her, there was fear in those green
eyes.

"I do not need to read the lines of a hand, nor the stars
of your birthdate," Thuramon said, quietly. "By my Art,
I will tell you this much. You have caused the death of
men, which is no very important matter in the eyes of
the gods; you have betrayed your sworn word, but so do
most people, sooner or later. You are neither better nor
worse than any other. I say this to you so that you may
remember it while you live, woman."

She continued to stare at him, her face growing paler;
her tongue suddenly darted out, moistening her red lips,
but she said nothing.

"Now," Thuramon continued, "I shall give you this.

85

You will find that which you have never possessed before, and you will wish for no other possession. You will be fortunate, more than most people are." He chuckled grimly. "Such is the justice of the gods that you will never pay any price for the sorrows you have already caused . . . except if you freely choose to pay."

Gwynna shuddered, her green eyes wide.

"I . . . don't understand," she said, in a low voice.

"Neither do I," Thuramon told her. He seemed to forget her at that, and turned toward Hugon. "But you . . ." The old man pulled his beard, scowling at Hugon. "I've no claim on you now, young man. I will compel nothing."

"I'm glad of that," Hugon said. "Since I've no doubt you could set me dancing jigs or crowing like a rooster if you wanted to. You've the air of someone who wants a service done, I think." Hugon spread his hands wide apart. "Good warlock, I'm entirely at your service. I've all the time in the world; no work would be too hard, for your magnificent hospitality . . . and for such a breakfast as I've just had."

"You'd best be careful with such offers," Thuramon said sourly. "You might be taken seriously. In fact . . . I do intend to ask a service. But more of that later. Now . . . I would bring you to meet a kinsman. He waits in my study."

"By all means," Hugon said. "Your kinsman . . ."

"No," Thuramon said. "Yours."

Hugon looked mildly surprised. Thuramon turned to the door. "Come," he said shortly, and went out; Hugon followed.

The warlock led him along a wide stair, up to a heavy door, which opened at Thuramon's lifted hand. Within, a huge room lay before Hugon's eyes. There were odd devices ranged on the walls and on tables; towering shelves of books and rolls, and narrow windows closed with iron shutters. The room was lighted by lamps, though it was day.

But the man who stood at the other side of the room,

86

his back to the door, was the central item in that room, to Hugon. As the door closed behind Thuramon and himself, he stared at the man's back with a queer chilled feeling of . . . familiarity. He felt that he knew that man . . . but not merely knew him; that he was in some way, unbelievably, a part of him.

Then the man turned and put down the roll of parchment he had been reading; he stared at Hugon, silently.

To Hugon, it was as if he were looking into a mirror; it was his own face, and more. Not merely likeness, but something more subtle; an inwardness that was his own self, duplicated. And yet, the other was not like him, not in everything. He was older, by a few years, Hugon thought, though no more than that. Yet his hair was gray, silver-gray.

Thuramon looked from one to the other, and nodded, slowly, as if satisfied of something.

"Hugon of Kerrin," Thuramon said, slowly, "here is your kinsman, Kavin of Hostan, now called Orm."

"Kavin . . . of Hostan," Hugon repeated. The other regarded him, gravely silent.

"I . . . have heard such a name," Hugon said with effort. "That prince Kavin who . . . no, of course not." He looked at Thuramon, and back to the other. "Kavin, who returned here to be Koremon's first king, long years ago. Who died and was most properly buried . . . or, according to you, Thuramon, did not die, but slept until this generation." Hugon stopped, and shook his head. "No, really, I can't believe that tale you told me, warlock. Who's this, who looks so much like myself? Come now, let's cease playing these games."

The man called Kavin smiled, and spoke. "It is the truth, Hugon of Kerrin. If you've trouble believing such things . . . well, so do I."

Thuramon grunted, sourly. "And while you both stand and gawk, I must wait. Listen, now. This is indeed the same Kavin who came back to this land only a short time ago; took the name of Orm, and became master to one of his own descendants, it seems." Thuramon glowered at

87

both of them. "And took a wife, too. Not any ordinary woman, but a lady who . . ." The warlock stopped, coughed nervously, and glanced around the room. "A lady of great intelligence and charm." he said. "In case she happens to be listening."

Kavin laughed suddenly. "She could be," he said.

"Listen, now," Thuramon went on. "It seems I have much to explain to both of you, and little time to do it. To begin . . . I would ask your pardon, Prince Kavin."

"For what?" Kavin asked. "But take it, in advance . . ."

"For a long deception," Thuramon said, slowly. "For all that I did not speak of, in our former acquaintance. For the devices by which I caused the course of your life to be changed, and therefore for this time."

He looked down at the long table, piled with books, and among them some of those tiny rolls from the island archive.

"I have nearly reached the secret I have been pursuing, for so long," Thuramon said, his hand touching the books. "But I have also found much more, here, in these. Prince, I was born . . . elsewhere. Not in this familiar world of yours, but in a place . . ." Thuramon passed and shook his head. "A place, that to you would be nightmare. A world brought down by . . . wise men. I fled, and saved myself. Then, I learned that the evil which destroyed my world was creeping into this one as well. I came to that land called Dorada, as you know . . ."

Kavin's mouth set into a grim line, and his eyes were bleak.

"Dorada," he said.

"You were only a wild boy, then," Thuramon said. "There was a ship, a white, beautiful ship; a sea-gift, found adrift and brought to Dorada. You named it your Luck."

"It lies here, in this city," Kavin said, his voice distant. "An ancient trophy now. I . . . went and looked at it."

"That ship came from another world, too, Prince. Not

88

the same world as mine . . . but another. This world of
yours is like a crossroads, where many pass through . . .
here, there are the lost ships and the lost tribes of a hundred worlds," Thuramon said. "But I used the gift of the
ship, as I used other events, to turn you to the work I
needed. Time and again, I turned the course of things toward the time . . . that time when you would do what
you did. You came to the place where evil entered this
world and closed the gate . . . and met the doom."

Kavin looked at Thuramon directly. "I lived. And I
gained my wishes. Doom, you say?" He glanced at
Hugon. "It seems I left enough of my blood to put a face
on this man that's more like me than I find comfortable.
I don't understand how that can be, since . . . well, there
it is, anyway."

"My ancestor was called Brahon," Hugon said. "He
was the son of . . . of your daughter, the lady Isa."

"MY daughter?" Kavin stared at him. "I left two sons,
but no daughters . . ."

"The Kavin who ruled Koremon, for all those years,
left a considerable progeny," Thuramon interrupted.
"No, wait. I must insist, for reasons I shall give you later.
He *was* yourself, in complete truth."

Kavin shrugged. "Very well, then he was," he said.
"He seems to have enjoyed himself, at least, kinging it
here in Koremon."

"Let me go on," Thuramon said. "You met certain mas-
ters of that place, the valley of the Gate. You saw a
body, one who seemed dead . . . and who resembled
you as much as Hugon here does. And who was also
yourself, Kavin; yourself, sleeping, not truly dead. But
not alive, either. You have lived before, as all men do,
and what you saw was the body you once were."

"I saw a good deal more, too," Kavin said in a grim
voice. "That was the worst trap of the journey."

"But you were not caught," Thuramon said. "You went
in, to face the . . . being called Ess, and you destroyed
him, with the light he could not bear. But, because he
was master of time and illusion, he nearly destroyed you

89

first . . . and then, in his agony, he . . . no, there are no words to describe it precisely. Ess broke time itself, tearing the fabric of reality as a cloth is torn . . . and you with it."

Kavin looked at Hugon, and then back to Thuramon. "Me? I feel . . . reasonably complete." He chuckled.

"I know well enough how difficult it is to understand these matters," Thuramon said. "But . . . there is the truth. One Kavin returned here. Then, after years passed, another . . . yourself. Believe it, Prince."

Kavin ran a hand through his gray hair. "If you insist . . . then I'll believe it. But luck be thanked, there's no need to call me Prince. I'm Orm, commoner and master of horse, and my unfortunate other self had all the pleasures and pains of king's work." He grinned cheerfully.

"I must tell you something which will not please you," Thuramon said, slowly. "The creature, Ess . . . is not dead. Nor are you truly free of his power . . . and this world is not free of him, either."

There was a strange chill in the warlock's workroom. The two men, so much alike, stood watching the old man as he looked from one to the other.

"The gate you closed, a way between this world and others . . . must be opened again," Thuramon said. "And you . . . must face Ess again. If you fail, black doom falls on this world, and not this world alone, but many."

FIVE

In a place which was not a place, where there were no stars and no light, Ess . . . existed. It would not be correct to say that he waited, because the idea of time itself was very different in that place. He was not uncomfortable, though that place beyond space and time would have been death to any human who entered it; nor was he impatient. The entity called Ess had come across an uncountable number of years, in both directions, before he had been flung into this odd place. The kind of time known to human minds and bodies meant very little to Ess.

It was not entirely correct to call Ess by the male article, but he had long ago decided to be what, for his kind, would be called male, and was still so. "He" could, if it suited him, become "she"; but if he did so, he would divide into others, like himself. And he preferred to be alone.

Now, from the unthinkable place where Ess was, he looked out into reality, and perceived . . .

There was a short-lived, two-legged mammal, one of those primitive life forms of the remote past. Primitive, but one of those creatures had caused Ess to fall into this empty place, he remembered. Not with anger; Ess was not capable of anger.

Their minds were weak, tiny, operable in only one time direction; their senses capable of a very limited reception. But in this world and time, there were no others that Ess could reach and control; all other creatures ex-

91

cept the dragon folk were too stupid, and the dragons were far too wise.

This creature would do, Ess thought. It was not as clever as most of its kind, but it had certain advantages . . .

He reached down, into the mind he had contacted many times before, gently and carefully . . . the mind of Sharamash, Thrice Glorious, Holder of the Throne of Thrones, Emperor of great Mazain.

Sharamash was asleep. He lay in the enormous bed, a fat and hairy man, with nothing particularly regal about the look of him; snoring gently, his black beard cased in a night-snood, but otherwise naked. The two concubines favored by the Emperor's command for the night lay curled at his feet, also asleep.

Outside, it was a hot summer night; through the arched windows, stars glittered, reflected in the lake that surrounded the King's House. Beyond, the lights of the great city still glowed, in spite of the late hour; Mazain never slept entirely.

Outside the royal bedchamber, a rank of armored men stood, shoulder to shoulder, axes in hand; while in a nearby room slaves pulled steadily at wooden handles, driving a fan that sent cool air through the room where the Thrice Glorious slept.

Sharamash grunted, softly, in his sleep.

He was standing in a wonderful place, lit by dim red light; great trees stood around, and there was soft turf under his feet. A queer, high pitched singing, wordless but somehow unbearably pleasurable, filled the air; and Sharamash felt a kind of strange ecstasy that was almost pain, a sensation he had never found in his waking life, though he had tried to find it through many odd pathways.

He had been in this place before, and he knew it well. As the dark glow began to form before him, he knew who was there to speak with him. With dream eyes, he watched as the shape of dark fire formed, and the scarlet eyes glowed down at him.

92

"Hail, O Lord of Night," Sharamash said, and knelt, bowing his head.

"Sharamash . . ." the humming voice said, infinitely distant and yet near. "You have done well."

"Your temple is nearly complete, Lord," Sharamash said, feeling the weird black ecstasy rising stronger within him. He knelt, moaning with pleasure, shaking.

In the royal bedchamber he moaned, and one of the girls woke, staring at the Emperor with terrified eyes. She dared not wake him; her hands pressed against her mouth, as she saw the expression on the sleeping man's face.

"Be swift, my servant," the Lord of Night told him. "I have promised, and I will fulfill . . . when the temple is complete, I will make you a god, immortal, capable of all things and all joys . . . and I myself will come forth and give the whole world to you to rule under my hand . . ."

"I shall hasten, Lord, I shall . . ." Sharamash said, still shuddering.

The dark world faded suddenly, and the red light vanished. The Emperor opened his eyes in the dim lamplight of his chamber, and sat up, suddenly.

The concubine who was awake stared at him, and suddenly she uttered a choked scream through the fists she had pressed to her red mouth.

Sharamash's face glowed strangely, and his black eyes were dilated as he stared at her; then he laughed, very softly. The girl had heard that laugh before; she went white and fainted.

The other concubine was awake now, too, but she was a girl of considerable self-control; she lay quietly, without a sign.

"Aaah," Sharamash said, with a long yawn, and swung his hairy legs off the bed. He clapped his hands, once. A door opened, and a silent slave appeared with a robe; and another with a tray of wine bottles.

The Emperor sipped the cool wine, and stared at the first girl, grinning.

"So," he said, softly. "Are you recovering, my pretty

93

one? Good, good . . ." He chuckled. "You've had an experience, haven't you? I'm sure you don't realize how remarkable an experience . . . but you have looked upon my face transfigured by the Dark Light." He nodded, still grinning, as the girl sat up. She stared at him with the terrified gaze of a bird held by a snake's eyes.

"So you'll understand," Sharamash continued, softly. "I'm doing you a great honor indeed, girl. I've just decided to give you to the Lord of Night, immediately . . ." He stopped, at the girl's strangled scream, and shook his head. "Really, now, let's have no fuss. Actually, whatever-your-name-is, it's hardly any pain at all, and you'll go straight to the Dark Kingdom. . . . What a noise, girl!" He snapped his fingers at the slaves. "Take her along, will you? Down to the temple, now . . . and I'll be along in a moment, as soon as I'm properly dressed."

The girl was dragged out, her terrified screams echoing in the outer halls as she went. The Emperor listened appreciatively while a slave dressed him in the black, jewel-studded garments of the High Priesthood of the Lord of Night. He had designed them himself, and as the slave finished, he cast an admiring glance at his reflection in a tall mirror, adjusting his tiara carefully.

The other concubine, who was much cleverer than she looked, gazed at him and emitted a sound of awe and admiration. The Emperor glanced at her and chuckled.

"Ah, thank you, my dear," he said. "As a matter of fact, I noticed that you seemed a shade more—well, *interested*, during the course of our games a few hours ago than the other wench. As you see, your Emperor notices everything." As he passed the bed, he gave the girl an affectionate slap. "All right, now, back to your quarters."

The Emperor passed out of the room, and the stately progress through the ancient halls began. The palace echoed with the clash of arms presented at his passage, and the sound of feet as the priests and guards moved in his train. Several high nobles joined the procession as it wound downward toward the Gate of Chariots; all of them wore carefully arranged expressions of zeal, with one exception.

The exception, Paravaz, First Chancellor of the Realm, wore his usual stony expression. He was growing bored with the new religion adopted by the Emperor, and doubtful of certain points; furthermore, he had been busy all day, unlike most of the court, and had not managed to catch enough sleep. The day's problems were, he felt, directly traceable to the new cult, which again robbed him of his earned rest. Paravaz was not pleased.

The sacrifices were all very well, he thought sourly, as he moved behind the Emperor and they passed under the torchlit arches of the Gate. Paravaz rather enjoyed a well-organized, properly emotional blood sacrifice now and then; he had never thought much of the modern god-ways, most of their rites asking nothing but an animal or two at best. Couldn't take that sort of god seriously, Paravaz thought. But on the other hand, this Lord of Night had quite unreasonable demands, much beyond the deaths of slaves.

All that silver especially, Paravaz thought, remembering the day's accounting of tax receipts. Not to mention some of the other materials, metals nobody had any use for till now, and costing more than gold, some of them. His mouth set in a hard line.

The King's House, an enormous and ancient mass of walls and towers, had always occupied most of the island in the lake, in the center of the sprawling city of Mazain. At the end of the island, until recently, a wide pleasure park had lain, a lovely place built by a remote ancestor of Sharamash; and around it a circular road, which had once been used for exercise of chariots. Now, where the groves had been, a squat, gigantic pyramid rose, a structure of black stone, lit with flaring torches. A gate opened for the Emperor and his train, and priests bowed before him as he entered the fane of the Lord of Night. Pipes wailed, while somewhere within the girl who had been sent for sacrifice shrieked again.

The interior of the pyramid was a lofty space, floored with shining obsidian blocks; so high that torchlight did not penetrate the dense shadow overhead.

Across one end of the wide space, the high altars of the Lord of Night were lit by the firelight, rising tier upon tier, gleaming whitely in glittering reflections . . . altars that were like no other that anyone had ever seen before. The Emperor himself had given detailed instructions concerning that strange structure, and had watched it built, step by step. Once or twice the builders had attempted to cheat a little, although they had been clearly told that the Emperor had received the plan directly from the god, and would tolerate no changes at all. Those builders had gone first to the sacrificial altar, and there was no more cheating now.

The altar structure was still not quite finished, Paravaz knew all too well. Though how anyone could tell when such a mad array was finished, he couldn't guess. Great rods of silver, inches thick, twisted in strange ceiling shapes around cylinders of rock crystal; webs of silver wire stretched from column to column, and queer cages of silver and copper rose around the whole insane array. Paravaz knew, to the ounce, how many loads of silver had already gone into that structure—not to mention the constant leakages of silver into various palms.

It looked, to Paravaz, like an enormous gateway, a barred gate that might be part of a birdcage fit to hold a bird twice the size of a dragon. Except that behind it there was only stone wall. A gate to nowhere.

Still, Paravaz reflected, it was unhealthy to oppose an Emperor's whims, even a mad Emperor.

Now, the priests were chanting, pipes and gongs were making a considerable amount of noise, while incense smoked. Everyone, including Paravaz, was kneeling, bowing repeatedly, while the Emperor himself stood with outspread arms before the towering mass of silver. Behind him, the minor priests were busily killing the girl, who had been flung down upon a huge black block that was carved with bloodstained channels. They were

96

doing it as slowly as possible, but with horrible inventiveness.

"Receive, O Dark Lord of Night, this flesh brought to thee, this soul given into thy hand," the Emperor was chanting. "We, thy servants, wait eagerly for thy coming, daily we toil at the task of building thy altar . . ."

Well, Paravaz thought, daily *someone* toils, that's true enough. And some of them were beginning to object, too.

Now the altar was flickering with those odd lights that Paravaz had never really understood, and the Emperor was finishing the chanting. The object of the sacrifice had stopped quivering, and it would appear that the weekly rites were over. Paravaz gave silent thanks for that, to whatever god might be listening; he rose, stiffly, and followed as the Emperor moved out.

Past the Chariot Gate, and within the palace again, Paravaz moved closer to the Emperor's elbow as they entered the Great Hall.

"Thrice Glorious," Paravaz said, in a low voice. "A word . . . I was unable to speak with your Illustriousness this afternoon."

"Oh, I was resting, Paravaz," the Emperor said. "In preparation for an enlightenment . . . and I received it, you know."

"Most wonderful lord," Paravaz said, "I am greatly pleased . . . but lord, I am concerned with matters that have less to do with the divine. Charged as I am with the burdens of state . . ."

"Oh, now," the Emperor said, petulantly. "This is going to be another complaint, isn't it, Paravaz? More trouble collecting tax moneys, is it? Or that matter of coinage?"

"Yes, my lord," Paravaz said. He was close at hand as the Emperor continued to pace; the other courtiers had deliberately fallen back a few paces to allow privacy. No one wished to annoy Paravaz by seeming over-curious.

"My lord," he went on, "the taxes have been raised as high as they can be raised. As it is, we cannot collect in every case . . . and there is always money required for

97

the usual business of state, beyond the sums your Illustriousness is devoting to the Lord's altar . . ."

"Oh, come now," Sharamash said, frowning. "A little twisting, and the money will come . . . we've plenty of soldiers to use in the tax collections, if necessary."

"I have twisted, my lord," Paravaz said. "Hard. As for soldiers . . . they must be paid, and the new coinage does ·not please many of them. As it does not please many of the merchant class, either. They have a foolish trust in gold and silver metal, my lord . . . and some of them are growing very difficult."

"Pah!" Sharamash said, angrily.

"It is a serious matter, lord," Paravaz told him. "There is the rebellion in Quenda, especially. It is the Quenda mines that have sent us' much of the silver . . . till now."

"But I must have the silver, especially!" The Emperor looked at Paravaz with a queer, wild expression. "The god told me . . . that when his altar was complete, he would . . . he would do much more. Only another few hundred weights . . . another month's work, at most."

"But there is no more bar silver from Quenda," Paravaz said, patiently. "We must depend on whatever we can collect in coins. Could we not wait a while for the completion of the altar . . ."

"Wait? How can you say that?" Sharamash snapped. "Why?"

"We must raise more soldiers," Paravaz said. "More ships, too. Unless we send gifts to the northern border lords . . . gifts that will cost much. I must tell you that there may be trouble there, too. And we cannot struggle on two borders at once, north and south." His face was grim. "My lord, if the kingdoms eastward . . . Meryon, or Grotha, or even Spathan . . . should look toward our shores, they might recall what has gone before. Seek vengeance for wounds not yet healed . . . while the Empire is thus tangled . . ."

Sharamash uttered a high cackle. "Paravaz, you are an old woman!" he said, grinning. "Let the kingdoms plot, for all the good it'll do them! And let those border lords do without their bribes for once . . . and for the rest . . . strike hard in Quenda. Take back those mines swiftly, whatever the cost. Get silver as fast as you can!" His eyes burned wildly. "Let every damned merchant scream his head off and plot against me, let all my dear false friends creep about hatching revolt! Paravaz, it will not matter! Have you no faith in Him, in the Lord of Night? He has promised! He will send forth all that I need, he will send a black doom on all my enemies!" The Emperor shrieked with delight, grinning as he spoke. "The whole world, Paravaz! All nations, all! And even the lands beyond, where no man has gone, all of it will bow before Him, soon!"

Paravaz stood watching as the Emperor withdrew; the ruler of Mazain capering with glee as he disappeared into the inner halls of the palace. And, at the Chancellor Paravaz' elbow, the gray-sprinkled beard of the Lord Chamaras, and his low voice.

"He is mad, Paravaz," Chamaras said, but not loudly enough for any ear but Paravaz'.

"Certainly," Paravaz said in as low a voice. "Like his grandfather . . . though he had no turn for religious matters, that one." Paravaz shrugged. "It runs in the blood, I fear."

"It becomes . . . impossible," Chamaras said.

"For the Emperor, nothing is impossible," Paravaz said.

"Is there nothing to be done . . ."

"For us?" Paravaz glanced at the other. "No." He smiled thinly. "For lesser lords, perhaps. But think, Chamaras. Think. We have our power . . . but it rests in the Emperor alone. We have given the commands, sweated the taxes, sent many to the axe . . . in his name. But in ours as well. If we . . . if some accident befell the Emperor . . . we would go down with him. No matter what, we must serve him, though the Empire falls about our ears."

"Must?" Chamaras asked, narrow eyed.

"Have you friends, Chamaras?" Paravaz asked coldly.

99

"If so, it is well for you. I have none any longer. Except
. . . that one." He stared at the doorway. "Mad as he
may be, he is all."

And in the state cabin of the Windbird, far east of Mazain in the dark sea, the captain chuckled, draining his
cup.

"Mad, of course, m'lady," he said. They sat around the
wooden table under the yellow lamps; the captain and
two mates, and the Lady Gwynna, at supper.

"Though I'd be obliged if you'd keep my maunderings
to yourself, lady," he added a little nervously.

"Of course, good Samavan," Gwynna said, with her
sweetest smile. "How can you think such a thing? That
I'd betray the confidences of such a fine man as yourself
. . . after you have done so much for a poor shipwrecked
woman, helpless as I was . . ."

She had paid, in good solid gold pieces, for her passage; but at the moment, the point was not essential.

"Aye, it's a queer port these days, that Mazain," one of
the mates said, and poured more wine. "Done well
enough this past year, trading east and southward . . .
but what I hear tell, we'll be lucky if the Imperial Customs don't tax the very meat off our bones."

The captain chuckled, and glanced around. "Well,
now, I'm no fool, you'll grant me that. Didn't you think
I'd taken the matter under thought, eh? We've made
hardly a coin's worth, if you go by the ship's book. Oh,
yes, it's poor men we are, unless the customs men have
more wit than I've ever seen 'em have."

"Wit?" The mate shrugged. "I hear there's a
demon-god in Mazain these days. Maybe they've witches
for customs takers, too."

"Ah, I doubt it," the captain said. "But the Emperor's
mad, right enough, and he's got a demon-god too.
Though it hasn't been much help, from all I've heard."

"I know little of the Emperor's new god, myself,"
Gwynna said. "My . . . late husband, the Lord Barazan,
did not wish to take any part in such things." She gave a
delicate shrug of ladylike distaste. "But I did not know

that matters were quite so bad in the Empire as you tell me . . . and so much worse in the short while I've been gone."

"Growing worse, day by day, m'lady," the captain said. "Rebel armies coming north, a dozen barons and lords rising against the Empire. I'll not keep the ship long in Mazain this trip. It might be that war'll come all the way to the city walls, and I'm a man of peace, I am. Go west, I will, and wait till all the important folk settle their quarrels."

"Might be your ladyship would be wisest not to have come at all," one of the mates said. "All's peaceful enough in the Kingdoms these days. If I was yourself, lady, I'd take a journey to some spot where there's no chance of house burnings and manslayings. Why not Meryon shore, for one?"

Gwynna stared at the man, and a sharp pain gripped her; but she kept her expression calm.

Armadoc, she thought, remembering the forest and the river in a swift, bright flash of tortured yearning, and thrust it back into unremembrance again.

"Ah, but I'll have much to do in Mazain," she said lightly. "Many things that I must take care of . . ."

In a courtyard, gray with dawn, the ape-servants of Thuramon were bringing out three horses, saddled and ready. Hugon, yawning enormously, swung himself into a saddle; beside him, Kavin waited, and Zamor. The gate opened, and the three clattered forth into the cobbled street, and down through the city of Drakonis. Fraak sat, perched on Hugon's saddlebow.

Beyond the walls, a wide road curved away toward the hills; westward, the sea glinted in the morning light, and a wind came, bringing the sharp salt smell of it. In the other direction, a village of thatched roofs began to awaken, and there was a scent of wood smoke.

Hugon stared around, on either side, as they rode; Zamor, too, examined the country. Kavin's face was oddly grim, with a look of tense foreboding; he stared

101

straight ahead as he rode, and seemed disinclined to talk.

"It's a beautiful land, this Koremon," Hugon said, watching a flight of birds. Fraak stretched his wings, and uttered a note; Hugon patted his head warningly. "No, Fraak, no hunt today."

"I don't wonder at the folk of Dorada settling here," Zamor said. "It's like Numori, hereabouts . . . those hills could be our own mountains."

"Dorada was more beautiful," Kavin said suddenly, almost as if he were speaking to himself. "But only one man lives now who remembers Dorada . . . myself."

Hugon glanced at the big man with the youthful face and the silvered hair, and remembered, with a strange chill . . . this man had been born generations ago. Common men had lived and died, while Kavin slept that strange sleep . . . and now he still lived.

"Thuramon," Hugon said. "He was with you then. He remembers your Dorada, too."

"He was not born there," Kavin said.

For a while the three rode in silence, the big horses at a steady canter, the only sound the jingle of metal and creak of leather. The sun rose higher, but the road was shaded by huge old trees. Now and again they passed a cottage, and once rode through another tiny village. Kavin kept silent, his eyes shadowed.

"That wench, now," Zamor said after a long while. "The old warlock said we could count on her word . . . still, I wonder." He glanced at Hugon, who rode beside him now, Kavin just ahead. "I'd never have guessed you were such a backward one, brother Hugon."

"Eh?" Hugon glanced at him. "How?"

"Why, you never bedded the lady at all, and there was time enough to do it before we put her aboard ship for Mazain," Zamor said, grinning blandly.

"I did not," Hugon said. "If I'd wanted a female leopard, I'd see if there were dealers in wild beasts about the town." He glared at Zamor. "And why should I? There's an abundance of willing girls in Drakonis . . . as you found out yourself, I think."

"Great Snake, there are!" Zamor agreed, with a broad grin. He closed his eyes reminiscently for a moment and chuckled. "And a scarcity of *real* men, they told me. Several times, in truth . . ."

"Spare me," Hugon grunted.

"But you should have given the noble lady something to remember the last night she was with us," Zamor said. "She would have been easy to persuade, I'd guess, from one or two of her looks at you."

"All that concerns me is whether she'll keep her word if we ever find a way into Mazain," Hugon said, frowning. "As Thuramon says we must. Getting into the Imperial City may be easy enough when the time comes. But if the Lady Gwynna betrays us, we'll never get out again. It'll be back to the oarbenches, if we're lucky."

"Not living," Zamor said grimly. "I had many months on that bench. But if you wanted to be sure of the woman, you should have eased her widow's woe. It's the only way to be sure of a female's word . . . or reasonably sure, anyway."

"Ah, now, don't forget, I still have the crystal charm," Hugon said, grinning. "I can enchant the girl with it whenever I need to. Keep her silent, at any rate."

"For a few hours," Zamor said. "We need more than her silence. She's our only key to the place Thuramon spoke of. With her help all will go swiftly . . . without it, who knows?"

"It was a fair oath," Hugon said. "She, to go back to her place in Mazain, and be ready to help us. And in return, Thuramon to aid her in going back to her Armadoc that she seems to yearn for." He chuckled. "Though I suspect the warlock's cheating. I can't think of any way she can go home to Meryon and live."

Ahead, the road curved upward around a hill; on the green slope, among the trees, a gray mass of stone showed. As they came closer, Hugon could see that it was a dolmen shrine, very ancient from the nearly featureless look of the stones, but bearing the familiar symbols of the Great Goddess. He kicked his horse and trotted ahead to where a path led up toward the shrine; drew rein, and swung down.

"A moment," Hugon said, as the other two drew up. He took his leather wine bottle from the saddle and patted Fraak. "Stay there, pretty one." Then, to the other two, "I'll pay my respects to the Goddess here. We'll need all the luck we can find, I think."

He went up the narrow path while Zamor and Kavin sat in their saddles, waiting.

"He may be wise at that," Zamor said in a low voice, watching Hugon's distant form. Hugon had knelt before the stone, and was pouring wine. Zamor glanced at Kavin, curiously. "I thought all of you of this land worshipped the Goddess."

Kavin shrugged. "I . . . have done so. But She may not be pleased to take anything I give her. I once . . . took a different view of such things. No, I find it better to remain away from Her shrines."

"In Numori, men are not even allowed near such a shrine," Zamor said. "The Goddess is for women, the Snake for men, in my land. It seems to work out well enough. If we need luck, we ask the women to get it for us." He chuckled.

On the hillside they could see Hugon, who had risen to his feet now. He still faced the ancient dolmen, but he was evidently finished with his offering; he was reclosing the wine bottle. Then, oddly, he seemed to freeze where he stood; and the two at the foot of the slope heard him utter a strange cry. Abruptly, he backed away, still facing the shrine; then he turned and came running down the path. As he came closer, they saw he was as pale as a man who has escaped a terror, and his eyes were staring wildly. He reached his horse and swung into the saddle, his heels thudding into the animal's ribs.

Zamor and Kavin spurred after Hugon, and after a time came up with him as he slowed his own horse to a walk. He sat in the saddle, hunched down and staring ahead; there were beads of sweat on his forehead.

"Here, brother, what's this?" Zamor asked, drawing closer. Kavin rode nearer too, studying the other man with narrow eyes.

"I . . ." Hugon said, shakily, and shook his head. "No. I can't say exactly what it was. Kavin, you should have warned me about the shrines in your land. In Meryon we worship Her too, but She doesn't speak." He glanced at one and then the other. "No, I'm not mad. I don't think I am, anyway. Look you, Zamor, Kavin, I only thought . . . a common custom, after all . . . a little wine, and a prayer for luck in our work."

"A Goddess spoke to you?" Zamor asked incredulously. "But I saw nothing up there, nothing but yourself, and the rocks . . ."

"What did she say?" Kavin asked with a curious intentness.

"I . . . cannot tell you," Hugon said. "Only . . . I heard a voice. She . . . laughed. If you had heard that, you'd believe me. It was no human laughter. And then She . . . told me certain things concerning myself and . . ." He looked at Kavin. "You, Prince Kavin. And . . . a great deal more. But I . . . cannot say what it was She told me."

"You mean this Goddess forbids you to tell us?" Zamor asked. "Was it something about our fate? A prophecy?"

"Damnation, no!" Hugon snapped, anger in his voice. "Look you, it was no prophecy, nothing like that . . . and no command to keep silent. I can't repeat what I heard . . . because there were no words, and I've got no words of my own for what I . . . saw."

Zamor's black face grew gray.

"May the Snake protect you, brother," he said in a low voice. "I have heard of this thing among my own people. If She comes thus to a man, he says that he has been spoken to, but he can't repeat what he's heard . . . as you say. We . . . fear such visitation."

Kavin was silently watching Hugon. He nodded, but said nothing. After a while, Hugon said, "That was it, as

105

you say. I heard and saw . . . something that cannot be said." He glanced at Zamor. "You say you've heard of others . . ."

"In my land," Zamor said. "They who have seen the Goddess generally go mad; some die. A few become witchmen."

Hugon shivered slightly. He looked at Kavin.

"One thing," he said. "The voice spoke a few words that were plain enough, of you. But I don't understand their meaning."

Kavin stared at him silently; then glanced ahead, along the road, and back at Hugon.

"You may as well tell," he said, grimly. "Though I think I can guess."

"The voice said, 'Let the Prince Kavin know that my daughter has returned to the place from which she came.'" Hugon said, slowly.

Kavin abruptly drew his horse to a halt, and his head bent over the saddlebow. As Hugon pulled up and looked back, he saw the expression on the other's face; the look of a black despair, a loss. Then Kavin straightened, his expression calm again, but his eyes grim.

"I accept this too," he said, and his horse paced on again.

They rode silently over a ridge, and looked over a wide valley where the road wound downward toward distant towers. The sea was visible again, far away; and on the other side, a glitter of water among thick trees, a lake in the forest. A narrow path wound away from the main road toward that distant lake.

"These are the lands of Hostan," Kavin said, pointing across the valley. "There, the manorhouse . . . where the present lord of this valley lives. And there are the horses bred here . . . see, in those fields. They were my charge . . . while I was Orm."

He reined in at the beginning of the narrow path, and turned his horse toward it, slowly, seeming to do so reluctantly.

"I lived there, near that lake," he said, but did not ride on. Zamor and Hugon both noticed the odd use of the past tense, but waited silently.

"When I . . . awoke, after that strange sleep," Kavin said, "I came here, as you know. I remembered this valley, and that lake, as a place of peace." He stared down the path. "Once, in my . . . other life, when I was Prince Kavin . . ." His mouth twisted wryly. "A prince, leader of a people, and all the other things one says of princes. There was a woman. A strange woman indeed . . ."

"All of them are," Hugon said. Kavin stared at him, then smiled slightly.

"True," he said. "But you cannot know how strange. Listen, now, and see if you can understand me. In that other life, long ago, I left two queens to rule Koremon while I went on that journey that ended with my long sleep. There was . . . another. A woman who was a voice, and no more . . . invisible. Whether her kind are mortal or not, I never knew, I don't know now. But she was real enough, as Thuramon could tell you."

There was another silence. Then Kavin went on.

"When I returned to this land, I found . . . her, here. She is there, in the house by that lake; she has been with me since I became Orm. But she is no longer invisible. She was there, and I . . . was very glad of it." He leaned forward in his saddle, his hands gripping the horn hard, his jaw set. "But I did not understand. I do not understand now. What she was, or how she came across that long span of time, while I slept . . . why she should have seemed to be . . . no more than any mortal woman." He stared at Hugon, strangely. "I did not want to understand, d'you see? She may have been . . . anything. A witch, a goddess, a being from another world . . . I couldn't ask. It was enough that she was here."

Hugon looked at Kavin, and nodded.

"She is no longer there," Hugon said in a quiet voice, but with a strange certainty.

"The Goddess said it," Kavin said. "Returned . . . to the place from which she came." He pulled harshly at his

107

horse's head, swinging the animal around. "There's no need for me to go back, now."

"Are you sure, Prince?" Hugon asked.

"I am sure," Kavin said. He glanced back along the path into the forest, and then away again. "I came to bid her farewell, and she's been wise enough not to wait." He spurred his horse, and the other two men rode after him, back up the road.

SIX

In the late afternoon, the three men rode once more across the causeway and into the landward gate of Drakonis. For a long time, riding back, Kavin had been silent and gloomy; then, for no reason that Hugon could understand, he began to change, as if the weight were lifting. As they drew nearer to the town, Kavin seemed his old self again, though there was a shadow in his eyes.

"Both of you must think I'm mad," he said, as their horses clattered on the paved street. "A day's journey for nothing at all!"

"It's given me a thirst," Zamor called out over the noise. "There, now . . . shall we stop a moment?" He drew up, and the others beside him; a boy came out of the inn and took the reins of their horses while the three dismounted.

"The sign of the Two Dragons," Hugon said, staring up at the brightly painted board overhead. "Eh, now, it seems a lucky omen."

Zamor lowered his bulk onto a bench in the innyard and grunted, "Omen me no omens. I thirst, man." An aproned man, fat and smiling, approached, and Zamor asked for cold wine.

Returning with tall pitchers and mugs, the innkeeper set them down on the table; then paused, looking with round eyes at Fraak, who sat on Hugon's shoulder.

"Ah . . . sir?" The innkeeper came closer. "Is . . . is it truly a dragon? So small?"

"I'm NOT small," Fraak said firmly, and puffed.

"It speaks, too!" the innkeeper said, amazed. "We have

109

seen dragons here, of course, but only those great ones on their island. May I touch it, sir?" He stretched out a hand.

Fraak uttered a low hiss, but allowed the touch, at Hugon's warning word.

"Could you think of selling it, good sir?" the innkeeper asked. "An inn that possessed such a curiosity would be known to all . . ."

"Fraak isn't a curiousity," Hugon said, in a level voice. "And it's he, not it. No, I wouldn't sell him, not at any price."

Fraak uttered a scale of notes, pleased sounds, and blew a long plume of fire which caused the innkeeper to retreat in some haste. He spread his wings and whistled gleefully.

"A little calmer, Fraak," Hugon told him. Then, to Kavin, "I wonder what those great dragons on that island would think of this one? What are they like?"

Kavin sipped his wine. "Those? Few men have spoken with them. I have, a long time ago. They're wise, and old . . . and not fond of any closeness to mankind. Man and dragon have a compact in this land . . . to let each other alone, as far as possible."

"The warlock said we must go there, to their island," Zamor said. "If they're no friends to human folk . . ."

"It depends," Kavin told him. "I have been there once. And by custom, certain men go there, to live and learn from the dragon folk. No, if Thuramon says we must go, then we shall go. But whether they'll aid him in any way . . . well, they are a strange kind. I don't know what they'll do."

They drained their mugs and went out into the street again. Swinging up into their saddles, the three slowly moved along the streets of Drakonis, back toward the warlock's house.

"They call this the Street of the Ship," Kavin said at the next corner. "Look there, at the other end."

There were white columns, and as the three rode closer, a high marble dome came into view, and columned arcades. Through a great open archway, the interior was visible; a block of stone on which something was mounted, a dark shape.

"It's a ship," Hugon said.

"Yes," Kavin said. "Mine, once. There she is, put up like a monument . . . and under that great ugly piece of rock . . ." He stopped and grinned strangely. "Myself. Yes. That's the tomb of the first King of Koremon, Kavin."

Hugon stared and shook his head. "I don't think I'd care to visit a tomb with my name on it," he said. "Not even if I felt positively sure I was still alive. Let's ride on, to our magician host, and supper."

They wheeled and rode away along the last streets toward the house of Thuramon.

The ape servants, swift and wordless, took charge of the horses; within, other servants waited with hot water and fresh robes. In the dining hall, platters of food appeared with marvelous speed. The three sat down and began to eat without waiting for Thuramon to appear; by now, they had grown used to his odd ways.

But they were hardly started when the door opened and the magician entered; he came to the table and sat down, leaning back.

"So," Thuramon said, looking at Kavin. "You bear it well, Prince."

Kavin looked at the magician. "You know, then."

Thuramon nodded. "Your woman . . . or whatever she was . . . is no longer here."

Kavin looked at Thuramon oddly, and then laughed, in a short bark. "So," he said, "even you are not quite all-knowing, are you, Thuramon?"

Thuramon looked puzzled.

"The gods be thanked, you aren't wise in all things, not yet, old friend," Kavin said. "Though you've learned much, it seems, since I've been asleep . . ." He watched Thuramon's face and grinned. "Yes, the woman is gone, as your magic told you. But I have a feeling she's not gone very far."

111

Thuramon suddenly looked nervous, and glanced around the room. Then, frowning, he looked at Kavin.

"As long as the matter's settled," he said, "I am content. Kavin . . . I could have told you that she would vanish again, but you would not have thanked me for the foretelling, would you?"

"No," Kavin said. He drew a platter toward himself and began to hack off a slice of meat.

"You two," Thuramon looked toward Zamor and Hugon. "Now, the work begins."

Hugon fed Fraak a delicate morsel, and scratched the scaly head, watching Thuramon. Zamor ate, silently.

"Tomorrow, we go to visit the Dragon's Isle," Thuramon said, slowly. "There, if they will aid us, we can find those things we'll need for the work we must do."

Hugon pulled an oar, and Zamor another, as the open boat turned outward, past the harbor mouth. Thuramon, muffled in a dark cloak, sat in the stern with Kavin, while Fraak perched on the rail beside him. The dragonet uttered small, excited cries; he had captured a fish, and was watching for another.

Ahead, shrouded in the morning mist, the gray bulk of the place called the Isle of Dragons looked shadowy and unreal; like an immense whale, drifting on the sea. The two men pulled steadily toward it, as Kavin steered.

"The galley . . . was easier rowing," Hugon said, in a strained voice, drawing at his oar in an effort to match Zamor's strokes.

Zamor appeared to have no trouble; he grinned as his oar beat steadily at the water.

"Your back would have been stronger, after a while, Hugon," Zamor said. "Stronger, or fishfood." He chuckled, grimly.

The boatman had been most reluctant, though he yielded at last to gold. But to row them to the Isle of Dragons? No, that he would not do for any amount of gold whatever. And as he had watched them go, his expression said plainly that he did not expect them back.

The dark rock grew closer, looming over them; Zamor and Hugon stopped rowing, letting the boat drift on a running tide that set toward the island; and Zamor narrowed his eyes, studying the rock.

"There's no harborage, Master Thuramon," Zamor said. "Not even a beach."

"If we are admitted at all, we will find an entrance," Thuramon said, shortly. Then Fraak exploded with a squealing cry.

A shadow crossed the boat, and returned a moment later. Hugon stared at the broad-winged shape that soared by close overhead, circling silently and ominously. A gigantic triangular head looked downward, and eyes, emerald spheres as large as a man's whole head, scanned the boat. Fraak, his own wings spread widely, teetered on the rail; he opened his jaws and a horn note came out.

The dragon overhead emitted a tremendous tone, Fraak's note amplified and lowered in pitch; then, the giant tilted and swept closer in a long spiral, touching the oil-smooth sea as lightly as a gull, though it was twice the size of the boat. It came close, sliding through the water till it was at the boat's side; the snaky neck lifted, and the monstrous head peered down. Zamor and Hugon sat, tense; each man's hand moved uncontrollably toward his sword hilt, though there would have been no real use in such weapons.

"Greetings, Thuramon," the dragon said in an enormous thrumming voice. "It has been long since you last came to us. What is it you seek, wise one?"

"We had an enemy, Arrakimok," Thuramon answered where he sat in the stern. "That enemy has returned and is at work again."

The dragon uttered a deep sound like a three-note chord, a sound of pleasure.

"You know me by name, Thuramon," Arrakimok said. "Few of your kind seem able to do that." The head turned, and the emerald eyes aimed at Fraak. "And a Small One! It is well that the Small One is not caged and

113

wears no collar, as I see. Are you the friend of Thuramon, Small One?"

"I'm Hugon's!" Fraak piped, and sprang across the
boat to settle on Hugon's shoulder; his golden eyes
stared up, boldly and unafraid, into the emerald ones.

"Oho?" the giant dragon said, and suddenly made a
sound, a deep-booming musical phrase; a question, apparently. Fraak tooted back, his tail lashing with
pleasure at finding another who could speak his language.

"The Small One is pleased with you, man," Arrakimok
said, his emerald eyes on Hugon. "And also with the
black man. He says that you are honest men." The
amused note came again. "He sees much in you . . . and
you are with our ancient friend, Thuramon, also . . .
who seems to have lived a very long time for one of your
kind."

The dragon stared now at Kavin, in the bow, for a
long moment.

"Another?" he said, slowly. "You too . . . you were
that Prince who came here with the other, long ago.
This is very strange, man."

Kavin's eyes were steady. "I am the Prince," he said.

The dragon hummed. "The gates will be opened, humans. It is certain that our Old Ones will wish to hear
more of all this."

The creature moved away from the boat, the enormous wings spread wide, and Arrakimok shot swiftly up
and into the air. Then he swiftly grew smaller, arrowing
toward the looming rock ahead.

"There!" Kavin pointed. "The gate opens."

In the wall of stone, a gap had appeared, an arched
space into which the sea eddied. Zamor and Hugon bent
to their oars again, and the boat drove through the opening.

Beyond, a stone quay loomed in the shadows under an
overarched dome of rock. A single brilliant light, a point
of bright gold, hung over the quay, a curious lamp such
as neither Hugon nor Zamor had ever seen before. As

114

Kavin jumped to the quay and made the boat fast, the other two stared at the light curiously, shipping their oars. But Thuramon rose, and climbed out, beckoning them to follow.

Fraak was wildly excited now; as the group went forward, he spread his wings and shot into the air, circling and swooping around Hugon's head and piping musically; smoke trailed from his widely opened mouth as he dived and swooped.

Zamor laughed, looking up. "He must smell his own kind, I think."

Ahead, a door opened, without apparent help; Thuramon and Kavin went confidently through it, and Zamor and Hugon followed. They felt less certain than the other two; both men kept their hands near their swords, moving watchfully. Here, they walked along a hall that seemed cut out of the rock itself; the strange lamps lit it at intervals.

Then, approaching them out of the distance, they saw a human figure, the first living man they had seen so far in this place. He moved slowly, pacing toward them; and as he came closer, they saw that he was very old, with a face that seemed made of brown leather. But his eyes surveyed them brightly under the shadow of a hooded garment he wore.

Thuramon stopped and waited, the others behind him. The magician stared at the newcomer, with an amazed expression.

"Are you . . ." Thuramon paused, touching his own beard in a gesture of puzzled thought. "Is it possible that you are . . . Arastap?"

"I am," the ancient one said; his mouth stretched in a smile. "And though this body is as you see it, much worn with time and use . . . I have no flaw in memory. I remember you well, Thuramon, though your beard was shorter then. And this other, the Prince, who once undertook a service for us. It would seem he alone has escaped the work of time . . ." And the old man chuckled. "Yes, I know much of what has happened. Even something

115

concerning you two." He looked at Hugon and Zamor. "A black king, and a knight of nowhere . . ."

Zamor stared at Arastap, his face stony.

"I am no king," he said, in a level voice.

"You have a king's blood," Arastap said. "Though that makes no difference in this place. But . . . it may be better not to waste time. The ancient enemy grows stronger. Come."

He walked away with long strides, and the others followed.

They came now into an enormous circular room, domed, lit by a misty glow of sourceless light. The floor was paved with odd designs, circles and shapes and letters in some unknown language, inlaid in jewels and metal; and the room held only one other occupant.

He lay, curled in a spiral of tail around a huge low table, his mighty head reflected in the black glass of the table's top as he seemed to look down at it. Then the head swung up, and huge glowing eyes regarded the newcomers; a ripple of movement stirred the blue-gleaming scales, and the dragon spoke.

"Welcome, Thuramon, and these others," the huge voice boomed.

"Greetings, wise and ancient one," Thuramon said, stepping forward to face the giant creature. For a long moment, they looked at each other, the small gray beard and the enormous saurian; and Hugon, watching, suddenly was aware of a passage of something between them, wordless, yet real. It was a recognition, he thought. They were alike in some way, the man and the dragon.

"I have long wished to return here," Thuramon said. "But without invitation it would not be the thing to do. Now . . ."

"It is most necessary that you speak with us," the dragon said. "Forgive us our need to be left alone. Few men are welcome here, as the Prince Kavin knows . . ." The great eyes looked at Zamor and Hugon. "You should also know the reason for our wish to remain alone. We

116

are few, and old, for the most part. Many of our kind have gone away to worlds where we are . . . more at home. We remain, to teach a few of your folk whatever we can, and to preserve the work we have done in this world . . . but we have no desire for commerce with mankind." The huge head bent over the glass table again. "Now, however, we need the hands of men, once again. Our ancient enemy is awake." The dragon stared down at the glass and the humans came closer, drawn by a silent order.

The black glass of the table was glowing and flickering, as though currents of light flowed deep within the material. As they watched, it cleared into a tiny perfect image of a great city, webs of streets and houses, walls and towers; a glimmer of sea, beyond, and the green hills that crowned the other shore of the Narrows.

"Mazain," Hugon said, and Zamor echoed the word with a grim look.

There was a lake, a long oval of shining water; reflected in it, the groves and the tall palaces that surrounded it. And in the midst of the lake, the enormous bulk of the Imperial House; tower rising upon tower, over ancient walls of solid rock. Just beyond, at the island's tip, among the trees, a second dark mass of building stood.

"The Temple of the Lord of Night," the dragon said. "So he has revealed himself to the Emperor, sending him dreams and visions. And the Emperor is now his servant, building that temple which is no temple, but a gate. As you know, Thuramon."

"I know," Thuramon said quietly. "I came here because of this. The Egg of Fire . . ."

"The Egg," the dragon said. "It is there, in the Imperial House. He has it, and will place it in its position in the silver gate, when the gate is complete. With the Egg of Fire in place, that gate will open to all worlds and places, even the place where Ess now lies."

"The Egg is a great crystal," Thuramon said to the others. "There were others like it, once, but as far as I know,

117

there's but one left here. How the Emperor obtained it, I don't know, but he has it." Thuramon's face was grim. "And he holds the world in his hand with that."

"There is still time," the dragon said. "The gate is not yet finished. If the Egg of Fire were gone . . ."

"Yes," Thuramon said. "That. Can you aid us?"

The dragon stared at him for a long time.

"We will give you what we can," he said at last. "It may be that we should not . . . but you have a Small One with you, and he has given his love to one of you, this one with the fair beard."

Fraak, sitting on Hugon's shoulder now, had been very quiet, as if awed; but realizing that he was being spoken about, he preened and uttered a low note.

The giant dragon replied with another sound, like a deep laugh. His enormous mouth seemed to be smiling.

"Small One, would you like to come here to live with us, your Elder Brothers, and learn to be wise?" the dragon said.

Fraak blew a long plume of smoke, and lifted his wings.

"I want to stay with Hugon," he said, firmly. "Why should I want to be wise?"

"Why, indeed?" the dragon asked, in a deep voice. He stared at Hugon. "When one of the Small Ones chooses a human friend, it is fortunate for that man. As it is most unfortunate for those who try to cage our Small Brothers against their will. Listen, Small Brother. Some day, your people will follow ours to the place where we will soon go . . . but not within your lifetime, so be as you are, and be happy." The deep laugh came again. "You are wise not to choose wisdom. We find it a burden, sometimes . . . and a burden that once taken up, can never be set down again."

The dragon turned its head and looked toward Arastap.

"After so long, the Law must be broken," the dragon said. "We shall give a few of our weapons to these humans. A few . . . though even this is against our wisdom.

118

Thuramon, you I need not warn. You have special knowledge of the evil of some things. And you, Prince Kavin . . ." The great eyes glowed strangely. "Yours is a special and strange fate, I think. There is no need to caution you. But you, black man, and you of the fair beard . . ." He looked at Hugon and Zamor.

"We of the Dragon people have long lives, and we remember many things," the deep voice went on. "We neither hate nor love you of the human kind, but we dislike the disturbances you cause, when you learn too many tricks. Now and again, we do what we can to keep you from growing too clever for your own good . . . and we have an ancient law that we must never give you knowledge of certain tools and weapons. A law I fear we must break, now."

Hugon tilted his head to look directly into the huge eyes; he scowled a little as he stared, and his hands gripped his belt as he stood stiffly.

"Now, my lord dragon . . ." Hugon said, in a loud, clear voice. "Though I may be breaking the law of hospitality by disagreeing with you . . . I must speak."

The dragon stared at him silently.

"You're wise enough, I don't doubt," Hugon said. "But you spoke of . . . as you put it . . . keeping we human folk from growing too clever. Wise as you are, I doubt you can do that. We learn, slowly I grant you, but we learn, year by year." He paused, and stared grimly. "But if what 'you say is true . . . that your folk have used some magic or other to keep my kind from true wisdom . . . why, then, I call you enemy of my folk and of me, though you slay me not!"

Hugon's voice rang loudly as he finished. Zamor glanced at him and shrugged grimly; his big hand dropped to his sword, and he whispered to Hugon, "You're a fool, brother." But more loudly, Zamor said, "I stand with my brother Hugon in all things."

Thuramon flung up his hands and uttered a harsh bark of laughter, and Kavin, too, chuckled. The big dragon made no sound, but sat, still grinning.

119

"The young man is bold," the dragon said, slowly. "But I would not have him for an enemy. He is one who seeks wisdom, I think, and therefore he is right to speak so. Listen, man; there is wisdom, and there are tricks. Ask your warlock here; he knows both magic and sleight-of-hand, I think. If your folk become too fond of tricks, they will have no time to learn true things. I tell you this because we of the Dragon folk have lived long enough to see the proof. Come here, and look."

Hugon came closer to the table, reluctantly; he still felt a deep anger, but he controlled it.

"Look," the dragon said. "This is a true record of a place and time when men had learned many tricks . . . but no wisdom. In a different world . . . but still men, like you."

The image in the glass glowed darkly as Hugon stared. He saw the tiny forms of men moving carefully among huge ruins . . . smoke drifted by, and there were dead men on the ground. No, not men only, Hugon saw, as he bent closer. There was a small dark form, a child . . . he shuddered as he saw that it seemed to have been hideously burned.

A dark shadow sped across the imaged ground, and something enormous and winged swooped past. Bright flashes spat from the ground, and from the winged thing, which Hugon saw now was something like a great machine, with men in it.

"I wish there were time to show you much more, seeker of wisdom," the dragon said, with a faint note of irony. "Much, much more. There, for example, you see a world where men slay most skillfully, with weapons of great art . . . for no reason that any of them can discover. In that world, they have neither wisdom nor any gods at all . . . and soon, for one reason or another, there will be no men there, either. I could show you many worlds where there are no men; in some, there are few beasts or birds, either, and even the sea is poison, now. And all done by man's tricks, seeker Hugon."

Hugon shrugged. "Because others are fools, as you

120

seem to say, why should we be fools too?" he asked. "I think we can learn, unless you prevent us."

"What do you wish to learn, man?" the dragon asked.

"What?" Hugon repeated, and scratched his beard. "Why, all there is to know. From the stars in the sky to the fish under the sea, for one thing, and the shapes of things, for another . . ." He stopped and laughed. "If I knew the name of the wisdom I seek, I'd have it already. But look you, Lord Dragon, I'm what I am, a man with a hunger and not knowing the word for meat, d'you see? But a Goddess . . . or somebody very like Her . . . promised me this much, that I'd die wiser than I am." He stopped, and grinning, scratched Fraak's scaly head.

"All men may die wiser than they began, if they wish," the dragon said. "But we must move about our work, man; the time grows shorter. The being called Ess must not open his gate, and you shall prevent him; you must steal the Egg of Fire."

"From the Imperial House?" Hugon stared. "Why not the Emperor's crown, too, while we're about it?" He glanced at Thuramon, and then at Kavin; both of them seemed gravely calm. "You mean all this, then?"

"You have wisdom, in the warlock Thuramon," the dragon said. "I shall give him a little more wisdom than he has, in a moment. And you have . . . luck." He stared at Kavin. "You will need that, Kavin . . . called Lucky Kavin once or twice in the past." The eyes turned to Zamor. "You have strength . . . of several kinds. You shall have more strength, but be very wary of how it is used; it can kill you as well as aid you. And last, you . . ." He looked at Hugon. "For you, the tools of your trade; a thief's tools. You will use them well, I think." The dragon's head lifted. "Arastap!"

The old man came forward, and waited.

"Take these others to the sea gate, and give them those things I prepared for them," the dragon said. "Instruct them in their use while I speak a while with Thuramon privately. Go, now." The dragon looked toward Fraak, on Hugon's shoulder. "You also, small one . . . but if you

121

wish, you may return to us whenever you desire." Suddenly, the great dragon uttered a rumbling musical phrase, and Fraak answered it with one of his own.

Arastap beckoned. "Come," he said.

They followed, leaving Thuramon. The old man led them silently through the same halls, down to that stone quay where their boat lay tied. There two other old men waited, carrying objects in their hands.

Arastap took something from one of the others, and held it in his own hands, turning it over with a low chuckle. He looked at Kavin.

"Luck," Arastap said, his voice echoing in the stone vaults overhead. "There's no need to instruct anyone in the uses of luck. Luck you've had, Prince; this will give you better. You know her, I think . . . you gave her a name, once." He held out a tiny ivory figure, a woman's form. Kavin took it, and stared at it where it lay in his palm.

"I know her," he said, quietly. He put the ivory figure into his pouch, silently.

Arastap had taken another article—a broad leather belt, very dark with age, with a huge metal buckle. The buckle was of silver, also age-filmed, with tiny odd figures twisted in strange designs upon it. On the rim of the buckle there were two small jeweled studs.

"Put this on," Arastap said, handing it to Zamor. The big man did so, and waited.

"Touch the buckle," Arastap said. "On the left, and on the right . . . there. If you press the left, the belt becomes . . . effective. The right, and it ceases to work. Now, before you try, listen." His voice became harshly earnest. "There is nothing of true magic in that belt, only art. What it gives you is taken from your own flesh and bone and blood; if you use it overmuch, you will die, withered and old before your time. For every moment that you use it, it is as though a day of your life is taken from you. Never forget that."

Zamor looked down at the belt, his mouth tight.

"I don't know if I like this gift," he said.

122

"You'll need it," Arastap told him. "But when you've made use of it, if you're wise, you'll toss it into the sea. Now, the manner of its use . . . press the left stud."

Slowly, with reluctance, Zamor did so. He waited, but nothing seemed to have happened; he looked at Arastap.

"Now, be very careful," Arastap said. He indicated a heavy iron post, one of several that were set into the rock along the stone quay to serve as bollards for the lines of boats.

"That post," Arastap said. "Take hold of it, and draw it up."

Zamor looked at it, and his teeth gleamed in a grin.

"Are you out of your wits?" he asked. "That? Man, I've the muscles I grew while I pulled that damned oar, but . . . come, you're joking."

"Go on," Arastap said, impatiently. "But carefully, now."

Zamor shrugged, and bent to grip the iron. His hands clamped, and his broad back straightened . . . and with a stony shriek of protest, the iron post began to rise as he pulled. He let go, and stared down at it with a look of total surprise.

"Why, the thing must have been weakly set . . ." he said, but Arastap shook his head.

"Look, there, where your hands held it," Arastap said. Zamor stared down at the iron. It was indented with the marks of his fingers, deeply.

"Great Snake!" he said in a low voice.

"That post has been set most firmly these nine hundred years," Arastap told him. "Now, press the right stud. Good. Listen, once more. That which you wear is most dangerous, to you as much as to any other. Use it only when you must, and never keep it active for long. Not only will it draw away your strength if you do, but you may slay someone without intending to do so with a mere touch. Or other evil things may happen, if you forget."

"By the Nine, Zamor," Hugon said, grinning, "Think. You're with a wench, and give her a friendly grip round

123

the waist, and there you stand, with the two halves of her at your feet."

"Ugh, but you've an unpleasant turn of mind, brother," Zamor said. He stared down at the buckle uneasily. "I'd as soon keep this elsewhere . . ." He began to open it.

"Better to wear it," Arastap told him. "If another took it, you'd wish you had kept it close."

Zamor shrugged and let the belt remain, though he did not look pleased.

"Now, your gift . . ." Arastap said to Hugon; he held up a flat leather pouch, like a book, and opened it, showing Hugon what it held. There were several small metal tools, a curiously shaped metal bottle, and other things which Hugon could not identify.

"Wait, now," Arastap said as Hugon reached out to take the pouch. "Each tool has its use, here. Now, these . . . they will open any lock you will find, I think. Put this rod so . . . I think you already know the simpler lock picks of your world. But this is more complicated." He took out a tiny metal bottle, small enough to fit into his hand; once more, he turned toward the luckless iron post. "Watch me."

He directed a thin stream of something like a clear liquid, circling the post. A moment later he tapped it gently; the post fell, like a cut tree.

"That's even better than your magic knife, Hugon," Zamor said, admiringly.

"Now," Arastap said, replacing the bottle. "This." He drew out an object that seemed to be a small mirror; it glowed and flickered as he held it up. "Let any man look at this, so . . ." He held it before Zamor's eyes. "And now . . ."

Hugon stared at Zamor, and then at Arastap. "What's this?" he snapped. "You've done something to him!"

Zamor stood, his eyes widely blank, staring ahead of him; his hands limply at his sides, frozen.

"He will recover within an hour or two, of his own accord," Arastap said. "But since we've little time . . ." He slapped the big man's face lightly several times.

Zamor's eyes suddenly snapped into focus, and he grunted, angrily.

"Hold your hand, old man!" he growled, his hand going to his sword. "What . . ."

"No, he meant no harm," Hugon said, grinning. "Merely a trial of one of these most marvelous tools. Are there more, Arastap?"

"One more thing," Arastap said. "This." He held up what seemed to be a reel on which a fine pale hair was wound. "This is a rope; hook one end this way, to your belt, and cast the other where it may catch . . . as you see, there's a hook. Now, it will hold the weight of ten men your size, though it seems to be so thin."

He closed the case, and handed it to Hugon.

"No thief in your world has ever been so well tooled; be wary, man," Arastap said.

"Why?" Hugon asked. "Does this gift also carry such dangers as Zamor's belt?"

"All that Zamor may lose, with strength, is his life," the old man said, somberly. "Or another's, perhaps. But you may lose much more. You may gain all the wealth you need, or more, with those tools, man."

"What would be lost by that?" Hugon asked, wonderingly. He fingered the leather case with a grin.

"I say to you what I have already said to your friend," Arastap said. "When the task is done, if you live . . . cast that into the sea. He who once used it should have done so."

"Did he come to a bad end, then, the former owner?" Hugon asked.

"He did," Arastap said. "He died old, rich, and much respected. But that was long ago, and doubtless his soul has passed through enough lives to remove the memories of that one."

Hugon stared at him, and rubbed his knuckles against his chin.

"There are times when I almost think I understand you," he said. "Do you understand him, Fraak?" he addressed the dragonet on his shoulder.

125

Fraak chuckled. "No, but he is a nice man. He told me a secret!" Fraak emitted a pleased chortle, and flapped.

"Oh, what secret?" Hugon asked.

"Can't tell!" Fraak sang.

"Certainly," Hugon agreed. "Otherwise, it would be no secret . . . ah, here comes our warlock at last."

Thuramon emerged from the gateway and came down the quay toward them. His face seemed very pale, and his eyes deep; he walked slowly.

"Well, now, Thuramon," Kavin said, going to him. "We've all received our proper tools . . . were you given wisdom enough, just now?"

Thuramon stared at him, and then at the others, with an odd look.

"Wisdom?" he said. "Oh, yes. Yes, I learned . . . quite enough." He was silent for a moment. "More than I wished to know, I think. Well . . . we must go. We shall start for the western shores, and the Imperial City, as soon as I have instructed my servants concerning my house." He spoke absently, almost as if speaking to himself; moving toward the boat, he climbed down, with Kavin's aid. Zamor and Hugon followed, taking the oars.

Arastap stood watching, his figure growing smaller on the quay as the boat moved out toward the open water into the brightness of day. The city lay ahead, a glitter of white wall and rooftops and the thin black lines of masts, on the horizon; Zamor and Hugon began to pull steadily. Overhead, three dark specks wheeled slowly in the sky, and a distant bugling note came through the air.

SEVEN

"And so my poor friend Barazan lies at the bottom of the cold sea, does he?" Izzanash, Justiciar of the Imperial Revenues, peered myopically at Gwynna, fingering his thin beard. He looked, she thought, somewhat like an otter regarding a hen. But she nodded, and dabbed lightly at her eyes with a perfumed kerchief.

"Yes, my Lord Izzanash," she said, allowing her full lower lip to tremble just a shade. She had noticed that this was always one of her better effects. "And I am alone, and unprotected . . ." She directed a large-eyed look at Izzanash. "Only by the favor of the gods did I manage to return to Mazain, through so many terrible dangers . . . and as I told you, my lord, I care nothing for wealth. My late husband's palaces in the city, the lands he held in the south . . ."

Izzanash's tongue touched his lips, thoughtfully.

". . . his personal treasure," Gwynna went on, watching the Justiciar. "So much gold . . . I am only a woman, and I am sure I know nothing of accounts and the managing of vast estates. If I knew a man of wisdom and honesty, who could do it all for me . . . but I am of foreign birth, and know few, except the lords of the Emperor's court . . . so, perhaps it would be as well if I simply allow my husband's relatives to divide the estate among themselves, as they desire." She shot another look at the Justiciar. "If only a little could be kept for me, as his widow . . . a few jewels, and enough to live on."

"No, no, of course not," Izzanash said hastily, squinting. She was really an extraordinarily handsome

127

young woman, he thought. And a widow . . . and, as she said, so . . . unprotected. Izzanash felt quite fatherly, in a way. At the same time, he began to calculate the precise difference in their ages; and remembered that his old acquaintance Varmaz the merchant had married a young wife only recently. A young wife without any special dowry, either, Izzanash recalled.

"But the laws are more than clear on this," Izzanash said, and ventured to pat Gwynna's hand reassuringly. "All of your late lord's wealth must go first to his wife, of course, since there were no children . . . I assure you, my lady, the matter can be settled with dispatch. Of course, should you wish, in pure kindness, to make certain settlements on some of these relatives who have raised this issue . . ." He shrugged, spreading his hands. "While they deserve nothing, considering their avarice, it would be easier to do this. Now, if the Illustrious himself should sign an edict confirming you as the heir of the estate . . ."

"Oh, but the Emperor couldn't be troubled with so small a matter!" Gwynna said, widening her eyes. "With all these terrible things happening, the rebellion . . . he has too much to burden himself with as it is, I'm sure."

"I happen to be, ah, quite close to the First Lord, Chancellor Paravaz," Izzanash told her, smiling thinly. "In many ways, my lady, my connections with the Imperial Court are very good. Mmm . . . yes."

"And you are well known to be a man of great honesty . . . skilled in the law and in . . ." Gwynna stopped, and looked at Izzanash with an expression of delicate panic. "Oh, no, I must not! I cannot ask a man so important and so busy . . ."

"To handle your affairs, my lady?" Izzanash said, rubbing his hands together. "But of course!"

Gwynna beamed at the Justiciar, and he basked in the glow as they settled the details. He would steal whatever he could, Gwynna thought, as they arranged their agreement. But she would have nothing to concern herself about in matters of the great estates that Barazan had

128

left. If I could give them all away for a few feet of the lands of Armadoc again, she thought . . .

". . . it is true that the rebellion may cause us all much difficulty," Izzanash was saying. "The lands your husband held in Quenda . . . they're now in rebel territory. But as soon as the Emperor has crushed this villainous sedition, all will be well."

"Have these rebels come so far, then?" Gwynna asked. "Surely they can never reach the Imperial City, can they?"

"Quite impossible," Izzanash said. "The Imperial forces are advancing against them daily. And a great fleet is fitting out, even now. Lord Barazan would have taken great joy in those fine ships." He sighed.

"Then we are agreed on the whole matter," Gwynna said, and rose. She gave him a final melting look. "I am sure all will be well, in your hands, my lord."

Descending to the street level, she entered the litter in which she had come; the bearers picked up the shafts and trotted away toward the palace of the late Lord Barazan. Gwynna, her hand cupping her chin, sat, thinking hard.

There was no way to tell when Thuramon and the others would arrive . . . if they could reach the city at all, she reflected. She knew much more than she had allowed Izzanash to guess; more than he did himself, probably. Half the Empire was now in the hands of various rebel forces; all of the southern coasts of Quenda.

All the sea between Mazain and the other coast was a hunting ground now; ships of the Empire and rebels contending, and pirates roving freely to seize such merchants as dared to venture through. It might be difficult to find passage to the city . . . and difficult for foreigners to enter.

But the magician Thuramon had promised, Gwynna thought. Promised the one thing she desired above all else, when he had completed the secret work he intended; to give Gwynna back the homeland she had cast away.

She stared through the curtains of the litter, as the bearers thrust their way through the crowded streets; her red mouth curved in a wry, bitter smile. Thuramon and his party would never come, she thought; and if they did, they would not succeed. Thuramon's promise meant nothing; it was beyond any magic to give back the years that had passed, to change what the Weavers had knotted into the web of time. Not even the gods could do that, she thought.

But . . . if they came . . . she would help them. Why not, Gwynna thought. Both of those men were young, strong, and . . . her red tongue darted out suddenly and moistened her lips. Which would I choose, if I chose at all? The strong one, with the skin like jet . . . he would be a lover to remember, that one. Or the clever one, with the wise hands and the way of looking at a woman that . . .

The stench of the city drifted through the curtains, and she wrinkled her nose. No, she thought. I chose this, all of it, Mazain and its crowds and smells, the court and the fawning lords, and that madman, the Emperor. She thought of Sharamash and shuddered, slightly, remembering that she was to appear soon at the court, to present herself formally upon her new status.

Ess, in the place where he was, stirred. Thoughts moved in his mind . . . an awareness came to him, and memory images shifted in that unhuman brain.

The biped that was called Kavin. He had other names, Ess thought, and other lives. Odd, that these bipeds should be so unpredictable, so dangerously clever. This one, the Kavin, was linked to Ess by a strange bond forged when Ess had been hurled out of space and time in a spasm of pain . . . by the Kavin thing's act. The link remained; even in the place where he was now, Ess was aware of Kavin.

The biped lived, impossibly, though the life span of his kind was usually much shorter. Lived, and moved

. . . toward the Gate, the Gate that Ess had caused to be built, with so much effort, the Gate which would release him.

The mind of Ess reached out, searching, desperately, feeling into that darkness that was more than darkness . . . there were biped minds to be reached, here and there. Few were right for his use; such a mind must be bent, twisted out of the normal shape, before he could send a touch into it. There were madmen who could feel his questing touch, and who shrieked at it; and here and there one whose mind was poisoned by disease or a drug . . . but these were men who were often ready to die, or otherwise useless. He needed another mind that belonged to one who held some power, as the Emperor's did.

And he found it. A mind that glowed with deep scarlet fire, asleep . . . as he wished it to be. Ess touched that mind, and held it, sending visions.

My name is . . . Gann

Cold, bitter cold, and the memory of his name; the mind had slept for a very long time, but now it woke, very slowly. The dreams that Ess created floated in the mind of Gann, dreams that were partly memory of real events, and partly the distorted images that were bent to the advantage of the thing called Ess.

The body of Gann still slept, but now it was aware of a little of the world around it; the cold, most of all. It could not awaken completely; the body was too badly damaged to bear the currents of life, as yet. But Gann dreamed, now, and thoughts moved in the mind that had been so long frozen into stasis.

Ess saw, as no human mind or eye could ever see; he regarded Gann's brain, and touched certain parts of it, delicately. There were cells, frozen . . . and they warmed, and lived again. Control was established; repair began.

To Ess, the mechanisms of simple creatures of this world and time were no puzzle; they could be manipu-

131

lated quite easily, under the right circumstances. This one, Gann, was a somewhat special case, but without real difficulties.

The body had been placed in deep sleep and intense cold, just after the infliction of the injuries that had "killed" it. The part that was its true identity was gone, of course, as Ess knew only too well; but there was quite enough left. Under the direction of Ess's mind, cell after cell grew into place; the ancient wound healed. And the part-mind dreamed slow scarlet dreams.

I am Gann.

I will NOT die.

"All men must die, Noble Gann," the priest said in the scarlet-tinted dream.

He stood at a window, staring out over a milky sea of fog that lay below. Out of the mist, the towers of the city thrust up, like the arrogant spears of a hidden army, their tips glittering in the sun. In the distance, a great ship drifted across the sky, a mere dot of light at this distance.

"Mystical nonsense," Gann said, his back to the priest.

"In former ages, Noble One, it was only a hope and a belief," the priest said quietly. "For a thousand years, men thought that the soul lived again, through life after life, as the Mysteries taught. But now, we *know* that it does, as the men of science have shown us. Yet, to live again, a man must suffer death. Only thus may he continue to ascend the long stairway . . ."

"Ascend?" Gann turned and stared at the priest. "For me, ascend? I have done so, priest. In this life, not another. I have turned away from pleasure; I've eaten bitterness, toiled like a slave . . ." His voice grew harsher. "I have betrayed friends and caused good men to die . . . but I build something that will stand, and now that I have come to a time when I may taste life, it is to be taken away from me. I will die, and be reborn a slave, a peasant, with none of the knowledge I bought at such a price . . . no. No! I will not die priest."

132

"There is no cure for the disease you have, Noble One," the priest said, "The surgeons have said it."

"Then they shall work till they have a cure," Gann said. "And I shall wait, till then."

"Noble One, it may not be," the priest said.

Gann stared at the robed man, and the priest grew pale, but did not move.

"I know what your order teaches," Gann said at last. "At the moment of death, my . . . soul, as you call it . . . flies free, to seek rebirth. Even though I command that my body be instantly plunged into the cold, to be preserved thus till the men of science discover how I may be cured . . . yet, according to you, I will already have entered the darkness, possibly already reborn. Your order says that this is true." Gann's eyes, fever-bright, held the priest's. "We have already proved it a lie."

"The subjects that your men of science have placed in the great cold have returned," the priest said. "To a seeming life. But not completely."

"Not completely?" Gann said, and laughed. "Five, so far . . . and each man walks, speaks, and is alive as he was."

"No," the priest said, stubbornly. "In each of those five, the true self fled into the darkness and seeks rebirth. We have the means of reaching such, as you know. What remains is only a part. And this is the true evil, Noble One . . ." His voice grew earnest. "A man should not be thus divided, a part in the world of the living and another in the darkness. Always, the divided parts will seek reunion . . . and think. Should the soul of such a man find rebirth, while another body still lives, what then? Listen, Noble One. Love and hate are closely allied, desire and repulsion, destruction and creation. In those two bodies with but a single soul, the forces of the universal power will cause a dreadful desire and a great hate. They will seek each other . . ."

"Babbling mysticism," Gann said. "Without proof. And without logic, even in your own terms, priest. Look you,

133

if there were two of me, on the day I wake from the cold, one would be a child." His eyes were grim. "And I would be as I am now. Need I fear a child?"

"How long will that cold sleep be?" the priest countered.

"Priest, we have learned this much in half a dozen generations," Gann told him. "All this." He thrust out an arm toward the mist-shrouded city. "We can tap the power of the sun. We can go out into that blackness to walk on other worlds . . . we can create, as man has never done before . . ."

"And destroy, too," the priest said.

"Yes, and destroy," Gann said. "We have no enemies any longer, have we? Priest, if my doctors have not learned the secret of this thing that destroys me, within a decade or two . . . ah, but they will. They must!" He turned to stare out the window again. "And then, I shall wake . . . and complete my work."

The priest silently stared at his back for a moment.

"Noble One, my order has charged me to tell you this," the priest said, at last. "When we learned of this plan, we sought by means of our Art to discover its consequences. Listen. The great state you have built will not remain for the lifetime of a man. It will go down in fire and destruction, and the whole earth shall be laid waste for a thousand generations. The few men who live shall live as beasts, unremembering."

Gann whirled and stared at the priest; then, harshly, he laughed.

"Prophecies of doom again? I've heard this before," he said. "What enemies have we to make this come about?"

"The enemy is here already," the priest said. "All that is built by force contains the seed of death."

"So your croakers have said, many times," Gann said. "But we acted as we had to act. Should we have meekly surrendered to those others? You and those like you would have died under their knives long ago if we had not struck back . . . or been slaving under their whips,

134

more likely. Now that their cities are ashes, you find it easy to preach, don't you?"

"But we never said that we feared death, Noble One."

Gann chuckled, and suddenly put a hand to his side, with a choked sound of pain.

"True," he said. "And I do fear it, do I not?"

"There is a greater evil to fear," the priest said. "I must tell you this. Your body will lie, sleeping and soulless, till a time generations from now. It will be taken to another world, for this one will be as I have told you, a desert and a wilderness. And in that world, your soul will already have found rebirth, while your body sleeps on."

"I think these are lies, priest," Gann said. "But go on. You amuse me, and I need amusement badly, now."

"There are many worlds, folded one upon another," the priest said. "As your men of science already suspect. In some, like this one, the gods are dead . . . as you would say it. In others, they live. In that one to which your sleeping body goes, the Great Goddess has decreed that man shall walk a different road . . ."

"We must have all the mystical claptrap revived then?" Gann asked, grinning ironically. "That primitive Goddess as well?"

"I must tell you what I am charged to tell you," the priest said. "It is not necessary that you believe me."

"I do not."

"Then let me say the rest," the priest said. "In that newer world, you shall sleep; but those that brought you there will attempt to build, as you have built. They will seek aid from the End of Time itself, and call evil into that world. And in time, you may awaken and face your own soul in a new body. And this is the worst doom any man may have, Noble One." The priest stared at him. "This is the time of your choosing, Gann, called Master of the World. If you choose to accept death, you will surrender wisdom and power, and gain much more than that. But if you take the other path, evil and dread will be your end."

135

The words seemed to echo, oddly. The room was dimmer, and the priest's face seemed obscure.

The dream shifted and moved, voices and images entangled.

Cold, cold . . .

". . . the stasis. At least as successful as the others . . ." a voice, very distant, was saying. "According to the instruments, the life force remains . . ."

And swirling darkness again.

Scarlet spots of light, glowing against blackness. Eyes.

"If we only dared awaken him," a voice said. "He knew every phase of their science. He could teach us enough to finish this work in days, instead of months and years . . ."

"He would die," another voice said. "Almost as soon as the cold ceased. At least we can reach his memories now, a little . . . enough to help. Ess will not heal him, because of the other . . ."

"So Ess tells us," the first voice said. "It may be a lie. The idea is madness. That another lives . . ."

"In this primitive world, the other would be only a barbarian, without any weapon we need fear," the second voice said. "But we cannot force Ess to do anything he doesn't wish to do, can we?"

Darkness . . . and the scarlet eyes.

And then, for a brief, blinding moment . . . a face. His own face, younger, and somehow different . . . staring down at him with a look of amazement. There was a queer, terrific sense of drawing, a pull . . . and then it ceased. The face had vanished.

A quiet, soundless voice, coldly unhuman, and enormous.

"You have seen him," it said. "He is called Kavin. He is a barbarian, a prince of a primitive folk, in a world that is as your own was a thousand years ago. He is your enemy, because he possesses you, Gann. Slay him, and that which he has will return to you, Gann. I will give you life again . . ."

"I will not die. I WILL NOT DIE."

136

"You will never die, as long as you serve me," the voice said.

Gann awoke.

There was light pouring through an opening above him, a jagged rent in a ceiling. Sunlight, he thought. It was cold, very cold. But it was not the cold that he had felt before; this was merely the chill of an unheated room in winter.

And there was pain burning in his body. But not unbearable now.

He stood up, his body aching and stiff, and discovered that he was naked.

The place where he stood was a great arched hall, rubble strewn, with holes in the ceiling through which the sun came; a bitterly cold wind came, as well. There was no sign of life anywhere.

Swiftly, the naked man moved, searching; in a few minutes he found a door, and entered the rooms beyond. There were bones, and thick dust.

Much later, Gann sat beside a fire made of broken sticks of ancient furniture; it burned against a stone wall, sending its smoke up through the broken ceiling. He was wrapped in a heavy brocade, gray with dust, that had once been a wall hanging. It had a queer stench about it, but he did not notice it.

He propped a stick over the fire, and the body of a small gray creature, a leaping rat, roasted there. In his hands, he held a tattered mass of paper, turning the pages carefully and peering at the faded writing. After a time, he laid the book aside and ate the rat; then he rose and began to explore.

The being called Ess had explained much, in that strange dream-voice. The journal had told him more. His thoughts moved with a strange passionless precision as Gann walked.

Outside the enormous building he surveyed the land. A bleak valley, surrounded by peaks on which snow glittered, and empty of life. At one end of the valley, a queer towering structure of girders and wire stood, at

137

which Gann started in cold wonder. The Gate, he realized; through which men had entered to this world. But it was dead now, without power.

They had begun well, he thought; there were many traces of the work, and there was the record written in the journal he had found. From this place, they could have gone forth to take this world in hand, build and make, as he had once done himself . . . but they had not. They were very few, of course, but they had an even greater command of some of the sciences than he himself had, and more than that; they had reached the creature called Ess, who seemed to have helped them greatly.

But the journal said nothing of how they had ended. Yet, somehow, Gann seemed to know, though he did not know how he knew it. Ess . . . spoke to him, silently.

It will be necessary to find weapons, Gann thought. And helpers. Then . . . to destroy that other, first of all.

He stood up, drawing the tattered cloth about him; he was aware of cold, and of the pain of that which lay within him, not healed, but controlled. Aware, but strangely uncaring.

I am Gann, he thought, again. Yet I am not . . . complete. I seem to possess all the knowledge I had, but I am not as I was. Perhaps the priest was right. That other possesses something that is rightfully mine, something that is myself. I must take it back.

Then he thought, If that unknown being told me the truth, I shall live . . . forever. Time. Time to rebuild, here in this primitive world, all that was.

That journal. It recorded the fall of the great state, too; how it all happened. As soon as I was out of the way, Gann thought, they betrayed all, everything we fought to make. Small men, weak, fearful and hungry for power, tore down the greatness, used the weapons against each other. Till nothing was left but that desert that the priest predicted. Strange, Gann thought. I should feel hate for those fools . . . though they are dead long ago. Yet, I feel nothing.

He turned, and re-entered the gigantic building.

Hours later, he found the entrance to the store rooms, deep under the foundations; and there, in the darkness, he moved slowly and purposefully, seeking and finding. He did not sleep much; and whenever he did, he entered the dim world of dream-visions, where the voice of Ess instructed him. Outside, the sun rose and set many times, but how many Gann did not know or care.

The other was named Kavin, Gann knew. He knew that the other lived, somewhere in this world; and a strange, drawing instinct told Gann that the other was at this moment somewhere in the easterly direction, but moving west and north. It was as though a compass needle turned, measuring the other's progress day by day, deep within Gann's mind.

But the other was far, and Gann knew that he would need a means of transport to reach him. He remembered the swift machines of his own world and time, arrowing through the sky; with one of those he could have reached the other in a day. And with the weapons of his world he would not need to know exactly where that other lay hidden. He could burn half a city . . . but those weapons were not available to him, nor those ships of the air.

No, Gann thought. This was a world of the past to him; and even such tools and weapons as he might find here, in the ruin, would be primitive enough.

The small hairy men who lived among the mountains, north of the valley, avoided the place out of a generations-old fear. An ancient tale spoke darkly of what had once happened there, but the tale also said that the terrors were slain. Therefore, a few of the braver tribesmen sometimes came close, following their shaggy herds of elami; there was better grazing in the pass that led to the Black Valley. But there was fear, too; ghosts dwelt there, it was said.

Yet, Mang Eelap and his herders dared to move always a little closer to the valley every season. Once, Mang Eelap had actually descended to the valley floor, and had returned, bearing strange and marvelous loot.

139

And no evil spirits had pursued him; his herds were not stricken with disease, and his wives bore healthy sons.

The grazing had been poor this year, too; and Mang Eelap determined not to let his herd starve while the grass grew so well in that pass above the strange skeletal towers.

So, on a certain morning, the little woolly, humped elami moved slowly down the valley, following the grass; and behind them, mounted on other elami, the men and women of Eelap's little tribe followed. This time they camped almost within the shadows of the skeletal tower; within clear sight of the squat, enormous ruin in the valley, at which they looked with fearful eyes.

It was noon; cooking fires burned in the camp, and Mang Eelap himself, and two of his sons, sat their elami, watching the herd. A woman, coming out of the skin tent behind them, glanced toward the ruins and abruptly screamed. Mang swung about in his saddle and stared.

A demon had emerged from the House of the Death and stood, gazing silently at the camp.

Mang Eelap knew a demon, though he had not actually seen one before. This one was tall, and made of metal that shone like copper in the sun. It carried a short metal spear, and it had no face, only a smooth dark surface of something that shone.

Then, one of the sons of Mang cried out, and kicked his heels into the woolly sides of his elami; the little beast sprang forward, charging, as the son of Mang fitted an arrow and fired it at the demon.

The demon did not move; the arrow cracked against the metal, and fell broken. But the son of Mang was almost upon him, a second arrow on the string. The demon lifted its staff and pointed. There was a flash of light, more brilliant than the sun; and then there was no man, nor mount. Only a blackened spot on the earth marked the place where both had been.

My fourth son was always something of a fool, Mang reflected. He stared at the immobile demon for a mo-

140

ment longer; then he raised himself in his saddle and cried out in a loud voice, offering the demon worship.

The demon did not speak. But when Mang finally came, very cautiously, closer, the demon did not strike him. He merely stood as Mang laid gifts of meat and milk at his feet.

Here are the helpers and slaves I require, Gann thought. I have few charges for the weapon; it is well that they do not need another demonstration. They are, of course, savages. It would be impossible to train them adequately . . . but they are human, and their bodies are all I require, not their minds. Also, they possess transport animals. Now, at last, I may go . . . to the other.

EIGHT

Her name was Golden Turtle, and Hugon, leaning over a forward rail to watch the sea against her bows, thought there was good reason for the name. She was a round-bellied, wide-beamed ship, and slow as troll's blood, too. The Turtle was very old, older than her most ancient crewman, who was a graybeard; her heavy timbers were split here and there, and her bilge reeked ominously of dry rot.

She had been at the coasting trade, up and down the world for a long time, bearing dried fish one way and half-tanned hides another, and the ghosts of such cargo hung about her blackened hold. She plowed forward now, under patched brown sails, rolling with the sedate, yet slightly lascivious pace of an old madam. To port, the coastal hills showed as a gray mist on the horizon.

Kavin stood there, in the waist, leaning on the bulwark and staring eastward. His sea cloak muffled him, except for the curious silver-gray hair, and his eyes were intent on the distance.

Zamor was aft, on the quarterdeck with one of the seamen; Hugon heard the big man's booming laugh come faintly from there. Thuramon, in the tiny cabin, was probably still poring over the strange books, of which he had brought quite a few along.

Hugon moved quietly down the ladder, and came to Kavin's side. He leaned on the bulwark beside the other and watched him, covertly.

"What's yonder, that you look so hard?" Hugon asked, at last.

143

"Eh?" Kavin glanced at him, startled. "Oh. There. Nothing, now. An empty place, where Dorada was, once. Deserted land, and ghosts." He shrugged, drawing the cloak closer.

Hugon was silent, knowing that there was nothing to be said.

I could indulge in a black mood or two myself, he thought, remembering Gwynna. What devil took me by the codpiece and prompted me to fits of honorable conduct about that fine, smooth wench? Gone she is, and the chances of getting my hands around her as slim now as . . . as our chances of ever getting to Mazain at all, he thought grimly.

Thuramon had paid enough gold for their passage to weigh the value of the Turtle itself. No ships were clearing for Mazain any longer, not since word came from the west of the sea's being full of warships and pirates . . . and not much difference between the two, as far as any merchant was concerned. Gwynna might not have reached the Imperial City herself, for that matter, Hugon thought.

And if she had . . . well, she'd be a lady of wealth and position, again, and would she notice a vagabond like himself? Lucky enough if she keeps her promise to aid us . . . or at least doesn't betray us. Though he thought she feared Thuramon's wizardry too much for that.

Hugon doubted very much that they would ever be able to enter the city in any disguise at all, and he doubted even more that they would be able to steal any Egg of Fire from the Treasury, thief's tools or not. In general, Hugon viewed the future darkly at this moment.

He walked along the swaying deck and found his lute; sat down on a capstan, and proceeded to play a bawdy ballad for the delectation of several members of the crew.

Even the captain, a leathery ancient named Garph, emerged from the after cabin to listen appreciatively as Hugon continued to chronicle the adventures of the yellow-haired girl who knew every word except "no."

144

"... then came a lad from the northern isle,
And a harpooner was he,
And the yellow-haired girl gave him a smile,
And asked his harpoon to see ..."
At which point Hugon was rudely interrupted.

"Sail ho!" the man at the foretop bellowed. "Three sail, and bearing close on the starboard quarter!"

And a moment or two later, the lookout added, with a slight quaver, "Ships of war they are, cap'n!"

There was a great deal of purposeful noise and running. The Turtle was not a ship meant for war; but she was not meant for a rapid escape, either. However, Captain Garph intended to put as many sea miles as he could between himself and those three ominous sails, without any curiosity at all about their nation or their intentions. More patched canvas went up, until the Turtle's masts carried every rag they could bear; the round-bellied ship swung about, to run directly before the wind, northward.

Within two hours, the three sails were nearer; they lay now south and west of the Turtle, and whatever they were, they had most obviously turned in pursuit.

Kavin was already on the quarterdeck, as Zamor and Hugon came up, armed and ready. The prince leaned on a long straight sword, and wore a plain steel corselet and cap borrowed from the ship's small armory; the others had also borrowed armor.

Zamor had found an enormous ancient boarding axe, a monstrous thing with crescent blades mounted on a four-foot shaft; he swung it, testing its balance, and grinned broadly as he did so.

"I'll have a chance to spill a little more Mazainian blood, it may be," he grunted.

"Always assuming those folk yonder are Mazainian," Hugon said. He wore a sword, too, but he had found a big crossbow as well, and was hastily smearing its channel with a lump of grease.

"That's a Mazainian galley, man," Zamor said, peering hard. "See that canted mast? Coming on fine, too; should

145

be on us before dark, that one that's so far ahead of the other two "

"If we keep off till dark," Captain Garph said, anxiously, "might be we can lose him, grant there's no moonlight." He glanced down at the waist where his motley crew were gathering, muttering and staring. "By the Nine, I can't fight a war vessel."

"I doubt we've strength to fight an angry rowboat," Hugon said, surveying the crew. "I've been wondering, these past few days, Captain Garph, seeing the crew you've got . . . is it a floating home for ancient sailors, this Golden Turtle? There's a gaffer there, calls himself mess boy, must be old enough to be my father, and he's the youngest of the crew."

Thuramon appeared, now; he stood and watched, his eyes keen under their thick white eyebrows. He seemed quite calm.

"We shall escape, I think," he said.

"Could you essay a bit of sorcery, lord wizard?" Hugon asked.

"If necessary," Thuramon said. "But . . . for reasons I know best . . . it would be unwise. I do not wish to call attention to our party. Attention that might be caused by . . . excessive use of certain forces."

Kavin looked at Hugon, and now he smiled, hard-mouthed.

"Have no fear, cousin," he said. "There are the three of us, armed men. We can make a fine ending of it, if we need to."

"I'd prefer not to make an ending, if possible," Hugon said, grinning. He twanged the crossbow string. "Not my ending, at any rate. I've several fine poems not yet written."

The dragonet, Fraak, had been asleep in the ship's galley, under the stone hearth; his favorite spot, warm and dry, where occasional goodies came his way as well. But now he came soaring across the deck to land on the rail, with an excited trill.

146

"Bad men!" he cried, and blew a tongue of fire. "Bad men, there! Put me in a wire cage, again!"

"Not if they don't catch us, Fraak," Hugon said. "If they do, we're for a cage ourselves, but they'll never feed us as well as they will you, pretty one."

"Don't LIKE cages!" Fraak said, firmly.

Now the war galley was clearly visible, a white bone of foam under its sharp prow, the tiny figures of men on its foredeck. The sun was on the horizon; it would be dark in half an hour, but the galley was gaining steadily.

"Aaah, HO!" The cry was faint, but audible, over the gray water. "Heave to, there!"

Garph stared aft, toward the galley, then up at the straining sails, clenching his fists nervously.

"We'll never . . ." he began, in a low voice.

Then a loud snap was heard from the galley. An arc of blue smoke appeared; a clay firepot struck the sea a few yards behind the Turtle, and burst with an oily flame.

"Why, the devils mean to burn us!" Garph said in a shocked voice.

"Meaning they aren't out to merely seize cargoes, it seems," Kavin said grimly. "We might have better luck if they'd been only pirates, instead of lawful men of war."

"I'd sooner meet pirates than honest men, myself," Hugon said. "A man loses less, that road. Now, a few yards closer . . ." He had cranked the crossbow to its full tension, and laid a short iron quarrel in it. He balanced it carefully on the rail, kneeling to sight.

"Now!" he said, and squeezed. There was a sharp twang and whizzing sound.

Distantly, they heard a choked shriek, and Hugon grinned as he cranked the bow again.

"Marvelous shooting, brother!" Zamor cried, grinning. "There's a man down, see there? Can you do that again?"

"I'll try . . ." Hugon said, kneeling once more. He squeezed again, and a moment later muttered a curse. "Damn them, they're down behind the bulwarks."

"Well, one's for us," Kavin said. "Let them come closer, and we'll take a few more."

Another firepot arched over, this time nearly aboard.

"If they come closer, we'll be baked like hens," Hugon grunted. "They've no intention of boarding, the motherless . . ."

Suddenly Fraak cried out, a sound that was not like any of his normal hunting cries; pure anger flamed in the sound. He sprang into the air, wings beating, and shot upward, in a wide circle, higher and higher; his body gleamed golden in the sun's last level rays. Then he dived, in a long slant, toward the galley.

On the galley's deck there was distant shouting, and a black speck shot skyward toward the flying dragonet, an arrow. But he was much too fast as he swooped through the upper rigging, slanted upward, and turned to swoop again. The deepening twilight had turned the shape of the galley to a towering darkness behind the Golden Turtle; but now that darkness was suddenly broken by a yellow flower of light. There was fire in the galley's topsail.

A second bloom of fire appeared, on the rushing galley's foredeck; Fraak had evidently dived upon the firepots that lay ready beside their catapult. The galley was turning, now, as men clawed down the flaming canvas and fought the fire; it slowed and fell behind into the dark.

A moment later, Fraak sailed back down to the deck, singing a wild triumphal chord as he thudded onto the wood. He strutted, chortling, as men gathered around him, kneeling to scratch his scaly head and offer him delicious morsels from the galley. He flapped excitedly, his claws scarring the deck, and his golden eyes blowed. Fraak was a hero, and humility was not in his dragonish makeup; he loved the compliments he was hearing.

In the midst of the triumph, Captain Garph struck a discordant note.

"Yon's but one," he said grimly, peering into the dark. "And she may rig new sail yet. Then, there's the other two. And all three of them feeling damned wrathful at

148

us, the way we've scorched 'em. Best press on fast as we can, lads."

Far astern, a star flickered in the darkness, the light of the galley's burning; but it was dimmer now.

The wind was rising a little; the tubby ship rolled more heavily, and seemed to be sailing a little faster. Captain Garph took a log line, and made a calculation of speed, which appeared to cheer him slightly.

"It'll be a near thing, however," he muttered, running the line through his hands as he coiled it. He came back toward the group who waited for him. "We're running due north, ye know. There's the Axe, rising ahead." He pointed out the polar star.

"North," Kavin said, frowning, and glanced at Thuramon, who nodded.

"No chance of turning westward to Quenda coast," Thuramon said, questioningly. Garph shook his head.

"Nay, Master Thuramon, we cannot risk it now," he said. "There'll be more of those damned galleys, closer we get to the southern province. That's where all the fracas is, you know that." He shrugged. "Not to mention the ships the rebels will doubtless have about, who'll be as glad to pluck us as any."

Thuramon glowered. "You were paid, man."

"You may have back your gold," Garph said, with a look of inner agony at the thought, but a firm voice. "I will not have my men slain and my ship burned." He stared at Thuramon, his jaw set. "Master, my men have sailed with me a long time. They're . . . my men."

"Don't press him, Thuramon," Kavin said. "He's in the right."

"We'll be as far from our goal when we land as we were before," Hugon grunted, sitting down on the rail with a disgusted expression. "Father to his men, isn't he? Hah."

Fraak, returning from a foraging trip amidships, sailed to Hugon's shoulder and sat, burping contentedly. Hugon stroked him absently; then glanced at the dragonet with a new look.

149

"One thing we can do, come dawn," Hugon said. "If we need to see beyond the horizons, to find those galleys . . . why, here's our eyes." He patted Fraak's head. "Unless he eats himself to such a weight that he cannot fly at all," Hugon added. "By the gods, he seems to be getting fatter, at that. Are you growing, Fraak?"

Fraak chuckled sleepily.

"I've seen others like him not much larger," Zamor said. He swung the axe thoughtfully, staring into the darkness. "He has his full growth, I'd say. But that's a grand notion, sending him aloft to see what's afoot."

The night grew deeper, and the Turtle went on, mile after mile, farther and farther past the point at which they should have turned toward the southern shores of the Empire. All night the wind held, for which the Captain voiced his thanks, as the dawn began to gray the eastern sky. Hugon, who had not slept well, found Garph on his hands and knees in the prow, bumping his forehead repeatedly on the planks of the deck. A small brass image of the Sea God, green with age, stood in a cavity under the jib boom, and Garph addressed him. He was making a number of unlikely promises as Hugon listened.

"Ah, Captain . . ." Hugon said, clearing his throat. Fraak sat on his shoulder, watching with bright-eyed curiosity as the Captain rose, his ancient knees creaking.

"Our friend Fraak will go up and scout the sea, now," Hugon said. "And let's hope the Sea God believes those grand offers you've been making. Fly now, Fraak, and come back swiftly, when you've seen all." Hugon aided the dragonet's takeoff with an outthrust arm; the creature went up and up, higher and higher till he was only a distant point in the brightening sky.

As they waited, Kavin emerged from the cabin and waited, silently. Zamor, a man who liked his sleep, would arise only when he sniffed breakfast.

Time passed. The Captain paced nervously; Kavin stood against a rail, immobile. Hugon occupied himself with a new string on his lute, which he tested with enormous care.

Finally, they saw the tiny speck growing larger, and then the wide-winged flight, as the dragonet arrowed down for his usual flamboyant landing. He was piping nervously as he came to a stop on Hugon's shoulder, and his tail lashed.

"Ship!" he cried. "The ship I fired yesterday, the same!"

"Easy, small friend," Hugon said, soothingly. "Not so excited . . . the same ship, you think?"

"Yes, yes!" Fraak piped. "Sail all burnt; they have patched sail, now, and men make new ropes. I sailed close, and they saw, tried to shoot arrows at me! They are wicked, and they are very angry, I think!"

"That seems likely," Hugon said. "No captain likes such handling as you gave them. They follow us, then?"

"Oars, rowing hard," Fraak said. "Soon they will have sail again, but with the oars, they go very fast. But there is only one, now," he added, puffing smoke. "Only one, that way. The others, the new ones, are there." He lifted a claw and pointed ahead and to starboard.

"Only the one, then . . ." Hugon began, and checked himself. "Others? Ahead? What ships are they, Fraak? What did they look like?"

"Two, small and black, but with tall sails," Fraak said, and then uttered a rather pleased noise. "One of them has my picture on his sail, all red."

"A sail, with a red dragon?" Garph had been listening, and now his leathery face turned a faint green-gray color. "It is a Thulin, a pirate. They carry such images on their sails . . . they have a god who is a dragon."

"That's *nice!*" Fraak said, in a delighted voice. "I must meet him!"

"He's a god," Hugon said. "Which means that he'll never be there when he's wanted, only when he's not. No, Fraak, I'm afraid those are bad men too."

"But they like dragons," Fraak said, practically.

151

"They eat dragons," Garph told him. "When they can catch one. Small ones, like yourself."

Fraak uttered a horrified croak, and blew a ball of black smoke. He sat on Hugon's shoulder, his golden eyes round with fear and anger, shocked into unaccustomed silence.

"Well, now," Kavin said. "It would seem that we'll pass between the two, with luck. Maybe they'll meet each other, and we'll be rid of both."

"It's possible," Garph said. He called out to the steersman, "Bear another point westward, there, and keep to that."

"Aye," the steersman said.

"Thus, we'll be exactly midway," Garph explained. "It gives the galley a small advantage on us, but we'd never escape it in the end." He scowled thoughtfully. "Though, should the Thulin pirates and that Mazain galley meet, there'd be a fine set to, indeed, and we might well be-gone, meantime."

"Like the mouse between two cats," Hugon said.

"Look you, young fellow," Garph said, "I've done what I had to, to save my men's lives and this ship . . . which is my own living, remember." His face was hard, now. "But if we're trapped, then we'll fight, all of us, old men that most of them be, and we'll cut many a younger man's life short before we go."

"Now, that's what I like to hear, Captain," Hugon said. "A little showing of teeth . . ." He glanced at the Captain, and added, "With my apologies, noticing you've got no more than three or four of 'em . . . I'm sure you'll bite hard enough when the time comes."

The Captain grunted, and stumped off. Kavin looked at Hugon, and shook his head, with a chuckle.

"You've a tongue in your head, cousin," Kavin said. "But you over use it."

Hugon stared at Kavin, silently; then, "Shall I tell you something, my princely ancestor?"

"Tell."

"I am as full of fright as . . . well, I was about to say a

virgin on her bridal night," Hugon said, in a low voice. "But the comparing's wrong . . . she knows well enough what to expect, and that pain's usually followed by pleasure. No, I'm simply craven fearful, prince; fearful of the pains of death, blind feared of the time after it . . . or worse, that there may be no time after it." He stared at Kavin. "I am no hero, and they'll make no ballads out of me, as they've done you. A man like you, all iron and gall and not a quaver in your soul . . . though you've had the small advantage of having tried death once, I hear. But myself . . . I'm but a disinherited son with a taste for poem-making and thievery, no hero at all . . . and fearful, down to my very toes, Prince!" He stared at the deck, shaking his head. "Now, how in the Nine's name could a coward come of your line, can you tell me that, Prince Kavin?"

Abruptly, Kavin laughed, and his big hand clapped down on Hugon's shoulder; he stood, grinning down at him.

"Easily enough, cousin," he said. "Most easily. Because I've a gift to keep my face straight, you think I have no fear? I fear now, as much . . . no, more, than ever. I've never fought yet that I didn't feel a fear's frostbite tooth in my gut, and I think it grows worse with age." He glanced out, toward the sea. "And what do I know of death, more than you? I slept. I saw nothing."

"The wise say we live again," Hugon said in a low voice. "Life after life . . . now, could I be sure of that . . ."

"If you were sure, you'd live a fool's life, and die a fool's death," Kavin said, bluntly. His deep eyes burned into Hugon's. "I have been initiated; I know the Mysteries. But even so, I do not know all. I believe we live, always . . . but I do not know."

"You are initiate?" Hugon said, staring. "I have the Third Grade, myself . . . but that is nothing, of course, as you know. There are few nowadays who go to higher grades . . . to the Mystery itself."

153

He made a certain sign with his left hand; Kavin, nodding, answered it.

"I promise you, cousin," Kavin said, quietly, "when we come to the end of this, I shall, myself, enter you in the Mystery. Not because you are of my blood, but because I think you are an honest man. I give you my word on that."

He turned and walked toward the cabin door, leaving Hugon staring after him. Hugon scratched Fraak's head softly, and spoke.

"I have been half around the world, and seen no prince I would follow with all my soul . . . till now."

Fraak crooned softly. He was still in a complete shock from the gruesome notion that anyone would eat a dragon.

"I smell breakfast," Hugon said, and went down toward the midships house.

The sun rose higher, and toward noon, the wind began to slacken appreciably. From time to time, a man would glance at the limp sails and mutter under his breath. The sea was growing smoother, with an oily look.

The galley appeared, soon enough; first a speck of something far aft, then a growing shape. She had every rag of canvas on, but also, Hugon saw, a tiny flashing whiteness that meant oars out. He thought grimly of those men, straining below, lashed on by whips; dying, as they drove the galley on, their hearts bursting with that effort . . . and there was every chance he'd join them, soon enough, unless he died.

Zamor, beside him, voiced the same ill thought.

"I will not be taken alive," the big black man said, in a matter-of-fact voice. "I've drawn oar for the last time. Though this magic belt might make the labor easier, it wouldn't make slaves' bread taste otherwise."

"Look yonder," Hugon said. "We're competed for. Makes a man feel quaintly, to have two shiploads of armed wolves come from either side."

154

Zamor peered across the sea, and saw the two dark shapes growing in the distance ahead.

Fraak lifted his wings and squalled defiance, staring out.

"Ah, Garph, a feat of navigation to be admired!" Hugon called out, as Garph emerged. Others of the crew gathered round, taking axes and swords as he served them out; he wore an old and rusty corselet now. One aged crewman sat, fiddling gloomily with a greasy skin bag from which pipes protruded; a strange strangled squall came from his work, and he laid the bag down with a black look at it.

"Why, may the demons fry me, but it's a warpipe!" Hugon said, and went toward the man, grinning broadly.

"Here, man, let me try . . . I had some skill, once."

He gathered up the pipes and fiddled with them for a moment; put them to his lips, and blew, mightily. A wild shriek came out, and Fraak leaped into the air, circling Hugon's head and the mast, and piping wildly in counterpoint. Hugon stalked solemnly along the deck, the wailing pipe crying out a Dalesman's warsong; a weird and dissonant thing, but with the eerie dignity of a skeleton dancing a saraband, stately and terrifying. Fraak's aid made it a stronger dose; he seemed able to join the pipe's drones with three separate notes at once, and his wings drummed in time.

"AAAAAhoo!" Zamor cried out, his eyes white and wide; the four-foot axe sang around his head, in whistling circles, as he stood spread-legged, watching the ships draw closer. Kavin had drawn his long straight sword, and held it now, loosely and lightly. Thuramon, Hugon saw, was nowhere about; wise of him, Hugon thought grimly. He drew breath again, and the pipes blared out once more.

A firepot arched through the air and thudded into a sail; it did not break, but slid down, to thump into a coil of rope, and roll across the deck, a trail of sullen fire following it. Hugon found it squarely in his path as he

155

strode forward, piping; he did not break his pace, but kicked, hard. The thing flew up, trailing fire as it arched over the side; before it struck the water, it burst with a dull boom.

Hugon marched straight on, across the fire line, and turned; a crewman hurled a water bucket at it, and the blaze died slowly.

But Garph had been at the steering platform all the while; craftily, he waited, and now he swung the ship, hard over. The Turtle heeled; as she came across the wind, the sails that bore a red dragon, the oncoming Thulin, went slack, barred from the slight air by the patched canvas of the Turtle. The Thulin pirate came about, but too slowly; the Mazainian war galley arrowed past its intended prey, like a hawk missing its stoop. And a moment later, a rending crash rolled across the sea, as the galley's metal-shod ram drove deep into the Thulin's black side.

The noise was tremendous; above decks, Mazainians and pirates roared, full throated as a hundred packs of mastiffs in hunt; and from the galley's lower deck, a monstrous wail of terror and agony erupted, as though the Pit itself was opened. The splintering oars flew upward and outward, and in those decks men died dreadfully.

The Turtle was lumbering slowly off, away from the grim scene; and Hugon, lowering the pipe, stared back with sickened heart. The galley could not withdraw; the black pirate, broken-backed, was canted far over and sinking swiftly, and drawing its killer down with it. Across their decks, a mass of men hacked and screamed and died, back and forth in the slime of blood under their feet, tripping in the tangle of cordage as they fought.

The pirate's other ship will aid her, Hugon thought, and in the meantime we'll be off.

But the second black ship slid swiftly past the tangled pair, with a roaring jeer rising from its decks, and an answering roar of rage from their abandoned comrades. They came on, straight for the Turtle's stern blood hungry.

Hugon put the pipes to his lips again and blew a wild call that stopped just as the pirate's sides scraped hard against the Turtle's hull. He dropped the pipes then, and sprang toward the rail, whirling his sword around his head; and heard himself crying out the ancient yowling battle cry of his folk.

Beside him, Zamor bellowed and the great axe swung, flashing; a bearded head that had just appeared at the rail sprang off, bodiless, and arched across the deck in a spray of blood.

The crewmen had gone mad, it seemed; the power of that pipe had stirred their old blood, and brought antique blood lust to warm their old bodies once more. They stabbed and chopped, cackling and squalling, as the pirates came aboard.

Kavin moved down the rail's length, the long sword circling and swinging up and down like the pendulum of death's clock. The pirates spread away and back, dodging that terrible blade, but meeting other blades among the crewmen as they did so.

But there were too many of them; they swarmed up, more and more, fresh swords to replace those who fell. Captain Garph fell backward, clutching at his belly, as Hugon bent to stab upward at the man who had killed Garph.

The pirate squealed; but Hugon's sword jammed tightly somewhere in the corsair's gut, and the man's writhing nearly yanked the blade from Hugon's grip. Behind the dying pirate, a gigantic spade-bearded man rose, and stabbed downward at Hugon; his blade sliced along Hugon's bicep, with agonizing fire in its wake.

Then the giant shrieked, as Fraak's claws found his face and tore; Hugon, rolling free, saw the dragonet swoop, clawing, and rise again, to dive and claw and burn.

157

Hugon clutched at his sword, the pain of his wound knifing into his arm, and hastily changed the blade to his other hand in time to parry another downward cut.

There were few crew members left, he saw now; and there were still at least a score of the pirates alive on the deck. But no more came over the rail. He grinned fiercely and moved forward, Zamor and Kavin on either side, a grim circle of crewmen with them. The pirates were caught against the rail now, pressed back. They fought hard; not a man surrendered. Then, one man sprang backward, to splash in the sea below; Kavin's longsword brought down another, and the great axe in Zamor's grip slashed down a third. Others began to jump; as Hugon lunged forward to miss one such, he saw there were others, below, in the black ship. They cut at the lines that held their grappling hooks to the Turtle, as anxious to be free as they had been to come aboard.

A stray pirate dodging rabbitwise as men cut at him, ran head-on into Zamor's open arms, and was grasped and held high in the air. Zamor, painted with red gore from neck to heel, roared a gigantic laugh, the wriggling pirate clutching vainly as he swung outward. Then, the pirate's hands clasped Zamor's belt, that broad, ancient belt which was the gift of the Dragon folk. The man was screaming in terror; he clawed, trying to drag himself free by the grasp upon the buckle.

Only Hugon saw it clearly; standing as he was, a scant yard away. The man had clutched the jewel stud as Zamor lifted him higher; Zamor laughed again, and leaned far over the bulwark.

"Here's the last of your men, Thulin scum!" Zamor bellowed. "Take him back, with our best compliments!" And he hurled the man, straight downward toward the open hull below.

There was a sickening sound, as of a giant melon cracking; a shriek of broken timber, and a howl of insane terror from the remaining pirates below. Then Hugon peered over, and saw the unbelievable.

The hapless pirate had been driven like a missile, clear

158

through the stout planks and timbers of the pirate's ship; water sprayed upward, red tinted, but there was nothing left of the man's body at all. But the others had seen, and wished to see no more; though their ship sank beneath them, they would not stay near the black giant of terror. The ship veered away, listing as it went; and now, lying half under water, it moved still farther.

"Get a man to that helm," Kavin called out, calmly enough, though his breath came in panting rasps.

The Turtle was still under way; a man staggered aft, and seized the staff. Others drew at the lines, bringing the sail around, still obedient though the Captain lay dead under their feet. Hugon clutched his shoulder, the pain growing now; and looked around.

There were no more than eight or nine crewmen left, he saw. Kavin, and Zamor . . . and where was that ancient devil, Thuramon, he thought for a moment. Now that we could use his wizardry . . . And myself, Hugon thought; well, I've still an arm, though it's my left one.

And there, by the God of Thieves and Luck, comes the Imperial galley, Hugon thought, staring aft. And that's the end of the lot of us, he added to himself; and balanced the sword clumsily in his left hand. He pulled a fragment of torn cloth tightly around the shoulder with his teeth. The red stain came through swiftly, but the pressure seemed to slow the agony.

The galley forged closer; most of the oars were smashed and useless, but some still beat steadily. Below, the timesman's gong clanged steadily, one, two, one, two . . .

A company of marines stood on the galley's foredeck, ranked stiffly as though on parade, in shining plates and scarlet cloaks; each pike slanted forward at the same angle, a fence of death. Behind, officers stood, grimly silent; there were bowmen in the tops, as well, but not an arrow was loosed. There was only the dull clang of the timesman, as the oars drove closer.

Fraak, weary at last, clutched Hugon's shoulder, and was silent, except for harsh panting.

They'll be for revenge, Hugon thought, watching those grim faces come closer still. Not to burn the old Turtle under us, with firepots . . . nor even to take her as a prize. They've gotten their prickles up, over their first scorching . . . it's proud hard men they are, as I know well enough.

So, they'll take us, if they can, for the oars. But not me, damn them, Hugon thought. And glancing at Zamor's stone face, he knew. Not Zamor either. Nor Kavin there.

He turned his head to Fraak.

"Fraak, little friend, listen," he said, low-voiced. "Do this, for me. Do it, if you love me, Fraak! Fly, fly free. The mainland's that way; you can gain it, easily. Go on, GO!" he hissed fiercely.

Fraak's claws set tightly, and the golden eyes glowed wide and fiery into Hugon's.

"NO!" Fraak said.

"They'll cage you again . . ."

"They must kill Fraak first," Fraak said. He uttered a low brassy note. "I kill many, first, then they kill me. I will not fly away. You are my friend."

The galley's high prow slid over the Turtle's bulwark; a hooked bridge clanged down, hooking firmly on. From the galley, trumpets blared suddenly, and the rank of marines moved forward, like a single man, across the bridge.

Kavin, Zamor, and Hugon took a step forward, blades up, to meet the rank. And then Thuramon's voice came, clear and high.

"Na' aamara, effa n'yaaam!"

The old man stood just outside the cabin door; he wore a shabby dark robe, and the wind blew his white hair and beard. His arms were spread widely, and his head flung back; his eyes seemed weirdly empty as he stared skyward.

The advancing men paid only a second's glance to the man who stood up there, if they thought anything, they thought him merely a harmless madman. They had business to attend to. The lances lowered; Kavin's long blade

160

met one iron point, with a clang, as Zamor's axe swung up.

Then, from overhead, the Sound came.

Later, Hugon tried to call the Sound by some familiar name. A whine, as of a broadsaw a thousand feet long drawn through hard wood by a giant hand? No, not quite. A squealing howl, as if a demon as big as a mountain drew a fingernail the size of a ship across a glazed plate as big as a city. That was close, Hugon thought.

Whatever the Sound was, it was not to be borne. Hugon reeled backward, the sword dropping from his fingers; on his shoulder, Fraak squalled, but could not be heard. Zamor dropped his axe, flinging up his hands to cover his ears; Kavin bent, clutching at a rail.

But horrible as the effect on their own side, it was much worse against the Mazainians. The iron rank of marines wavered and crumbled; each man fought to find his way back, away from the Sound. Men fell into the sea, mouths open in unhearable screams of terror, while others fell and crawled back toward their own deck.

Hugon, staggering, looked up and saw It; the source of the Sound, apparently.

It hung, like a whirling shadow, centered over the galley. It was indistinct; it had too many colors, and yet no color, and it spun with such speed that it could hardly be seen at all. Yet, somehow, Hugon had the awful conviction that he saw . . . eyes, deep within It, staring calm and terrible.

The Sound rose higher, louder; it was impossible to hear any other sound, though those open mouths were obviously screaming. But above the Sound, there was indeed another sound. The voice of Thuramon, faint but clear, speaking to It.

The wizard chanted a line, and then another, in that strange choke-voiced language.

The Thing sank, lowering itself down upon the doomed galley. Hugon lurched forward, pain lancing through his head, and hacked at the boarding bridge; beside him, he saw Zamor's agony-twisted face, and the axe

161

swinging, up and down. The galley was free, now; but Hugon dared not look, because It was there, over the ship.

Abruptly, the Sound began to die. And then it was gone. Hugon sat on the deck, clutching his head, as hearing slowly came back.

Somewhere far away there was a continuous noise of voices; but there was something quite odd about those voices, Hugon thought. Nearer, he heard an occasional groan or curse from those around him; he managed to rise, with some trouble, and stared off toward the galley.

The Thing, whatever it was, was gone, with the voice in which it had cried out.

But the galley turned, slowly, oars trailing. There was no man at its helm.

But men still lived there. Hugon saw a white, mad face, glaring unseeingly toward him from an upper deck; then there was a distant twang. An arrow had been loosed from above; and the man fell out of sight. More arrows flew, from below as well as above, but even at this distance, Hugon saw that they were not aimed well, if aimed at all. It seemed as though men were using whatever weapon came to hand, but in the manner of blind men.

He saw a figure fall, now, and then another, into the sea. The cries and screams were those of madmen, meaningless; a voice rose in discordant song, till it stopped with a hideous gurgle.

Kavin was on his feet, and hung onto the railing beside Hugon, staring.

"They're all mad, yonder," Hugon said, hoarsely. "Was it . . ."

"Thuramon," Kavin said. "He . . . said that he would use his Art, at the last, if no other way would do. You see now why he hates to use such . . . weapons." Kavin's shoulders shuddered.

"A demon?" Hugon said.

"Or something worse," Kavin said. "Tanit! Those men!

162

They are not only mad, Hugon!" He stared, wide-eyed. "They are blind!"

On the galley, farther away now, lines of flame appeared; a madman with a torch ran, screaming faintly. Fire climbed higher, and spread wider.

The Golden Turtle rolled, and moved a little faster, before the wind, leaving the sinking galley far behind.

NINE

"To the Thrice Glorious Sharamash, King of Kings, this, from Harmazz, Commander of the Imperial Army in the South, hastily, hastily, hastily.

"Know, O Emperor, that I have put forth all my strength in fulfilling your commands. Having, at length, been caused to withdraw our force from the pass of Imshag southward and from the castle that commands that pass, I determined that we would also let go hold of the town of Shamgraad, which lies below, and hold only the river crossings. Know, Lord, that my heart was bitter within me, and I abase myself, calling upon your Gloriousness for mercy, because I did this; yet, it was a needful thing.

"Concerning the pass of Imshag; the castle overlooking it was held under your hand by the Lord Kazzarashik, cursed be he, with men at arms of his own house as well as men of my own force. Upon the fourth day of the month Imok, the traitorous Kazzarashik caused the gates of the castle to be opened, and those who would prevent this he ordered to be slain. Thereafter, the forces of the rebel lords came up into the pass, and having nothing whereby I could oppose them, I called back such as remained.

"Thereafter, having closed the gates of the town of Shamgraad, I began to cause its defenses to be strengthened. But many of the townsfolk fled; others hid all that they possessed, and none could be brought to work upon the walls (these being much in decay), except unwillingly and with little effect.

165

"At this time, I caused many of the more loudly speaking spreaders of rebellion among the townsfolk to be taken; these I ordered slain, some by impalement, others by hacking to death, that the manner of their deaths might be instructive to others.

"However, upon the ninth day of Imok, the rebels appeared below the town in great force, and with siege engines, wherefore it appeared to me that the town could not be held. Also, I saw that the hearts of the townsfolk were hardened against your Glorious rule, and that neither words nor deeds could alter them. So I withdrew the Imperial force out of that place, first permitting the houses and goods which remained to be plundered for one day. (Unfortunately, many of your Glorious Majesty's forces ignored or did not receive my orders, and remained overlong in the town; these were taken upon the entry of the rebels, and doubtless done to death through their unwitting greed.)

"Know, therefore, that I now lie upon the northern bank of the river, together with four thousand men at arms, and one thousand of the Imperial cavalry. Of the Numorian spearmen sent me, I have none, these having fled to the rebels in the night, and of the household riders of the Lord Warden Taramashak, no more than a score or two remain.

"This being my whole force, I am opposed by near upon nine thousand of the rebels, many horsemen among them, well supplied and armed. I have seen that these will come against me within the week, striving to cross the river; should they do so, nothing bars them from the plains toward your Imperial City itself. Yet will I strive against them, most loyally. But it would be well if your Majesty could deign to send much aid, and especially food and beer for the men; many, in greed, desert nightly. Also, there are few horses, which are much needed.

"Let the Thrice Glorious consider the action of the traitor, Kazzarashik; it is said that he possesses two sons dwelling under your Majesty's just hand, in the City, and

166

these have wives and children of his line. I append to this letter as well the names of others, men of the town of Shamgraad and near it, who now serve the rebels. May the Thrice Glorious hear his servant Harmazz; let not the Imperial clemency soften your heart, but let all who have the blood of rebels, the relatives of these, be taken and publicly given to death, that others may be warned.

"Concerning the letter received from the Imperial Treasury; alas, there is no silver to be had, not so much as an ornament or a single coin, and as far a cartload, it would be as well to ask for the moon. The coins with which I must pay my troops are called of no value by the merchants, and they refuse to receive them, except at sword's point.

"Once again, Thrice Glorious Emperor . . . your servant Harmazz, lying now in great peril, yet loyal, will fight to the death. Yet if more soldiers could be sent, horses, and supplies, I can still hold here, where I stand now."

The messenger reached the city gates in the early morning, his lathered horse thundering through and on toward the Palace.

In the afternoon of the same day, a dozen riders on big horses, lances glittering, galloped to the farther end of the stone bridge that lay at Mazain's southern gate; the guards, lounging at the inner end, stared at them with dull curiosity. The leading rider drew rein and stood in his stirrups; his brawny arm swung an object the size of a man's head, and slung it. With a derisive yell, the riders whirled around and fled south, out of sight.

The object was a man's head; the head of General Harmazz, that rolled to the feet of the gate guards, leaving a dark trail. It grinned up at them, mustached and sardonic, the blank eyes open.

"That fool Harmazz," the Emperor said when they brought him the news. He walked in the wide gardens below the King's House, under the trees, with gorgeously robed courtiers about him. Gwynna, on the arm of a leer-

167

ing fop called Orashaz, was close by when the message came, and she watched and listened.

"Well, Paravaz, that solves one question, doesn't it?" the Emperor said. The Chancellor shrugged.

"I mean, you've nagged like an old marketwife to send more men and arms to this fool's army," the Emperor said, grinning. "It seems he couldn't keep what he already had . . . nor even his head." The Emperor giggled. "Where's the head, messenger? At the south gate? Have it brought, I'd love to see it . . . unless it smells. Does it smell? I can't bear smells."

Orashaz, beside Gwynna, looked down at her, simperingly solicitous.

"If my lady is unable to bear such a sight . . . of course, we men are of stronger mold," he began, twirling his long mustache.

Men? Gwynna thought. Ha, boy, I know of men that could have you for breakfast and call for a second helping. But she lowered her eyelashes delicately, and looked uncertain.

"Violent matters are so . . . *violent*," she said. "But if the Great Emperor desires to look upon anything, even something not usually entertaining, why, it becomes enlustered merely by his looking thereon, does it not?"

Sharamash heard, and beamed at her.

It is amazing, Gwynna thought; I can say these things, and neither vomit nor laugh, and more amazing, they even sound as though I meant them. Had I not been born of proper lineage, I might have made a great career acting on a stage. She smiled, thinking of it.

"My lady is amused? A thought, perhaps?" Orashaz asked.

"Oh." Gwynna looked up. "I . . . recalled a joke, told at the theatre."

"Ah?" Orashaz leered slightly. It was doubtless a bawdy joke, he thought, considering that there was little on the stage in Mazain of late that was otherwise. Perhaps the lady was beginning to yield a little, Orashaz thought, and eyed her. A beauty, a widow, and a rich

168

widow . . . what more could a man require, except a little less stout resistance. But, he considered, no woman could be long near himself without sooner or later melting; it was but natural, poor creatures, moths to his flame. He leered again, and laid a hand on her bare shoulder; but somehow she managed to slip away from it, to his surprise.

Paravaz was speaking in a low, urgent voice; his words, to Gwynna's ears were nearly inaudible, but what she could hear sounded even more dour than the Chancellor usually did.

". . . at the very gates, even in the . . ." she caught. But the Emperor merely sniggered, and turned away.

". . . so little of real interest in the theatres," Orashaz was saying. "Though I hear a company has been sponsored by a certain noble, whose name escapes me . . . they intend to revive some of the comedies of Gerovan the Elder." He rolled his eyes upward. "The great classics! Ah, my lady, you must not think of me as merely one who cultivates the body to the exclusion of the mind . . ."

"I would never have imagined such a thing," Gwynna said sweetly. Out of the corner of her eye she saw the Emperor's queer look in her direction; an unreadable look, she thought. In any but a madman, she would have been able to guess at his thoughts, but of late, no one knew what the Thrice Glorious was thinking. None would have dared to ask, either; the Emperor was becoming stranger in his whims with every day.

"A woman with a certain amount of wit," the Emperor said, suddenly; he was definitely looking at her, she realized. "And quite pretty, too." He nodded, grinning. "You do know you are good to look at, don't you, Lady Gwynna?"

She turned toward him and smiled, slowly, saying nothing.

"Even wise enough to keep silence," the Emperor said, and uttered his odd chuckle. "I have too many wives already, Lady Gwynna. I cannot offer you that honor, alas.

169

But . . ." He stared at her. "The Lord of Night speaks to me, you know. He says that I shall become a god, like himself, and live always. Would you like that for yourself, Lady Gwynna?"

"I . . . am not sure, your Majesty," she said. "Life is good, but for a woman, to grow old . . ."

"The Lord of Night has promised me youth, as well," the Emperor said. "But to all who do not serve him, when he comes, he promises only night and darkness, forever. When His gate is opened, terrible things will happen, you know." He giggled. "All my enemies will know, too. But I will try to keep my friends, my true friends. Not you, Paravaz, you old croaking vulture." And he glared at the Chancellor, who remained impassive.

The Emperor returned his eyes to Gwynna's. "So many will die when the Gate is opened. There should be a few women kept alive, don't you think?"

"A woman alive is much preferred to one that's dead, your Majesty," Gwynna said, a little daringly. "By most men, at least."

Sharamash snickered, and rocked back and forth on his heels, studying her.

"Perhaps the Lord of Night would grant you life if you came to his temple and bowed before him," Sharamash said in a tone that was, possibly, inviting. "Many of my court have come, and sometimes he has granted a prayer or two. And the rituals are most interesting, my lady."

"I have heard so," Gwynna said, with a coy look. Interesting, he calls it, she thought. Last time it was said that the Emperor himself and all the other worshippers were dancing about in a circle, naked and slashing away at each other with whips. Now, whips I don't care for, at all, Gwynna thought. And besides, she remembered, the Emperor had abruptly decided that an unfortunate courtier had been too enthusiastic with those whips; the man had been abruptly placed in a new and fatal role.

"I shall most certainly consider your Majesty's kind suggestion," Gwynna said. "Though I have so little free

170

time, I fear . . . my poor husband's affairs, his estates, all
in such a muddle, I must spend many hours trying to
make some order in them. And since those terrible rebels
took away much of the lands of the estate as well . . ."

"Ah, but there's no need to worry your head about all
that, lady," Sharamash said. "No, not at all. Paravaz
keeps telling me that the rebels are at our gates, but he
cannot see that it will not matter. The Lord of Night will
come forth, soon, and all that . . ." He snapped his
fingers expressively. "They will be swept away!"

The afternoon sunlight seemed suddenly colder there
in the magnificent gardens; Gwynna looked at the Emperor, and slowly the conviction came to her . . .

. . . it was true. Something not quite human was there
in the man, something that was daily less human. God or
demon, but not man.

The headland rose out of the sea's rim, distantly ahead
of the Turtle's prow, like a giant ship's prow itself. The
crewman on watch nodded, with a satisfied grunt.

"Poor old Garph could've done no better, good sir," he
told Hugon. "There's the Grothai cape, and Grotha port
the other side of it." The man glanced at the patched
sails. "We'll come round, handily. Before sunset, if the
gods will. Then we'll all have time for sleep, at least."

There had been so few men left alive, at the last, that
even with Hugon and Zamor's help, the clumsy old ship
had been hard to work. The survivors were weary, and
gloomy, though they knew their luck in being alive. And
to Hugon and the others of his party, Grotha was a poor
substitute for their original destination; nearly as many
miles of sea still separated them from Mazain as there
had been when they started.

Hugon knew Grotha well; and it was possible, he
thought, that there might be those in Grotha who still
knew Hugon. He sincerely hoped that there were none
such; but it had not been too long since he had sought
knowledge there, among the famed scholars who taught
in the ancient schools of Grotha.

Unfortunately, there were many sorts of knowledge, and Hugon had sought to delve in fields in which no degrees were granted, the burgess's daughter being one such field. A girl of expensive tastes, too, as he remembered her; he had promised her a necklace, and a necklace was what he brought her, obtained at some difficulty and danger. Highwaymen were customarily displayed, swinging odorously in their chains, along the west road out of Grotha town, as Hugon remembered all too clearly. Even now, the thought chilled him a little.

Strange that he could no longer remember the name of the girl, though she'd been a nicely shaped, high-colored lass. Not as slim as the Lady Gwynna, of course, Hugon thought critically.

The Golden Turtle came up the wide channel and round the seawall, into Grotha's wharves; with the late tide, as the crewman had predicted. There was much conversation with the officers of the port; they bore a somewhat curious feeling toward a battered old ship that arrived without cargo, with only a handful of crew still alive, and the signs of battle upon her. Yet, when Thuramon had judiciously let a few coins drop into the right places, the inquisitiveness waned. After all, other ships had lately come in, with wild tales of the turmoils going on southward, and some ships expected had never come at all.

The Turtle would be sold, for whatever she could bring, and her price distributed to the surviving crewmen. The late captain had no heirs, it seemed. That disposed of, the next problem would be to find a way to reach Mazain, across the Middle Sea, and that problem seemed insoluble indeed.

All four, Thuramon, Zamor, Hugon, and Kavin, sat in a quayside public house, under the flickering lamps, after fruitless hours of search along the quays. No, not until the Middle Sea was safe again, was the repeated verdict of a dozen captains; not for gold in any quantities.

The public house was well-filled, many out-of-work

seamen among the patrons. These sat, grumbling, telling strange tales, sometimes wandering off in search of rumored berths to be had on coasters or on the river trade. Some of them found Fraak a mighty wonder, and came to where the dragonet sat curled on Hugon's shoulder, to admire him. This Fraak enjoyed enormously; and even more he enjoyed the bits of fish and ripe sausage they brought him, eating the gifts swiftly and repaying the donors with small fire-spectacles and smoke rings.

After Fraak had finished an especially garlic-laden bit, Hugon sniffed meaningfully at the dragonet's pointed snout.

"Gods, Fraak, you'll be able to slay a man soon with that breath," he said. "And I'll swear you've gained half again your own weight, this night."

"Oookh," Fraak said, softly, and closed his eyes.

"A handsome beast," a voice said behind Hugon, and he turned in his seat to look at the speaker.

There was something slightly familiar about the man; a tall, dark man with a spade beard, dressed most elegantly in scarlet and silver and wearing a sword. Then Hugon placed the familiar look; the man was a Mazainian, in dress and accent. Zamor, across the table, saw the look of the newcomer too, and sat, stone faced.

But Thuramon did not seem at all disconcerted; he looked up and smiled, stroking his silver beard.

"Greetings, Lord Admiral Farzakk," Thuramon said. "Will you sit, sir?"

The Mazainian stared at Thuramon, and his face grew tight.

"You are a sorcerer," he said, low voiced.

"I have some knowledge of the Art, yes," Thuramon said. "But it needed no magic to know your name and face. I saw it once, long ago. And I have learned that you have been proscribed as a rebel by the Emperor."

The tall man sat down between Hugon and Thuramon, leaning closely toward the magician.

"I would prefer no loud words, sir," he said. "I am not known here, fortunately."

173

Thuramon nodded.

"There was a certain acquaintance of mine," Farzakk said, staring at Fraak. "A lord Barazan, who had purchased just such a beast as this, at a ridiculously high price, but a year or so ago. But he was drowned, I've heard, and doubtless the beast went also."

"Doubtless," Hugon said, calmly.

"If a man had slain that Barazan," Farzakk said, "I would bear that man no ill will at all. I considered that lord an arrogant and overbearing fool; and he would have been my enemy today, if he had lived. He would most certainly have gone on serving that madman who calls himself Emperor."

"I believe that Barazan drowned by mere accident," Hugon said, calmly. "Not by any man's hand."

The other glanced at him, and teeth shone in a grin.

"Then I owe no one thanks," Farzakk said. "Indeed." He looked from one face to another, Kavin's, Zamor's, and Thuramon again.

"A man came to me and said there were travelers who would go to the Imperial City," Farzakk said. "A rare thing, just now. By another odd chance, it happens that I have been seeking just such intrepid travelers to . . . ah, do me a small service." He smiled.

"A service," Thuramon said, thoughtfully. "And for what pay?"

"Well, now," Farzakk said, "If those same men desired to reach Mazain at all, I might be able to aid them greatly there. I could, for example, find them a small swift ship that might land them somewhere in the north, past the Narrow Sea. From there, it would be easy enough to make their way to the city, since the place is not yet encircled."

"Not . . . yet," Thuramon echoed, drawing his hand down his beard. "Has the rebellion gone so far, then?"

"All of the south is lost to the Emperor," Farzakk said. "Now, if the madman were cut off from both the sea and the northern provinces . . ." He shrugged. "But of course, the whole fleet of the Mazainian force is out at

174

sea. It would take much force to break through that
wooden wall. Many ships . . ." He paused, and gazed at
Thuramon. "Perhaps . . . even a little of the Art itself."

"If I were myself a sorcerer of skill," Thuramon said,
serenely, "and my lord will notice . . . I said if . . . I
would much advise against the use of the Art in war. I
have heard that magic is sometimes used so, in desperate
cases. But plain steel slays as certainly as any spell, and
a man at arms demands a small enough price for his
work. But the price of magic is very high, and a man
may pay, again and again."

Farzakk stared at him, with a strange look. Then, after
a moment, he spoke.

"I see."

Kavin, who had been listening with a grim look, said,
"Do you, sir? You're fortunate. I myself learned the truth
of what the old man says, once . . . but it was an expensive lesson."

Thuramon chuckled. He looked at Farzakk.

"So, apart from whatever weak aid my Art might give
you . . . none, probably . . . what other service did you
have in mind?"

Farzakk spoke very low.

"There may be certain ships," he said, obliquely. "A
few being made ready here and elsewhere. Or even such
ships as are now in the service of a certain king, who
might bear a grudge of some standing against the Emperor. If many ships drove, all together, against the fleets
of Mazain in the Middle Sea, a breach might be made.
What might follow is in the hands of the gods, of course,
but the city could be encircled; it might be that the king
I mentioned might feel it worthwhile to send his own
men to the rebellion's aid, also."

The High King of Meryon, then, Hugon thought. A
grudge, indeed; hate, since that betrayal and slaughter at
Armadoc. Yet, a king borne on the shoulders of wild
mountain barons and restive lords, who would not strike
too rashly lest he fall himself. Rebellions were mischancy
affairs, Hugon thought. Till the High King knew how the

175

dice would fall, he would be the enemy of neither side, openly, though men like Farzakk might build and arm fleets in full sight, in the King's own lands.

"Then, should that small swift ship you spoke of bear a small party to the other shore," Thuramon said, "to Mazain itself, as it might be . . . what would you like in return?"

Farzakk's eyes suddenly grew wild though he kept a calm face.

"There is a woman and a boy," he said. "The boy is the son of a rebel lord. He never wedded the woman, in proper form . . . he had no time, and she was not of high blood in any case. But the boy is . . . his. They dwell in Mazain. The woman was . . . she is a weaver, and keeps a shop, close by the Fountains, in the Street of Three Lanterns. Her name is Elanak, and the boy is called Zaraz. She is a handsome woman, pale with black hair . . ." He stopped.

"What would you have us do with your son, then?" Thuramon asked.

"Yes," Farzakk said. "He is mine. And the woman, too. I'd have had her to wife, if I had dared oppose custom . . . but enough. If I'd wedded her, she'd be slain by now, as the madman's done to all who are related to any rebel. He does not know of her, I think. But she must go out of the city. She must!"

Thuramon nodded.

"Simple enough," he said.

"Is it, then?" Farzakk said, wryly. "Wait till you try. I desired her to flee with me six months ago, and she . . . oh, but she's a stubborn woman, that one. Spoke of her workshop, the five weavers there, and work agreed upon; put off the leaving, again and again. But now it may be too late, unless she is made to go, soon."

"The Emperor knows nothing of her," Thuramon said.

"He may discover her relations with me," Farzakk said. "But there's another matter, too. Mazain will soon be under siege; a city, starving perhaps, and later to be looted and burned, it may be."

176

All at that table knew what the black-bearded man meant. A city under siege . . . a place of doom, often enough.

"We have business in the Imperial City," Thuramon said. "If we could reach it, quickly . . . why, I'm sure I can speak most persuasively with this woman Elanak. Aid her to make haste in leaving, it may be." He pulled his white beard, and a glint appeared in his eye. "For such uses as that, I may use my Art freely. You'll remember, Hugon, I gave you a certain crystal toy to silence another woman?"

Hugon grinned. The pendant was still in his pouch.

"I may have use for it again," Hugon said.

Farzakk came to his feet. "Good," he said. "I did not set a time, concerning that fleet I spoke of. I was not sure of you, then. But now I must tell you . . . we are ready, and have been these last ten days. The ships waited only for the wind's change, that comes every year about this time. So, you understand, you sail at once if you accept my bargain."

"Ugh," Hugon said. "I'd hoped to spend one night in a bed that didn't move save when I caused it to. A proper bed . . ." He gazed gloomily at a round-formed innkeeper's girl, who passed through the crowded room bearing a tray of mugs, swaying as she went. He sighed deeply and with feeling. "Well, then . . . away." He thrust back his bench, and rose, draining the mug that had been sitting before him.

"Oooh," Fraak fluted, on his shoulder, opening a golden eye. "Aaah," on a lower note, and closed the eye again. Fraak, Hugon thought, could sleep soundly in an earthquake if he chose to.

The person called Gann walked with long, steady strides down a winding trail that clung to a mountain side. He no longer wore the battle armor he had rebuilt back in that ruined valley; the coppery metal was bundled on the back of the wooly beast that followed close upon his heels. He was wrapped in a thick, hooded cloak

177

of gray wool, though he had already learned that he did not really care whether he was cold or warm. Yet, the thin snow blew about him as he went, and the temperature was low; this body might not yet be overdriven. There was still the pain, too, the pain that never left. That did not change, no matter whether the air was warm or cold.

Behind him, five other cloaked figures moved, and a dozen of the little, sure-footed beasts called elami bore heavy loads, following the men. Gann did not look back at them; nor speak to them. He did not need to.

The leading man of the five was, or had once been, Mang Elap. Behind him, four others of his tribe walked, and each man's face was as empty as a skull's. Their eyes were blank, and none of them spoke as they went, plodding steadily down the long trail toward the known lands at the base of the mountains.

It had been simple enough to perform the operation needed to make these simple creatures into useful workers. Gann knew the procedure well; in his own world it had been common. Now Mang and the others were no more than machines, less free than the beasts they led, but much more useful. As all such should be, Gann knew.

There was a second advantage gained from the thing he had done to the hillmen; he now possessed a great deal of what they had known, knowledge of great use to him. Their language, for one, a tongue which, with variations, seemed to be nearly the same in the more civilized areas where Gann must go. Strange, he thought, a world where so many different peoples speak the same basic tongue. It would imply that this was truly a young world; yet, from other evidence, it was immensely old. There should have been time for a mighty civilization to grow here, Gann thought.

That strange internal compass pointed toward the west, where there was a seacoast, according to the maps he had found. The Other was there, but moving again,

178

steadily away. Perhaps that Other was on a ship again; if so, it would be necessary to cross the sea after him.

Gann would do so, then. He knew that he ought to feel some anger, some sense of fury directed at his quarry; the Other seemed almost to sense his coming. Yet he could feel nothing. It was strange, he thought, but it had advantages, this utter cold that lay upon him. He remembered incidents when he had allowed rage or caution to seize him for a brief moment, and had thereby erred in judgment. Or even worse, compassion. Now, he need fear those enemies within no longer.

The trial turned, and the land below began to be visible. Deep pine forests stretched downward in long slopes toward a distant river; and many miles away, he saw a thin blueness of smoke, and a tiny pattern of rooftops. A town, Gann thought. And a river, that might prove a road to the sea, and to the Other.

He strode on, steadily, and the human machines followed.

TEN

On either side, as far as Hugon could see, the gray ocean was dotted with ships. To port, a covey of slim fighting galleys plowed swiftly, while starboard there lay a huge war galleon that was unmistakably of Meryon build. It was triple decked, and from shuttered ports on its sides, the bronze cannon that were still rarely found in the world could fire. A dreadful and untrustworthy tool of war, Hugon thought; by the favor of the gods, the fashion for those monstrous things had never spread far, though the black powder had been known for a long time now.

Hugon, whose agile brain possessed a truly remarkable assortment of information, had once delved into the mysteries of chemical art. Though the exact means of mixing black powder was a guild mystery, he knew that it required three elements, two of which were easy to find. The third, the white salts, were not easily gathered, and therefore the art of making the black stuff was, to his great satisfaction, little practiced.

Also, only in Meryon were really strong cannon cast; their smiths had secrets known to no others. Even after the black powder had been acquired, with much trouble, a war lord might find that a badly cast cannon could slay more of his own men than those of the enemy.

But at such times as this, the cannon came again into use; those great galleons were their most suitable home. Hugon watched the giant, under towers of sail, plowing steadily along; and there, behind it, another, and then a third.

181

Farther away, toward the horizon, he counted seven big vessels, warships of Grothan make; and in the other direction, nine more, these of varying rigs and sizes.

Every one of them was filled with fighting men, Hugon knew. Some were mercenaries out for loot; but many more were exiles of Mazain, ruined men and landless now, whose relatives had been slain by the mad Emperor, men who would take joy in slaying any who still served Sharamash. Also, men of the Meryon Kingdom, who had come to the ships with no command of their own king to send them, but none to forbid, either. These would fight with almost as much fire as the exiles and rebels; the memory of the landing of Imperial force on the soil of Meryon was fresh and new as spilled blood.

The ship on which Hugon and the others now sailed was a slim, swift little vessel, with hardly any cover from the weather, crewed by four dour men. Both the ship and the four crewmen had a distinct air of having once been engaged in much less respectable trades; but Hugon thought it would be just as well not to ask about that.

It was fast, this little boat; it bore a rather well-made carving of a winged girl at the prow, and the name Swift Virgin. The virginity Hugon took to be merely symbolic; the speed was a fact. And, like other virgins, Hugon noticed, she gave a rough ride; he was forced to keep a hand close to a rail, even in the light winds that presently drove her.

One man was at the helm, and a second squatted, watchfully, atop the foremast step, one arm around the mast. Then that man rose suddenly, hand over his eyes, peering.

"Signaling, up ahead," he called to the helmsman. After a moment, he added, "Three smokes . . . and there, the galleon's running up a pennant."

"Below, there," Hugon called out. Zamor's head emerged from a hatch, and he looked inquiringly up. "The Imperials. They're close ahead, might be."

Zamor came up, yawning, and dragging up the long

182

axe which he had kept from the fight aboard the Turtle. He had declared it a fine weapon indeed, and he had ever begun to ornament it with small and intricate carvings on the haft. Behind him, Kavin came also, and Thuramon followed.

"There's a strange whiff below there," Kavin said, moving toward the rail. He grinned. "It must have been a queer mixture of cargoes that this ship held last."

"Best not to ask," Hugon said. "One thing is plain enough; what passes for a bed down there was never meant for human bones. Fraak liked those bunks well enough, but he's not as fragile as I am." He groaned, and stretched. "I'd sell my honor for a night in a real bed, even a night alone in one."

"If you could find a buyer for honor," Zamor grunted.

"If I had it to sell," Hugon answered. "Ha! Look there! Sails!"

Zamor peered, and uttered a low curse.

"We'll have no chance at all to let blood with them," he muttered.

"None," Hugon agreed, "I'm glad to say. The rebel admiral, our friend Farzakk, upon whose head the sea-god should send a special protection, made that absolutely clear. We are to slip by, with the light footed discretion of a virgin in peril of her purity, avoiding all combat as a virgin should. Thus, our vessel's name will be kept honored," and he rolled his eyes upward.

"I want to try my Steel Moon again," Zamor said, and twirled the axe slowly around and around.

"Kindly remember, friend, there's little room to dodge," Hugon said, moving back. "Could you arrange for that Moon of yours to suffer eclipse for a while? There'll be ample chance of blood once we're ashore in Mazain. I ask the gods that the blood should be somebody else's, only that."

The distant sails were taking shape now; swift galleys, single bankers in a broad half circle ahead, at least twenty of them. But behind, a line of what could only be two and three banked ships, from their size, massive and

183

huge hulls filled with armed men, on whose decks weapons bristled. There would be arrow engines that could spit a death storm of shafts; catapults, to hurl round stones, or firepots and dolphin throwers, that could cast a gigantic fish-shaped metal bolt up and over, to crash through a ship's keel.

Trumpets blared nearby, and were echoed by others farther away. The ships of the rebel fleet moved into a new pattern, one planned much earlier by the cunning of Farzakk. The huge galleons turned, one this way, another that, moving out toward the wings of the Imperial line. It was entirely against tradition; it was usual for fleets to encounter, line upon line. For a fleet to thus open its center, and permit an enemy to enter its midst, must have seemed clumsy foolishness to the Imperial commanders.

It was a long, slow, stately movement, this sea-fighting. Hugon, watching, found it enchanting, but he was a chess player. Zamor muttered and paced the deck impatiently, while Kavin sat, relaxed and impassive.

The apparent errors of Farzakk were not to be ignored; the Imperials lunged forward, like a pack of hounds into a wood. Their line had become a wedge, its point forward, the swifter galleys far ahead. Meanwhile, the Swift Virgin had tacked down away along the outer edge of the whole melee. She was far past her own fleet by now, but it seemed that no Imperial vessel wished to notice so small a prey.

By now Fraak was awake, too; he flew high over the Virgin, returning occasionally with bits of news. However, much of what happened was clearly visible, even from the distance.

Like hounds the galleys had come, and now they were hounds in a wood, encircled by leopards that they had not expected. Each galley found itself drawn off alone, and swiftly set upon, in a series of actions that had obviously been most carefully planned. As soon as a galley was cut off, two or three rebel ships would turn toward it, and come slashing down on either side, reaping a har-

184

vest of broken oars. The wind was with the rebels; their own galleys sailed.

Then, the attackers would claw the victim between them; a ship grappled at either side, and often a third to aid them, and a roaring horde of swordsmen poured into the doomed ship. But, again and again, as soon as the armed men had boarded, the rebel ship would swiftly draw away, and turn to a new engagement, leaving those she had sent to fight on.

Hugon, soon enough, caught the sense of it. The Imperials outnumbered the rebels in ships; yet, by this means, they were repeatedly outnumbered themselves. And the rebel ships had been packed, shoulder to shoulder, with fighters; though dangerously overloaded, none had been swamped. Yet, that had allowed them to hurl a mass of men into one ship after another, as they had been doing. The maneuver allowed boarders no chance to retreat to their own decks, but to many of these desperate men, that mattered not at all. Here and there a galley testified to the success of the method, as the ship turned to fight beside its recent enemies, taken over by its boarders.

But now the heavier Imperial ships should have been able to plunge into the conflict. They lay, turning slowly, in a disorganized mass like penned cattle; unable to charge, ram, and board as they should have done, because the cannon of the galleons were well able to pound them to matchwood first. Two that had tried to charge lay burning in the water southward, and a third was already gone.

Among the others, chaos increased; their lighter and fewer cannon were intended only to fire at close ranges, and were useless now. Nor could catapults and firepots help much. Slowly, the huge galleons edged closer, turning in a stately dance; as each side came about, the cannon thundered. A sheet of orange flame swept across the Imperial ships, and death shrieked about their falling masts.

The thunder of the guns was fainter now, like the rumble of a distant storm, as the Virgin sped onward. The

185

men on her deck could see only a low cloud of drifting smoke behind them; the rumble of broadsides seemed less frequent, as well. It was likely that other rebel ships, having made their first victories, were flocking in toward the doomed fleet, to board, ram, and burn. There would be little mercy there, in the cold sea, either from the sea's grip or man's weapons.

The rigging creaked, and the water hissed beneath the Virgin's keel; seabirds cried hoarsely in the air, where Fraak sailed over the mast top. But on the deck, the group of men stood silent, each watching.

Far astern, a smoke-hazed shape came, moving slowly in their track; a light galley, masts gone, bulwarks broken away, drawing a tangled trail of wreckage as it moved. A few oars still beat, in irregular, wild strokes, like the kicking legs of a dying spider. Zamor straightened, with a hopeful growl, and Hugon dropped the lute at which he had been picking idly, and rose.

But it was obvious that the galley was not pursuing them; it had simply blundered out of the slaughter, like a dumb beast, to prolong its life by a few more minutes. They saw it, trailing smoke as it came, listing more and more, till one oar bank lifted clear of the water, and the other must have gone below the water line. The stern lifted, higher, till the distant galley stood for a moment, like a monumental column, straight up; then it dived, and was gone.

"He's broken them, by the Snake's teeth," Zamor said, in a low voice. "That admiral's a man of his craft. But I still wish we'd been able to take a little of that for ourselves."

"Never mind, you blood-drinker," Hugon told him. "We'll be ashore before dawn, if we're lucky. You can slay the first fool we meet, and give his liver to the Great Snake. That's the custom, isn't it?"

Zamor glanced at him and laughed. "The first fool we meet? Shall I let you off that list, brother?"

Hugon scratched his chin, thoughtfully. "I never thought of that point, brother Zamor. Damn it, I'd best

186

not come with you to your Mumori land after all if they
sacrifice fools *all* of the time."

"Only during full moon," Zamor told him calmly.
"Fear not, we've as many fools in Mumori as you do hereabouts. And we'll look after you well, little brother;
you'll be a rarity. Most of our own fools are black like
myself." He chuckled, and began to polish Steel Moon
with a rag.

Kavin stood at the rail, looking aft; now he turned,
and leaned there, his silver-gray hair blowing. He
seemed to be deep in thought; his eyes were distant.

Hugon, dropping to a comfortable squat on a coil of
rope, had taken up his lute again; he held it on his lap
and watched Kavin, thoughtfully.

The prince seemed to be listening to something. Odd,
Hugon thought. To what? Hugon cocked his head,
trying to hear if some sound came. A whisper, a voice
that was hidden under the sea's sounds . . . Hugon was
not quite sure.

He plucked a string, tightened it a trifle, still watching
Kavin. There was something disquieting about the silence, and the faint moan of the wind did not help. And
Hugon felt something. A presence, as though there were
another here, on this ship. A faint prickle ran along his
back, and his hair seemed to lift a little.

I may be growing unhealthy, with too much seagoing,
Hugon thought. A disturbance of the natural elements,
perhaps; the salt water about me calls to the aqueous hu-
mors of the blood, thinning it, and thereby causing a
vapor to arise toward the brain. Thus, a feeling of melan-
cholic discomfort, an illusion of hearing faint voices in
the air, and the commencement of superstitious fears.
And the remedy, Hugon thought; solid ground under
foot, a decent horse between the legs, and such other
simple cures as might occur. A masterly diagnosis, he
told himself.

He tried a chord or two, and sang a line, half remembered.

"Come to the window, sweet maid, come and see,

187

Where I wait . . ."

A very old song, Hugon knew, though he could not guess how old. He dimly remembered various versions of it, sung by one or another, back in the dales where he was born. Some versions were sweetly romantic, others bawdy. But all of them had a common theme, and were intended to be sung back and forth, by a girl and her lover.

He sang another line, softly, feeling his way through the fragmented memory of the words. Then he heard the other voice. It was faint, distant, and without direction, but clear . . . a woman's voice.

"Go from the window, fair rider, go far,

For I shall not fly down, neither shall I come see . . ."

Automatically, Hugon's fingers took the chord line; but his eyes were wide and staring, and he felt an icy chill. The voice sang the answering lines, and Hugon replied; and again, in chorus with his own voice, the invisible singer joined him. Fraak still circled high over the mast; and that voice could never be the dragonet's, in any case.

For a moment, Zamor had listened, his broad face smiling; he liked Hugon's ballads. But then it suddenly dawned upon him that a second voice had entered. He snapped to an erect stand and his fist gripped the axe, lifting it, as he stared around the deck.

"Hold!" Zamor roared; and the song ceased, cut off in mid line. The big man glared at Hugon. "Have you two voices in your throat, brother?"

"No," Hugon said, in a shaken voice.

"There's an invisible demon here, then," Zamor said. "I thought I heard . . . have you a woman hidden aboard, you lecher?"

"Now where would I hide one, tell me?" Hugon countered. "I heard her too, Zamor. But she hadn't the sound of any demon." He turned his head. "Are you there, girl?"

There was no answer.

"Frightened her off with your roaring, Zamor," Hugon said reproachfully. "A sea ghost, it might be . . ."

"No sea ghost," Kavin said, from where he leaned on the rail.

Hugon stared at the prince. "Oho, cousin," he said, at last. "I begin to remember a part of that tale about you, now."

Kavin nodded. "The tale was true enough," he said. "I have known that I have . . . a companion, who cannot be seen. But she is neither a ghost nor a demon, and you will take no harm from her, my word on it. As to what she is . . . you know as much as you'll ever know, at this moment, and that's not much less than I do."

Zamor stared at both of them. "The pair of you are mad, I think," he said, glumly. "Spirits, ha! Since I came south, among you pale folk, I've never seen so much superstition. I'm growing infected with it myself." He stared around the deck, darkly. "If I find there's been one of those cheapjack tricks you like so well, Hugon, I'll . . ." He looked grim.

Fraak came circling in, to land on a bulwark; he carried a large flat fish in one claw, delicately, though it still kicked.

"I brought a fish," Fraak announced, unnecessarily. He held it up, balancing himself, toward Hugon. "For you."

Hugon chuckled. "Thank you, Fraak," he said, and took the creature. "It'll make a fine dinner. You are a great hunter, little friend." At which Fraak preened, his snaky tail curving up and around him. Suddenly he opened his golden eyes wide, and stared around, as if remembering something.

"Where is the pretty lady?" he asked.

There was a silence. Finally, Hugon asked, as calmly as he could, "The pretty lady? Ah, yes. Did you . . . ah, see her clearly, Fraak? What did she look like?"

"She had long, long hair," Fraak said, confidently. "She waved at me. I like her." He chuckled, and settled his wings around him. "She had no clothes on," he added. Then he hopped down, to the deck, ambling toward a dry spot below to sleep.

"Long hair," Hugon said. "And of course she wore no

189

clothing. Certainly. What else might one expect? Obviously!" He rose, and picked up the fish, taking out his broad dagger. "Now, friends, I intend to clean this fish," he said, staring at Kavin and Zamor. "This perfectly ordinary, visible, fish. I'd rather hear as little as possible about less material matters, myself. This fish, now . . . properly fried, these can be delicious. Let's speak of fish, and bread, and wine, and good beef . . ." He stopped, and grinned at the others. "Shall we do that, then?"

"There was a woman," Zamor said, in a puzzled voice. He glanced at the two others, and his expression was puzzled, and a little distrustful. He grunted, and moved away toward the deck shelter where there was a cooking-hearth of brick. Hugon and Kavin saw him kneeling, cracking small sticks to start a fire. His broad back was turned toward them, and his attitude made his annoyance plain.

"It would seem that dragons have very good eyesight," Hugon commented, looking at Kavin. His knife slid expertly through the fish, and scales flew.

"Yes," Kavin said from where he still leaned on the rail. "Do you know, I never knew that Fraak could see . . ." He stopped. "Listen, cousin. I did not know she was on this ship until the moment at which she whispered to me. Nor do I know how she can go from place to place as she does, nor . . . what she is, woman, ghost, demon, or illusion of my own mind." He shrugged. "Nor have I ever wished to know," he added, with a level look at Hugon. "Cousin, she speaks to very few, and I have reason to know that she wishes not to be spoken of. It would seem that you are truly of my own blood, or she would not have sung."

Hugon laid the cleaned fish out carefully on a piece of board, and wiped his knife; he nodded, but said nothing.

"There's no doubt that this young man is your descendant," Thuramon said; he came, out of the shelter deck, past the squatting form of Zamor, toward the other two. He was carefully wrapping a bundle in oiled canvas as he walked, tying it tightly. "It will probably rain be-

190

fore dawn," the warlock said, glancing at the sky. "Even *my* tools sometimes rust."

Zamor had laid charcoal on the hearth, and it now burned quietly with a blue vapor; he came back to hear Thuramon's words, and grinned.

"Why not use your arts, Master, to give us one more dry day and a fairer wind?" Zamor asked.

Thuramon stared at him under thick white eyebrows. "And where thought you this wind we now have came from?" he asked. "Such steady wind as this, bearing so toward the coasts, is not common at this time of the year."

"Now that's true," Zamor said, frowning slightly. "Yonder man, steering, told me as much an hour ago, while we were still in sight of the battle. He was certain that the gods favored the rebels greatly, because of that." Then he laughed. "But I've heard such things said before, too often. If a man's lucky today, then the gods favor him, or a sorcerer's helping him; and tomorrow, he's cold meat, the gods having changed their minds. No, I believe what I see. We have been lucky; that should be enough." He looked at Thuramon. "Perhaps you offered a prayer for a good wind, Master, and received one. But surely you don't say you *made* this wind, as a man might belch one out, so to speak?"

Thuramon said nothing. He turned, and pointed toward the southeast, his fingers twisted in an odd gesture. He pursed his lips, and a faint whistle, a queer little three-noted tune, came out.

Behind Hugon, there was a deep rattle and clap, and he turned to see the sail drooping, loosely, swinging against the mast. The deck slowly came to a level position, as the Virgin slowed. And the sea was assuming an odd, oiled look, he saw.

The crewman at the steering oar called out to the other, across the deck, a rattling Grothan curse; he leaned back and made a gesture, spreading his hands out and letting the oar hang free. The ship was almost stationary now; there was no reason to steer any longer.

191

"It would not be wise to wait here too long," Thuramon said, looking at Zamor. "Not even for a demonstration to enlighten the mind of an unbelieving one." He chuckled, and turned to make that pointing gesture again, and utter the whistled notes in another order.

There was a crack, as the sail filled abruptly, and a whine of wind in the rigging. The steersman snapped hurriedly up out of his relaxed posture; whitecaps appeared on the sea around them as the Virgin seemed to spring forward.

"Hold, hold, Master Thuramon!" Zamor said, staring at the taut sails. "I never said I didn't believe you, did I? But in the Snake's name, don't overdo it and whip up a gale!"

"It will lessen in a moment," Thuramon said.

Hugon gathered up his fish and went forward along the rolling deck; he knelt, wrapping portions of fish in the broad leaves of a sea-plant that drifted in these waters, which he had brought aboard earlier. There were thagga roots in the food-bags, a round, brown-skinned plant grown in the coast Kingdoms, and Hugon placed these in the wrappings as well, with other spices. One by one he laid the wet packets on the charcoal, where they began to steam busily; he stood up, and held to a stanchion against the rolling, admiring his work.

Thuramon's words were true; by the time the fish had baked a little while, the wind was less, though still strong and steady. The other two crewmen came on deck for their night watch; the sun was almost down, now. They took their share of the food, with the glum silence that all four crewmen seemed to have as a common law; and a jar of the bitter yellow wine that Grothans liked was opened for all.

"Eh, now," one of the crewmen said, suddenly. He picked the last bit of fish from the leaf, and wiped his mouth with the back of his hand, looking at Hugon. His expression was much less sour than usual. "Now, that's a tasty bit, young fellow. I thought you was some sort of

192

lord, when we was hired out for the trip. You a master cook, might be?"

"Thanks, friend, but I'm neither lord nor cook," Hugon told him with a grin.

The other crewman, who seemed as nameless as any of them, was looking their way, also wiping his mouth with a satisfied look. He came closer, and spoke to Hugon.

"Ye're cook enough, and more though you've a landsman's look about you," he said. "Listen, you may have thought we're a bit . . . uh, unfriendly, might say. Keep to ourselves, as it were, we north coast men. Y'understand, it's our way." He reached down and got the wine jar; when he finished, it was much lighter. He belched, and squatted down.

"Man came to us, said he'd pay well to run four travelers across to the shore," the crewman said. "Right. The gold pieces in hand, and no questions. Ask us none, we'll ask you none." He took another pull at the jar. "We're not asking where that damned wind came from, either," he said, pointedly. "Nor what you'd be doing in the Empire. We've had a sight of queer cargoes aboard the Virgin in our time, haven't we, Yonn?" He grinned at the other man, who grunted in reply, and took the jar.

"Me . . . my name's Yorgan, by the way . . . me and the others, we've had the Virgin since she was built, just the four on us, doing such business as came our way," Yorgan said. "Small, she is, but fast. And us coasters, we know more of the sea than most folk. We can go anywhere, and damn few can find us if we don't want to be found, you understand. As there might be, well . . . things to be took here, there, and about, something light but worth a good deal, and somebody might need a fast boat with good, silent, men . . ."

"They damn bastards, Mazain folk, made themselves a great list of things to be taxed," Yonn said, with a broad grin. "More of 'em every year, stuff folk would like to buy, but with the taxes and all, too dear. So, we used to

193

bring 'em what they required, and our prices hadn't a tax on 'em. Of course, business isn't too good now, what with the fighting and all . . . that's why we were lying in port when we was asked to do this trip."

"There's always work for us, one place or another," Yorgan said, with a philosophical shrug. "Them other two, Ullof . . . he's the one with the flat nose, steering there . . . and Bungt, the fat one, and us, we manage pretty well. We've a bit of gold put away to buy something a bit bigger than the Virgin, if we've a mind to. Or maybe for other uses . . . we haven't decided. Been talking about it, now and then." He stopped and looked at Hugon, then at Zamor and at Kavin, one by one, thoughtfully; and at Thuramon, last.

"Whatever you've got to do ashore there I'm not asking," Yorgan said. "This village we'll be coming to, now . . . there's friends of ours there. If you're there a month or two from now, we might have the Virgin there to take you off, or there might be somebody else in our line of business dropping by. You'll understand, we keep no regular schedules in our line of work, eh?" He grinned.

"Anyway, whenever you're back, if you ain't hung or sliced up, the way those bloody Imperials like to do a man in," he went on, "we'll be about, if you look for us. Now, I was just now thinking . . ." He took another dram of wine. "You, the name's Hugon, ain't it? Yes. Anyway, you seem a handy sort, know your way around a ship, and maybe you even know how to use that sword you're wearing, eh?"

"Hold on, friend Yorgan," Hugon said. "Here, let me have a drop of that jar before you finish it off." He swallowed a gulp, and made a face as he set it down. "Grothan wine; whale piss. Ugh. Look, I am only a fair hand with a blade, and maybe a decent shot with a crossbow . . ."

"He's better than a fair hand with a crossbow," Zamor grunted. "You forget, I've seen you shoot, Hugon."

194

"But I'm a man of peaceful habits, in spite of the way I seem to be getting into brawls lately," Hugon said.

"Now, I may be putting the matter wrongly," Yorgan said. "I'm not a man as is handy with words, you'll see. We're a peaceful lot ourselves, avoiding bloodshed unless somebody makes it needful. We be men of business, purely. Now, I've been thinking. Spend a lot of time at sea aboard the Virgin, we do, and none of us has ever been much of a hand with grub. Times the food's been so damned grim as to make a man think of giving up the sea, that it has." He shook his head sadly. "Well, we tried to mend matters a while back. Bought a plump wench as was said to be a fair hand at cooking and all, which was true enough. Thought she might be handy with a few other things, as it might be. And we agreed, like we do in other things, 'twould be share and share alike, no advantage to any one of us; the lass could bunk with each man in fair turns."

Hugon chuckled, listening with fascination. "It didn't work out, then?"

"It didn't," Yorgan said, glumly. "She cooked well enough, but after a bit, she weren't even doing that, not regular. What she was doing, she kept setting one of us against another, stirring things about . . . oh, I don't want to be talking about the way it was. We near came to knives, after a bit. So we sold her, took a loss on it, too. Made up our minds to bear with things as they were. But, well now, I was wondering . . . the way I told you, we might be taking our gold and seeing about a bigger ship. If we do, we'd need one or two more lads at least, handy folk. Full shares, it'd be." He looked at Hugon. "You being such a hand with cooking, now . . ."

Hugon laughed, and shook his head. "I'm a landsman, friend. And I've already promised my large friend here to go to the North, to Numori, and see the sights there. No, thanks . . . I'm not a seaman at bottom, not a bit of it."

"Well, if it comes to that, we could fair enough use the

195

both of you," Yorgan said. "Looks like he could be a useful one, he does."

"I've no special love for salt water either," Zamor said.

"Eh, now," Yorgan said. "Maybe I didn't put the whole of it out for you to be considering. Spoke of a bigger ship . . . well, we've reasons, y'see." He scratched his head thoughtfully. "Can't tell you all about it, but there's business to be done. A place pretty far off, where a man might pick up treasures. More than you could think, enough to make a lord out of a man if he liked, and no trouble at all, beyond going there and taking it. But it's a long way, into seas that few men have traveled . . ." Yorgan stared at the darkening sky. "Now, it happens we know the road there, and we'll go when we have a bigger ship. If you'd like to join us, you and your big friend, we'd be glad to have you."

The man stood up and stretched. "Time to take the watch, anyway," he said. "But remember what I've said when you're done with your business." He stumped off toward the steering oar, and Yonn went forward.

"Now, there's an offer," Hugon said, stirring the last of the charcoal to make it burn away. He chuckled ironically. "From my lowly condition as vagabond, ballad singer and thief, I may rise to be ship-cook, pirate and smuggler."

Kavin, in the shadows, chuckled. "Cousin, your fish dinner was excellent. Cooks are much rarer than either poets or heroes. Accept the compliment Yorgan paid you and be content."

When Yonn called below, to rouse them, it was still black darkness outside. But the sails were down, and the Virgin rode at anchor, rubbing her side against a rough wooden pier. There was a dim light in the eastern sky, a hint of dawn; a couple of torches burned on shore. By their dim light, it was possible to make out dark houses, and silent men who moved nearer to the wharf; there was also a strong smell of drying fish.

"This village lies near the highroad, and the city is no

196

more than half a day's riding, southward," Yorgan told them. "There is a man called Klamash, the innkeeper here . . . he comes, now. He has horses, for you, and anything else you might require; and if you wish to send word to me, he is trustworthy. Leave any message, at his inn; it's called the Green Girl."

The man called Klamash was a cheerless-looking individual, gaunt and gloomy. He led the four men to a torchlit yard, where horses were waiting; aged nags, but rideable, Hugon thought.

"Best we can do, sirs," Klamash said, looking at the mounts. "Hard enough to get horses, now, the way things be, and the prices . . . you'll have gold, I suppose."

Thuramon counted out pieces, and Klamash took them; but he did not seem to be cheered, even by that.

"Mind you, I'm not asking why you're heading for the City," he said. "But I doubt you'll be back. Most folk that value their hides are going the other way these days, going up into the northern provinces. Mazain now . . . if the Emperor's taxmen don't strip you, or the soldiers chop you, you'll be finding the city under siege any day now, so you'll starve a while. Before the rebels come in and hang you for managing to stay alive."

He re-entered his inn after that cheering pronouncement, and the four men prepared to mount and ride. Hugon, groaning, swung into his saddle, and noted that Thuramon seemed to mount as lightly as a much younger man might do. The others were mounted, and two extra horses led behind to carry the baggage. They rode in single file, out through the darkened village and toward the highroad.

Fraak slept peacefully on Hugon's saddlebow as they jogged along. Hugon rocked uncomfortably in the saddle; the bony nag he rode was not the easiest of steeds to mount.

The road was a good one, wide and well kept; yet it seemed curiously empty for such a highway. It was not till mid morning that they saw any other travelers; and this was a caravan of carts, that trundled by in grim silence. The passing riders made no friendly greetings and kept to their own side of the road as they passed.

"Merchant folk," Kavin said thoughtfully, peering back at them. "With their goods and families, too. That's no good omen for any city when those folk leave it."

There were other such carts, now and again; but no one seemed to be going their way. The farms, on either side of the road, were rich-looking, with fields and groves near ready for harvest, but there seemed to be no farmers about. Twice they passed peasant houses with doors wide open, empty of life.

"You'd think this country had been plundered already," Hugon said. "If it weren't for the harvests there, not touched . . ."

"Apples!" Zamor said, suddenly.

Ahead, on a hillside, apple trees were ranked closely together, and the scarlet gleam of ripe fruit shone among the leaves, and on the ground. Zamor pulled his horse around toward the slope.

"I've hungered for apples since I was thrown into the galleys," he said, and spurred his mount up the slope.

"Well, now, I could enjoy one or two myself," Hugon said. "We're near the city, and we might as well enter with full bellies." He turned to ride after Zamor. After a moment, Kavin and Thuramon followed.

As the riders cantered toward the orchard, Zamor had already dismounted, and was biting down on a big apple. He looked toward them with a grin as they approached, and held up a red prize, half eaten.

"As good as the apples at home," he called out. "Try one!"

Fraak sailed off Hugon's shoulder and into a tree above Zamor's head, where he snapped at a fruit, gulping it in two bites. From his pleased note, he evidently liked it; his tail curled around a branch, he swung his scaly head, seeking another.

"What's become of the farmers?" Kavin asked. Still in

198

the saddle, he reached to take an apple, and bit it. "These are cultivated, not wild."

"Fled, as those others seemed to be fleeing," Thuramon said, getting down from his horse. He sat down and opened a saddlebag, extracting cheese. "We may as well eat now, before we enter the city. It can't be more than another hour's ride to the gates."

At that moment, as Hugon prepared to swing a leg over the saddle and dismount, a wild scream echoed in the orchard. He paused and stared, trying to locate the source; Zamor, dropping his apple, came to his feet with a grunt, and Kavin's horse backed, wildly.

"That way!" Kavin cried out, and yanked at his horse, pulling it round; he kicked it, and plunged through a wall of brushwood ahead. Hugon followed, clattering after Kavin as the dismounted Zamor ran in their wake. The screaming continued, a woman, wailing in wild terror, and as the two horsemen careened through and out into an open space, they saw its source.

There was a wide clearing in the trees, and at one side there were three big carts, brightly painted, parked with shafts down. Near them were ragged tents, and at the center, a small fire crackled. Near the fire, two big men in red cloaks held a writhing woman, who shrieked insanely as she tried to break free. Four other men, also red-cloaked, wearing cuirasses and helmets, sat their horses near the carts, lances lowered, holding half a dozen ragged people at bay.

The seventh man stood over the fire, laughing loudly; a child, a naked boy of two, was held head downward over the crackling flames, swinging back and forth, his ankles gripped in the big man's hand. The child screamed in terror and pain as the fire touched his hair, and the woman shrieked again, wildly.

Hugon, behind Kavin, saw the entire scene in a flash, as his horse crashed into the open space; his hand dragged at his sword, and he thumped his heels into his horse's ribs, hard. Kavin, ahead, already had his sword out. Kavin's horse leaped forward, and Kavin leaned from the saddle, grasping. His hand caught at the child, as his horse's shoulder struck the man who held it, knocking the man off his feet as Kavin galloped past.

A moment later, Hugon was upon the man, who was scrambling to his feet with a curse, dragging at his sword. Hugon's blade sheared down and into his neck; he screamed and fell.

Kavin pulled up, and carefully lowered the child to the earth, leaning from his saddle. He straightened, and swung round as Hugon drew rein beside him; the two men faced the others, grimly.

"Why, you motherless dogs . . ." one of the two men on foot, those who held the woman, began. But she had managed to bend far enough to sink her teeth into his arm, and he released her with a maddened yell; she ran for the child.

At that moment, the four lancers swung their horses and came into a grim line, facing Kavin and Hugon; their lances swung down, level, and they crouched for the charge.

Behind the four lancers, Zamor loomed, his axe swinging high; and a lancer suddenly flew from his saddle as the curved blade struck. But the remaining three shouted and spurred forward; while the two on foot ran toward Zamor, swords out, between the three horses.

Hugon felt a stab of fear as he saw two lancepoints, both seemingly aimed accurately at his chest; and a momentary flash of resentment at their choice of himself. Then, he had no more time for thought; he was too busy. He parried one lance, slamming hard with the flat of his sword to deflect it, and twisting his body to avoid the second. The lancer crashed into Hugon, shoulder to shoulder, and both men fell earthward with a crash.

Kavin, meanwhile, had managed to swing his left arm over the thrusting lance that came at him; he seized and yanked hard, drawing the unfortunate rider up out of his saddle, and down, onto the lifting point of Kavin's sword. But the sword, impaling, had been twisted from

200

Kavin's hand as the rider fell, and now he was weapon-less.

Meanwhile, the third lancer had pulled his horse back, and high on its hindlegs; his lance aimed downward to where Hugon and the second man rolled, clutching at each other's throats. The rider stabbed and missed, raised the lance to try again.

Then, as Kavin rose in his stirrups, reaching for the other rider, a winged bolt of lightning erupted from the trees. Fraak, screaming, shot straight into the lancer's face, claws out; the man rolled from his saddle, yelling with pain as blood spurted.

Zamor's axe swiftly put an end to the first man who had charged him; the second, more cautious, was crouching and circling, in an obvious effort to pass the big man and flee. On the ground, Hugon had managed to hold his man for a moment with his left arm across the fellow's throat; he thrust upward, and managed to get his point under the heavy cuirass, grunted, and leaned hard. The man groaned, bubbled blood, and died.

Hugon, panting, got to his feet and saw the end of the performance. The blinded rider had crashed into a tree, and then Fraak struck again, beaked jaws and iron claws outward, in a flying blow. The man folded up, his throat open.

"Damn it," Zamor growled at the other side of the clearing, "Stand still!" He lunged forward, dropping his axe, and his huge fist swung to slam against the man's head; the other fell as if he had been struck with the axe itself.

"Nine Gods!" Hugon said, catching his breath. "Now, here's a f-fine slaughterhouse!" He stared around, and grasped his horse's neck to support himself. Fraak sailed around him once, piping in an anxious tone, and settled on the saddle above him.

The woman had the child in her arms and was sooth-ing it. She stood up, and came toward the men. She was a tall, handsome woman, with black hair and a tawny skin, dressed in a strange bright garment. The others,

201

who crowded behind her, seemed of the same sort, dark folk with big noses.

Thuramon appeared, and was coming across the clearing with a slow, dignified walk, stepping around the gory evidence of the recent struggle with complete indifference. The woman saw him and cried out, in a strange language, a series of queer clattering words.

Thuramon smiled, and answered in the same tongue. The woman, clutching the child, dropped to her knees and bowed; the others behind her did the same, muttering in awe.

ELEVEN

"Tinker folk, we are," the black-haired woman was saying. She brought a piled platter of food and set it cautiously before Fraak, who sat curled within his tail, looking regal. The child patted Fraak, as the dragonet uttered his odd purring note of pleasure; the woman watched, her eyes wide.

"He will not hurt my child?" she asked, anxiously.

But Fraak had selected a bit of meat from the plate, and was eating it, with dignity, as the child crowed at him. Hugon grinned from where he sat.

"He's harmless, except when he feels the call of battle," Hugon said. "Gods, I never knew you had such a fierce way about you, friend Fraak."

"How is that you know our language, master?" the woman said to Thuramon. She still seemed in great awe of him.

"I have met other tinkers, from time to time," he told her. To the others, he said, "These are skillful smiths, in iron or brass especially. Tazala," he addressed the woman, "what were these men doing?"

"They are soldiers of the Emperor," Tazala said. "They thought we had silver hidden." She laughed scornfully. "We! We are fleeing north now, out of this mad realm, and as for silver . . ." She dug into a pocket and produced some dull-looking coins, holding them out. "These are coins of the Empire, their new coins. We would use such metal to mend a pot, perhaps."

The tinkers had been bringing food to Zamor, who sat

203

on the man he had knocked down last, grinning happily as he ate. The tinkers edged close to him, and some touched him curiously.

"Are you of the folk that live in the north?" one of them asked, and Zamor nodded.

"I am," he said, and as he spoke the man he sat on uttered a groan; he glanced down, with an annoyed look, and clouted the fellow once more into silence.

"We're afraid of the north," Tazala said. "They say that there are folk who eat men there. But we dare not stay here; the signs of evil grow stronger every day." She made a queer gesture with a finger.

"You needn't fear the north," Zamor said. "We are a kindly and peaceful people . . ." The man he was using as a seat tried to return to consciousness once more, and Zamor grunted, "By your leave, I seem to have skimped my work here." He rose, and took the fellow's legs, swung him into the air, and hurled him into the bushes. He squatted again on the ground. "These tales about we of the Numori country are all Mazainian fables. You are smiths? We'd never hurt any who can do such work." He grinned at the tinkers. "Why, you'd be rewarded well up there, I give you my word."

"He speaks truth," Thuramon said. "You need not be afraid."

"When you reach the highlands," Zamor added, "Say to my brother Zarram, of the Amanor Numori, that I sent you. If he asks for a sign, tell him that he lacks half an ear, which he does, and that I bit it off when we played, as children. He will remember that." And Zamor laughed.

Tazala stared at him, with a strange look. Then she made a gesture, like a curtsy, with her hands held outward.

"I believe you, noble sir," she said. She made the same gesture toward Kavin. "You are both kings, is that not true?"

"Not I, as far as I know," Zamor said. Kavin shook his head.

"Nor I," he told her. But she smiled, unbelievingly.

"It's not possible to lie to a seeing-woman of the Tinkers," she said. "But if you wish, noble sir, we will say you are not a king."

"You come from Mazain," Thuramon said. "How do things stand there?"

"Not from the city, sir," she said. "We dared not go there, not for many months. But it is said that the Emperor is mad, and that other lords come soon, to besiege. All the signs are very evil, for that city." She looked at him. "Surely you do not go that way?"

"We have business there," Thuramon said.

"Noble sir, do not go," she said, earnestly. "Listen, you know our tongue. Perhaps you know of the Book, too . . ." She dug into a pocket and showed him a packet of greasy cards, tied with a cord.

"The Book of Truths," Thuramon said. "Yes, I know it."

"Casting for the city, I found the Demon, who led the Lost Man by the hand," Tazala said. "And at last, the Tower lay under the Single and the Three . . . of Swords. Can you read that?"

Thuramon nodded. "The Book is probably right," he told her. "But we must go there. We shall leave again, before the time of the Tower."

She nodded, but still looked worried.

"We are poor folk," she said, "but you have saved us from death . . . and my son. Whatever we have is yours . . ."

Kavin, putting down his plate, chuckled. "Your food's repaid me well enough, lady."

"And me," Zamor said, and belched. "Hugon, get the secret from the lady as to how this dish is made, will you?" He grinned at Tazala. "We're a most remarkable company, good lady. Two kings, a warlock, and a man of

205

all talents—master cook, luteplayer, and swordsman among other things—my brother Hugon there."

"Your brother?" a tinker asked, incredulously, and Zamor's laugh boomed out.

"Our mother kept him wrapped, out of the sun, till he was fully grown," Zamor explained, gravely. "This the odd pallor of his countenance."

But Thuramon wore a thoughtful look.

"I know you are poor folk," he said, "so I'll pay you for what I wish to have, in good gold . . ."

"No!" Tazala said, firmly.

"Yes," Thuramon said, and stared at her. "Take out the Book of Truths, and ask if you should do as I say."

She dropped her eyes, and touched the pack of cards in her pocket; after a moment, she brought them out and slid them in her hand, shuffling. She drew a card and looked at it; muttered, and put it back.

"I shall pay you, then," Thuramon said. "Gold, we have enough; and we'll need little of it for our work." He stood up. "There . . . a cart, and two of our horses may draw it. And possibly a few other small things, such as you can spare . . . a garment or two, suitably colorful, befitting our new professions." He grinned at the others. "A troupe of mountebanks. Myself, as juggler and teller of fortunes . . . there's not too much difference there." He looked at Zamor. "And you, of course, wrestler and strong man. Ballad singer, teller of tales . . . our good Hugon, there. And finally, Kavin . . ." He paused, and pulled his beard. "What skill shall we assign you, Kavin? I find it a puzzle, I fear . . ."

Kavin chuckled.

"The Dragons' gift was luck," he said. "I remember a game or two, played in the market places in my youth . . . good lady, have you three cups, wine-cups, say?" Tazala brought three small clay cups, and Kavin set them upside down on the earth. "Under one, I place a coin, thus . . ." he said. "And now, around and around, and once more around . . . now, you watched carefully, did you not?"

"It's under that one," Zamor said, pointing.

"It is not," Kavin said, upending the cup. "Shall we try it again?"

They tried it several times. Thuramon watched, and nodded.

"Yes," he said, at last. "Yes. A most unprincely occupation, but it seems certain that the luck is there, Kavin. Since you had never an opportunity to gain skill at a certain means by which the outcome can be made certain . . ." He chuckled. "No, luck it is, surely. And it must apply to all games, then."

"Good," Kavin said. "I'll be your gamester, then. And as for unprincely . . . that's a prince's work, to play the swindler, often enough." He laughed, a little bitterly.

"Good, then," Thuramon said. "Tazala, take this." He counted out gold pieces. "And those six fine horses there . . . I think you can use those, as well."

"Why, damn it, I'd hoped to take one of those myself," Hugon said. "My mount's a bone-rack. And these poor dogs don't need their horses now." He glanced at the dead men.

"Yes, these, now," Thuramon said, glancing at them. "It would be wise if your people gave those men decent burial, Tazala. If any comrades of theirs should chance to find them, unpleasant questions might arise. As to the matter of the horses, Hugon, you, as our elected thief-in-charge, should know a prime law of thievery . . . not to wear a stolen cloak in the marketplace. Those horses are cavalry mounts, and might be known in the city."

Hugon led two horses to one of the carts, and Tazala aided him, hitching them to the shaft. She showed him the cart's interior, fitted with bunks and closets, into which he peered with interest.

"A fine way to live," he said, a little enviously. "Had I not given my word, I'd be off with your folk to the north, I would."

"Come, when you're done with whatever it is you must do," she said. "You will always be welcome among the tinkers. And your great black friend . . . whom I do not believe is truly your brother, is he?"

"Of course he is." Hugon said, gravely.

"He I would like to see again, especially." Tazala said, and her black eyes ·urned toward the place where Zamʳr stood, with an expression that Hugon knew well. He chuckled.

"I think he's a much wedded man already," he said. Tazala laughed.

"I did not speak of weddings," she said, pointedly Her tongue touched her red lips, briefly. "We nave a saying . . . some horses can be ridden but once. out the ride is equal to owning a hundred lesser horses."

Zamor came toward the wagon, bearing a sack, and flung it into the back.

"Apples," he said, and laughed. "I'll never get my fill of 'em, I think. Are we ready to ride, ᴅhen?"

The cart rumbled through the pasture below the orchard, and down onto the highroad; Thuramon had established himself within, and Zamor with him, while Kavin and Hugon rode in the box. The other horses were led behind.

"A good meal, as is usual before going to the scaffold," Hugon grunted; Fraak sat above, on the cart top, looking like a carved decoration. Kavin glanced at Hugon.

"We'll succeed, I think," he said. "We must."

"We've little time, I suspect," Hugon said. "Look, more of those carts. Ah, those red cloaks have a familiar look."

Behind the carts that rumbled past, riders in steel and red cloaks came, slowing as they came abreast of the painted cart. They stared, curiously, and one turned to ride beside.

"You're heading cityward, are you?" he said.

"Yes, noble sir," Hugon answered, pulling his forelock with a fawning grin. "We've heard there may be need of entertaining folk, like us, to lighten the burdens of the war and all, you know. We're poor traveling folk, and we haven't got ought but what you see, my noble sir . . ."

The rider guffawed. "You might not have that, either, when Rarashaz, on the gates, gets through with you. He's picking them clean these days, going in and going out." He turned and clattered away.

Ahead, the road curved toward a high wall, that stretched away in either direction into the distance. At regular intervals, square towers rose along the wall, and below a deep ditch ran. The road ran down, into a huge gate, topped with loopholed towers, and flanked by gigantic black statues.

"The outer walls," Hugon said, looking ahead. "And beyond, the second wall. Strong, those old walls; strong enough to hold any enemy off . . . as they've done a dozen times."

"No wall is any use without men behind it," Kavin said. "I have a feeling this one is weaker than it looks. But about this matter of the gate watch . . ." He leaned back and spoke into the cart. "You heard that rider, Thuramon. Best hide what gold we can."

Thuramon, invisible, chuckled. "I have a better way. Let gold be found . . . enough, just enough."

There were guardsmen lounging at the gate; they looked glumly at the cart, and one man climbed inside to look about. He poked into various corners, in a lackadaisical way; it was obvious that he had little hope of gaining much. Meanwhile, the gate officer walked around the caravan, studying it thoughtfully.

"You'll not have twelve besans apiece, entry fee, I suppose," he grunted at Hugon.

"My lord, we are poor folk, as you see . . ." Hugon began. The officer shrugged.

"Well, then, if you'd enter, we'll have to have something," he said. "You've horses, now . . . two on the cart, four behind . . . let's see, now. Four of you makes . . . uh, fifty. And there's the cart fee, of course, so that's another ten, and we'll allow you six apiece on the beasts. Though they look as if they're no use even for meat . . ."

"But your honor, we'll have need of the beasts," Hugon began.

"Well, you're in trouble, me boy," the officer said, with an unpleasant grin.

"Perhaps we'd best turn back," Thuramon said, looking out of the cart.

"If you do, you walk," the officer said. "The fees are due now. Whether you turn around or not."

"I've found nothing in the cart," the other man said, climbing down. "Not a bit of coin."

"You say we cannot enter without payment, sir?" Thuramon asked, looking most pitiful. The gate guard nodded. "And if we have no coin, we lose even these few poor things we have? Have you no mercy on us, noble sir?" He was whining now.

"The law's the law, old croaker," the man said roughly. "It says plainly what the fees are. Now, then . . ."

Thuramon came down and hobbled close to him. "Why, then we must pay, must we not?" he said. He held up a leather sack, and peered into it, with a nearsighted gaze. "Ahhh," he said, and pulled out a coin, then another. He laid each coin in the man's palm, with great reluctance, one by one, till there were enough.

The officer, obviously the renowned Rarashaz, watched Thuramon's performance with increasing puzzlement, and greed began to show on his features. As Thuramon brought out the last coin, he reached out and took the leather sack, with a grin.

"Here now, it feels as if there're a few more in there," he said, squeezing it. "Probably just barely enough to pay your city tax." He dropped the sack into his belt pouch. "On your way, then, the lot of you." He stood, chuckling, and watched the cart go through the gates.

Hugon drove through a twisting tunnel-like archway, and out into a broad square; ahead, the gates of what was certainly a drover's inn, from the smell, opened on the square. He turned the cart that way, and heard Thuramon chuckle behind him.

"Much we've got to laugh about, wizard," Hugon said. "That lizard fingered guard took all we had, did he not?"

"Of course not," Thuramon said. "Even such gold as he thought he received was no more than an illusion, as he'll find when he seeks it in his pouch." Thuramon chuckled again, balefully. "But he went farther and took the leather sack, thinking there was more within. There is, but not gold. No, not gold."

Hugon steered the cart into the innyard and drew rein. He looked back, puzzled.

"I don't understand the mazes you like so well, Thuramon," he said. "If you've power to fool the man's eye, why not give him as much as he wished, and have done?"

"It was necessary that he follow the path of his greed," Thuramon said. "And in the matter of the sack. . . I work under a Law, master Hugon. It is a Law of Balances . . . and it forbids me to act as I sometimes desire. That man deserved what he has received, but he had first to seize his doom with his own hand, of his own will."

"Balances?" Hugon shrugged. "I can't say I understand . . . and what doom, except for a notable shortage in his pocket?"

"I told you," Thuramon said, with that unpleasant chuckle. "He will put his fingers into that sack, in search of gold. And he will find a small, very angry, scorpion."

Hugon shuddered. "I see," he said.

"This inn looks as though it might welcome customers," Kavin said, swinging down off the cart. "Thuramon, I would prefer that you paid the innkeeper in true coin, if you will."

"I always pay in true coin," Thuramon said. "The scorpion was as true as any other coin, for value received."

The palace of the late lord Barazan, now the property of his beautiful widow, was a great white pile of towers and domes behind a wall that encircled the whole noble quarter. There was a marble stairway that ran down into the lake from the palace, and in the lake beyond, the King's House rose hugely on its island.

The message was delivered to the lady Gwynna, as she sat in her bath, a great shell of bronze in which water steamed. She had lolled in the hot water, sleepily; she had not found her bed till dawn, because the Emperor had caused a great celebration of nothing in particular, a feast that had gone on and on. She suspected that he had some twisted reason for the almost constant feasting that was going on, but she could not guess what.

The maid had gone in search of fresh towels while Gwynna lay luxuriating. She had few servants left; they were vanishing all over the city, it seemed, from every house.

Fraak sailed in, through the high window, and circled, to come to a landing on the bronze end of the tub; he stared down at her with his big yellow eyes, and uttered an appreciative cry.

"You!" Gwynna said. Fraak chortled.

"You are pretty!" he said, and blew a smoke ring.

Gwynna already knew that. Fraak's golden-eyed stare made her a trifle nervous, though; it was necessary to remind herself that he was a dragonet, not a man.

"Where's Hugon?" she asked. "Is he here in the city? The others, too?"

"He's here," Fraak sang. "He told me to say so, he did. I think you're almost as pretty as the other lady."

"What other lady?" Gwynna snapped. "Oh, never mind. And must you eye me so, you lecherous lizard?"

"I am NOT a lizard," Fraak told her, sounding hurt. "Hugon and the others wait, at the great inn by the North Gate. They say that you may come after sunset."

"Tell them I'll be there," Gwynna said. "Now go, quickly, or my maid will come back and think you're some giant insect, perhaps." She waved him off. "Go, shoo!"

212

The innyard was fairly crowded, as were the market squares beyond. But not as crowded as it had been in the time before the city lay under the lengthening shadows of siege. Still, a few farmers came with their produce, a few bold traders still brought goods; but only a handful, compared to the swarms that once came to the Imperial City. There were too many soldiers in the crowds, and not nearly enough folk with fat purses; and such coin as circulated was the dull metal of the new kind.

Torches flared, lighting various booths and flickering over the faces of people who came and went about the huge innyard, and in the market square outside it. In one place, a pair of acrobats skipped and tumbled on a rope; in another, a tent was up, and a fattish dancer revolved in front of it, while the proprietor spoke loudly of the unspeakable delights within. Other booths sold various and curious goods; everything from the brown and gummy candy that caused a delightful unconsciousness, called hashazz, to the weird erotic toys that seemed to please the yokels so much.

But there seemed to be little of any real value for sale, Hugon noticed. No cloth, and not much food; only one baker's booth was open, and that held little of any value. Even the girls who plied their trade about the square, he noticed, were hardly as appetizing as he would have expected, in the great city. And there seemed to be an air of gloom, unexplained, because no one seemed to know much of how the wars went. There were a dozen tales, all different; the rebels had surrendered en masse, they had all taken ship for the west, or they had all been slain by a mighty attack of the Imperial forces. These tales were dispensed by many, usually persons with excellent and apparent reason for their inventions.

Some of the other tales seemed more likely, to Hugon. The rebel forces held a number of points south of the city, that was certain; and now, likely enough, large bodies of the rebels would be moving around, in a wide circle, to ultimately cut all the ways out. Now that there was no Imperial fleet, even the sea would be closed. The thought did not please Hugon greatly.

In the cart, the four had consulted together earlier, just as the night's torches began to be lighted.

"I went to the shop in the street of weavers," Hugon said, scowling, as he fiddled with a lute string. "The woman, Elanak . . . she was not there. Nor the boy, either." He controlled his voice with difficulty. "That foul lump of toad's excrement, the Emperor. He makes war on women and children, it seems, as a regular preference."

"Where are they?" Kavin asked.

"In a prison, toward the sea wall," Hugon said. "If they live. That harbor fortress is said to be a hellish place, where none live long; and daily, a few are brought forth for execution, as a few more are added." He looked up, with a black glitter in his eye. "Old men, women, and babies, most of them; any who may be denounced, for any reason."

There was a grim silence in the darkened cart.

"Well," Thuramon said, at last, "Fazakk's woman is dead, or as good as dead, then. I wish we could have done his will in this, but we've other work that must be done swiftly . . ."

"No," Hugon said, and Thuramon glanced at him, surprised.

"Our word was to help the woman flee the city, you'll recall," Hugon said, in a low, hard voice. "I do not know that she is dead, or the child either. Fazakk did his part of a bargain; I will do mine."

"Listen, Hugon," Thuramon began, "we must hasten, I tell you. Unless we lay hands upon the Egg of Fire within a few more days, the Gate will be complete, and Ess will be free to come forty." In the shadows, Thuramon's eyes glowed. "Then . . . such black evils as you cannot imagine will come with him. He has many servants, in many worlds, fools like this Emperor . . . but not all of them human fools. First, the Gate will vomit out those

214

legions of his, and they will spread across this world, to make it theirs . . . and his. Then worse will come, till no man lives in the world any longer . . . and he will go through that Gate to yet other worlds."

"I gave my word . . ." Hugon said, stubbornly. He shrugged. "Look you; I've heard other things about this city today. I think those gates may close at any moment. Rebel horsemen have been seen on the road north of the wall. Then we will be penned here, like rabbits in a hutch, plucked forth for dinner when the rebels choose. They may break in swiftly, at that, and all our problems solved at once." He grinned in the shadows. "Suppose they do . . . why, their first troopers will push toward that imperial Treasure at once, as any man of sense would do. Break in, and see that jewel, too large for any one man. A blow or two with an axe edge, and it's fair divided, and no more use at all to anyone." Hugon chuckled. "Well, then, you'd be locked forevermore within this world, as you told us, Thuramon. Is it so bad a world as that, that you cannot make the best of it? And we have great need of wise men here, too."

Hugan looked at Thuramon, who shook his head gloomily, and then at Kavin.

"But to destroy the Egg . . . whether we or another do so . . ." Hugon said, again, "Would that not accomplish all our ends, except yours, Thuramon . . . and absolve you of promises to Gwynna, as well?"

"To destroy that Egg?" Thuramon shook his head again. "No. Fool, that crystal contains a power locked within it that would burn the whole world to a smoking cinder, release it thus. Nor would this world's doom affect Ess; he has other ways, in time, to gain his freedom. Unless I lock him in forever . . ."

"So, I am wrong once more," Hugon said with a shrug. "But I have my given word to think of. And this tool-sack, Dragon gift. Am I not thief-in-charge, official opener of locks, and the rest? And prisons have locks, I imagine."

"That one has guards as well," Zamor grunted. "But I
am with my brother Hugon, here. We were given passage by Fazakk's wish. We said we would free his
woman."

"I must say so, too," Kavin said. "We must find a way
to do both tasks, then."

Thuramon grunted sourly. "I am burdened by such
henchmen as I wouldn't wish upon an enemy," he said.
"Very well, then. But we must first speak with that lady,
Gwynna, if she comes tonight; she will be our key to the
King's house." He looked at Zamor. "Now, keep in mind,
large one . . . that belt is as dangerous to you as it is to
others. Use it sparingly, if at all."

"Great Snake, I know that," Zamor said. "On the one
time I did use it, I was weary as a sick cat for hours afterward." He stood up, his head bent under the low roof,
and stretched. "I think I can do without its use, after
seeing these weaklings hereabouts. At least, most of the
time."

One by one, they climbed out, and began their prepa-
rations, under Thuramon's direction. He had mapped
each step with care, and nothing was left unconsidered;
first, it would be necessary to become known, so that the
Emperor's spies would have a proper explanation of all
they saw and heard. Gwynna would bring a new and entertaining group of mountebanks to show on the steps of
the palace on the lake . . . or better still, in the King's
house itself. But they must be real, a troupe that had
been seen and known already.

Gwynna came alone, wearing a hooded cloak, through
the narrow alleys and streets of the dark city. She came
into the square and moved quietly along the stalls,
watching to find the four she sought. Then, at a distance,
she saw them.

Zamor was standing, high on a platform, above the
crowd's heads; he lounged against a post, grinning with
magnificent insolence at the upturned faces. He wore

216

only a loincloth, and his shining black body was painted with strange stripes and slashes of color; in his hair, he wore a gaudy knot of feathers.

Hugon, in front of the platform, was bawling energetically over the shouts of other showmen and peddlers, as he walked to and fro.

"Look ye, look ye," he was roaring. "The Mighty Mangler, Man of Iron, who has defeated every champion in nine kingdoms, offers to meet any brave lad who fancies his brawn, and give odds of ten to one, ten besans to your one, that you'll not stay on your feet for the fall of the sandglass, here!"

Gwynna, in the shadows, watched as Zamor took a muscular farm lad in hand. She suspected that he could have snapped the man's spine in the first moment of their encounter, but he prolonged the bout with a showman's instinct, to the last grain of sand in the glass. Then he pinned the lad down, with a triumphant shout.

Gwynna came closer, next to Hugon, as he continued to shout his challenge; she turned, enough to let him catch a glimpse of her face, hidden under the hood. He did not pause in his roaring for longer than it might have taken him to draw a deep breath; but in that space, he whispered, "The cart. Go there."

She saw the painted wagon he had indicated, and went in that direction. As she came to it, a young pair emerged, a man and a girl with dazed, happy expressions, who passed her hand in hand.

Gwynna pushed aside the curtain and saw Thuramon, cowled, sitting over a low table, his hands folded. He looked up and smiled, with a curiously bitter look.

"I have been telling fortunes," he said, and sighed. "Lies, of course. Those two have little joy before them . . . but I lied, so they are happy, for a little time." He indicated a stool. "Sit, lady, and let's lay plans."

"You took long enough to come," she said, staring at him. "I wonder if you know how black the future looks at this moment for all of us, soothsayer."

217

"I know," Thuramon said. "But there are things I do not know yet. Listen. We must gain access to the King's house, in any way we can, and soon, very soon."

"That might be possible," she said, putting her chin on her knuckles, and staring down in deep thought. After a while, she nodded. "Yes, it may be . . . but you wish to steal the Egg of Fire, as you told me, in Koremon. I must tell you . . . that may not be possible."

"Possible or not," Thuramon told her, "it is necessary."

She looked troubled. "I have seen it," she said. "It is large . . . no man could take it out. But there's another point . . . the jewel lies visible, where the Emperor himself comes, almost daily, to gloat over it. He would go mad . . . madder than he now is . . . if it vanished."

"Leave that all to me," Thuramon told her. "For the rest, this is what I wish you to do. You have seen certain amusing things here . . . or you will, if you wander about. A wrestler of enormous strength, a fortune teller and maker of illusions . . . myself. And our servants, a skillful pair of rogues, as you will also see. Now, the Emperor has been most lavish, lately in his entertainments . . . and you are of his court, anxious to please him further . . ."

"I see," Gwynna said.

The torches guttered out, one by one, and the last booths closed. Here and there a drunken citizen snored in a gutter, or rambled homeward; and a patrol of City Guardsmen clanked by.

Zamor, who had had the hardest work, lay snoring in a bunk in the cart, while the others made ready to follow his example. Hugon, yawning hugely, gave Fraak a tasty bit from his plate.

Then, in the distance, there was a deep rumble, and Hugon stared out the tiny window, puzzled.

"Thunder?" he said. "But it's clear . . ."

Another boom rolled, echoing in the night. Kavin sat up.

"A cannon," he said.

Somewhere, not too far away, there was a tremendous crash, and a sound of shouting. Torches flickered in the night, and Hugon went to the cart door.

"I'll take my oath that was a catapult," he said, staring into the dark. "Aha, and there go the guardsmen to the gates. Thuramon, I think we've less time than before. The city has been besieged, at last."

Out there in the darkness, another stone fell with a crash, and somewhere southward a cannon thundered once more.

TWELVE

By dawn, the siege was well under way. It was plainly not a simple siege, an affair of waiting, but an assault, continuous and bitter.

For three hundred years the City had never once been taken by any army. Century after century the walls had been strengthened, built again and again. Within those walls were sources of water, and warehouses of food; unless assault succeeded, an army could lie before Mazain for another century and never enter.

But this time the sea was closed. Those few ships that had limped back from the battle were in the harbor now; and in the Narrow Sea, without, the rebel galleons lay, their guns run out. On the southern plain, the rebel armies lay encamped in a broad circle that ran clear around to that highroad to the north.

Stone throwers stood, dangerously close to the walls, before each gate and near every major tower; their arms swung up, and huge stones sailed over, to crash into the roofs and streets. The cannon, too, were laid level with each gate, and their iron missiles clanged again and again against the stonework. Twice, balls slammed into the gates themselves, and splinters flew, though the bronze-shod doors remained in place.

As the sun rose higher, the first major rebel assault of the day began, with the advance of siege towers and rams against the southwest walls, near the sea. Here, a slight rise overlooked a gate called the Gate of The Dolphins. Where a portion of wall and a tower had been battered nearly to rubble by stones, there were fewer defenders. The siege towers rolled down toward the wall, rumbling monsters covered with wet skins; ahead, men hurled bundles of faggots into the ditch, as they rode swiftly by under a spatter of arrows. In two places the ditch was almost filled, now; and here the siege towers rolled closer to the wall. Meanwhile, a ram came slowly toward the half-shattered gate, inching its way.

There was a desperate engagement atop the wall, and in and out of the swaying towers. At that moment, the gate creaked open, and steel-clad lancers thundered out, rank after rank of men; and behind them, mailed pikemen, who swarmed against the towers' bases with torches. The ram stopped and flamed, as the lancers swept by and over it, and now the lances went toward the hill.

Then, over the hill's rim, other lances glittered, and bright pennons flapped in the sun; the armored riders came down, and met the city's defenders in a crashing line of death.

Some of the lancers managed to turn and ride back through the gates, but not many. The towers burned sullenly, and the dead lay still, in rows where they had fallen. And around the city, the cannon thundered again, and the stone-throwers' arms rose and fell.

In the late afternoon, in the white palace beside the lake, the sound was distant, but steady. There was also the sound of harpists and flute players, who floated in a barge that was rowing by the marble steps; and the sound of light laughter among the trees. Half a dozen elegantly carved boats lay at the steps of Gwynna's palace, and she walked, with others of the noble class, near them.

Orashaz, dressed with even more extravagance than usual, hovered at Gwynna's elbow. Once or twice a louder boom would cause him to jerk slightly and lose the thread of his conversation for a moment; however, for the most part he was managing rather well, Gwynna thought.

"Indeed, my lady, I am sure that your plan will please

222

his Glorious Majesty greatly," Orashaz was saying. "I myself had found several unusual dancers . . ." He simpered, and rolled his eyes. "A group of extraordinarily flexible creatures, though a little shocking . . . ulp." Three heavy detonations had gone off in the north. "However," Orashaz went on, "they seem to have disappeared, with the usual cowardice of such creatures." He sighed. "Poor fools, they would have received a sizable reward if they had pleased our glorious monarch."

"There seems to be a frightful amount of disloyalty about," another lady observed. "My maids came back from market today with the most dreadful stories. It would seem that there was some silly irregularity . . . apparently the food warehouses were not filled, by some clerk's error, and there's a stupid panic going about."

"I can't see any cause for alarm," Orashaz observed. "My own storehouses, in the palace, are quite filled. It seems very unlikely that those rebel swine will make their way past the walls, but even so, we have the inner wall around the noble quarter." He tittered. "It might be just as well if the city's common herd were to feel the rebel whip on their backs, for a while; they'd soon know how much better off they are now."

Another noble joined in. "Have you not heard the latest? The real reason our Sovereign has commanded tonight's feasting?"

Gwynna turned to listen. The noble smiled, and lowered his voice.

"He plans to loose utter destruction against the rebels, this very night!" the man said. "He has been merciful, till now, hoping they would see their error, but now!" The man shuddered, elegantly.

"Destruction?" Gwynna asked, arching an eyebrow in bored interest. "Of what sort, tell me?"

"Sorcery!" the noble said. "Mighty sorcery, known only to our Emperor, given him by the Dark Lord himself. But there's more!" He leaned forward, and his voice went lower. "At dawn, he will call forth the god, as he's promised for so long! All of us will see, with our own eyes, as we knew we would! The Dark Lord will come, and sweep away all opposition, before the Emperor!"

"Then the altar is finished?" Gwynna asked, trying to keep her voice devoid of interest.

"The last work is done, needs only to be fitted into place," the man told her.

I wonder where those fools have gone, she thought, with a rush of terror rising within her. They've been caught, flung into prison, or hacked to death. Or a stone's crushed them all. They should have come an hour ago or more . . .

I'll die here, in this foul magnificence, she thought bitterly. That madman will loose his demon, perhaps . . . or the rebels will break in, as they must sooner or later. And there will be a few men of Meryon among them, I don't doubt at all, she thought. It may be that a man of lost Armadoc will find me . . . at least that will be a clean death. And a just one, for what I've been and done.

She bit her lip and gained control again, with an effort; a voice was coming through, Orashaz's.

". . . most interesting, to see those sacrifices which will be performed tonight . . ."

The Harbor Fortress was a squat mass of stone, windowless, stained with age and dirt; its walls were washed by the stagnant waters of a broad canal on two sides, and there was a narrow, filthy alley along a third side. On the fourth, a gateway of iron faced the streets, well guarded.

"During my short stay in this city beforetime, I happened to learn one or two interesting bits of history," Hugon was saying, as he walked on the other side of the canal with the others. They stayed well within the shadows of the moldering warehouses, and watched for possible guards. There were none about; every man who carried arms was busy at one part of the walls or another.

But there were still guards at the prison, plainly; several men moved behind the barred gates. A few minutes before, the four had seen lancers ride up, a dozen or more of them, and their mounts were still tethered at the gates. But there was no way of knowing how many still lived there, within those blackened walls. Many had been dragged out already, to executions that were still going on.

"A sewer," Hugon said, thoughtfully. "It opens there, on the canal bank. It's barred, of course, but I have these tools." He patted the leather pouch. "Now, once inside, there's a courtyard, large and fairly dark, because of a roof over it. The prisoners would be there, since the place hasn't room in cells for so many. Besides, I made inquiries. The guards are few . . ."

"What about the lancers, a while ago?" Zamor asked.

"That puzzles me," Hugon admitted. "It may be that they came to fetch some especially important prisoners . . . thought they've been the damndest long time about it. Perhaps they can't find whoever it is in the crowd." He stared across at the stone pile with a frown. "Yes . . . that's a question. Those lancers . . . I understood that there were few guards, old men mostly, who seldom looked down into the prison proper, except to fling down a little food and water. They can spare no able men, now especially. And most of those in there are women, children, or old men, as I've heard."

"Listen!" Zamor said, suddenly.

There was a sound of horses on the stone street. Hugon listened, and grinned.

"Those lancers, leaving," he said. "Well, then." He walked toward the canal's edge. Over his shoulder, he said, "Zamor. That beast, Fraak . . . I had an hour's work to persuade him to remain in the cart, so much did he wish to come with me. If I should not succeed, take care of the creature. He has a foolishly tender heart, and needs a friend."

Zamor grunted. "You? You will live, no fear. Only the good meet early death, brother. In you go."

Hugon slid into the fetid water, and swam toward the distant sewer opening, a faint streak on the oily surface.

225

Thuramon looked after him with a strange expression; and Kavin too. Zamor turned away from the water's edge and joined them.

After a long while, Thuramon glanced at the advancing shadow of the building; it lay over the canal, now. He pulled at his white beard.

"We must reach the gate of the inner city before dark," Thuramon said.

"He intends to find those two and show them the sewer's entrance," Zamor said. "A woman and a child. They would be fearful, and slow."

"Not that slow," Thuramon said.

"He may have decided to bring some others out, as well," Zamor said. "It's not been long, yet."

Thuramon glanced at the big man.

"It's been too long," Kavin said.

"Then I'll follow him in," Zamor said. He unbuckled his cloak, and dropped it. "If he's dead, I'll slay a few."

"No!" Thuramon said sharply. "Remember our agreement."

"Damn our agreement, warlock," Zamor said, and took a step toward the canal.

"Hugon took your oath," Kavin said, in a hard voice. "He swore you not to follow him, remember that? And you gave it, in the name of friendship."

Zamor stared at him, his eyes gleaming oddly.

"I swore, too," Kavin said. He stared at the black water with eyes that were dark with pain.

"I break the oath, then," Zamor said.

"You need not," Thuramon said, in a relieved voice. "Look, he comes."

Hugon, dripping, climbed wearily up the bank. He was masked in filth and mud, and shook as he stood; his eyes looked out of the gray-black mask, wide and blank, the eyes of a man in a state of shock.

"You're alone," Zamor said, staring at him. "Here, you'll freeze, you fool." He flung the cloak around Hugon, who continued to stand and shiver.

226

"Come, then, let's get away from here," Kavin said, and Zamor, glancing oddly at Hugon, nodded. They moved off, Hugon walking like a machine, stiffly.

"There were . . ." Hugon started to say, and stopped. He turned and leaned against a wall, head down, and vomited.

After a while, he straightened.

"I need to wash, quickly," he said, in a curiously calm voice. "There's a fountain in the next street."

He walked ahead of the others, and found the water; kneeling, he sponged the filth away, and rose again, to wrap the cloak around himself.

"Let's get to business," Hugon said. "We're late, I think."

He would say no more, until much later; then, as they rode toward the gates of the area of palaces called the inner city, he broke his silence.

"Fazakk must be told, if possible," Hugon said, as if to himself. "The woman is dead, of course. And the child." He stared at Kavin and Zamor with a slightly mad look. "All of them were dead. It was the lancers, those we saw; but many had been dead already, for a long time. The lancers were merciful. They finished the work."

"All dead?" Kavin asked, with a look of horror.

"Starved, I think." Hugon shook his head. "Gods. I don't wish to remember what I saw there. This is no longer a city of men. Demons!" He spat.

Behind them, a thundering crash echoed, and a column of dust rose.

"It will not be a city long," Kavin said, glancing back.

At the end of the street, the white gates of the inner city loomed; guards in jeweled armor barred their way.

"We are sent for, by the lady Gwynna," Thuramon said from the seat of the cart.

The guards waved them on, and the cart rolled into the parks among the white palaces. Beyond, the lake glimmered through the trees, and ahead the white towers of Gwynna's palace shone.

227

As the night fell, campfires bloomed on the hills around the city, lines of bright points like stars. Within the city, there was a thick odor of smoke and death; here and there, fires burned in slow orange flares. In the Street of Coppersmiths, there were dead men and women piled against the walls, while living wounded moaned in the gutters. Here, troopers had battled with city folk over an empty warehouse. In another quarter, a street riot raged.

A door, low in one of the wall towers, opened and closed, very quietly; in the darkness, a man ran swiftly toward the rebel camps, his feet padding silently and his breath rasping. He carried a message from the commander of seven towers on the southeast side, who had finally made up his mind.

On the lake, the torchlit barges drifted, in procession, to the sound of music. On the great portico of the King's house, the Thrice Glorious Emperor Sharamash sat on a throne that flashed and glittered in the lamplight, a large winecup in his hand. He giggled incessantly, and sometimes he choked with laughter.

The courtiers who stood about him joined his laughter from time to time; but they glanced uneasily at one another, where he could not see them. The sky, in two quarters of the city, was lit by a red glow, and there were more distant thuds than earlier.

Zamor had been on show a little earlier; he had thrown three wrestlers sent against him at once, lifted great weights, bent bars, and the like, all to the Emperor's open delight. Sharamash looked now to his left, and saw Gwynna; he beckoned, chuckling.

"Ah, my dear, you're a wise girl," he said, pinching her arm. "You knew I have a taste for low, common, things, didn't you?" He burst into a mad guffaw, spilling half his wine. "I do, you know," he said, drawing her closer with a grip on her forearm. "That young oaf who sang the naughty ballads was delightful, too, and the old man

228

with the beard, who made such delightful tricks . . . but I can do real magic, Gwynna, do you know that?"

"If you tell me so, I believe it, Majesty," Gwynna said.

"Of course you don't, my dear," Sharamash said, and snickered. "You'd be a fool to believe it. I've never shown any learning in the magical arts before, have I? So, how could I learn so quickly?" He beamed at her. "I have, though. He showed me, the Dark One. In a vision, I was taught . . . because of those filthy rebels, you see. I was afraid they might come and prevent me from finishing the god's work, so I asked him what to do, and he told me. It's all arranged. They'll know, soon." He giggled wildly.

"The rebels cannot come here, Majesty," Gwynna said.

"Oh, yes they can," Sharamash said. "I've no loyal men, none; I know, believe me." He cackled and drained his cup, which was swiftly refilled.

Among the trees, in the park that lay between the King's House and the huge temple, shadowy figures moved. The blank wall of the Treasure House rose above them, like a smooth cliff; swiftly, a thin rope rose into the air, and clung. A figure rose along the rope, like a spider, to a distant narrow window.

It took Hugon several minutes to actually reach the guarded inner chambers; and he climbed in, at last, thoroughly winded. He paused in the darkness, catching his breath; the round package he carried strapped to his back seemed to weigh as much as a calf.

Here, where he stood, there were no guards; all of them were outside those heavy doors on which the Emperors of Mazain had always relied, to guard their jewels. Swiftly, Hugon padded forward, toward that inner room where the greatest jewels of all would be.

At the door, an open arch seen dimly in the starlight from overhead, he paused. It seemed too easy, he thought. There was no door in that arch, only blackness; he waited, and stared at it.

After a moment, he decided. He slipped off one soft

229

leather boot, and gently, carefully, tossed it at the door.

As it passed the arch, there was a sudden flash; the boot, sliced nearly in two halves, fell to the floor.

A blade, suspended. Hugon moved carefully, searching the sides of the door; there was a curiously shaped projection. He touched it, and moved it; studied the arch again. A second boot sailed through; this time, no blade sliced through.

Clever, clever, Hugon thought, and stepped inside. His hands moved quietly along the walls, finding boxes and caskets, touching each and passing on. Then he touched a shape under a heavy cloth; the right shape, a huge ovoid. He unslung the package from his shoulder, and placed it on the shelf; removed the cloth, and made the exchange.

In the darkness, as the cloth was moved away, the Egg of Fire glowed with a cold green radiance, and vanished again into the sack.

The new Egg glowed as brilliantly, until the cloth was over it again. It was made of glass, by a craftsman of the city, who had been mightily puzzled . . . but well paid. The glow within, Thuramon had induced in some way; Hugon had not asked his method.

But for a while, till that glow died, as it would, the new Egg was as close a counterfeit as would be necessary. Hugon turned back and headed for the narrow window once again. He stopped there, and flattened himself against the wall, staring down into the dark trees below.

Beyond the trees, the lake glittered with torches; the feast was continuing. And farther away, the sky grew redder, with fires that spread in the city. Hugon waited a moment longer, then slid through the window, and out.

At the bottom, he unhooked the rope with a deft flip, and curled it again into the kit. A shadowy shape came up in the dark, and he heard Zamor's whisper.

"Done?"

"Yes," he answered softly. "Now, where's my winged friend?"

230

An orange glow appeared in the dark, as Fraak let a small puff of flame emerge; Hugon heard his wings flap excitedly.

Hugon knelt down beside the dragonet, and put the huge egg on the ground.

"See if you can lift it, Fraak," he said. "Try . . . but remember, if you fly with it, it's a long way."

Fraak uttered a soft note, and Hugon heard his wings beat, with a rapid rattle. Then he rose, up, and up higher, circling. He was holding the sack firmly in his claws as he flew, and now, circling back to the ground, he made a triumphant horn note.

"I can do it, Hugon!" Fraak said, and chuckled. "I can lift it and fly!"

"Good!" Hugon said, and found the scaly head, to scratch it. "Now remember, hide the jewel well when you reach the village. You remember the way, don't you?"

"Dragons have *good* memories," Fraak said firmly. "It smelled of fish, anyway."

"Watch for that little ship we came on," Hugon said. "If it returns, speak to Yorgan, and say we will come soon, but remember, say nothing about this jewel. Humans have strange habits about such things as this. Hide it till we come, and remain out of sight yourself. I wouldn't want to find you caught and put into a cage, or worse."

"I'll do exactly as you say," Fraak said, and clutched the sack. "Hurry, master," he said, and then his wings beat hard, and he lifted into the blackness.

"Trusting the Egg of Fire to that talking lizard," Zamor grunted. "I don't know if that was wise."

"It was the only way," Thuramon said, invisible in the shadows. "We will almost certainly have to flee, and we may be searched at any moment. The madman Sharamash plans to go to his temple at any moment; we were barely in time as it was. Now, soon enough, he will find that the gem is counterfeit."

"And from the looks of that man," Kavin said, grimly,

231

"he'll be monstrously unpleased about it. Thuramon, hadn't we best consider a way out of here?"

"I think so too," a woman's voice came, whispering.

"Gwynna?" Hugon said, seeing a cloaked shadow.

"Yes, of course," she said, tensely. "Master Thuramon, it's high time to go. Listen . . . the gongs of the temple."

A deep, thrumming clang echoed in the trees, again and again. Distantly, a sound of chanting came.

"The Emperor is waiting at the water gate of the King's house until all the nobility is assembled with him," Gwynna said, hastily. "He plans something, I know not what . . . something devilish. He spoke of magic, something he has learned from his demon god. After he's done it, whatever it is, he wishes to lead his nobles and the court to the temple, to open the gate."

"He will take the false jewel, then," Thuramon muttered. "He will know it's false, too, as soon as he attempts to place it on his damned altar. But this magic he spoke of . . . I wonder about that." He moved away. "Come, all of you. We may be able to cross the lake, if there are no torches to show us. As for getting away through the city . . . well, we'll attempt that when the time comes."

They went quickly through the parkland, toward the island's shore; reaching it, Hugon glanced toward the lighted front of the King's house, and the mass of people gathering there. Boat after boat came to the steps, and nobles emerged, with their servants and guards, their women, and bearers who carried some of their possessions. They were fleeing from the great houses around the lake; word must have come of rebel advances in the fighting beyond.

The feast seemed a feast no longer, but a fevered flight, though musicians still played on the balconies, and the Emperor still sat among his folk, regarding the growing crowd with a strange smile.

"I've found a boat," Kavin called, from the darkness.

The others came closer, and saw a boat drawn up on the gravel bank; but the mass of torches at the King's house landing sent a broad glare across the water. If

232

they moved out into that light, they would be seen at once.

From their hidden vantage among the trees, the group could see the distant figures, brightly lit as though upon a stage; the looming mass of the structure behind them, black against the reddened sky, where flashes of light came now and again as a distant cannon boomed. The water, magnifying sound, carried the babble of voices, and, farther away, the deep boom of the temple gongs in the place of the Lord of Night. The Emperor rose, standing like a tiny glittering toy figure at this distance; the black-robed servitors of the temple were gathering around him, and the crowd of panicky nobles was moving back, to clear a wide space.

Thuramon muttered something in a strange language; to Hugon's ear, it sounded like a prayer.

Then, he spoke, as if to himself.

"I must," Thuramon said, and his voice sounded as though he were in pain. After a moment, he said, "I must. Though I never return again . . . Mistress of Men, why must I take this burden, too? Have I not borne enough?"

"Thuramon?" Hugon moved closer. He saw the old man's shoulders, bent as if in pain. Kavin stood on his other side, and his eyes glittered at Hugon's.

"Say nothing," Kavin said, in a commanding voice.

Far away, Hugon saw the Emperor stretch out his hands, and there was suddenly a great silence. The music ceased; the babble of terrified voices stopped. Black-robed figures moved in a wide circle at the Emperor's feet, moving in a silent, hieratic pattern; and in their center, something that seemed to be a pale vapor began to eddy upward.

The Emperor's arms were still outstretched. Now they heard his voice, tiny but clear, crying out a word in an unknown tongue.

Overhead, it seemed to Hugon that there was distant lightning, a blue flash; yet the sky had been clear, he remembered.

233

"What I must do, I shall do," Thuramon said, in a deep voice, and straightened. Hugon could see his face, profiled against the light, as he stared toward the distant scene. His eyes seemed to glow with an inner light.

"All of you," Thuramon said. "Go back, away from me. What I must do . . . is most perilous. Go there, to the boat, and wait."

Reluctantly, the other three moved to the shore where the boat lay; in the darkness, they could not see Thuramon, though there were odd sounds, as he seemed to be busy at some work.

But the Emperor was clearly doing something as well. The strange words he cried out came again, and then a third time; and each time it seemed to Hugon that a strange flicker of light passed by, sourceless, but immensely brilliant. The moving black-robed shapes had begun to move more quickly, and the smoke that rose in the center of their circling was thicker, almost solid.

Then, across the water, a concerted cry rose from those who watched, a sound of blind terror. The gaudily dressed nobles and their women, guards and servants all began to drop, crouching and covering their faces from the Thing that they saw. They screamed and wailed; and the black-robed servants of the Lord of Night were themselves obviously in terror, as they stood encircling the creature that they had brought forth. Only Sharamash seemed unafraid; he stood with arms out, staring down at the thing. It was too far away to see his expression, but they heard his mad laughter ringing across the water.

"What is it?" Hugon asked, hoarsely. He stared, trying to see, but the thing seemed to have no certainty of outline; it was like a pillar of smoke, twice a man's height, that swayed slowly, turning and turning. Even at such a distance, there was something more than terrifying about the Thing; to look at it turned his stomach, as though its very existence made man's life of no worth.

"I thought he couldn't raise his damnable demon without the Egg," Zamor said. "Have we failed, then?"

234

"That . . . Thing . . . is not Ess," Kavin said, in a tight voice. "It is called a Simbavada . . . an elemental form, drawn from another world. It is . . . a hunger, a demon if you want to call it that."

"You seem to know more of the Art than I'd known," Hugon said.

"I know a little," Kavin said. "But not enough to send that monstrous thing back. To call it forth at all, a man would be mad . . ."

"Yonder Emperor's mad enough," Zamor grunted. "Here, now, that creature's growing! Damn it, my axe is in the cart on the other shore!"

"No weapon would protect you against that," Kavin said. "Wait. Thuramon knows."

The smoky thing was indeed growing larger. Now it moved, slow-seeming because of its size, yet with terrifying speed; it passed through the groveling crowd, toward the marble steps that swept down to the water. For a moment, it paused among the crowd; and where it stopped, the figures of those nearest seemed to fall, like empty bundles of clothing, to the pavement. But it moved again, and swept out across the lake, seeming to walk on the water. As it went, it grew larger again; and though it seemed not to touch the water, the lake's surface seemed to be stained in some sickly slime where it had passed.

There was a sudden dim glimmer of light where Thuramon had stood; and Hugon heard the old man groan, a sound of agony as if he had been stabbed. He stared into the dark, and saw a queer glow that seemed to hover above the ground for a distance of a few paces; and in the dim light, Thuramon's body, stretched out.

Hugon ran toward the old man and knelt; he felt the chest, under the gray robe. There was no beat; Thuramon's eyes were closed, and he did not seem to be breathing.

"He's dead," Hugon muttered. His eyes burned, but he stood up, and his mouth hardened.

"Dead?" Gwynna said, at his elbow. "Then we're lost,

235

all of us." She stared down at the body. "And Armadoc, lost for me . . . though I didn't think he could keep such a promise." Her voice shook.

"Dead, then," Zamor said. "But we still live."

"Not for long, if we're caught," Hugon said.

"Not at all," Kavin said in a harsh voice. "If that demon is free for long, no man will live."

Against the red sky, the smoke-shape stood, tall as a tower now. It moved from the west toward the east, across the city, as though it stalked across the tops of the houses.

"It was sent to kill, and it's killing, now," Kavin said. "It will walk, on and on, circling outward and slaying as it goes . . . I don't know how long. But long enough. Long enough to slay every rebel, and his own men as well . . . he does not care. Long enough to walk out into the lands of men, even across that sea . . ." The Prince stood looking down at Thuramon's body. "He tried a mighty magic to thrust it back. And it killed him."

THIRTEEN

Zamor bent down and lifted the body in his arms.

"We'd better get off this filthy island," he said, "and no friend of mine lies on this demon's soil. That other demon, yonder, moves outward, you say? Then, like a forest fire, it's safest to follow him." The big man strode down to the boat and stepped in, laying Thuramon's body carefully on the floor.

The overloaded boat moved, cautiously, into the lake, keeping to the shadows as they rowed.

The brightly lighted front of the King's house was dimmer now, as torches burned out; and they saw that the Emperor was gone, and many others as well. There were still a few who wandered there, apparently too terrified to follow their lord to his black temple; but most of them had gone with him. From the temple itself, the gongs were booming again, with a heavy, insistent clangor.

"I think none will see us," Zamor said. "They look as mazed as a kicked anthill over there. Row, man."

The boat came closer to a landing step, bumped gently.

Then, in a strange voice, Kavin cried out, "Look!"

In the sky, two towering, smoky shapes stood facing each other; swiftly, they seemed to move toward each other. They met, and swirled together in a monstrous embrace.

There were flashes of that sourceless light again, and now, in the darkness, another sound . . . and Hugon's hair lifted, listening. It was that woman's voice that he had heard before . . . and it wailed in sorrow. Kavin heard it too; he stood up in the boat, and his arms stretched out in a strange gesture.

"I'm here!" Kavin called, in a low, almost pleading voice. "Return! I call you to return . . ."

Then, suddenly, the wail ceased, and there was an eerie, high laughter, a sound of almost unbearable joy. At the same moment, the towering shapes in the sky seemed to burn with a glare of scarlet fire, brighter and brighter. Then, there was a shriek of pain, but a shriek of monstrous volume; a sound that tore across the sky itself, and seemed to break the sense of hearing.

"By the Great Snake's Nine Thousand Children," Zamor shouted, "it's gone!"

Both towering smoke demons were gone; the sky was clear of any sign of them. Then, at their feet, Thuramon sneezed.

"You're alive!" Hugon said, staring down at him.

The old man sat up, and his eyes opened; he stared at the others bending over him, with a look of enormous weariness.

"I . . . am . . . alive," he said, very slowly. "Kavin . . ."

Kavin came close.

"You . . . know where my . . . tools are kept," Thuramon whispered, in a voice that seemed an effort with each word. "I require . . . the leaves. Hurry." His head dropped again, but he still breathed.

Kavin glanced up, desperately. "Gwynna, where are we? His things, in the cart we brought with us . . . I need them, swiftly."

"Not far," Gwynna said. "Come . . . the cart was in a carriage yard, behind the palace there." She sprang ashore, and Kavin followed, pausing only to speak a word to Hugon and Zamor.

"Guard him!"

Then he was gone, into the darkness.

"The old man seems to breathe, at any rate," Zamor said, as he touched him.

238

"But he seemed dead, there," Hugon said, puzzled. He laid his own cloak around Thuramon. "He seems very cold, too."

They waited, and at last, Gwynna and Kavin returned, Kavin carrying something and running swiftly. Arriving at the boat, he knelt beside Thuramon, and held a vial to his lips.

After a moment, the old man opened his eyes again, and coughed.

"He'll be well enough in a while," Kavin said. "But we must try to gain the outer walls. The cart is ready."

Zamor gathered Thuramon up, and carried him as they went.

"Thuramon . . . left his body," Kavin said as they came to the cart. The horses stamped and whinnied; they seemed as terrified as the humans had been. Zamor lifted Thuramon in, and the party moved toward the inner wall.

"Left his body?" Hugon asked, as they walked beside the cart. "Then he was truly dead?"

"In one sense," Kavin said. "He had to do it. Though it cost him more than you yet know, Hugon. A fearful price . . . that second smoky thing in the sky. That was Thuramon, himself."

"They'll all die," the Emperor said, capering. His laughter rang out again in the stone corridors, wildly. "All of them, all of them! Where's Paravaz?" He stopped, and stared at the glittering crowd around him. "Paravaz?"

"Alas, Majesty, the Lord Paravaz did not return from the walls of the city," someone said. "He must have been slain."

"But I don't need a Chancellor any more, do I?" Sharamash said, and giggled. "No, not any more. It's a new world, now, all new."

He embraced the cloth-wrapped object in his arms with a sly grin. "Here . . . the key to a thousand worlds

239

beyond, the jewel above all jewels . . . the Egg of Fire!"
He stared down at the cloth and caressed it. "To the
Temple of the Lord of Night, and the Gates!"

The procession moved down through the palace and
out into the night, toward the open doors of the Temple.
It had become a crazy, hysterically excited rout, almost a
mob. Guardsmen at the lower gates and in the halls
watched as the nobility of Mazain poured past them,
shouting and wailing; a few of the men at arms remained
still at their posts, though many had already slipped
away.

But the maddened throng was swept up in belief now;
the advent of the Lord of Night was all that there was
left for them to believe in. As they passed through the
gardens, they could see the ancient and lovely palaces
that lined the lakeshore, the homes of their great clans;
and fire leaped from the windows of one and then another of those palaces. There was a gleam of armor and
spears there, and shouting.

Unless the Lord of Night came to Sharamash's call
. . . unless the Dark Gate opened, and the power was released . . . they were all doomed. They had to believe.
But not all of them did, even now. At the water gate, a
dozen men stood, swords in hand; their women and
slaves about them, waiting for death. These watched the
boats that were putting out from the shore, and spoke to
one another gravely, bidding goodbye.

In the temple, Sharamash advanced with slow steps
toward the enormous silver construction; in his outstretched hands, he bore the cloth-covered ovoid. Light
flickered, blue and lambent, over the twisted columns
and through the crystal globes; the altar lived, with a
new and dreadful life.

Before him a cavity in the structure waited, shaped to
receive the Egg; he knelt, and laid the glowing crystal in
its place.

Rising, he spread his arms, and cried out as silence
fell.

"Lord of Night, Lord of Darkness! Now is your Gate

240

opened, come forth! Come forth and rule us, even I, thy servant!"

The Silver Gate glared as the glow about it grew brighter; a high, humming sound came, rising in pitch, and those who knelt before it moaned in awe. Sharamash fell to his knees, and bowed low.

Then the glow became intolerably brighter, till the whole Temple was lit up as if by the light of day. The silver columns and twisting rods glowed brighter and brighter, with an intense heat that radiated out into the Temple; crystal tubes suddenly cracked, with loud explosions. And the Egg of Fire itself glowed scarlet for a moment; and then disintegrated into a heap of smoking fragments with a tremendous sound.

As the false Egg collapsed, the altar itself began to sag strangely; droplets of hot metal fell from the work, and a smoke of burning rose. A spatter of the hot silver flew across the wide area of the Temple, and worshippers screamed in pain; and one drop struck Sharamash himself on the arm. He leaped up, with a maddened yell, and stood, staring at the melting ruin before him.

And beyond, in his own place, Ess knew that the defeat of this tool was accomplished. He was not angry; he was not capable of anger. He sensed the mind of the biped called Sharamash; it had become a ruin itself, as that Gate he had built had been ruined when the intolerable power had flowed into it . . . without the true crystal to control that flow.

The biped Sharamash is no longer controllable, Ess thought.

He must be abandoned. There is the other, however; the one called Gann. He remains.

The power source, the crystal; it will be taken to another Gate, that old Gate which was used at another time. The biped Gann may take control of that situation, then. He may be able to destroy these other creatures; and he possesses the skill to open that Gate for me. He himself is curiously without the . . .

Here Ess imaged a Something. The Something was a

factor which he perceived in those bipeds he touched, but which he did not in the least understand. It was, to him, something like a color, or a quality. Whatever it was, Gann, alone of all bipeds that Ess had touched, did not have it.

He does not have the Thing, Ess thought. This is strange. In another time, he had it. But now that he does not have it, he wishes to destroy his double, who does have it.

The matter was of no concern. Ess turned his attention to other matters.

Sharamash lay, writhing and shrieking, on the floor before the altar; his voice came, babbling words that no longer had meaning or connection, as he clawed at the stone. And behind him, swords rang, as armed men thrust their way into the Temple, hacking and slashing as they came.

Among those who came through the doors were men who had been high in the Empire. Nobles and lords, and others who were of no high birth, fought shoulder to shoulder. Within the Temple, there was little resistance left; steel-clad men herded the mob within against a wall, while others hacked down those few who fought back.

A tall man in chain mail, with mad eyes, splashed with blood from his helm to his boots, thrust through, and stopped to stare at the writhing figure that lay there before the altar. Behind him, another man, gray-bearded and cloaked, came.

"He is there," Fazakk said, staring down at the Emperor. "Look at him." The Admiral began to laugh horribly, a choking, coughing laugh; he thrust out an arm to halt those who came behind him, and he turned his mad eyes toward the gray man.

"D'ye see him, Paravaz, there? The Thrice Glorious Lord of Lords, King of Kings, Emperor of Mazain!" Fazakk glared madly. "Mazain! Mazain, a sty for swine to wallow in . . . and he, there . . . killer of babies. Look, how he soils himself in fear, like a beast!"

"I had a wife, too, lord Admiral," a man at his elbow said, in a voice colder than ice. He lifted his sword. "Let me make an end."

"Was yours dearer than mine, then?" Fazakk grated. He laughed again, and the laughter echoed in the high roof of the temple, like the sound of shields crashed together.

"No," Fazakk said, grimly. "He shall not die. I wish to place this beast in a cage . . . a silver cage." He stared at the Emperor. "I shall lift him up above the market square by the harbor, where I may see him daily in his cage. He shall live long, long . . . as long as my hate shall live!"

Paravaz glanced at Fazakk with a strange look. The Chancellor was a wise man; he had changed sides only barely in time, with all the troops he could bring over. Now, plainly, he could see his decision had been wise. And yet . . .

"Your pardon, lord admiral," Paravaz murmured, and stepped forward to kneel beside the pitiful creature that had been an Emperor. His hand rose and fell, with the flash of steel in the torchlight; and he came to his feet again, to face Fazakk.

"At the last," Paravaz said, "I remembered that I had sworn service to him." He stared at Fazakk's lifted blade, and saw that death was there before him. "But it was the last service I could do him. I would that I had done it sooner."

The cart rattled northward, along the highroad; a fine rain fell, and the horses' breath blew white mist in the chilly dawn. Gwynna remained with Thuramon inside the cart; he still seemed very ill. Hugon sat on the box, driving, while Kavin and Zamor rode behind on the other two horses.

Their ride through the streets of dying Mazain had been a nightmare, lit by the torches of burning buildings.

243

The North Gate no longer existed; a vast moraine of broken masonry lay across the road, and the cart had had to be drawn carefully over and around the wreck; past a basalt statue of a long-dead king that leaned, headless, over the path; and past dead men, in the ditch and on the road.

There was a foul smell of smoke and death in the air; crows flew by in the gray dawn, crying harshly.

Gwynna looked out of the cart, her face pale; Hugon, on the seat, glanced at her.

"Is he better?" Hugon asked.

"He sleeps, sometimes," Gwynna said, in a low voice. "But then, he speaks strangely, like a child. Hugon, he may be mad."

Hugon said nothing; only drew his cloak closer around him with one hand, and jerked the reins to speed the horses.

The mist was clearing a little, though the rain still fell; Hugon, peering at the roadside, thought he recognized landmarks that he had seen on the trip southward. It could not be much farther to the coast village.

Then, overhead, there was a familiar brazen music, and Fraak sailed down, out of the mist, to career around the cart with joyful pipings. He left circles of blue smoke in his excitement, before he came to a stop on the wooden edge of Hugon's seat; there, he teetered back and forth, wings spread, shaking water drops in all directions.

"Calmer, calmer, Fraak!" Hugon said, grinning down at him and stroking him with one hand. "You're wetting me down with that flapping . . . is all well?"

"Yes, yes!" Fraak cried, excitedly, finally managing to close his wings. He leaped up to Hugon's shoulder, where he clung, making a deep purring sound. "I was afraid!" he said.

"Well, you see we're all alive," Hugon told him.

"There are bad things," Fraak said. "Humans dead all around, many men with swords! And . . ." He tried to remember the word cannon, and failed; instead, he emit-

244

ted a realistic miniature booming sound, and a puff of smoke.

"Did you see the ship, Fraak? The small ship, the one we came here on?"

"It was there, in the sea," Fraak said. "Coming to land. I hid the shining thing," he added. "In a chimney. Nobody can find it, except me!"

"That's very good, Fraak," Hugon said. "You're a clever dragon." He glanced back into the cart. "Now, let's hurry on to that village, eh?" He whistled at the horses, and slapped the reins against their backs.

The cart rattled into the innyard, and drew up. There was no sound from the inn, and the village itself seemed empty, as though everyone had fled, though there was no sign of fighting. Hugon climbed down from the box, and began to unhitch the horses; beside him, Kavin was unsaddling his own horse, while Zamor came up and dismounted.

"There seems to be no one here," Kavin said, glancing at the shuttered windows of the inn; he threw the saddle into the cart, and began to rub down the old horse with a rag.

Then a door opened, and the gaunt innkeeper appeared; he looked as gloomy as he had before, no more and no less. He bore a cocked crossbow in his hand, but he lowered it when he saw Hugon and Kavin.

"There are a good many masterless soldiers about," the innkeeper grunted, as he put the crossbow carefully against a wall. "Man's got to be careful."

"No apologies needed," Hugon said. "We're leaving you a gift, my smiling friend. Not merely these magnificent steeds you sold us, but a cart as well, a carriage fit for nobility." He glanced toward the narrow street. "Do you expect our friend Yorgan and his ship, soon?"

The innkeeper stared glumly at the horses and the cart.

"There's no money about," he grunted. "Can't buy 'em."

"Now, did I mention selling them?" Hugon asked, with

a hurt expression. "Do you take me for a horsedealer? I, sir? I, a poet, hero, and housebreaker of note? I don't lower myself to common trade, I assure you. No, these things are a gift, because I like your cheerful smiling face, sir innkeeper. You remind me of a vulture's breakfast I saw on the road yonder."

The innkeeper's eyes were wary; he evidently thought Hugon was a trifle mad. Hugon thought so, himself.

"A gift, eh?" the innkeeper said.

"Exactly," Hugon told him. "Now, if you felt moved to fetch a pitcher of that . . . ah, I suppose you'd call it wine, I'd be most pleased with you, my man." Hugon shivered, feeling the damp beginning to soak through. "Perhaps you should make that two pitchers, considering everything," he added. "And if you warmed them well at the fire first, I would not mind at all."

The innkeeper made a curious noise which was possibly a sound of assent, or it may have been only wind in his gut; however, he went slowly back inside, taking the crossbow with him. A couple of minutes passed; then he returned, with pitchers of hot wine, which he handed into the cart solemnly.

"Ugh," Hugon said, swallowing a mouthful. He handed the pitcher to Gwynna. "Give our wizard a little. Kill or cure, perhaps. It may be wolf urine, or it may be wine . . . my tongue seems to have lost all skill at telling which. But it's hot." He glanced out. "Ha, Zamor comes, with none other than Yorgan at his heels. I think we may be away and out of this earthly paradise ere long."

"I grow more and more tired of the sea," Hugon said, watching the foremast sway slowly. Gwynna, who sat on a coil of rope, sewing busily, looked up at him and laughed.

"I could sing that song for you, Hugon," she said, plucking a thread between her white teeth. "I've heard it so often of late. Let me see. Could you but place an oar on your shoulder, and walk inland, then some day you

246

would come to a fair city; there, the folk would regard your oar with wonder, and ask 'What's that strange tool you carry, and what's its function?'" She laughed.

"Exactly, sweet lady," Hugon said. "Just as I would tell it, and shall again, till I make a ballad of it."

He regarded her, carefully. It wouldn't do at all, he thought, to make his growing thoughts too clear to this wench. She had no wealth now, nor any high place, no more than he . . . still, such a match would be unwise, Hugon thought. And he had lately acquired a profound desire to find less turmoil in his life. Gwynna, now . . . where she was, there would be turmoil, without a doubt.

She had grown browner, and of a warmly healthy color, these long days at sea; and her eyes had lost a certain wild and bitter look, too. She seemed no longer a great lady, accustomed to servants and unable to aid herself in small matters; instead, she had quickly begun to serve herself in all things. She had brought away only the clothes in which she stood; and now, from odds and ends, she was swiftly making a new wardrobe. But more than that, she had done all such work as was needed, without complaint, swiftly and well; and she had nursed Thuramon, day after day, with skill.

"Has he spoken this morning?" Hugon asked. Gwynna nodded.

"But only a word or two," she said. "Yet, he seems so much better, in body at least."

Kavin emerged from the tiny cabin and stretched himself, staring southeast; he glanced at Gwynna and Hugon, hearing them.

"He's not young," Kavin said. "But I think he'll be himself again. I hope soon . . . we may see the shore tonight."

"Prince . . ." Hugon said, slowly. "You seem to know what ails our warlock, but you've kept your counsel about it."

"I do," Kavin said. "I am also a little learned in the Art, and I have been Initiated, as you know. I don't know if

247

you would wish to know certain things, or how much I may lawfully speak of." He bit his lip, staring at Hugon, and then at Gwynna.

"Very well," Kavin said. "Listen. There are many who have some small skills in the Great Art—from those who cast spells to dry up a cow or bring a wench to bed, to those who have learned all. All the secrets . . . of which the greatest is this." He stopped, considering Hugon for a moment, with an ironic smile. "That it is best not to work magic at all; but only to *know*. To know, without using the thing known . . ."

"Man, that's witlessness!" Hugon said, indignantly. "To wear a sword, and never draw it? To own a fine horse, and never saddle it? What's this?"

"I suspected that you would not understand me," Kavin said. "Well then . . . Thuramon has grown wiser, year after year, and yet never filled with wisdom, seeking more. And at last, he learned that he had come to a place in his wisdom where he must . . . stop, in a certain sense. He has a certain desire . . . a desire that each of us four has, in one or another way. He wishes to return to the place from which he once came."

"That ought to have been more than easy, for a wizard," Hugon said.

"No," Kavin told him. "That place is farther than you can dream of, farther than any land on earth . . . on this earth. It is a stranger journey than any you will ever take, Hugon. And now . . . Thuramon has barred his way home, to himself."

"Barred? How?"

"Certain great acts of high magic . . ." Kavin said, slowly. ". . . these are forbidden to him, because of his . . . Law. His compact with other forces, if you will. He has earnestly restrained himself from all such acts . . . yet, at that last moment in Mazain, it was necessary. That monstrous thing that walked there would have laid half the world waste . . . and Thuramon went out of his body, into a new state of being, to slay it."

248

Hugon shook his head, puzzled. "So, you say his . . . his gods, perhaps, or the Goddess herself, will now punish him for this?" Hugon asked. "Is this the Law you'd have me believe, that a noble and brave action can lead only to what Thuramon must bear?"

Kavin nodded. "Sometimes . . . that is the Law. Quite often."

Hugon shook his head. "No, I will not believe that. No! If I thought thus . . . why, there'd be no use in poem-making, nor in love, nor in honor at all."

Kavin looked at him with a curious expression. "You're a man of greater luck than mine, though I was the one the dragons gave luck. You'll never rule men, or need to."

Hugon laughed. "Or want to. But Thuramon . . ."

"I am myself again," came Thuramon's voice from the hatchway. He came, slowly, onto the deck; his face was very pale, and his eyes deeper set than before, but he seemed to be completely rational, at last.

He held to a taut line for support, but stood; Gwynna rose and went to his side, with a concerned look."

"Thank you, lady," Thuramon said, "but I need no more nursing." His eyes rested on her, for a moment. "You did well and I thank you." And now, he looked toward Kavin and laughed, in a curious way. "Your lady was also of much help to me, Prince. Especially while I spent a certain time wandering, half in this world and half in another, these last days." He came forward and leaned on a rail, stroking his beard.

"She was there, then," Kavin said. "You saw her, as . . . as she was, when she was with me in the light of day?"

"She was there," Thuramon told him.

"Hold," Hugon cried out, and came to his feet, staring around. "I begin to feel most uneasy, friend wizard. That lady, now . . . if she is Kavin's mistress that was, or a ghost that follows him now, or the Goddess herself . . ." He stopped, and grew a little paler. "I remember a voice that spoke to me in Koremon," he said. "I thought it was

249

the Goddess . . . not an invisible nymph." He walked, uneasily, across the deck, his hands searching. "Which is she, then?"

"You'll not catch her that easily," Kavin said, and laughed. "I could not. Yes, she's the same. I have known her long . . . and yet not at all." He spread his hands apologetically, and grinned at Hugon. "She may be the Goddess, for all I know. But each day I seem to learn something new about her, this matter of her passage into that place where Thuramon's mind wandered last . . . that's new, to me."

"I think you're too inquisitive, sometimes, Hugon," Gwynna said. "Even an invisible woman must be spied upon by you." She giggled. "Could you but see yourself, feeling your way there, like a blind lecher . . ."

Hugon turned, and glared at her.

But before he could speak, Kavin cried out, loudly, "There!"

Ahead and to port, a mountainous cape was rising, and farther, a line of breakers showed like a white glimmer on the horizon.

"We'll come ashore there, where there was a town . . . once."

Kavin's voice was so strange that Hugon thought, for a moment, that he was about to choke on something; it was as though the words were forced past some obstruction.

"It is Dorada," Kavin said, and turned away, to stare up at the masthead.

"Dorada?" Gwynna asked, looking after him.

"Once, the people who are now the people of Koremon lived there," Hugon told her. "A land called Dorada . . . Kavin's birthplace. In the end, they all fled, Kavin leading them, and left Dorada empty, a desert. It's all there in old songs . . . how the land was destroyed by war and plague." He glanced aft, toward Kavin's silent figure. "It will be strange for him; to see it again. Empty, for so long . . . though I have heard that men have returned

250

there, in recent years. A few farmers and fishermen, it may be."

"But to go there, to such a place!" Gwynna's eyes were wide. "To see one's ancient home . . . like that! I couldn't bear to see Armadoc so . . . why must we go by this route? Are there no other ways to that valley Thuramon seeks?"

Hugon shrugged. "None shorter. Thuramon's maps show a path, beyond Dorada and up into the mountains. The first time that journey was made, it took a long time; they went from Koremon inland."

"Poor Kavin," Gwynna said.

The breakers opened, and smooth water lay ahead now, a wide bay that ran inland, narrowing as it went. Low mountains ranged on either side, green with pines.

Kavin had gone to stand beside Yorgan, at the steering staff; and Thurmon remained amidships with Hugon and Gwynna. Zamor came on deck, and saw the nearing land. He called out, toward the upper air, "Fraak, you scaly clown, return!"

Fraak sailed down, and landed on the deck. Zamor regarded him with a grin.

"Can you see the land, ahead there?" Zamor asked.

Fraak rattled his wings, and settled himself. "I have been there, today!" he said. "There's a man on the shore!"

"I'd hope there'd be a number of them," Zamor said. "We'll need horses, and food. Hugon, is that place as empty as I'd heard it was, then?"

"I don't know," Hugon said. He extended an arm, and Fraak leaped into his favorite position. Hugon grimaced. "Gods, the fish diet you've been on has given you both weight and . . ." He sniffed at Fraak's triangular, fanged mouth. "Phew, a certain air as well."

"I *like* fish," Fraak said.

"There's no doubt of that," Hugon said. "But you'll have to try another diet for a while; we're faring inland." He glanced shoreward thoughtfully. "You saw men on the shore, there? Fishermen, perhaps?"

"One man, big, wearing scales like mine," Fraak said. "He was Kavin."

Hugon's head snapped round, and he regarded the dragonet with a puzzled look.

"Kavin?"

"He's standing on the shore," Fraak said, confidently.

"No, he isn't," Hugon told him. "Look, there he is, on the deck above us."

Fraak allowed a thin eddy of smoke to curl from his nostrils, and opened his yellow eyes wide. Then he said, "He's there, *too*."

"Wait, now," Hugon said, and considered the matter. "You saw a man who looks just like the Prince, and he is standing on that shore beyond us?"

"Just like," Fraak said. "He wears scales, like me. But he's very bad, the one there."

"Oh, he's bad? Why? Did he shoot at you?"

"No!" Fraak said. "He only stands, waiting, and looking out to sea. But he has no . . ." Fraak stopped, searching for the word. Then he emitted a rippling series of notes, in the dragon tongue. "He has none," Fraak added. "I never saw a man who had none before. Except dead men."

"Thuramon?" Hugon called to the wizard, who turned toward him. "Listen to this. Fraak, what is that, the word you used? The thing you noticed about the man on shore?"

Fraak uttered the notes again. "He had none," Fraak repeated. "But he looks like Kavin, except that his hair is dark."

Thuramon bent a dark gaze on the little dragon, and his fingers touched his beard, pulling thoughtfully.

"This man . . . who looks like Kavin," Thuramon said. "He is alone?"

"No, there are more like him, but little men, hairy," Fraak said. "As many as . . ." He held up a clawed foot, and counted. "That many," he said, extending all five claws. "They haven't got any . . ." the musical phrase again ". . . either."

Thuramon glanced at Hugon and Gwynna. "He means a certain quality, an ι . . . object, which those men don't possess," the warlock said, in a tense voice. "Do you know what that is? No? I can't find a word that describes it, except . . . a soul." His eyes held Hugon's. "That would be the common word, but it is inaccurate. A true self, the eternal and permanent reality of a man. And these men, who wait for us . . . yes, I think it is for us they wait. They have no souls. They are, in one sense dead. But they can move. And slay, I think."

The Virgin's sail slatted as she came about. The bay had narrowed; a broad river entered, and the shore was green with trees and grass. Among the greenery, old walls stood, broken by time and nearly covered; and up river, there were roofs, a village of some sort.

But there, on the bank, figures stood, still as statues. The foremost figure was a man, in a garment that seemed to shine with a coppery glow in the sunlight; it was too distant to see his face as yet. But he stood, with an inhuman stillness, waiting, as the ship drew nearer.

FOURTEEN

Gann waited, and watched the small vessel as it tacked toward the rivermouth. Wind driven, he thought. Nowhere in this world was there any power other than man's muscle, the strength of beasts, and the force of wind and water. Weakness. That would change. Man was meant to bend the forces of nature to his will. The phrase echoed in Gann's strange dead mind, a record of words heard long ago in another world.

He felt the presence of the other, close now . . . so close that it was as if life flowed into him, out of that one, warming him, easing the pain that still burned in his flesh. He had known that the other would come here, and had traveled far, to this place, far and fast.

There were only a few charges in the weapon, Gann thought. It was most necessary that the body of the Other not be damaged in any way; of course, the people with him were of no account in the matter. But at this range, accuracy might be difficult.

And yet . . . the wind-driven ship was moving outward, toward the other shore, and up into the river. It was possible that the primitives aboard it feared strangers, and were fleeing him, Gann considered. He estimated the growing distance. The vessel must be brought closer.

He lifted his arms and called, loudly, in the language he had learned from his human machines.

"Ship!"

Distantly, heads were visible at the rail. One of those was the Other, Gann knew, and the hunger welled within him. He cried out again.

"It's the Other," Kavin said, in a low voice. "He that I saw lying in a tomb of ice, dead . . . my other self. Thuramon, it's he!"

"It is he," Thuramon said, coldly. "Now I know what new tool Ess has sent against us."

"He is myself," Kavin said, his eyes on the shore. "Myself!"

"Yes," Thuramon said. "In a certain sense. You owned that body once, and you left it; that which is truly yourself fled out of that flesh, and sought rebirth. But in that world, that body was not allowed to die completely. Against the Law of Life and Death, it was kept, half-living, as you saw it once before."

The ship was close to the high banks of the far shore, and Yorgan called out, to one of the other men, to keep watch as they moved. On the other bank, Gann walked with steady strides, keeping pace, while five shambling figures followed him.

"He has acquired those poor creatures, too," Thuramon said, almost to himself. "Made them . . ."

"He is myself!" Kavin said, in a voice filled with agony. And suddenly, he clutched the bulwark, and lifted his body, half over the top rail; he twisted, swinging a leg over, ready to plunge into the river and swim to that bank.

"Zamor!" Thuramon cried out, clutching at Kavin's belt. "Hugon, quickly!"

Hugon came, running, and got hold of Kavin's arm; but the other pulled free, with unnatural strength. Kavin's eyes were strange, glazed and mad.

Then Zamor reached him, and his huge arms clamped about the prince's waist, heaving; they fell to the deck, and rolled in wild struggle. Then Zamor's fist rose and fell with a meaty thud, and Kavin lay unconscious.

"I had to strike," Zamor muttered, rising to his knees

256

beside the other. His big hand touched Kavin's face. "By the Snake's mercy . . . no, he will not be hurt too badly." He got to his feet, looking apologetic; but Thuramon nodded.

"That was well done, Zamor," he said. "Had he reached the other bank, the Other would have him now." Thuramon turned, to stare at the distant mailed figure, which had paused.

"He could make himself one with Kavin," Thuramon mused. "That cold and monstrous mind, in a soul and a body that could live as other men do . . . it's not strange that Ess could seize him so."

"We'd best bring the ship in, up there," Yorgan called down. "There's a landing, and a village, see there?"

On the other shore, Gann waited. He called to his Other; but the Other could not come. It would be necessary to use his weapon, he thought. The ship was nearly out of range, and in a moment it would be. Gann lifted his arm, and sighted the thing he carried, carefully.

There was a glare of violet light, and a crash of sound.

The bolt struck the ship's side, high and near the stern; it burned a hole the size of a man's head through the stout timbers and planks, upward, and out through the decking. And also through one crewman, who screamed, and burned like a torch before he fell to the water. In the blackened hole, small flames burned.

"Douse that!" Yorgan barked to the other seamen, setting example with a bucket. They threw water on the flame, while Yorgan ran to the rail, uttering a curse of magnificent complexity.

"May the gods rot my gut, that filthy bastard that did this is out of range!" Yorgan snarled, sighting a crossbow. But he loosed the bolt anyway; it struck the water, halfway across.

"Killed poor old Bungt, the motherless dogsgut!" Yorgan grated. "Yonn, lash a line to the bows, and come help me get the boat overside! I'll tear that scum's foul eyeballs out with my fingers, damn him!"

"Wait!" Thuramon thundered, commandingly.

Yorgan paused, his fury-flushed face turned toward the warlock.

"Wait? For what, till he burns my ship about me?" Yorgan's voice broke, and tears streamed on his leather face. "Bungt! He sailed with us these five years, man! The dog threw fire and killed him, and not a challenge out of us or that one!"

"His weapon can slay you before you reach him," Thuramon answered, calmly. "But he is no longer close enough to fire it a second time, or he would have done so. And he cannot cross running water."

Yorgan stared at Thuramon, and his face paled under the sea tan.

"He . . . cannot . . . cross running water?" Yorgan knew well enough what it was that could not cross a running stream. He shuddered, and uttered the word, low. "Vrykol!"

"No, not that," Thuramon said. "But nearly. Yorgan . . . let me manage this. I have the skill." He touched the man's arm. "I know your sorrow. Be wise, though. Remember the safety of this ship, and the others."

Yorgan uttered a wordless sound, and turned away.

"I must set a stronger barrier between us and that thing," Thuramon muttered. He glanced at Kavin, who still lay unconscious on the deck. "Especially since the creature will call again."

The others had gone to the shoreward rail, and were looking down toward the houses that lay along the riverbank. They were low, log and wattle buildings, thatched; a few chickens wandered among them, and farther along the bank, small boats lay under a shed. All in all, it seemed a typical fishing hamlet, Hugon thought. But it seemed odd that no one had come out of the houses. He saw a faint eddy of smoke from a chimney, and pointed it out to Zamor.

"They might be afraid of us," Zamor said. "There have been pirates, in these seas."

"They would have to be blind not to see we're no such thing," Hugon muttered.

"We could go and see," Gwynna suggested.

"We?" Hugon looked at her. "My lady, this is man's work. If you'll excuse me . . ." He swung himself up and over the rail, to drop to the river bank; he laid a hand on his sword, and moved forward, but did not draw. It might be best to seem as friendly as possible, he thought, moving slowly toward the house where he had seen the smoke.

Behind him, he heard a faint sound and whirled; then glared at Gwynna, who came toward him. She carried a crossbow, with a competent air, and smiled sweetly at Hugon.

"Well, if you must," he said, and turned. But before he could move, a new sound intruded.

Thuramon's voice rang out, in a thundering shout, strange words that meant nothing to Hugon's ear. As Hugon stared toward the ship, a cloud of white vapor eddied up out of the moored vessel. Thuramon's voice echoed out again, and the cloud swelled larger; it poured, like thick milk, out and over the river.

The cloud spread, and stood like a white wall; the other bank vanished, hidden completely.

"It seems Thuramon is about his craft again, thank the Goddess," Hugon grunted. "That would be a barrier to any more lightning bolts from that demon on the other bank, I hope."

He turned toward the house again, and reached its door; pushing it open, he looked inside.

"Nothing but a fisherman's hovel," he grunted, and stepped in.

On a stone hearth, a fire smouldered, nearly out. Pots and plates stood in disarray, as though a meal had been interrupted. And other objects, scattered about, seemed to say that those who lived here had departed in haste, gathering up whatever they could carry. Hugon turned and went out again; Gwynna was coming from another house.

"They've all run away," she said in a puzzled voice.

"Something to do with our mailed friend over there," Hugon said. "Though Thuramon said he couldn't cross here . . . but there may be a way for him, farther up the river. I wonder if he's been here, and the villagers ran . . . like wise men, at that."

They went back toward the ship; Zamor came toward them as they approached, and Fraak as well, sailing down to the ground.

"The dragon says he saw men, fleeing out to sea, in small boats," Zamor said. "They went by another channel, eastward, so we didn't see them. Those would be the village folk." He stared about. "I wonder what could frighten fishermen so much. That creature over the river . . . he doesn't look any more than a man, to me. He's got no more than five others with him."

"He is more than a man, Zamor," Thuramon's voice came from above, at the ship's rail. "Or less than one, if you wish. But you cannot fight him with your hands alone. He carries a deadly tool, for one thing; and both he and his creatures will not die as easily as a man might, though you break them into pieces." Thuramon laughed wryly. "Die, indeed. They are long dead, in a way, already."

"Well, then, we'd best leave them as quickly as we can," Hugon answered. "Ah, Prince Kavin! Awake again?"

Kavin stood at the rail, rubbing his head with a rueful grin. Zamor looked up and spread out his big hands in a gesture of apology.

"I tried not to strike too hard, Prince Kavin," Zamor said. "But it was most necessary. You were about to leap into the river."

"I know," Kavin said. "And I thank you, Zamor. You've my leave to do that again, as hard as you like, if that spell takes me again." He shivered.

260

"You're right, Hugon," Thuramon said. "We should move as quickly as we can. Perhaps there may be another village upriver, and horses; but as it is, we'll walk." He swung himself over the rail, lightly, and dropped to the bank. In one hand he carried a heavy sack, which he swung over his shoulder; there, Hugon knew, the Egg of Fire lay secure.

"My ship," Yorgan said, gloomily, gazing at the burned hole.

"If you're wise, Yorgan, you'll patch that with a sail, and set out again," Thuramon told him.

"Not if there's any chance to set my hook into that damned demon over there," Yorgan said, but shuddered. "Oh, curse it . . . you're right. If he's what you say he is, I'd have no way to do him properly. It's bitter in my mouth, it is. Bungt dead, and my ship wounded, and not to see the rat's son dead that did it." He spat. "But I'll sail. I will. And good luck, warlock. Kill me that thing, that's all I ask."

"If it can be done, it will be," Thuramon said. "Or he will kill us. There's no third choice. But we must reach the Black Valley first, and he must do so too."

The old man swung the sack to his shoulder, and turned to stride away along the river bank; behind him, the others came too.

On the other side of the river, Gann stood absolutely still, his cold, empty eyes fixed on the whiteness of the mist that lay on the river. He could not sense the presence of the Other. The mist . . . sang. It was as if a sound came from it, a low, soothing murmurous chant. He did not wish to move. The sound seemed to make the lance of pain within him duller.

Gann continued to stand, watching the white mist; and the sun moved, across the sky, and downward, into the western horizon. His five companions sat or stood, as immobile as himself.

261

Then the darkness deepened; and the mist thinned, and vanished, as the light went. Gann moved.

I was tricked, he thought. A hypnotic effect of some sort . . . indicating a slightly higher degree of technology than I had thought this world possessed. One of them, the natives in that ship, is a man of some skills. That would be logical, if he intends to attempt the operation of the mechanism of the Gate. He, then, is also to be killed, as quickly as possible.

They walked, in single file, along the narrow trail that followed the river; Thuramon ahead, then Kavin, who walked with a strangely stiff air, eyes ahead, as though he could not bring himself to look around. After them, Gwynna, carrying her share of the provisions and walking with as long a stride as any of the men, and last, Zamor and Hugon. Zamor whistled happily, and swung the long axe lightly; Fraak, sometimes in the air and sometimes on Hugon's shoulder, replied to Zamor's whistled tune with a rippling counterpoint of notes as he flew.

There was no sign of their pursuer yet; Gwynna glanced toward the distant bank of the river, on the other side, and saw nothing moving. Ahead, the remnants of a stone bridge rose from the water, and just beyond it, part of a fallen tower still stood above the trees, roofless.

"Prince Kavin," Gwynna called. He glanced back.

"The bridge and tower, yonder," she said. "It looks much like the ward tower on the Brynn, at home. And this great valley . . . why did your people not return here? There seems to be no reason to fear it."

Kavin's eyes were guarded. He flicked a glance toward the bridge, and his mouth tightened.

"You forget, lady, I was no longer with those people, the Doradans, after they reached Koremon," he said. "Not for long, at any rate. Perhaps they couldn't bear to return here. There were memories connected with this

262

land that might be difficult to bear." He continued to walk, silently; then, "That tower was part of a manor called Muronik. I was there many times; a fair hall, filled with good and happy folk." He looked to either side, where pines grew densely along the trail and up the slope of the river bank. "You can see it. This was farmland, where we ride now."

It had been so long ago, Gwynna thought. But to Kavin, it was as if it had been yesterday. That must be strange, she thought, as strange as if she were to return to Armadoc and see naught but empty fields, and ancient ruined walls. She shivered at that thought.

"There, ahead of us," Kavin said, in a low voice as if he spoke to himself. "Only a few more hours journey along the river, and we will come to the falls of Granorek. And the castle, below the falls . . . the hold of Granorek. It was there that the best man of Dorada died a long time ago, fighting the beasts that had been loosed against this land." He stared ahead grimly. "Loosed by Ess and his servants," he said.

Behind Gwynna, Hugon heard Kavin's words.

"A fall?" he asked. "Then how does the river turn above it?"

"Eastward," Kavin answered. "Yes we'll have to cross there, and then there'll be no barrier between us and that one."

"He is a full day behind us," Thuramon said, serenely. "And on foot, though he walks swiftly."

"So are we," Hugon said, and grimaced. "As both my feet could tell you, if they could speak."

"And if you used your eyes, master Hugon," Thuramon said, "you'd look where your feet are walking. There's a sign there, that we may not need to walk much farther, if we're fortunate."

Hugon glanced at the trail, and uttered a short bark of laughter.

"Blind, I am!" he said.

There were fresh droppings, and hoofprints on the

263

path; looking carefully, Hugon saw that they were shod hooves, as well. Not wild horses; so much the better.

And then, around a bend, they came out into an open space, and saw the wall. It was made of stout pine logs, topped with small platforms here and there, and with a heavy gate in it. The gate was closed, by a stout wooden door. There seemed to be no movement at all visible; but there was a smell of wood smoke in the air.

"Wait," Kavin said, sharply. The group came to a halt; Kavin went forward, walking deliberately, till he reached a point midway in the clear space before the walled village. There he stopped, and looked toward the closed gate.

"You, within!" he cried out.

Somewhere inside a horse whinnied loudly. Then, from the wall, a short spear flew, and thudded into the ground at Kavin's feet. He did not flinch, or step back. He stood, waiting.

"Go away, demon!" a voice cried from the wall.

"I'm not a demon," Kavin answered. "I am only a man, like yourselves!"

There was a sound of argument behind the door. Then, slowly, the door opened, a space wide enough to allow a man to slip out. The man who emerged was a thin, long-legged fellow, in a tunic of skins, with a head of wild hair that stood out like a furze bush. He wore a heavy chain of what looked like gold around his neck, on which a curiously ornamented disk hung, and he looked very frightened.

He came toward Kavin, very slowly and cautiously, step by step; Kavin noted that the fellow's teeth seemed to be chattering.

The man paused, and stared at Kavin with wide, frightened eyes. He looked deeply puzzled, as he studied the other.

Then he said, slowly, "Are you—you are not the demon, then."

"My name is Kavin of Hostan," Kavin said. The man's

264

eyes widened even more. He turned, and cried out, toward the wall.

"He's not the demon! He's a man!" The fellow paused, and added, "He bears the name of Hostan!"

"As you bear the clan-sign around your neck," Kavin said, as the man turned back toward him.

"We are Hostan, also," the man said. "I am Gred. But sir, you resemble a certain demon who passed this way three days ago." He stared at Kavin, hard. "Greatly do you resemble him, except the hair . . . and you do not wear the strange mail he did. But your face is not as his was, either, though much alike."

Kavin nodded. "I know the creature you mean," he said. "He pursues us, and will slay us if he can."

The gate swung open, and revealed a knot of nervous men, holding spears and axes; village houses, from which women peered with frightened curiosity. Kavin called the others to come forward, and they went into the village.

The locals' nervousness wore off quickly; in a matter of minutes, they were talking freely.

The "demon" had passed, going downriver; and he had casually killed three of the people of the village, apparently for no better reason than that they were overcurious about him.

His followers, demons as well, according to the local view, seemed to have killed a farmer farther up the river, and in the same reasonless manner. The creatures were somehow visibly evil, creating terror simply by their appearance. The folk of the fishing villages had fled already.

It puzzled the villagers greatly when they saw the strong resemblance between Kavin and the "demon"; but they evolved a kind of explanation that did well enough, saying that the demon had merely taken on a man's appearance, to confuse folk. But before Kavin had been with them for more than a few minutes, they knew him to be of their own blood.

265

They were descendants of peasants, once peasants of Kavin's own clan-holdings; their ancestors had hidden, or fled, during the terrible destruction of the valley of Dorada. Then, with a peasant's tenacity, they had crept back, one by one, and begun to live on their ancestral lands once more. There were only a few of them, scattered widely over the land; but still, Dorada was not wholly dead after all.

"We have many horses," Gred told Kavin. "You must ride quickly. The demon is terrible; he strikes men down with lightning. If he pursues you, you must go quickly."

There were horses, the short-legged, muscular little horses Kavin knew well. They were saddled and mounted before another hour had passed, and riding north again, with half a dozen remounts following behind them.

As they came at last to the ford above Granorek, and crossed the river, there was still no sign of the pursuer. Ahead, the land rose in long sweeping meadows toward the mountains, and they rode on toward that range.

Miles behind, Gann strode on, tirelessly. He came to the ford, and saw the muddy hoofprints; he stood, and stared at the distant mountaintops, red in the late afternoon sun. Then he went forward again, steadily.

It was the third day since they had entered the mountains. They had ridden along trails no wider than would accommodate a single horse at a time. Sometimes there were no trails at all, but only precarious scrambling across slopes of loose rock, and snowdrifted gorges to be negotiated with great care. Above them, the huge peaks rose into the cold sky; and everywhere there was snow, though they were by no means as high as the highest ridges.

Thuramon seemed completely certain of the paths he took. Once or twice he consulted notes he had about him; but he seemed to know the way without trouble.

There were humans living in the mountains, as was

clear from such evidence as burned spots where campfires had been, and the tracks of the elami they rode. But they seemed invisible, even to Fraak's sharp eyes, when he sailed high overhead.

This time, Fraak saw something more disturbing; he came down, in a swooping rush, chattering his news.

"The bad man!" he said. "He is close! He is walking, fast, in the valley behind us!"

Hugon spurred his horse up, to ride beside Thuramon.

"Master Thuramon," he said, "that creature behind us. Could we not make a stand? I dislike this constant fleeing. Can't he be killed at all, or hurt at least?"

Thuramon stared from under thick white eyebrows, and said nothing for a long while. Then, he spoke slowly.

"Yes, he can be killed, like any man. But he wears armor that is proof against most blades and almost any arrow, even a crossbow bolt. And he has the weapon you saw, that he used against our ship."

"I've been considering that," Hugon said. "Look you; he had more than one chance to let fly with it, yet he missed every chance save one. Now, that's the way of it with a man who's got only a few arrows in his quiver. Could it be that his weapon's the same way, with but a few bolts to it?"

Thuramon nodded. "That's possible," he said, musingly. "Yes, quite possible."

"Another thing," Hugon said. "His purposes. He seems to wish to reach prince Kavin, more than anything else. But not to slay him, if what you say is so. He needs Kavin alive, to make this damnable exchange of souls, or whatever it is. Am I right?"

Thuramon nodded. "Yet, he'll slay any other he can," the old man said warningly.

"You kept Kavin from yielding to whatever devilish spell the creature cast, back there," Hugon said. "Can you do that again, if need be?"

Thuramon seemed troubled. "I don't know," he said.

267

"Not always, I fear. It may be that Kavin himself may have to fight that black glamoring, without help."

Kavin, just behind them, was listening; his face was set strangely, in a look of cold determination.

"Thuramon," Kavin called, and the warlock turned in his saddle to look back at him.

"Ahead, there, where the ground is more level," Kavin said. "Draw rein there. I wish to speak with you."

The horses clattered into the level space and pulled up. Kavin reined his mount beside Hugon and Thuramon, and leaned forward, gripping the horn of his saddle, his head bent for a moment. Then he looked up, his eyes strangely dark.

"There, above, that doubled peak shaped like a wolf's tooth. You see it? That lies above the Black Valley." He smiled, without humor. "I should know it well, that landmark. We're no more than half a day's ride from the pass that leads inward."

"We've only an hour or two of light left," Hugon said, glancing up at the sun.

"Use it, then," Kavin said. "Waste no more time. Thuramon, you have the Egg of Fire. The Gateway lies before you. And you need no help from me in binding Ess. Do you, warlock?"

Thuramon shook his head. "None can do that last work, except myself," he said.

"Yet that other who follows will reach us before we reach the pass," Kavin said, looking from one to another.

"Prince Kavin!" Hugon said, suddenly. "No!"

"Yes," Kavin said. "I must remain to meet him. He is my fate, as I am his." He looked at Thuramon. "I remember now, old master. Even the name I bore, in that other life. Gann, I was called." Kavin turned in his saddle, to look toward the ridges behind. "And there, beyond that ridge, Gann's body . . . *my* body . . . comes to greet me."

"Not alone," Hugon said. "The wizard needs no help

268

from me any longer." He loosened his sword, and bit his lip to control a certain nervousness in his voice. It was necessary, Hugon thought; if a man's to sound brave, though he's not, he must not squeak or quaver. For once in all my rogue's days, Hugon told himself, I've found that time at which I can be a man of honor. Or be mistaken for one, at any rate.

"My Lady," he said to Gwynna, "take this talkative beast . . . since I stole him from you in the first place . . . and keep him in memory of me, if I come not again." He grinned at her. "Know that I've had a fine passion for you, but I've no wish to offer you my slightly soiled hand. And I could afford no other gifts, alas . . . till now." He dug into his pouch and brought out a small sack. "Take this as well, and use it, if you regain Armadoc or not."

"I am staying with you!" Fraak cried out, his tail curling around Hugon's arm for a better grip.

"But you're my friend, small scaly one," Hugon said gently. "And if I ask you, as friend, to do me the service of going with the lady, what then?"

"Now, hold!" Kavin snapped. "I need no help. You fool, you'd be cooked like a chitterling before you had a chance to lay blade on that Thing."

"I had another notion, Prince," Hugon said. "This . . . Gann, I think you called him . . . is not entirely invulnerable." He pointed to the narrow pass ahead. "He'll have to pass there, as we will . . . and I'd had a thought or two . . ."

"Kavin, if you're to be burdened with my wordy friend here, you'll have no time for anything else," Zamor broke in. "Look, I'll stay as well. If only to keep Hugon from getting in the way. But then, if he wishes, he might talk that demon of yours to death."

"I want neither of you to stay," Kavin said. He looked at them both. "There's neither need nor use in it. Listen, now. I told you that creature yonder is *myself*. All my

269

life has led toward this place . . . and the former life, when I was Gann. I must pay my way, and the time of payment has come."

"Kavin," Thuramon said, "he may seize your mind, as he nearly did before. Remember; when you saw him first, in his tomb of ice . . . even then you nearly fell."

"I remember," Kavin said. "I saw . . . what I had been, in that life. The power of that drew me, but I remember more, now. There was glory, and we were like gods . . . but we were growing less than men, as well. That world died, Thuramon. Gann should also have died. Because he did not die entirely, he and I must meet and only one will . . . be." He stared at Thuramon. "I think I can hold against him, now," he said. "And he dares not use his weapon against me, as you said. But I can use mine against him." His hand dropped to his swordhilt.

Thuramon nodded. "It may be that you can resist," he said. "But may the gods help you if you cannot." He glanced at the others. "Come . . . be reasonable. Kavin would meet Gann . . . alone."

He pulled at the reins, and his horse clattered toward the narrow pass ahead. After a moment, Gwynna swung her mount around to follow him, with a swift, strange glance at Hugon. But Hugon waited, his mouth set in a stubborn line, till Zamor reached across, and slapped his horse's flank a mighty blow with his open hand.

Hugon's horse whinnied, and sprang away, galloping toward the pass, Zamor following. But once through the gap, a slit in the rock that was as narrow as a door, Hugon yanked furiously at the reins, bringing the horse back on its heels as Zamor reached him. He swung down from the saddle, and flung Fraak free, to sail up and circle around; he himself headed doggedly toward the slope of rock beside the narrow trail.

"Hugon, you fool!" Zamor called out, and slid out of his own saddle. He undid the lashing that held the long axe, and twirled it, staring up at Hugon's climbing figure.

"Since you've made up your mind to leave your damned bones here," Zamor called, pleasantly, "I may as well stay too. Wait for me, brother."

FIFTEEN

He was very near, Gann knew. He lifted his head, and
his empty eyes stared toward the trail that wound up
ahead. Yes, the other was there . . . and he waited, no
longer fleeing.

Gann moved with long strides around the turn, and
into the open space among the rocks. There were long
shadows now; the sun was nearly set. And the other
stood there, silently, a tall figure in that primitive cloak of
his, leaning on a long straight sword whose point was set
in the ground.

A sword, Gann thought. He stopped, and his arm went
out, gesturing at the five who followed him; they too
halted at the command.

Gann stared at Kavin, and the hunger grew stronger
. . . like a leaping fire, up and up. And the pain, too; it
lanced through him. His hand went to his chest, and he
clutched at it in an involuntary gesture.

And, most strangely, Kavin's hand moved in the same
way; the mirrored face twisted into lines of agony, as
Gann's did.

We are linked already, Gann thought, staring at the
other. He stepped forward, slowly, very slowly, his eyes
on the other.

"You . . . know . . . me," Gann said. His voice was
hollow, and the words came with great difficulty.

"You are Gann," Kavin said. "You are myself."

"No," the other said, in that strained voice. "I am
Gann. You are Gann. WE are Gann." He took another
step forward. "Yield. Yield, and we . . . shall . . . be . . .

one." And suddenly louder, "ALIVE." And another step.

"I remember the pain," Kavin said, quietly. "I should have died when the surgeons did their work. But I did die, Gann. Gann is not real." He stared at the other. "Gann is merely a remnant. As though I had cast away an old cloak, torn and of no use . . ."

"I . . . LIVE!" the other said, in a deep, hollow shout. His eyes glared.

Kavin's sword came up; he stood, legs slightly apart, his cloak wrapped around his left arm, the long blade moving and seeking. His eyes moved over the scaly armor that covered Gann, studying it with a swordsman's skill.

"One of us must die," Kavin said, in a completely calm voice. "You died a long while ago. In another world, Gann."

"I AM GANN!" the other said, and stood, with the curious weapon in the crook of his arm, watching the lifted blade. "I AM GANN. I WILL NOT DIE!"

Kavin moved forward a single step.

"You . . . know . . ." Gann said. "It . . . was . . . the great age. What we . . . had done. So . . . much. Power. To . . . know . . . all . . . things." He stared at Kavin, and the sword point wavered slightly. "I cannot kill myself," Gann said. "You. Cannot do that either."

Then Kavin lunged forward, and the point struck, sliding toward a nearly invisible joint at the shoulder. It went in, and the other staggered back; he fell to his hands and knees, and remained there, head downward.

Kavin staggered, and fell back a step. His face contorted; the pain that was Gann's now struck Kavin's body as well.

Then, Gann's face came up; he stared at Kavin, from the position he still held, on all fours. Blood, dark and strange in appearance, welled from the corners of his mouth.

"We share . . . even that," Gann croaked. His face contorted into a horrible parody of mirth. "I CANNOT DIE," he said, and began to crawl toward Kavin.

274

Kavin lifted the long blade, and . . . froze. He could not strike again. The dead eyes that had once been his own stared at him; the empty shell that was himself crept, bleeding in great drops that splashed in the dust, toward him. And Kavin stepped backward, foot by foot.

Again he tried to strike, and could not; and once more he stepped back. They were within the narrow cleft in the rock, and still the dead thing crawled on, toward him.

Kavin backed away again, a distance this time; he flung back his head, and cried out in the dreadful pain that clawed at his flesh, wordlessly. Then, as he began to feel his very self dissolving, flowing back toward that other . . . there was a cool hand touching his face. A voice, whispering.

"You . . ." Kavin said, swaying dizzily.

"I am here," the voice said.

Gann was there, in the narrow space, framed by the columns of rock on either side; he crept, still, and bled. And now he lifted his head, and the dreadful eyes glared; and he laughed, a sound like no laughter heard on earth.

"I HAVE YOU!" he said.

Then there was an enormous thundering sound. Dust billowed up, in a outward rolling wave, as rocks cascaded into the cleft. Amid the roar of the fall, the voice of Gann came in a long, terrible, scream . . . and then was silent.

Kavin, his face gray with dust, stood and stared.

Then Hugon came sliding and slipping down the rock face, Zamor behind him. Fraak arched across the sky, high above, screaming a wild cry of triumph and leaving a trail of smoke.

"Kavin!" Hugon came, running. "Gods, man, are you hurt badly?"

Kavin stared at him and drew a hand across his face.

"I'm . . . not hurt at all," he said, and his voice sounded strangely to him, in his ears.

"You look nearly killed," Hugon said. Zamor grunted agreement.

"I'll never doubt Thuramon's word again," Hugon went on, as he helped Kavin walk toward the waiting horses. "That . . . thing. I saw your point go into it, and I thought that was the end of it; nothing human could take a foot of steel in the weasand and go on . . . but that creature did. Saw it crawling, like a broken-backed snake . . ." Hugon stopped, with a shudder.

Zamor laughed. "Hugon was near ready to foul his breeches, I thought for a minute. But I *felt* the damn thing, and I was as fearful as he was." His big hand touched his belt. "But the Dragon's Gift here did it. I used that strength; pushed a rock the size of an oxwain, and the whole top of that peaklet, there, fell on the demon."

Kavin looked from one to the other as he pulled himself into the saddle.

"I was ready to refuse your help," he said.

Hugon swung into his own saddle. "Let's ride, before the darkness comes," he said. He glanced back. "'I wonder what's become of those others with your demon brother, yonder?"

Fraak, sailing overhead, cried out, "They fell down!"

Hugon looked up. "Scaly clown, come down here!" And as Fraak landed on his shoulder, "Fell down? How?"

"They fell down, they don't move," Fraak said, settling down. "They are all dead."

"They moved by his will," Kavin said over his shoulder. "And he is gone." His face suddenly changed, oddly, and his eyes widened. "Gone?" A shudder passed over him, and he closed his eyes for a moment; then opened them. "Yes, he has. I'm sure, now."

After the sun had set, it became increasingly difficult to thread their way along the narrow trails. They had caught up with Thuramon and Gwynna by this time; Gwynna, turning to see them galloping after, uttered a

276

low cry as she saw Hugon. Then, when he came nearer, she gave her firm opinion of fools who tried to get themselves killed for no very good reason that anybody could see. She continued on the subject for some time, while Hugon merely grinned quietly.

Now the sky was starlit, and the rocky path was utterly black. Thuramon would not stop, however. He manufactured an odd torch, out of materials he extracted from his leather bag; a stick that smoked and flared with an eye-hurting white light. Carrying this, Thuramon peered ahead, as his horse cautiously picked its way. Twice, a horse nearly fell; but at last the path broadened, and became easier.

"We are in the upper pass now," Thuramon called out. "See, now that the moon's rising, we'll have enough light."

"Great Snake, what's that thing?" Zamor cried out, reining in. "A gallows for giants?"

Behind the gaunt framework, the moon rose, making the skeletal shapes resemble some cyclopean gallows.

Thuramon cried out, hoarsely triumphant.

"The Gate!"

The horses clattered down the long slope toward the tall framework. It was farther away than it had seemed, and much larger as well. Before they reached it, the moon was still higher in the sky, and the whole valley was bathed in silver light.

The valley was like a great bowl, with a level bottom; in the end nearest the riders, the framework stood, and not far away, an enormous building rose. The building was windowless, dark, and apparently a ruin; Hugon, gazing down at it, thought it was a miracle of ugliness. He wondered if men could build with such an apparently deliberate desire to offend the eye, as he studied its squat enormity.

"A Temple to Badness," he said aloud, as they drew rein at the foot of the framework.

"What?" Kavin asked.

"That building," Hugon told him. "If there were a spe-

277

cial guild for the making of pure grim ugliness, they built that. What is that place, anyway?"

"The workshops of those others, the servants of the creature called Ess," Kavin said. He stared at it, with dark eyes. "There I came, and met them . . . and met Ess, afterward. And there I stayed, gripped in some sort of magical sleep, for these long years."

Thuramon had dismounted, and taken down his gear from the saddle. He was busy about the gigantic metal framework's base; he knelt, examining something, and emitted a harsh laugh.

"They built well, those Lords of Death," Thuramon said.

The others dismounted, too, and gathered around him. He had risen to his feet, and now kicked a metal pillar with his foot, and chuckled.

"They built it to stand," he said. "But they were no fools either concerning human nature. They covered the lower standards with common iron, knowing that otherwise they'd need to guard their Gate by night and day. Do you know what's beneath those rusty plates? No? It's silver, pure silver." Thuramon stared up at the towering thing, and laughed again.

"It's a most remarkable Gate," he said, in a low voice. He glanced at the others, and nodded, slowly. "Yes, I know . . . not one of you could wholly understand this thing we stand before. I'll not even try to explain. But it is a door to other worlds . . . and a door to other times, as well, depending on how it is opened."

Thuramon knelt, and carefully brought out the Egg of Fire. The huge jewel shone with a pale fire, almost brighter than the moonlight that illuminated the scene. He took the Egg to a metal column, and felt carefully along the iron plates; a plate sprang open, like a cabinet door. Thuramon placed the jewel in the dark space within, and closed the plate again.

Suddenly, lambent violet flame seemed to run lightly up the skeleton of metal, leaping from girder to girder;

spheres of blue light danced on the tips of the columns.

A wide sheet of light spread across the open space between the columns, a glowing pane of light that shimmered like a curtain, but hung steadily in place.

"The Gate is opened," Thuramon said in a shaken voice.

Hugon gazed at the curtain of light, speechless for once. Then he heard Thuramon's voice again.

"The first task is that most important of all . . . to bind the being called Ess forever in the place where he cannot touch man's mind again." Thuramon stopped, and stared at the light for a long time before he spoke again.

"This, I must do alone," he said. "Wait here. If I do not return, I have failed. Remove the Egg of Fire, and the Gate will close again; take the Egg to the Dragon Isle and give it to them, to guard forever. Thus, this world will be safe from Ess for a time, and perhaps another will finish my task." He lifted a hand. "In the Goddess' name, I bid you farewell." And Thuramon stepped into the glow, and was gone.

The universe had run down, like an ancient clock left at last unwound. Here and there, a few dim red stars still glowed, floating in the utterly black cosmos together, as if huddled close for warmth.

Matter itself was aged; energy gone from the spinning particles, and in the enormous empty darkness, not even a frozen planet was left.

There was a single huge red star, near the center of all. Around it, certain highly unlikely and very wise beings moved, in a way that no human mind could ever understand. The beings were separate, and yet they were one; they possessed duration, in a way, but they could bend time as a man twists a rod of soft metal.

One . . . or perhaps several . . . of these beings communicated with another . . . who was perhaps also the same being.

A communication is received, the being said.

279

A being, made of archaic materials, has caused a message to be recorded. The being is-was-will be in a different time and place.

The message refers to the Portion called . . . Ess. (The name was unspoken, because sound was no longer possible in that place.)

The Portion is moving in an uncontrolled manner. It is necessary that the Portion be reintegrated.

End of communication.

The creature that was called Ess was suddenly drawn out into an unimaginable place, along a direction of travel that was at right angles to every other direction in the universe. It flashed out and away, and time folded behind it as it went.

The Portion has been reintegrated. Entropy is once more in balanced flow.

And in the curious place where Thuramon was, he knew that he had succeeded at last; he groaned, and his ancient bones protested, as he finished the last step of the work. Then he turned, and went back through the curtain of light.

Broad daylight poured down over the valley; Thuramon stood, swaying slightly with weariness, and saw the tethered horses, and the figures that waited. Zamor saw him first, and shouted for joy. Then the others saw, and came running toward him.

"It is done," Thuramon said. He closed his eyes. "Done . . . at last."

After a minute, he opened his eyes again.

"Now, the rest of our work," he said, briskly. "I gave my word to you, Lady Gwynna, that you might see your home again in Armadoc, and that your crime might become as if it had never been."

"Can you do that?" she said, her eyes wide.

"I can," he said. "But remember. You will know what

280

you did, though it will never have been done in the memory of any man. Do you understand me?"

"No," she said, but her hands were gripped into tight fists. "No, but whatever the price, do it."

Thuramon's eyes were holding hers. "You will return, through time, to that year in which you betrayed Armadoc to the Empire. You will be there, and you may lead whatever life you choose. Be that woman who betrayed her trust and broke her oath . . . or anything else."

"But," she stared at him. "If I go there . . . to step across years in that way . . . I don't understand. Will there not be another Gwynna, my younger self, there in my place, ruling Armadoc?"

Thuramon nodded. "Your logic is clear," he said. "So, indeed, there will be. Yet, all you need to do is touch her hand with yours, and in that moment, you alone will exist; she will vanish."

"Thuramon!" Zamor stared at him, wide eyed. "Look you, man. Give the lady this; she goes, as you say, to another year. Then where, in the Great Snake's name, am I? Where's Hugon? Why, you're about to change the web of things that have *happened!*"

Thuramon chuckled. "I'd never thought to find so much wisdom being thrown about so carelessly. Yes, time will change, Zamor. But you need not change. You will stand here, exactly the same as now."

"You're certain?" Zamor asked, scowling. "I'd not like to find myself back in the galleys, for instance. Or . . . hold, now. Would there be two of me, as well? I'm growing weary of this affair of twins hither and thither."

"Only one of you, and free as you now are," Thuramon said. "How could this world have room for two such?"

"Now, one more question," Hugon broke in. "D'you know, master wizard, this fiddling with the clock gives me a most uneasy feeling. Look, now. Mistress Gwynna returns to her home in Armadoc, as she wished. Good. She leads a most exemplary life, does *not* betray her wardenship, and doubtless contracts a fine and fruitful marriage with some good gentleman . . ."

"Hugon, you damned rhyming jackanapes . . ." Gwynna began, her eyes flashing. But Hugon plowed on.

"Thereafter, Ess being absent, the Emperor retains what wits he had, which seemed not too many as I've heard it. Yet, there is no rebellion, no burning of Mazain . . ." He flung out his hands in a despairing gesture. "Gods! No, Thuramon, don't attempt to explain it to me. Only assure me as you assured Zamor. I wish to remain Hugon, the one and only Hugon, unique in a world of lesser men."

"You will," Thuramon said. "And, if you choose to travel in time as well, you may remain unique in the same manner as I gave the lady. Touch your double's hand, and you are one again."

"Travel? In time?" Hugon shook his head. "No, thank you, but no."

Thuramon turned to Kavin. "And now, Prince . . . our last work." He stared at Kavin, and suddenly Thuramon seemed to look much older and wearier.

"It was said in the old tale," Thuramon said, "that the Prince returned to Koremon, having defeated the dread evil of the Black Valley. There, he ruled wisely and well for many years, until he was buried in that mighty tomb." Thuramon's voice grew lower. "It was said, also, that there was a certain wizard who stood always by that king's right hand, and lived long years after him."

"I begin to see," Kavin said. "I must return. The king who came back from the Valley was . . . myself." He laid his hand on Thuramon's shoulder. "You know I do not want this. Even with yourself to stand by me. Almost I'd rather take an oar in a galley, as these two did, than rule a kingdom."

"You must," Thuramon said.

Kavin laughed, suddenly and a little harshly. "Oh, must I? Why should I not turn and go back to my house by the lake? Did I not give enough of myself to earn that?"

"That house is empty," Thuramon said. "She is not there."

Kavin stared at him. "She is here, somewhere, with me," he said. "I know it. I have heard her, felt her hand. I never knew what she was, wizard. But she appeared, and became like any other woman, there in Koremon, beside that lake. She will do so again!"

Thuramon shook his head. "She will not," he said. "But . . . if you return to that other time, she will be there. She is . . . under the Law that the Goddess has given this world we live in, here. By that Law, she has already returned to the beginning of the cycle. She is there."

Kavin groaned. "If I could only think you were lying . . . but no. It's too neat, well-made, this trap. I yield, I yield." He flung out his hands. "Open your Gate, and I will enter the prison called kingship."

Thuramon nodded. "Yes . . . but understand. You will step through that Gate, and you will stand, at that moment at which you were caught in the sorcery that Ess flung at you. You thought, at that moment, that he had been slain. But you were cast into sleep, and you lay asleep while the years went by. Now you will be there, at the same moment, just after this has happened."

Kavin nodded. "Those who came with me will be there, I suppose," he said. "My old friends and comrades." He looked a little more cheerful as he considered it. "So, we mount and ride home, and there's an end to it all. And you, Thuramon . . . will you deal with your double as you told the lady here to do?"

"I am not coming with you," Thuramon said.

"Wait, now," Kavin protested. "If you're to be with me, in Koremon . . . oh, I see. The other, earlier, Thuramon, then." He stared at Thuramon and laughed. "May I tell him of what's to come, and earn credit as a fortune reader?"

"You did," Thuramon answered.

There was a silence, as the others tried to hold the dizzying thought. Kavin shook his head, as if to clear it.

"Enough!" he said. "I told you, I yield."

"Very well," Thuramon said. He turned toward the Gate. "I myself will go last; mine is the farthest journey.

You, Kavin, will go first. Then, as the light alters, the Lady Gwynna . . . by the way, lady, you should lead your mount with you. When you come out, you will find yourself among these same mountains, and a long journey awaits you, to Armadoc."

She looked at him with glowing eyes. "I would not care if it were across the world's width, so Armadoc lies at the end." She reached out, and took her horse's reins, patting its neck.

"But through the mountains, alone . . ." Hugon said, doubtfully.

Gwynna stared at him. "I can defend myself well enough," she said. "Of course, you may lend me that crossbow if you like. But there are only a few wandering herdsmen in the mountains, peaceful folk. Not pirates, who'd think to sell a woman like a market pig."

Hugon laughed. "Now, there's the old Gwynna again," he said. "Oh . . . have you my small gift about you, still?"

"Yes," she said, and pulled out the sack. "Why, do you wish it back?"

"Why, no," Hugon said. "If you'll look within . . ."

She opened the sack, and uttered a low gasp. Jewels glittered with cold fire in her palm.

"When I was in the King's Treasury," Hugon said, innocently, "I happened to run across these, and bethought me, some pretty lass might look well in them . . . better than a mad king would, at any rate."

"You may have them back," Gwynna said. "I have my own jewels . . . at Armadoc."

He stared at her. His hand dipped into his pouch, and brought forth something which he held concealed in his palm.

"No," Hugon said, reflectively. "It would not be fair. Thuramon, I have here a pretty thing, a toy which could render the lovely lady here speechless and docile, as you recall." He smiled at her, and tossed the crystal to Thuramon. "Take it back. I prefer her as she is, talkative and tart as sea-wine. My Lady Gwynna, will you accept my comradeship in your journey?"

She looked at him in a peculiar way, but said nothing.

"Oh, those pretties," Hugon said, glancing at the jewels she held. "I'd thought to offer them as a bride-gift . . . small as they are. And in despite of my brother Zamor's warnings about widows . . ."

"In that time and place, I am no widow," Gwynna said, in a small voice. She looked at him. "Come then, fool, if you will."

"Not without me," Zamor said, loudly. He looked toward Thuramon. "Wizard, this damned lute player wouldn't last a day without me to drag him from the pits he falls into. Can you let him ride back all those days, with a widow, and alone?"

"You're going somewhere!" Fraak cried out, suddenly, and flapped his wings excitedly. He had been sitting on Hugon's saddle, but now he leaped to his shoulder, and clung, determinedly. "I'm going too," he said, firmly. "Wherever it is."

Thuramon looked from one to another; and laughed, quietly.

"Go, then," he said. "All of you, quickly, while I may still hold my temper. Now . . ."

Hugon and Gwynna strode together to the shimmering curtain, leading their horses; they moved into it . . . and were gone. Fraak, as he vanished, uttered a last bugling three-note call. Zamor, with his own horse, and the long axe on his shoulder, hurried to follow them through.

Thuramon moved a control on a column; he looked at Kavin, gravely.

"Goodbye, wizard," Kavin said, grim faced. "At least . . . if she is there, as you say . . . there's one reason for this. Though, for the rest . . ." He groaned. "And the tale said I lived another half a hundred years, did it not? A throne can grow hard on a man's bottom in all that time, Thuramon."

He stepped into the light, and was gone.

285

Thuramon stood, alone. Once more, he reset the control.

He stared into the shimmering curtain and sighed; his hand touched his white beard.

"So long," he said, softly. "So very long. I have done all, as the Work required. Again, and again . . . from each of the Twenty-Two Signs, in turn. Is it finished this time?"

He stared at the flickering curtain of light, and took a step forward.

"Is it finished?" he said, again. "Or is there another road, there?" He picked up the leather sack, and was about to sling it over his shoulder; then, suddenly, he put it down again, and stared at it where it lay. "There's wisdom," he said. "Books full of it, paid for. Paid for, a thousand times over. And they who gathered it, dead and less than dust, ten thousand years ago." Abruptly, he kicked the sack, and it rolled away. He flung back his head, and the wind whipped at his white beard; he laughed, once, loudly. Then he stepped forward into the light, empty-handed, and was gone.

CPSIA information can be obtained at www.ICGtesting.com
Printed in the USA
BVOW02s1200020415

394471BV00001B/4/P